She stayed with him as he slowly revealed the secrets of his research. She drank it in eagerly, reading his manuscripts, asking probing questions, rewarding him for her education with nights of passionate delights. He invited her to be his assistant on his Tantric quest for magickal powers, and she accepted. Tied up, shackled, teased, she became his experimental sex toy. Her lustful writhing from denied orgasm captivated him. Between experiments, their courtship continued; he was falling in love. She continued her studies.

Then came the morning when Count Felipe awoke, not in his bedroom but in his laboratory in the dungeons beneath his castle, naked and shackled. Tabitha smiled her secret smile. "Don't worry. We are going to continue our search together. You see, darling, I know a thing or two about arousal that you don't know. I'm going to introduce you to the secrets of Valentine College."

Also by ROBIN WILDE:
Tabitha's Tease

TABITHA'S TICKLE

ROBIN WILDE

MASQUERADE BOOKS, INC.
801 SECOND AVENUE
NEW YORK, N.Y. 10017

Tabitha's Tickle

Copyright © 1997 by Robin Wilde
All Rights Reserved

No part of this book may be reproduced, stored in a retrieval system, or transmitted in any form, by any means, including mechanical, electronic, photocopying, recording or otherwise, without prior written permission of the publishers.

First Masquerade Edition 1997
First Printing February 1997
ISBN 1-56333-468-2

First Top Shelf Edition 1997
ISBN 1-56333-894-7

Manufactured in the United States of America
Published by Masquerade Books, Inc.
801 Second Avenue
New York, N.Y. 10017

Book 1
The Initiation

1

Sharon's fingers crawled slowly up Bobby's leg. "What are you thinking about?" she teased.

Even with his eyes closed, he began to blush.

"Was it being in Orlando with a thousand cheerleaders? Did you like that?" She giggled as she watched his erection lurch in his pants. Bobby went wild for cheerleading outfits, and Orlando was the site for the National Cheerleading and Dance Team Competitions. They were returning from a long week there in which Sharon's team had been second runner-up.

Bobby opened his eyes and glanced furtively around the train compartment. There were few people in the car. "Shh," he complained. "You're embarrassing me."

Sharon laughed again, throatily. "It's not *me* that gets

hard every time a cheerleader walks by. Some of the girls in my squad nicknamed you 'Woody.'" His blush grew deeper, but his erection continued to swell under her teasing fingers. She shifted her position to face her boyfriend as he slipped down in his seat, legs falling open. She smiled with smug superiority. He was so predictable and helpless when she teased him. She pressed the palm of her hand against his shaft through his pants and rubbed in a slow circle.

"Mmm, that's nice," Bobby said. "I wish we were alone in a hotel room right now."

"Me, too," Sharon replied, "but we're on a rocking train instead. Like the movement? Like how the car sways?" Her hand continued its slow rotation. Bobby's lips parted as he succumbed to her touch.

"Don't tease me, Sharon." He rocked his hips to press harder against her hand. "I thought I'd die from not getting you alone last week."

She pouted prettily. "It wasn't my idea. All the girls had to room together. Besides, you wouldn't be so nuts if you didn't have a raging cheerleader fetish. Sometimes I think that if it wasn't for my costume, you wouldn't want me at all."

"That's not true," he replied hastily, distracted by the continuing motion of her hand. "You're the sexiest girl in the world. I love you. I love everything about you."

"Yeah, especially my costume," she said sarcastically. It was a cute costume. A very short pleated skirt with two-color contrasting pleats—purple and white, the school colors—a tight high-necked sleeveless sweater with "Kittens," the team name, in bold letters, also purple and white. Tennis shoes, ankle socks, and matching purple panties that flashed with nearly every move. It showed off her athletic, trim dancer's body very well.

Sharon had long, wavy brown hair, now tied up with a red scrunchie. Currently, she looked great in a short red skirt, open-toed white sandals, and a midriff-length white T-shirt that hugged her shapely breasts. Bobby wore madras shorts, tented out with his hard-on, an oversize T-shirt, and tennis shoes without socks. He was tall, with light blonde hair and a good runner's body.

They had been dating for about six months. Their sex was good, but restricted by college life's lack of opportunities, especially with the various cheerleader road trips. Sharon made up for it by teasing Bobby at every opportunity, which she enjoyed a lot. She assumed he did, too—at least given the lack of other options most of the time.

Bobby's cock was giving him fits. It was true that being around so many costumed cheerleaders had driven him crazy. Worse, he also had a roommate, so he hadn't even been able to jerk off. And he needed to. He could already feel the first ooze of precome fluid. Just her hand could make him spurt buckets, and soon. "Let me get some tissue, and then you can finish me," he whispered. "I really need it badly."

"Finish you?" she said with mock anger. "Who said anything about finishing you? I'm pretty horny myself, and I don't know why I should do you when I'm going to have to wait too."

"I'll do you next," he whispered. "It'll be great. Or I'll even do you first. Right here. OK?"

"I don't think so," she smiled, not releasing the pressure on his cock. "It's too public and too messy. You'll just have to take what you can get."

He moaned as the rotating motion of her hand drove him slowly to the brink of much-needed orgasm. "Please..." he moaned. "Please..."

She regarded him with careful scrutiny, watching his muscles tense with his approaching climax. "I don't think so," she repeated firmly. "You'll just have to wait until tonight."

"Please!" he begged again, opening his eyes to plead for his orgasm. He looked into her lovely blue eyes, sparkling with cynical amusement. She enjoyed her sense of control, her sense of what she was doing to him. The brief smile playing about the corners of her red lips was nearly enough to trigger him right there.

Slowly, slowly she continued the circular motion of her hand grinding against his cock. She could see a slight wet spot where his precome had leaked through his shorts. "Almost time to stop," she teased.

"No...please...just a little more...I'm almost there... I need it so badly...yes...yes...yes..." He gasped as the inevitable moment arrived; he was so close...

And then she stopped.

He moaned with sensual agony; his balls were sucked up and taut with need; his cock twitched and pulsed in desperate rhythm. "Please...please..." his voice croaked. Her hand was still resting on his cock, so he squirmed up against it. She pulled away. Her skirt had ridden up to the tops of her thighs so he could get a brief glimpse of white panties; then she shifted position, pulling her skirt down.

Before he could continue his desperate plea for an orgasm, the train's PA system announced, "Next stop, Valentine College Station! Valentine College Station!"

Sharon giggled. "Sorry, Bobby baby. We're almost here. Maybe later."

He groaned with frustration and some embarrassment as he began to shift his cock around in his shorts so he could stand up without advertising his horniness to the world. Sharon was no help, standing on her seat to reach the overhead racks with their backpacks, showing off her long legs in her miniskirt. She looked down at him, catching him staring at her. She smiled wickedly. "Time to get ready. Just wait; you'll meet even more cute cheerleaders!"

Valentine College was a heavily endowed private all-girl academy with a reputation for producing models, actresses, and high-powered female executives, all with unusual self-assurance and a sense of their own sexual power. Their varsity cheerleading squad was nationally recognized for excellence; their dance team was always in contention for every award. The school was selective about admissions, and Sharon was pleased not only to be asked to apply, but also to pledge Tau Zeta Rho, the most exclusive Valentine sorority. It had all happened quite suddenly at Orlando, and the invitation included train tickets to the small town where the college was located.

Bobby wasn't happy about her attending an all-girl school, but Valentine College was only about two hours' drive from Tech, where he went. Plus, there were the cheerleaders to watch, and the thought of Sharon in a new cheerleading outfit.

The train pulled into the station.

A pink Cadillac convertible, license plate TZR, was waiting. Bobby's eyes bugged out just a little bit at the sight of the occupants—three fully costumed cheerleaders who were totally hot.

The first had long, silky, light blonde center-parted straight hair, a long, athletic body with endless legs, piercing blue eyes, and a wide, sensual mouth. The second was short and voluptuous, thick waves of raven hair spilling over a round face, deep red pouting lips, large, pillowy breasts and hips, curved thighs holding rich promise. And the third—the third had a sensual little rosebud mouth and laughing blue eyes, golden hair cropped in a pixie cut, cupcake breasts and hot legs, and a strange radiant energy promising cruel delights and wicked games. She was no more beautiful than the other cheerleaders—certainly no more lovely than his Sharon—but he couldn't take his eyes off her.

And the outfits: Valentine's cheerleading uniforms were scandalously sexy—a hot scarlet with white trim, flouncy pleated skirts barely twelve inches long, midriff sweaters just a size too tight with a slashing "Valentine" in white script that drew your eyes to breasts threatening to burst free any second, white athletic kneesocks, and red tennis shoes—so sexy that they radiated total confidence. "I know you want me. You can look, but you can't touch." Bobby's cock was again rampant in his shorts just from the sight of the uniformed cheerleaders, made even harder by Sharon's train tease.

The girls were perched on the top of the backseat, lively and gorgeous in the bright sunlight. They waved and cheered at the sight of Sharon. "C'mon," Sharon said to Bobby. "Here's our ride." She glanced at his pants with a giggle. "Shove your hands in your pockets. You're sticking out big time."

Bobby reddened with embarrassment. "Sorry," he mumbled.

Sharon took pity on him. "'S OK. They're really hot. But just wait till you see me in that outfit. You'll totally die."

The poleaxed look on his blushing face as he visualized her was the confirmation her ego wanted. She laughed, rich and deep. "I guess that doesn't help your woody, does it?"

Bobby shifted their suitcases in front of him to conceal his obvious erection and followed her to the car. She bounced ahead cheerfully; her skirt revealing her beautiful legs and emphasizing her lovely rear. By the time he reached the Cadillac, the girls were hugging each other and exchanging introductions.

"This is Kelly," Sharon said, introducing the tall long-haired blonde, "and this is Tiffany," the raven-haired one, "and Susan," the hot pixie blonde.

"Hi," he said, his face deepening in redness, and shuffled around to the trunk to load the luggage.

It was Susan who said, with wicked glee, "What are you blushing about?"

Of course, that only made his face flush crimson, and worse, he had just lifted the final suitcase into the Cadillac trunk. He had to turn, and the unmistakable evidence of his desire tented out the front of his shorts. Susan noticed it immediately. "Oh, he's got a huge woody! What's the matter? Are you a cheerleader freak?" His mute redness and downward glance confirmed it and all the girls, including his own Sharon, began laughing hysterically.

To his further embarrassment, Sharon began describing his cheerleader fetish in humiliating detail to the girls as he stumbled into the backseat of the Cadillac. He was in the middle; Sharon on his left and Susan, worse luck, on his right. Kelly drove and Tiffany rode with her in the front.

"He was right up front for every dance competition," Sharon laughed, "drooling over the outfits. Actually, he was quite an inspiration for my squad. They nicknamed him Woody, and he was nearly our unofficial mascot."

"Ooh, Woody!" Susan teased, leaning up against him. "That's a great name for you. Would you like to be our mascot?"

The torture of embarrassment and arousal had overloaded his blushing mechanism, and he was permanently red, but the thought of being a cheerleading mascot sent his cock into a dangerous lurch. To his utter amazement, Susan looked boldly down at his lap, reached over, and gave his cock a firm squeeze. Sharon just looked on in amusement; to his surprise, she patted his arm and laughed. "He'd be your mascot anytime, wouldn't you, Bobby?"

"Yeah, Woody," Susan whispered in a mock-bedroom voice. "Why don't you be our mascot?"

Bobby glanced over at Sharon, who simply patted his red face. "Just enjoy yourself." She smiled. "You're at Valentine College now."

He didn't understand her lack of possessiveness; although his cheerleader fetish was a running joke, she wanted him to confine himself to "look, but don't touch." Susan's hand now rested on his bare thigh, inches from the swollen tip of his shaft. He glanced down and was suddenly aware of a growing wet spot, a sign of his leaking arousal, on his shorts. This was some sort of tease, some sort of trick, and Sharon was in on it. He was still embarrassed, still a little bit humiliated, but if it wasn't upsetting Sharon he realized he'd just have to deal with it…and it was very sexy. Susan's perfume, sweet and slightly musky, filled his nostrils. Miles of bare girl-leg were visible on each side of him; scantily clad coeds were paying attention to him. There was probably some hidden trick, but how bad could it be?

The two-lane road wound into the countryside through miles of trees and fields; the wind swept through the open car. Tiffany pulled a joint out of the glove compartment and popped the cigarette lighter. "Here," she said with a tight voice, holding in her toke. "Have a hit." Susan took the joint and toked deeply, then passed it to Bobby. Marijuana always affected him strongly, especially his sensuality, which was all he needed under the circumstances, but he felt he couldn't refuse easily, so he took a hit and passed the joint to Sharon. Sharon seldom smoked, but this time she did, as did Kelly in the driver's seat.

The first joint was followed by a second and then a third. Soon all the car's occupants were high. Both Sharon and Susan snuggled with Bobby. Feeling like king of the world, he draped an arm around each girl. They didn't seem to mind. Susan's hand crawled up his leg and up over his shirt, rubbing gently. He gave up worrying about his hard-on until Susan found his nipple under his T-shirt. He had excruciatingly sensitive nipples that seemed to be tied directly into his cock, and he moaned as she flicked her fingernail over the hard nub. Susan grinned at Sharon, who attacked his other nipple immediately. The erotic overload was too much, especially under the influence of the pot; it began to tickle.

He tried to squirm away as the fingers tickled his nipples and his face returned to its beet-red condition, but Susan wouldn't let him. "Are you ticklish?" she asked with surprised glee.

"You wouldn't believe how ticklish he is," Sharon giggled knowingly. She dug her fingers into his side and he yelped with surprise. Then he convulsed as suddenly two sets of fingers began to tickle him senseless in the backseat of the pink Cadillac.

"Oh, God, stop! Stop! Oh, God! Ha-ha-ha-ha! No!" Bobby choked out his pleas for mercy in between bursts of convulsive, helpless laughter, but mercy was the last thing on the minds of his seatmates. They were getting into it, goosing his ribs, wiggling their fingers around in spite of everything he could do to twist and turn and escape. He was not very well coordinated, and the two girls were trained athletes; he could not defend himself successfully. Laughing and pleading and struggling, he no sooner defended one portion of his ticklish anatomy when they found another—ribs, kneecaps, stomach, nipples, armpits. Kelly just kept driving; Tiffany leaned over the front seat to watch and encourage the girls in their attack.

Soon Bobby was out of breath, gasping, on the verge of hysteria. His cock was still an iron bar, but now it was seized with a nearly uncontrollable desire to piss; he was terrified that he would wet himself in the car, a humiliation from which he'd never recover. "Uncle!" he cried. "I give up! I surrender…ha ha ha! Please stop! I'll do anything you like! Ha ha ha ha!"

The girls finally decided to accept his surrender. "Anything?" Susan demanded, clawing above his helpless torso. "Sharon, what do you think?"

Sharon looked at her helpless boyfriend and laughed. "I think you've got yourself a new mascot. Right, Woody?" She emphasized the humiliating nickname.

Bobby was wheezing and panting with his near-hysteria and looked up into the face of his girlfriend. She was still smiling, smug and in control. This was a game, a trick. Suddenly he was frightened, but it was too late. He had already been set up for whatever mischief she had planned, and the alternative, clearly, was to be tickled to death.

"O-OK," he gasped. "I'll be your mascot—anything—you want if you just don't tickle me."

"No deals," Susan said domineeringly, giving him a quick tickle in the ribs as proof. "Unconditional surrender—that's what we want."

Over the back of her seat, Tiffany chimed in. "Welcome to Valentine College," she said in her husky contralto. "Enter freely and of your own will."

Sharon and Bobby looked up. A high brick wall surrounded the campus. The iron entry gate swung open silently. It had tall brick pillars on either side, "Valentine College" in metal script in an arch. The pink Cadillac pulled into a tree-lined drive, and the metal gates swung closed behind them with a clang.

2

They put the young couple up in an old ivy-covered brick dormitory. The entire campus had the air of old money about it, careful elegance showing in the landscaping, the ancient trees, the architecture of the buildings.

"We're a girl's school, so we don't have a special men's dorm. We'll call this a coed dorm for right now," Kelly said. "I guess we'll just trust you two to behave." She smiled knowingly as the two students looked at each other. Bobby's cock was still half-hard; the beautiful girls in their springtime clothes walking through the campus had stimulated him further, and the effects of the marijuana hadn't yet worn off.

"Tabitha—she's the sorority president—will want to see you soon; she's at the Tau Zeta house right now," she told Sharon. "Unpack and get comfortable, and one of us will be up to get you in about twenty minutes. Woody, you can join us for lunch in the cafeteria."

As soon as Kelly left, Sharon and Bobby were in each other's arms. Bobby was more than desperate after all the teasing, combined with a week's frustration at the cheerleading contest in Orlando. Sharon had gotten turned on from teasing Bobby on the train and from team-tickling him in the Cadillac. It was very sexy to watch him squirm with desire; she liked the feeling. Right now the feel of his iron-hard pole pressing against her mound under her thin dress sent a thrill of lust and power through her young body. She ground her hips against him as his tongue invaded her mouth. His hands slipped up over her cropped T-shirt, cupping her entire breasts in his firm grip. Her nipples were already hard, her pussy wet. She moaned into his mouth with desire.

In between deep kisses, Bobby kissed her nape, her neck, her ears. "I've got to have you right now," he panted with earnest desperation.

She nearly agreed with him, but caution prevailed. "I need you, too," she moaned, "but we've only got a few minutes and I have to change. Tonight—tonight I promise!"

"No…now!" he panted. His hands pushed up her top, fumbled for the zipper of her short skirt, slid up her bare leg.

But she pushed him away. "We can't. We really can't. Not here. Not until tonight."

He grabbed her hand and pushed it against his erection, straining through his shorts so hard that it threatened the material. "Feel that! I've already got balls so blue they're about to burst! Please...please...it doesn't have to be elaborate. Just a little quickie. Here—let me lick you first and then you can suck me off. Believe me, it won't take long."

His desperate persuasiveness made her laugh. "OK," she smiled. "A quickie. And you do me first. Deal?"

"Deal!" he said enthusiastically. Within seconds, Sharon found her skirt pooling around her ankles and her panties sliding down her legs. Kissing her madly, Bobby pushed her backward on the double bed with her legs hanging over the side. Her tennis shoes and socks were still on; her T-shirt was pushed up over her bare breasts.

Bobby knelt on the floor and spread her legs gently. He loved to lick pussy. He kissed the inside of her thighs gently, working slowly up to her pouting labia, now glistening with the moisture of her arousal. He unzipped his shorts and pushed them down with one hand, pulled his underwear down to free his cramped, aching cock.

With one long lick, he traveled the length of her slit from bottom to top, then swirled his tongue in wet circles around her clit. As her netherlips parted under his probing tongue, he went deep, probing into her vaginal opening, then upward to the bottom of her clit and back again, building her arousal before capturing her in his mouth and flicking his tongue rapidly back and forth, drawing growing gasps of pleasure from her. His hands slid up to stroke her breasts, rubbing the hard nipples. She was hot and wet and getting closer by the second. Her hands tangled in his hair as she murmured, "Yes...yes," with increasing speed and passion. Unconsciously, Bobby began fucking the air with his hips, his cock developing beads of moisture. She was close...closer.... "Yes! Yes!" came louder and faster as her orgasm arrived in waves, a long orgasm that caused her to urge him faster and harder, to lick and lick and then finally to push his head away gasping when the excruciating pleasure was too much.

She panted with the afterglow as Bobby's heart pounded in his chest; he identified so strongly with her in the process that her orgasm was nearly his own...but not quite. His cock tormented him so strongly that he couldn't keep his hips or his legs still. More than anything, he wanted to stand up and slide his cock right into her, fuck her until his come spurted, but she had something else in mind.

"L-let me catch my breath for a second, then I'll give you a blowjob you won't forget," she said, wiping a bead of sweat away from between her lovely round breasts. She sat up slowly. He was still kneeling beside her. "Take off that shirt," she urged. He threw it over his head and to his delight she reached down to stroke his ultrasensitive nipples. They had a direct line to his pulsing cock. She teased them for a minute, sending delicious waves of pleasure through his needy body, then ordered, "On the bed, legs spread, and smile."

He hopped to obey. His tall body covered the length of the bed, and she knelt between his legs. Slowly, she captured his leaking shaft in her tiny hand. It was purple and the veins stood out in sharp relief, signs of his long arousal. He moaned at her touch. She smiled wickedly as she moistened her hand with her tongue, then used her wetness combined with his precome ooze to make his shaft glisten with desire. The few short strokes were enough to bring him gasping into preorgasmic territory. "That's nice, Sharon," he said as his eyes and voice glazed over with passion.

"Play with your nipples," she ordered. His eyes opened with surprise—that was a game they normally played when there was time, time to tease and then please.

"Baby, we don't have much—"

"Shush," she ordered. "Play with your nipples or I'll stop right now. After all," she laughed wickedly, "I've already got mine."

He reached his hands up to his own nipples and rubbed them, bringing him close in a hurry, but the slow, slow movement of her hand on his cock let him know she planned to tease him.

"Sharon, we don't have time," he complained.

"Then don't waste it arguing. I could always just stop."

"No...no...please keep going. I'll behave."

"You bet you will. Now, tell me which of the Valentine cheerleaders you like best."

This was dangerous. Very dangerous. Was she seriously

mad at him? Was this her revenge for Susan feeling him up in the Cadillac? His cheerleader fetish was a joke, but had it gone beyond that? His lust-dazed mind wasn't processing very well, but he had sense to say, "You're my favorite cheerleader…the sexiest in the world." He meant it, too.

Her hand continued to torture his cock with the slowest masturbation he'd ever experienced. She smiled. "That's nice, but that's not what I asked. How about Kelly? She's lovely, and those legs are to die for."

He was mute under her torment; he didn't know what to say, and he was desperate for the orgasm she might deny him.

"Tiffany? She's really cute. How'd you like to feel those lips around your cock right now?" His cock lurched dangerously in her hand.

"Oh? You like Tiffany. How about Susan? Did you like it when she squeezed your cock. Did you like being tickled by her?" He flashed back to the scene in the car. Combined with everything else, the stimulation set him off. His hips rose uncontrollably from the bed as he bucked them for the final stimulation he needed to trigger uncontrollable spurting.

"Ah, ah, ah!" she chided, releasing him. "So, it's Susan," she mused. She waited for him to calm down, then resumed her slow motion. "Would you like to be her mascot? Would you like her here right now, helping me relieve your blue balls?" His desperate moaning and the clear drizzle of viscous seminal fluid were all the confirmation she needed.

She laughed. "Good boy. Very honest. Now you'll get what you deserve." With that, she leaned forward, her lips parted and wet, her eyes fastened teasingly on his. Grasping his cock at the very base, she licked slowly up the length of his shaft. "Ready?" she asked with teasing innocence as she drank in his look of desperate tension. He couldn't take any more.

Finally she began to devour him with her mouth, sucking hotly and wetly, sending waves of unbelievable passion through his overteased body, driving him crazy. He struggled not to come, to make it last for a while, but she overpowered him. Inexorably, she drew him to the edge, then backed off a bit, then began again. He was in heaven, his body one large sex organ, every nerve filled with indescribable pleasure. And then it was here—the final build, the wave of passion, an eruption to rival Vesuvius—

"Are you two decent?" A girlish voice interrupted the culminating moment. The room door flew open and there were the three cheerleaders: Kelly, Tiffany, and Susan. In a moment of desperate shock, Sharon let go of his cock and sat up. Bobby rolled over and off the bed on the side away from the door to conceal his erect nakedness.

"Oops!" Tiffany giggled, but made no move to close the door. "I guess you aren't decent. Now we know how Woody got his nickname, don't we?"

The girls laughed and after a moment, Sharon joined in. All four looked at poor Bobby crouching behind the bed. Susan walked boldly into the room and around the bed to look at the crouching boy as he tried to cover his dripping erection with his hands. "Oh, the poor baby still has his woody," she cooed with wicked glee. "What's the matter—didn't your girlfriend spank your hamster fast enough?"

The blush that originated in Bobby's face burned its way visibly down his body. His cock began to wilt, aching from its frustrating brush with deliverance. In the space of an hour his embarrassment circuits had become so overloaded that his blush seemed a permanent part of him. Susan found his underpants and dangled them in front of his eyes. "Red briefs," she observed mockingly. "Shows what a stud you are." Her cutting comment sent another blush through him.

Trying to conceal himself, Bobby slipped on his briefs when she dropped them on the floor before him, then scrambled for his shorts, crawling on the floor to dress. When he finally managed to dress under Susan's scrutiny, he found Sharon already dressed in a short plaid jumper over a white short-sleeved turtleneck and white sandals. She looked innocently desirable.

"Kelly is going to take me over to see Tabitha," Sharon announced. "Tiffany and Susan are going to take care of you for the afternoon. Make sure you do whatever they tell you. I'll see you tonight and then we can take care of your little problem"—she licked her lip with deliberate sexiness—"or should I say your *big* problem?"

Tiffany and Susan each took Bobby by one of his arms. "Don't worry; we'll take good care of him. It'll be pretty hard, though," Tiffany said with a meaningful look at his pants.

"And if Woody doesn't behave," Susan added, "we'll take care of it. We won't let him be our mascot." That drew laughter from all the girls at his expense, and he could feel another hot blush travel down his face as Sharon left him in the hands of the two Valentine cheerleaders.

"That was really a mean trick. I don't know about this," Sharon said, shaking her head as they left the room. "I mean, it's OK that he gets initiated along with me, but he's really strung out right now."

Kelly smiled mysteriously. "If you think he's strung out now, just wait until you get him back."

Curiosity and arousal mixed with slight guilt. "Really? What are Susan and Tiffany going to do with him?"

"Just tease him to death. Susan likes to tickle, and Tiffany likes to be watched."

"I don't know," Sharon repeated as they walked down the single flight of steps to the dorm lobby and out into the springtime weather.

Kelly stopped. "Sharon, it's OK. Tau Zeta has an initiation program that's a little bit different. Part of the initiation is that you loan us a boy. Preferably a boyfriend, though some girls have tricked their brothers or platonic buddies into the role. We get the fun of driving a poor guy wild with desire, and you get the benefit later—and we get to watch."

Sharon shivered with renewed erotic feeling. "I

know, and I also know he'll probably really dig it. I just feel a little funny setting him up like that."

"Not as funny as he'll feel when Susan's tickling fingers get him for real," Kelly laughed. "Besides, you've got your own initiation to worry about now." She led Sharon back to the pink Cadillac.

"So," Kelly continued, "were you impressed by our timing?"

"God, yes," Sharon exclaimed, "I was so embarrassed! What were you doing, peeping?"

"Yep," Kelly confirmed as she pulled another joint from the glove compartment and lit it. "We've got you on videotape."

"No way!"

"Way," Kelly said firmly. "We want a horny boy, and you delivered. Congratulations. You must have been a great little prickteaser."

Sharon took a deep toke, leaned back in her seat, and laughed. "Yeah, well..."

"Turn you on? Prickteasing, I mean. When you do it deliberately."

"Oh, God," Sharon said. "I usually have to get myself off a couple of times. I'm pretty good. I can tell within a few strokes when a guy is ready to shoot. I love the begging; it turns me on a lot."

"Yeah?" Kelly encouraged. "Ever tied a guy up to tease him?"

"Well..." Sharon murmured.

"Come on, 'fess up," Kelly urged.

"Well...I did tie Bobby up, but he did me first."

"Did you like it?"

"Yeah, it was hot, especially because he's such a great pussylicker."

"We noticed." Kelly laughed. "I like that in a guy."

"But I really liked it the other way around. I kept him tied and hard for about two hours. I kept promising that this time I meant it, he could come; and then, at the last minute, I kept quitting. First he begged, then he got mad, and then he figured out if he pissed me off, he wouldn't get it at all. By the time I finally made him come, I think I could have made him do anything I wanted."

"We'll have to try that with him," Kelly said. "I'll call the girls."

"Yeah?" Sharon looked at Kelly with increased curiosity. What had she gotten herself and Bobby into? Right now it was all so sexy that she felt herself getting aroused again; the marijuana helped. She wanted Bobby's cock inside her, wanted to feel him pulse. Part of her imagined the come spurting from his cock; another visualized the desperate look he wore just at the end. There was a sexual spell on the Valentine College campus, and she was falling under it. She hoped Bobby would enjoy it—tied up and tickled by cheerleaders! Wouldn't he just die if he knew she set him up?

"How long have you two been together?" Kelly asked.

"About six months now," she replied. "He was always hanging out at cheerleading practice, and it took him about two months to work up the nerve to talk to me. It took him another month to ask me out, though his interest was obvious."

"Woody?" Kelly asked.

"All the time." Sharon laughed. "I thought it was cute. Once he asked me out, it took about two months before I finally decided to fuck him."

"Didn't he try earlier?"

"Yeah, and I let him feel me up a few times."

"You prickteased him, didn't you?" Kelly said accusingly.

"You know it!" Sharon laughed. "I drove him nuts, and I even played with his nuts a few times. Sometimes, when a guy figures out I'm just teasing, he stops calling, but Bobby just kept on."

"Some guys like to be prickteased," Kelly said. "Bobby is our kind of boy. Don't worry. You teased him, you tied him up, you just drove him nuts for a week, and he's ready for more. He'll love his initiation—at least, most of it."

Sharon took the last hit off the joint and stubbed it in the ashtray. She was flying in a fog of sensuality. Yes, it was OK about Bobby. The girls would prickteased him some more, but he'd like that. She wished she could watch. Maybe Kelly would have that videotaped, too—they probably would. She turned to ask her about it, but the pink Cadillac turned into a gravel drive leading to a large mansion. The Greek letters T Z R hung outside.

"Ready for your initiation?" Kelly asked with a sinister grin.

Sharon's nipples were hard with anticipation and

arousal. Suddenly her stomach had a feeling like going over the top on a roller coaster. The marijuana had blurred her sense of control; she felt overtaken by events. It was sexy and scary.

With a nervous laugh, she replied, "I'm ready for anything!"

"Sure, you are." Kelly smiled as she escorted the newest sorority pledge into the Tau Zeta house.

3

"You can wait in here," Kelly said as she ushered Sharon into a well-appointed parlor off the formal entrance. Tau Zeta was obviously a rich sorority; the house was built in the formal antebellum style, with an ornate curving staircase leading from the entrance to the upper floors. Sliding wooden doors on either side revealed the formal parlors. The parlors had large windows with sheer curtains, letting in wonderful golden light. Sharon looked around, impressed. Were those real Louis XIV desks?

"Just think," Kelly said, taking Sharon's arm, "all this can be yours—after the initiation."

Sharon looked up at the taller cheerleader with wide eyes. "W-What's going to happen?"

"Lots of things." Kelly smiled. "Don't worry. I'll protect you." With that, and to Sharon's amazement, Kelly's arm slid around Sharon's waist and pulled her close. Without thinking, Sharon closed her eyes and found herself lost in a warm, wet kiss. It was the first time she'd been kissed by another woman, and she was surprised to find herself accepting it so easily. Maybe it was the dope—or maybe it was the eroticism that permeated the entire campus. Somehow it was stronger in the sorority house.

She let herself be kissed and felt the sensation of a female body pressing against her own, warm and soft. She began kissing back and her arms went around her partner. Her nipples, already stiff, tingled as they pressed against Kelly's large breasts. If this was her initiation, OK.

"Mmm," Kelly said as she broke off the kiss. "This is going to be fun." Sharon stood there, aware of nothing but her own sensuality, as Kelly ran a slim finger slowly over her lips and down over her body through the valley between her breasts. She shivered with pleasure.

"I'd better tell Tabitha you're here. Look around all you like," Kelly said with subtle emphasis, "but don't touch anything." She slid the doors shut as she left.

Sharon hugged herself. She had never particularly thought about making love with a woman; she had no fundamental objections to it, but it had never come up before. She liked the look of the female body and appreciated a sexy demeanor, but her interest had heretofore been theoretical and aesthetic. Now it was becoming practical, and the thought was very pleasant. She looked around the room aimlessly, admiring the various objets d'art and the obviously valuable furniture, but not really paying close attention. There was a door at the other end of the room; without thinking, she opened it.

Her heart began to pound loudly in her chest and she started with surprise and another rush of sudden lust. The inner room was a library of some sort, with dark wallpaper and rich carpet. The furniture had red upholstery and gold trim. There were no windows, and the room gave off a red glow. It was as if she'd opened a door to another world. On the wall directly in front of her was a man—naked, chained to the wall with shackles spreading his arms and legs into a giant X. Another chain was fastened to a silver ring attached to a leather collar around his neck. A leather bit in his mouth gagged him effectively.

She moved toward him as if in a trance. His cock was imprisoned in two silver bands: one at the base of his cock, another forming a loop around the top of his balls. Only half-hard at first, his cock began to quiver with her nearness, swelling helplessly as she approached.

Kelly's words came back to her. "Look around all you like, but don't touch anything." She couldn't help herself. His cock was already rigid, saluting her. She touched his chest gently, and he moaned through his gag. His eyes pleaded; he needed her. A sense of erotic power surged through her. She liked the feeling. She liked it a lot.

Carefully, slowly, she rubbed her hand over his chest and found his right nipple. As she touched it, she glanced down. His cock lurched with sudden passion.

"Is your right nipple sensitive?" she asked, smiling with delight in her absolute control over her helpless victim. "How about your left?" She pinched both nipples, pinched them hard. His eyes were wide open, staring at her with helpless need, begging her. She could feel the wetness growing below; tying up Bobby was nothing compared to this.

She delighted in his moans of passion and pain as she stroked and pinched his nipples. Kelly's voice echoed in her mind again. *You're a prickteaser, aren't you?*

"I'm a prickteaser," she whispered aloud to her helpless victim. "I'm going to tease your prick now."

Dirty words turned her on. Without breaking eye contact, she reached down to take his cock in her hand, trailing her fingers over its twitching length.

"You've got a hard cock," she whispered. "Hard cocks turn me on. Your cock needs me, doesn't it? It needs my hand. You'd prefer my mouth or my pussy, wouldn't you." It was a statement, not a question. His face was taut with the agony of his need. "Do you want to fuck me? Fuck me with your cock? I'd fuck your cock, but I want to tease it even more. I like feeling your cock twitch. Maybe I'll want to see it spurt some come. Would you like to spurt your come in my hand, or all over my dress? I'd have to take off my dress before I made you come; then I'd have you spurt your come all over my body. I'd rub your come in with my hand; maybe I'd lick it all up. I'll bet your come tastes good. I want to see you come, just a little bit. Come for me. Make your cock spurt. Yes. Spurt your cock while I hand-fuck you."

The dirtier she spoke, the hotter she got. She took her hand off his nipple and rubbed her own breast through her sweater. Some part of her mind couldn't believe what she was doing, but the strange erotic atmosphere had taken control of her. She could feel the come building in his cock. Part of her wanted to feel his come spurting.

She looked into his face. What did she want to do? Her hand did the work for her. He was close, pulsing. His cockhead was swelling in her hand. She released him. "But I told you I was a prickteaser, didn't I? Mustn't fib."

The deep moan from under his gag filled her with cruel delight. She had never done anything quite like this before, and she was more turned on than she'd ever been.

Again, she stroked him toward the moment of crisis. There was precome oozing from the tip of his cock; she wiped it off. Holding her finger in front of his face, she licked it with a swirling and sexy tongue sliding over her lips. She flashed her eyes at him and pursed her lips. "Tastes good. Want some?" She dipped her finger back in the viscous fluid and smeared some on his helpless lips. From the expression on his face, he didn't like it, but didn't dare protest. The third finger went to his nipple, wetting it, then rubbing the wet, white-hard nub with her finger as she began to pump his stiff cock again.

"I told you I'm a prickteaser, and I am. But even prickteasers like to see come every now and then. I like cocks. I like hard cocks. I like wet cocks that spurt and spurt. I like your cock. I think I'll let you this time. I will. I'm going to let you come this time. I want you to come. Come for me. Come for me. I'll let you. You can trust me. How do you want it? Want me to hand-fuck you like this? I'll suck you off if you prefer. Just nod. Hand-fuck? Yes or no. Blowjob? Yes or no. Oh, you want a blowjob. I thought so. Dirty little boy wants to stick his cock in my innocent mouth and have me suck all the come out, drink it down. Do you want me to swallow all your come? Do you?"

Helpless, not knowing whether to trust her, he nodded. "But I think I want to hand-fuck you this time. Is that OK, or would you prefer not to come at all? Nod your head. Hand job? Yes or no. Or prickingtease? I'm sorry, I didn't get that. This time you have to say the words. Say 'hand job.' Say it, or I'll assume you want prickingtease. You're not saying anything. What's all that moaning? You must want prickingtease very badly. Oh, you're almost there! I can feel it! Speak up. Tell me what you want. Tell me. Tell me." Faster she stroked until the final moment, then stopped.

"I do prickingtease very well, don't I," she giggled.

"Yes, you do." The sound of another voice startled her. She swiveled around to see Kelly with another woman, one of the most beautiful women Sharon had ever met: Tabitha, president of Tau Zeta Rho.

TABITHA'S TICKLE

Tabitha was a tall, statuesque blonde with a luscious figure, wearing an amazing red leather dress with a lace-up bodice that showed her ripe cleavage down nearly to her navel. A long side slit revealed a long, shapely leg, the foot arched in red stiletto heels. Stunningly beautiful on a physical level, but what was most captivating about her was her eyes—royal blue and twinkling with secret amusement—and her lips, ripe and red and sultry, smiling with utter self-assurance and control.

Sharon knew she was hot, boys had often told her so, but in the presence of Tabitha she suddenly felt callow, childish, and clumsy. Caught and humiliated in the act of toying with the naked boy, she could only stammer apologies. Tabitha's knowing smile grew.

"We knew—or guessed, at least—what would happen," Tabitha smiled, cutting short Sharon's attempts to excuse herself. "It's the beginning of your initiation. Boy-toys like poor Robin here are part of life at Tau Zeta, and we need to make sure you'll fit in."

Sharon glanced back at her shackled victim. If this was part of Tau Zeta life, she was ready. "Really? Did you just tie him up, or did he volunteer?" she asked with curiosity.

Tabitha laughed as she walked over to her prisoner. "Oh, Robin found his way to us." She smoothed back the shackled boy's tousled hair. "He got himself admitted as one of the first male students to the school. He thought he'd be in for nonstop sex, and he was absolutely right…just not in the way he expected."

"We caught him masturbating while spying on the cheerleaders," she continued, "and of course we had to punish him thoroughly. Though if it hadn't been that, it would have been something else." She smiled directly at Robin. His pleading eyes never left her, and his cock quivered at her nearness. Sharon was fascinated and aroused.

"He was so cute as a prisoner, we turned him into a permanent boy-toy. He's on punishment right now."

"Punishment?" Sharon asked.

"Yes, he was very bad. We were using him to help work on one of our female toys, and he tried to get her off prematurely. Himself, too, of course. Or trying to, at least." Tabitha took his cock in her hand. It pulsed and quivered as if it had a life of its own. She pointed to the silver ring. "That's a special cockring; it really controls his orgasm. The girl nearly reached orgasm when Kelly caught him, and I sentenced him to another three weeks before we'd consider letting him come."

"Three weeks?"

"He had an orgasm only three weeks before." She dropped his cock. "Tonight's the end of his three weeks, but that only means I *consider* letting him come. Sometimes I wait longer—maybe even another three weeks. Sometimes I don't know whether I'll make him come or not." She smiled wickedly. "I like to keep him in suspense."

Sharon was amazed. Six weeks without an orgasm—she couldn't take it. And this thought about female tease victims: could it happen to her? Bobby was nearly

Tabitha's Tickle

desperate, and it had only been a week for him, and he wasn't being teased constantly like Robin. Tau Zeta took teasing seriously, that was for sure.

"Enough about Robin for now," Tabitha said. "We invited you here to consider pledging Tau Zeta Rho sorority. You've gotten only a glimpse. Do you like it so far?"

"Oh, yes," Sharon said fervently. "I do."

"Would you like to become a sister of our sorority, with all the rights and privileges thereof?"

"Yes," Sharon replied.

"Will you follow the guidance and direction of your officers and consent to the rules and regulations of our sisterhood?"

"Yes."

"You must undergo our initiation and trial to be considered for our membership. The ritual is secret, and you must consent blindly. Do you accept initiation into Tau Zeta Rho?"

"I do."

"Take off your clothes."

Startled, Sharon looked at Tabitha, who smiled knowingly. Was she slated to be a tease victim? Is that what all the girls went through? Her stomach took a sudden dip of fear. Her hands were trembling, but she followed orders, slipping off the shoulder straps of her jumper and unzipping the skirt, then pulling her turtleneck over her head. She was down to panties and sandals; she unfastened the sandal straps and slid them off; then, after a pause, slid off her panties.

Robin Wilde

She was naked, just like Robin. She looked over at the young boy shackled to the wall, his needy cock pleading for mercy. She had no idea how long it had been for him, or how desperate he really was. She had really tortured him. Surprisingly, the thought didn't fill her with guilt, only with a confused sense of power.

Being naked in front of two clothed women, including the first girl to ever kiss her in an erotic fashion, made her feel particularly helpless. Tabitha and Kelly moved toward her, pinning her between them. The touch of leather against naked flesh in the front, and the combination of brief cheerleader sweater and skirt along with Kelly's bare flesh in the back was exciting. She closed her eyes and tilted her head back as Tabitha kissed her. Kelly's hands slipped around to cup her breasts. She moaned with pleasure. Even if they did mean to make her a sex slave, this was fun. She surrendered to the erotic sandwich.

The sorority girls toyed with their pledge for a few minutes, then let her go, wet and trembling with desire.

"That was your welcome. Now, for the first part of your initiation, punishment for disobeying Kelly's order about not touching." Kelly took a wooden sorority paddle with the T Z R Greek initials from a hook on the wall. Sharon gulped, but she expected something like that.

"Move over toward Robin," Tabitha ordered. At their commands, Sharon placed her hands over Robin's shackled hands. Their faces were within inches; he could feel her breath. She spread her legs and leaned into Robin; if it weren't for his gag, they could have kissed. Her breasts brushed against his chest. His cock, fully extended, tickled her pubic hair.

Thwack! The first blow of the paddle made her lurch forward; Robin's stiff cock slid along the length of her sopping-wet pussy, stimulating her clit. It stung, but not too badly. The feeling of cock sliding across her wetness was arousing. The combination was devastating. She stuck her ass out again to greet the second *thwack!* and then rocked her hips back and forth under the paddling. Soon the stinging grew into pain; she felt herself getting red. She gazed into Robin's eyes, filled with desire and need. *Thwack!* She quickly lost count of the blows as she concentrated on rubbing his cockhead against her clit on each move of her hips. It was devastatingly sexy, all the more so because of the torment she could see on his face.

"Fifteen!" Kelly announced. It was over.

Regretfully, she moved away from the wall. She couldn't help it, she rubbed her ass where the paddle had left its impression. She reached for her jumper.

"No," Tabitha chided. "You get to stay naked for the rest of your initiation."

Sharon nodded. It wasn't such a surprise. As horny as she had become, her nakedness was becoming less of a concern to her.

Kelly was unfastening Robin's gag and unshackling him from the wall. "Say 'thank you' to the nice young pledge for giving you a hand job," Tabitha ordered.

"T-thank you," Robin whispered, sore and uncomfortable from his imprisonment and frustration.

"You're welcome," Sharon said with a smile. She thought the boy was cute. "I hope we can do it again sometime."

Tabitha chuckled wickedly. "Oh, I think we might arrange that, but only after your initiation. Then you'll have a better idea what to do with him."

"I've got a few ideas right now," Sharon replied lustfully.

Tabitha and Kelly laughed. "I'll bet you do, and I'll bet Robin would love them. Just wait until later, though. You'll discover possibilities you never even knew existed!" Tabitha stated firmly.

"Go, Teasers!" Kelly laughed in agreement.

Kelly then produced a leather collar with a ring to fasten around Sharon's neck, and put leather bands, also each with a ring, on her wrists and ankles. Robin wore similar bands, making it easy to tie them up in any position their mistresses chose. "Pledges have to learn what it's like to be slaves, so when they become slave mistresses, they know better how to deal with their toys. Don't worry: your initiation lasts only twenty-four hours," Tabitha stated. Still, the imprisoning bands increased Sharon's sense of helplessness and delicious fear. She and Robin were identical, both slaves and tease toys. The difference was that soon she'd be able to call the shots, and Robin would stay a slave.

Robin's hands were fastened behind him with a metal clip that joined the two rings; they left Sharon's hands free. They clipped a leash to each collar. Sharon felt particularly humiliated to be led around like a dog. Robin seemed to treat it as something inevitable.

Tabitha's Tickle

"Are you still sore?" Tabitha asked. Ruefully, Sharon nodded. "Robin, I want you to kiss it and make it better."

To Sharon's surprise and delight, Robin obediently knelt and began kissing her paddled ass, gently and tenderly. She bent over slightly to give him better access and slid her legs apart. He kissed her rosy mounds and finally dipped between her legs to plant one delicious kiss on her wet lips.

"That's not her ass!" Kelly laughed, giving Robin a tug on the leash. "Good try, though."

"I think the next idea is to show you around," Tabitha announced. "You need a better idea of what Tau Zeta is all about. Then we'll proceed with the next part of your initiation. Any questions?"

Sharon's mind was overwhelmed with lust, bizarre sexuality, and marijuana smoke. For a second she couldn't think of anything, then she blurted out, "What about Bobby? If you're doing this to me, and Robin is an example of what you do here, what are you planning for Bobby?" She was more curious than worried—the thought of Bobby shackled and teased like Robin was suddenly very appealing to her.

Both her captors laughed. "Oh, Woody is in for quite a treat," Kelly giggled. "Don't worry; you'll get your turn with him before it's all over."

Tabitha added, "It's always most fun when you bring your own toy to the party. Girls who don't have to undergo extra initiation. But you're sharing the pleasure—and the surprises. We'll tell you all about it while we show you a few of the other surprises this house has in store. Kelly, do you want to run Robin back down to the dungeons while I take our initiate to meet the Count? Then meet us upstairs."

The dungeons? Sharon thought with shock.

"Oh, yes, my sweet young initiate. Dungeons. And much more. Welcome to Tau Zeta Rho. You're in for the ride of your life—and so is your cute little boyfriend."

4

Bobby's humiliation grew with his hard-on. As soon as Sharon and Kelly left the room, Susan and Tiffany continued to tease him.

"Poor baby," Susan giggled as she pressed her lithe body against him in a teasing manner. "How's your woody? All tingly from your blowjob?"

The touch of her skimpy red cheerleading outfit was maddening. He was seized with the desire to grab her, tear off her panties, and bury his needy organ deep inside her, to spurt his long-delayed and pent-up sperm. It was just a tease, though. She could do anything she wanted. He could just look, lust, and suffer.

She brushed her hand lightly over his tented erection, inflaming it again. "Ooh, looks like Sharon didn't finish the job, did she?"

Bobby's blushing mechanism should long since have overloaded, but it seemed his capacity for embarrassment knew no limits. He could feel the hot redness in his face, advertising his humiliation to the little blonde who took such delight in tormenting him.

Tiffany was in on it, too. She slid behind him, making a sandwich of his body. Her fingers and hot breath teased the back of his neck.

"Please!" Bobby moaned. "If you're not going to do anything for me, please don't tease me anymore."

Both girls stepped back. Susan wore a look of mock horror on her face. "What do you mean, 'if you're not going to do anything'? Did you think we were going to do something? What a dirty-minded boy you are. Were you thinking that we might lay you down on that bed, take your shorts down, and suck your cock together? Is that what you were thinking? Tiffany and I, taking turns licking your shaft, sucking it deeply into our mouths, then finally sharing all your come when it spurts out? Really! Sharon's been gone only a few minutes, and already you're trying to cheat on her! What do you think about that, Tiffany?"

The voluptuous raven-haired cheerleader walked over beside Susan and looked at their victim. "I think Woody's a lech. Maybe we should tell Sharon he tried to fuck us."

Susan laughed wickedly. "Yeah; she'd be really pissed then. Maybe she'd cut it off; she sure wouldn't do anything for you."

"Wait...I didn't mean—" Bobby stammered.

TABITHA'S TICKLE

"What? Did you say something, Woody?" Susan demanded imperiously.

"I mean—I didn't mean that—I was just—"

"Come on, come on, out with it!"

"I'm sorry. I apologize. I wasn't trying to make a pass or anything, I just—"

"What?" Tiffany interrupted. "You weren't trying to make a pass? What's the matter? Aren't we sexy enough? Don't you want to fuck us?" She pouted her lips in exaggerated sexuality and then inflamed his lust even further by rubbing her hands over her own breasts, cupping them while cocking her hips in a model's pose. Bobby stared helplessly.

"Yeah, Woody," Susan chimed in. "If you don't want to fuck us, what's that woody all about? Are you some kind of tease or something?"

"I—I—" Bobby could only stammer at the two-pronged attack. "Yes, you're very sexy, I'm just—"

"You're just what?" Susan demanded. "Just horny? Just being a tease, showing off your hard-on to turn us on, then not coming across?"

"Just…involved," he blurted out.

"Oh," said Tiffany knowingly. "That's different. So you do think we're sexy, right?"

"Yes, yes I do," he sighed. "Very sexy."

"And you'd fuck us if it weren't for Sharon, right?"

"In a heartbeat," he said passionately.

"You'd like to fuck us right now, but you just can't. Is that right?"

"Yes, that's right. God, that's right."

"Well, what if we helped you just a little bit," she smiled, an expression of heavenly sensuality spreading across her face. "We wouldn't want you to be unfaithful to Sharon, but maybe there's something we could do that wouldn't be unfaithful." She moved toward him; he was paralyzed, like a deer caught in a car's headlights. She slipped into his arms, pressing her pillowy breasts against his chest, and tilted her head back to kiss him. He couldn't help it; he closed his eyes and leaned into the kiss. It was warm and wet and sweet and sexy. Sharon came into his mind, but he rationalized that this was only a kiss. Only a kiss.

He was breathless when Tiffany pulled away. "Mmm," she said, eyes sparkling. "You kiss good. Susan, try him out." Then he had an arm full of pixie blonde and a hot tongue probing his mouth, hips grinding against his erection.

When Susan finally broke the kiss, she stayed in his arms, but slipped one hand down to massage his cock. The other played with his neck. "Looks like you have a problem." She smiled.

At that moment, Bobby knew he'd do anything to get his rocks off. There was nothing else in his head but that. Not Sharon, not anything.

Susan studied his expression carefully and squeezed his erection. "We could help you out, you know, if you asked nicely. Nothing too elaborate, nothing to get you in trouble. Just helping out a friend. Would you like that?"

He nodded passionately. "Yes. Please. I need it so much!"

"Yes, you do," Susan said. "I can tell. Tiffany, feel this boy's need." She stepped back so Tiffany could fondle and squeeze his erection. His legs were trembling; he was nearly ready to spurt in his shorts.

"Oh, he *does* need some attention," Tiffany whispered. "This will be fun. Would you like us to help you out?"

"Yes, yes, please. Yes." Bobby couldn't think straight or see straight anymore.

"Then ask nicely," Tiffany commanded, continuing her stroking.

"Please, please, help me out, I need it."

"Need what?"

"To come. I need to come. Please make me come."

"How should we make you come?"

"However you like. Your mouth, your hand, anything. Please. Please."

"What do you think, Susan?" Tiffany asked.

"I don't know. Beg some more, Woody."

He put his heart into it. "Please, I beg you, make me come. However you like; I need it so badly. Please, you're so beautiful, so sexy, please...I beg you."

The girls listened to his begging with amused expressions.

"What will you do for us if we make you come?" Susan asked.

"Anything you like, just name it. Please, I beg you."

"All right, then. Kiss my feet."

He looked at her with surprise, but something in her face said she wasn't kidding. He knelt before her, bent over, and planted a kiss on the toe of her white tennis shoe. He couldn't take his eyes off the shapely calf. He kissed her shoe again.

"Now me," Tiffany giggled. Bobby crawled over and kissed Tiffany's shoe as well. He looked up expectantly.

Both girls looked at him with expressions of superiority; somehow, that turned him on even more.

"Show us your cock," Susan ordered.

Although the blunt command renewed his embarrassment, and he suddenly became aware that the door to the hallway was still open, he had gone too far. He started to scramble to his feet, but her order, "Stay where you are," kept him on his knees. He unzipped his shorts, pulled them down, and then his briefs. His straining purple cock leapt out. "Show us," the order came again, and he took his cock in his hand, holding it out as a thing for their inspection.

"Cute," Tiffany said.

"Yeah," Susan agreed. "OK, Woody, that's enough. Time for lunch."

He couldn't believe what she said and sat there dumbly for a minute until she repeated it.

"Please—" he started to beg, then suddenly both girls burst out into peals of laughter.

"You really believed we were going to do it, didn't you?" Susan said through her helpless laughter.

"Yeah, Woody," Tiffany added, "like we would do anything behind Sharon's back."

"You are a horny little boy, aren't you?" Susan laughed. "Let's have lunch, and before you know it, Sharon will be back. Your woody will hold out till then, I'm sure."

Tabitha's Tickle

He had no choice but to slip his shorts back on. His hard-on was so large, he couldn't fit it back into his briefs; the girls were amused, watching his every move. Finally, he scrambled to his feet, his face threatening to become permanently red. His teased erection throbbed uselessly. He should have known he couldn't trust the girls, but now he couldn't get them out of his mind.

Lunch was a typical cafeteria affair; the three sat at a table in the center and ate mediocre food off a tray. Bobby sat mute through most of lunch as a parade of gorgeous young Valentine students came through, many stopping to say hello to their friends. A few other cheerleaders came by briefly. Bobby's erection continued to throb undiminished; it had begun to ache. The girls chattered away as if he weren't present. The arousal gave way to more humiliation, his embarrassment at resorting to begging, kneeling, exposing his cock merely to be laughed at. He focused his attention on his food rather than on the parade of beauties. He wasn't sure whether he wanted Sharon here, after all.

"Hey! Space cadet! Woody, I'm talking to you." Surprised, Bobby raised his head from his tray to see Susan snapping her fingers in his face, trying to catch his attention.

"All the blood must have rushed away from his brain," Tiffany observed cruelly.

Susan chortled as Bobby looked down. "Must not be much blood left for the rest of his body. Hey, come on. Cheer up. We're just teasing you."

"OK," Bobby pushed back his tray. He resolved to be a good sport, no matter what they did next.

What was next was a campus tour that ended at the gym. Their prattle during the campus tour was mostly innocent, with a little teasing thrown in; Bobby was finally able to relax and his erection diminish, although the throbbing ache remained. The beautiful young coeds in their summer outfits—brief dresses, shorts, halter tops, even a bikini or two for sunbathers on the quad, were a constant goad to his overheated imagination.

The gym had brick walls, ivy-covered, and the girls led him around to a side door, away from public view, concealed by large bushes. "Time for a toke," Tiffany said, pulling another joint from the waistband of her brief pleated cheerleader skirt.

Bobby regarded the joint with an element of horror; all he needed was another renewed attack of the hornies, which he tended to get in place of the munchies, but he couldn't refuse easily. The previous smoking hadn't completely worn off. Soon he felt the red fog of a renewed high rolling over his brain.

With the new high came painful awareness of his lovely companions—Tiffany's lush breasts pushing out her thin cropped sweater, the gleam of perspiration on her naked belly, the long curve of her shapely legs vanishing under her tiny skirt, the waves of her jet-black hair spilling erotically over her shoulders. Susan's body seemed to quiver as if it were impossible for her to ever be completely still. There was something about her that made him even more aware of her nakedness under her clothes. The final few inches of her legs kept trying to keep out from under the short hem of her skirt; her brief top was loose enough to show the bottom curve of her breasts; her navel drew his eyes to her flat stomach and curving hips; her rosebud mouth held wicked promise and amused cruelty. He felt a pre-erection tingle; soon he'd swell up again. He tried to think about something else with little luck.

"Let's go inside," Tiffany suggested.

Susan opened the door and they found themselves in a narrow hallway, office doors on either side. "Where to?" she asked her partner.

"Um, I've really got to go," Bobby interrupted, suddenly seized with the need to piss.

"OK. Wait—there's no boy's room in here. It's a girls' school, remember?"

Tiffany touched Susan's arm. "There's the girls' locker room. Nobody's in there; Woody can use that."

"OK. Woody, you get to boldly go where no man has gone before: into the girls' locker room." Susan giggled. "Are you ready?"

"Yeah." He was embarrassed once again. "I'll hurry."

The locker room had bare concrete floors, walls lined with lockers and benches, a large shower, and a row of stalls. A series of cheerleader, majorette, and dance-team outfits hung on a long bar. He could visualize the room full of half-dressed girls. He was excited.

"Hey, don't memorize the place, silly. Piss and let's go!" Susan ordered.

He looked around for a urinal out of habit, then

shuffled off to the last stall. "Be sure to lift the seat, and put it back down again," Tiffany called after him.

Inside the stall, he unzipped himself. His cock was swelling once again; it was always troublesome to piss through a hard-on. He aimed it carefully; he didn't want to get the floor messy, not with his tormentresses around.

He couldn't do it, not in the girls' room, not with his erection. Everything hit him at once and he realized he had to masturbate, right then and there. He reached one hand up to rub his nipple and started pumping his cock with his other hand, quickly, needing to come before they started calling for him. Just a few seconds, and the worst would be over; he'd have the relief he so desperately needed. His eyes closed as he whipped the skin back and forth along his swollen shaft; his finger strummed his rockhard nipple; his mind filled with the images of his recent humiliation; he could see himself down on the floor, kneeling, begging, holding his cock out to be toyed with…he was going to unload buckets of come right now…he was…

"Gotcha!" Hands behind him pulled his shorts down to his knees. A bright flash went off. He swiveled around. More flashes. Tiffany was snapping pictures as fast as she could while Susan, who had pulled his shorts down, laughed as his cock bobbed up and down, leaking the evidence of its near-explosion. He tried to grab for the camera, but tangled in his own shorts and stumbled to the cold concrete floor. Tiffany hid the camera quickly.

"Well, Woody, what do you have to say for yourself?" Susan demanded sternly.

TABITHA'S TICKLE

Tiffany rejoined them. "Yeah. Jerking off in the girls' locker room. Woody, you're in deep trouble."

He could only stammer and stutter again; the combination of shock, humiliation, marijuana, and arousal had completely overloaded his mental circuits.

The girls cut short his excuses and explanations and apologies. "Woody, the pictures don't lie. We've got you. You had better do what we say, or not only will the pictures go to sweet Sharon, but also to the authorities. You've had it. Your fate is in our hands."

He was still crouched on the floor, unable to cover himself, nearly in tears.

"Please don't get me in trouble. I'll do anything!" he whimpered.

The girls smiled knowingly at each other. "Anything?" Susan said.

"Yes, anything. Please. I'm sorry. I couldn't help it."

"Anything at all?" Susan probed.

"Yes, anything."

"Are you sure you mean anything?" she asked again.

"Yes! Yes!" he cried.

"OK. Take off the rest of your clothes."

With trembling hands, he removed the rest of his garments. He was naked and erect.

"Now stand up."

He did. The girls circled him like cats stalking their prey. He trembled with fear.

"Well, Tiffany, what do you think we ought to do with him?" Susan asked.

"I don't know, but he deserves some serious punishment.

Waxing his woody in the girls' locker room. What a dirty boy!"

Tiffany stroked his naked rear end. He moaned and rocked his hips under her teasing touch. She spanked him, hard. "Stand still!" she ordered. "Absolutely still. Put your hands over your head."

With that, the girls embarked on a new campaign of tantalizing, making him stand absolutely still as they teased him. Susan toyed with his nipples; then Tiffany goosed his rear. Tiffany stood with her body so close to his that his cock brushed the rough fabric of her skirt, then Susan played spider's legs with the inside of his thigh. He couldn't help moving each time, and each time another stinging blow landed on his rear end. Their repeated commands couldn't make him obey; neither could the spanking.

They escalated their attack, exploring his nude form, caressing his ticklish sides, his tiny erect nipples, his dangling testicles. Susan snickered at his increasing discomfiture, tickling her soft hands over his naked torso, touching his nipples, sending waves of shameful pleasure coursing through him. His shame and vulnerability were evident. She petted his nipples slowly, rubbing the rigid nubs in a circle. He let out an agonized moan of frustration.

Her fingers neared the head of his cock, then pulled away at the last minute. She played a game of avoidance, caressing every part of his groin except the one most needful.

The nearness of her hands drove him crazy. "Oh,

Tabitha's Tickle

God!" he pleaded. "Oh, God…oh, God…please…yes…touch it…oh…yes…oh…"

"Horny little bastard, aren't you?" Tiffany commented. He nodded shamefully and groaned with mortified desire, but neither tormentress showed him any mercy.

The devilish teasing continued. He was red-faced and gasping for breath. He was rocking back and forth on his knees, dangerously close to falling. His mind was reeling as the coldhearted vixens continued their slow, devastating stroking. Clear seminal fluid began to leak from the purple cap of his untouched penis.

Finally Tiffany commented, "I think he's had about all he can take."

Susan regarded him carefully. "You're probably right. Still, Woody, you're not off the hook yet. Better keep doing exactly what we say, or you'll end up in even worse trouble."

Bobby could only nod his consent. His stricken face must have earned some sympathy because suddenly Susan patted it and said, "You're cute. I really like the way you blush. We've teased this boy enough—don't you think so, Tiffany? I think it's time to be nice to him."

"I think you're right," Tiffany said.

"C'mere, Woody," Susan said, sliding against his nude body for another delicious tongue-kiss.

"My turn next," Tiffany said, and took her turn in his arms. Bobby's cock was alive with delight.

"Let's go to the exercise room. We should have some privacy there for a while," Susan said. Each girl took an arm and they led him back through the locker room, leaving his clothes behind on the floor. He thought briefly about them, then surrendered to his overwhelming lust.

The exercise room was accessible directly from the locker room through an inside door. Besides the normal weight machines, one wall was a huge mirror with a ballet barre, obviously for practicing. Bobby got a glimpse of himself—a tall, naked blonde boy in the company of two devastatingly sexy cheerleaders.

A long leather-covered bench was connected to a weight-lifting machine. "Lie down," Susan said, grasping his cock in her firm little hand, making him gasp with pleasure. He stretched himself out on the leather and looked up with delight at the scantily clad beauties towering above him. They pulled up stools on either side of the bench and sat beside him. Susan grasped his cock in one hand and began tongue-kissing him; Tiffany began to lick his nipples. He closed his eyes in a sea of sensual delight. "Put your arms over your head," Tiffany whispered, "so I can do you better." He obliged.

Susan's hand continued a slow, devilishly delightful masturbation as she continued to neck with him. Tiffany got up, and walked behind him. He could feel her hands grasping his, stretching him out, slipping his hands into loops at the top of the machine, then stretching his legs into stirrups below.

He didn't think very much about what was happening until suddenly she pressed a button. The loops began to tighten around his wrists and ankles, imprisoning him. Startled, he jerked his arms and legs, only to find he could not move. Suddenly Susan stopped kissing him, let go of his throbbing cock, and sat up with a wicked smile on her face.

"Hey! Wait a minute! What are you doing?" he cried.

Then, to his shock and humiliation, the outside door to the exercise room opened to reveal two more Valentine College cheerleaders.

"Welcome, girls," Susan said. "This is Woody. He's our new mascot." Her hands slipped back over his stomach and, to his horror, began to tickle.

5

Count Felipe de la Roche was a student of sex magick. He believed that the special energies surrounding arousal and orgasm tapped into the underlying magickal energies of the universe. Research in the great alchemy and thaumaturgical libraries of Europe had allowed him to piece together elements of the puzzle. The Philosophers' Stone, the semimythical creation that would turn base metals into gold, was real after all, but its transformational power source was Tantric—erotic—in origin. That power source, Count Felipe believed, would not only unlock the secrets of the elements, but provide mystical access to power, wealth, and wisdom. Like many students of That Which Man Was Not Meant to Know, he ended up with a fate he did not anticipate; unlike many such students, his fate had its delightful side.

His studies revealed that he needed a vessel for the transformation, a sex partner whose building arousal, never relieved by orgasm, would serve as the transforming engine to make him all powerful. A beautiful American coed, traveling for the summer in Spain, became the target of his quest. Her name was Tabitha.

Heart-stoppingly lovely even in her jean shorts and white T-shirt, a backpack hoisted high and no makeup, she seemed to possess that quality of sexual drive and all-American openness essential to his quest. Distinguished, handsome, sophisticated, an accomplished seducer of women, Count Felipe found it easy to approach her. He swept her off her feet, out of the dust of the Barcelona streets, and into a suite. For their first dinner together, he insisted on buying her an elegant new gown. When he saw her walking down the steps of the hotel, her body poured into a chic French creation, her cascades of thick hair piled high, his heart was pounding. She was even more exquisite than he had imagined.

From caviar to oysters, champagne to Chablis, the courses of a formal meal passed through to the flaming dessert and cognac. The seduction proceeded according to its ancient script. She accepted the rituals of courtship with a secret smile; she cooperated fully in her own seduction. Then the drive in his Porsche up the winding road to the ancient castle of the de la Roches, the servant pouring sherry, the first warm kiss beside the stone fireplace, the slow seduction, the exquisite sex...

She stayed with him as he slowly revealed the secrets of his research. She drank it in eagerly, reading his manuscripts, asking probing questions, rewarding him for her education with nights of passionate delights. He invited her to be his assistant on his Tantric quest for magickal powers, and she accepted. Tied up, shackled, teased, she became his experimental sex toy. Her lustful writhing from denied orgasm captivated him. Between experiments, their courtship continued; he was falling in love. She continued her studies.

Then came the morning when Count Felipe awoke, not in his bedroom but in his laboratory in the dungeons beneath his castle, naked and shackled. Tabitha smiled her secret smile. "Don't worry. We are going to continue our search together. You see, darling, I know a thing or two about arousal that you don't know. I'm going to introduce you to the secrets of Valentine College."

Tabitha had her own spells, he quickly learned: spells of exquisite teasing, tantalizing frustration, sensual stimulation that built him up to heights of arousal he could never have imagined. Yet it was not only about the sex, the turnabout. She was serious about the magick as well. He learned the truth: there was real power in the ancient manuscripts—but it was woman's power, not man's.

She created her own instruments: an enchanted silver ring that could withhold orgasm or trigger it with a secret word, love philters to captivate and enslave, and more. She experimented with new spells, gaining in power. Still, she needed more. She told him of Valentine

College and the sorority of teasers. "There is a source of power that will enable all these spells to become reality," she said, a wicked smile of delight filling him with pangs of love and fear.

Even without her love philters, Count Felipe was fully under her spell. "Marry me," he murmured in his shackles. "I'm yours no matter what. Marry me and you'll have all the international fortune of the de la Roches at your disposal."

Tabitha was pleased. "Yes," she said. "I will marry you. I'll tease you and torment you and use you, but remember—I love you, too."

Count Felipe sent his new fiancée back to America, back to school to turn her secret sorority into the new laboratory for their magickal research, and turned his attention back to business. There was a difference: the silver ring that owned his cock kept him under her control. Every three months he flew to America to renew their liaison; their marriage would be postponed until her graduation at the end of this school year.

With each liaison, Tabitha had new surprises and torments ready for him. The anticipation kept him hard on the long transatlantic flight until his arrival at Valentine College, where he was greeted with the latest refinement of Tabitha's wicked imagination.

Sharon thought she was beyond being shocked. Her nakedness quickly ceased to be a problem; she felt natural and unashamed. She had a good body and she knew it, and somehow the erotic spell cast by this strange house had entered her. Tabitha took her leash and

TABITHA'S TICKLE

escorted her from the library through another door. Her bare feet padded silently in the thick, rich carpet. Tabitha commented on the age of the house, its ancient history, the ghosts that supposedly inhabited the castle.

With each step, the corridors grew darker. The house indeed had a gothic feel. In her imagination she could hear moans of sexual pleasure, laughter, even screams of passion and pain. She felt herself falling into an enchantment.

They climbed up the winding back staircases to the suite of apartments Tabitha kept as her own. "Would you like something to drink?" Tabitha asked.

Sharon nodded. Suddenly she was thirsty. Tabitha opened a locked cabinet and produced a silver goblet, into which she poured a strange liquid. "Drink it all!" she commanded.

Sharon paused. "Go ahead," Tabitha urged. "It's a special mixture we prepared. It's part of your initiation."

The beverage had a bitter taste. "What's in this?" Sharon asked.

"Oh, the usual. Some Ecstasy, some THC, a drop or two of LSD, and some witchcraft. It's the ultimate aphrodisiac. For the next twenty-four hours, you will become a creature of pure sex—exactly what we want."

Sharon looked down at the empty goblet with a slight shiver. Then she laughed nervously. "I already *was* a creature of pure sex," she said.

Tabitha smiled. "I know. I believe you'll make a great sorority sister. Before then, you have to learn about our secrets, and this is the best way to experience them."

She took the goblet from Sharon's unresisting hand, smiled, and kissed her. The naked young coed moaned at the touch of the lovely woman in the red leather dress. Tabitha caressed her, rubbing her hands over her recently spanked rear, and slowly worked up to her breasts, kneading them softly in her warm hands. Sharon moaned through deep tongue-kisses and didn't resist when Tabitha's hand dipped teasingly between her thighs to probe at her wetness. She had never been touched there by a woman before; she was surprised at how easily she accepted it.

When the kiss finally stopped, Sharon was panting. Suddenly the room began to quiver, to mutate in color and shape. A deep and total feeling of sensuality took possession of every nerve in her body. Tabitha regarded her with a smile. "I think you're ready to meet my fiancé," she said, and led her into the next room, her bedroom.

The distinguished man had Spanish features, a trim, muscular body with hair beginning to whiten in curls on his chest. Some white hair was part of the thick mass surrounding his erect penis, imprisoned like Robin's with a silver ring. Naked and spread-eagled, arms and legs lashed with silken scarves to the four posters at the corners of the large canopy bed, sweat beading on his forehead and hips twitching helplessly, he strained at his bonds as the two young girls on either side teased his cock with slow, deliberate motions.

"Count Felipe de la Roche, may I present Sharon, our newest pledge," Tabitha said, stroking his cheek gently.

He stared at her with an expression filled with need

and desire. "Forgive me for not rising," he smiled, the effort of politeness taking all his remaining energy, "but as you can see, I'm all tied up."

The young girls continued playing with his twitching penis. "Sharon, meet Zoe and Mandy." Zoe was petite with flaming red hair and a tiny figure. She wore a red Lycra teddy with a diamond cut out of the center. She smiled at Sharon. Her gleaming teeth and wicked sparkling eyes somehow reminded Sharon of a vampire. Mandy's innocent blue eyes, soft, wavy blonde hair, and ripe girlish figure made her seem the very opposite of her partner; she was every boy's backseat fuck fantasy. Sharon was surprised at her own body's response to the two girls; she knew she could take them on individually or together and still have energy left over for the bound man. She stared at his cock with hungry lust. *A creature of pure sex*, she thought. *God, that's me.*

"How is Felipe behaving?" Tabitha asked.

Zoe giggled cruelly and gave the Count's cock a hard twist, her hand rubbing underneath the sensitive head. He moaned. "So far, he's promised us a car and a trip around the world for a single orgasm." General laughter greeted the remark; the Count blushed.

"Oh, he did, did he?" Tabitha said. "Well, Felipe, I'll have to think of an extra-special punishment for you this time. It's only been three months since your last orgasm; there's no excuse for begging. I know; I'll have Sharon suck you off."

Sharon tore her eyes from his jutting hard-on to look at Tabitha with surprise.

"Would you like to suck this hard cock?" Tabitha asked. Zoe and Mandy sat back to watch with amused delight.

"Yes...I mean, if you want me to," Sharon stammered. She wanted his cock badly. She was salivating. She liked sucking cock, but she had never experienced desire like this before.

"Oh, I do," Tabitha said. "You'll find this extra-special." She produced a silver vibrator from the bedside stand. "Zoe, would you prepare him for me?"

Zoe grinned her vampire grin and carefully slid the vibrator into the bound man's asshole, then turned it on. He moaned at the first buzzing sounds. Tabitha then took out a jar of strange-looking salve and rubbed a thin line down the ridge of his cock, over the silver ring, and to the jutting edge of the vibrator protruding from his rear.

Finally she produced two more large silver rings that she placed on both Sharon's and the Count's head, like crowns. Sharon looked at her questioningly. "It enables you to feel what he feels," Tabitha said. "I want you to know what a needy cock feels like."

Tabitha unhooked her leash and Sharon crawled up onto the luxurious four-poster and crouched between Felipe's outstretched legs. Zoe and Mandy kneeled on either side of her, watching her while playing idly with their prisoner's rockhard nipples. Tabitha looked on from bedside. In spite of being surrounded by gorgeous half-clad girls, Count Felipe's attention was riveted on his beautiful fiancée.

TABITHA'S TICKLE

At Tabitha's command, Sharon bent over, took the shaft of his cock in one hand, tossed her hair aside, and gently began to lick and moisten his straining organ, teasing both of them with anticipation.

Suddenly a wave of new sensation swept over her. It was as if a penis had suddenly sprouted between her legs, a teased and tormented penis throbbing with desperate need. The wetness of her mouth warmed her penis. As Tabitha promised, she was feeling what he felt. She was sucking her own cock. Her mouth opened wide and she devoured it, her moans echoing his. With the instantaneous mental feedback, she sucked his cock perfectly, the waves of pleasure washing over both sucker and suckee. She knew what it was like to be teased as a woman, but she had never felt the absolute desperation of a cock denied its orgasm. It was unbearably strong; she sucked harder, faster, deeper, devouring it with her hot mouth, her own hot imaginary cock sending out its signals of desire.

For some reason she could not fathom, he was trying to hold back, to save his orgasm, but she would have none of it. She was going to draw every drop of sperm from his cock no matter how hard he tried to resist. She needed it. She needed it badly. She swirled her tongue around his shaft, sucked it in and out, pumped the shaft while stimulating the sensitive head, forcing out his orgasm, bringing him unwillingly to the edge.

"No...careful...you don't understand!" The Spaniard moaned, but she paid no attention. His vibrator was echoed as an imaginary vibrator in her ass, driving her even wilder with desire. Both their orgasms were close, so close…. Finally, her mouth overwhelmed the resistance of his cock.

Under the control of the silver cockring, his orgasm hit, but with a fiendish difference: she could feel the pulsing and clenching, but there was no sense of relief, no jets of spurting come and then…. "Aaaah!" both victims shrieked with the pain of electric shock as the vibrators—his real, hers imaginary—delivered punishment for the unauthorized orgasm attempts. With each pulse and clench of his cock, another jolt of electricity coursed through them; it took several jolts before the worst was over. She was gasping and so was he; their audience laughed cruelly at their expressions of shock and lust and pain.

"Want to suck him again?" Tabitha laughed.

Sharon could still feel her cock and vibrator through the magic of the silver headbands. Without conscious awareness, she reached between her legs to play with her cock, and was startled not to find it. The powerful aphrodisiac coursing through her system had so disoriented her that it took time for her to return to some sense of focus. She was burning up with desire; she needed her own orgasm nearly as much as the Count or poor Robin. She looked up at Tabitha. "Oh, God!" she whimpered. "That was so hot! I'm burning up!"

All three girls laughed as Tabitha helped the weak-limbed Sharon climb off the four-poster and remove the silver headband. Zoe removed the vibrator and headband from the Count. They began to stroke his prone and trembling body, returning to the slow, cruel teasing their visitors had interrupted.

"My darling, I'll see you this evening," Tabitha said, leaning down to kiss her fiancé. She stroked her hands down to his cock and caressed him for a moment. "Be good, suffer for me, and I'll come back to torture you some more tonight. Sound good?"

He could only nod weakly in response. "I love you, dearest," he said.

"And I love you, too," Tabitha replied. "But now it's time to continue Sharon's initiation." She took the trembling girl by the arm and escorted her out of the bedroom.

Back in the parlor of Tabitha's suite, Sharon said, "May I ask a question?"

"By all means, darling," Tabitha said.

"What was that—magic? A-Are you a witch?"

"Yes, it was, and yes, I am," the sorority leader said. "Tau Zeta Rho is also a coven, but our magic, you see, is utterly real. We have Count Felipe to thank for that, in part. The source of our power is orgasmic denial, especially male orgasmic denial, but sometimes female denial is useful. That's why we keep mostly boy-toys with occasional girl-toys. Most of the girl-toy need is satisfied by initiating new members. Right now, you're contributing to the sexual energy of this household, and those of us who are trained initiates in the ways of sorcery can use that power. We're still learning, but the toys you just played with are examples of what we're able to do. So is the potion you drank. The drugs are part of it, but some of what is happening to you is pure witchcraft.

"Your initiation serves several purposes," Tabitha continued. "You give us female sexual energy, which is part of our power. You are tested for membership in our occult society. If you pass, you'll learn how to use spells and potions yourself. Not all our sorority members become full witches, though they all learn at least some of the basic sexual magick. And finally, we enjoy the initiation rituals ourselves. You're cute. I think Kelly really likes you, and I'm pretty sure what she's going to do with her time with you." Tabitha smiled prettily. Sharon gulped with a combination of fear and desire. She knew what Kelly was likely to do, too.

"Speaking of Kelly"—Tabitha looked up—"here she is!"

Sharon turned to see the tall blonde enter the room. Her piercing blue eyes twinkled with sexual delight; her wide, sensual mouth smiled with pleasure.

"I'm going to put Kelly in charge of the next phase of your initiation," Tabitha announced. "I have some special errands to run before tonight's party."

Sharon stood eagerly, placing her hands behind her back to open her body for Kelly's inspection. The blonde sorority officer looked pleased. "I think we'll go on a tour of the dungeons next," Kelly said.

"I think that's a fine idea." Tabitha smiled and handed Kelly the leash. Kelly snapped on the leash and then took a spring-loaded clip and fastened the rings on Sharon's leather wrist cuffs together. Sharon tugged

TABITHA'S TICKLE

experimentally. She was caught. Kelly walked in front of her and slowly ran her hand over Sharon's naked torso. She moaned and arched, showing herself off, wanting to be taken and seduced by the lovely cheerleader.

"Eager little thing, isn't she?" Kelly smiled. "What have you two been up to?"

"Just a little drink and a game with the silver headbands," Tabitha laughed.

"Oh," Kelly said knowingly. "I think she's trying to seduce me. Think she's primarily into girls?"

Sharon blushed in confusion. She wanted to be seduced by Kelly, but she wasn't ready to do the seducing herself.

"We'll find out, won't we?" Tabitha said. "Right now, I don't even think she knows, herself."

Kelly laughed. "We'll see how she reacts to the dungeons. See you a little later."

"Bye-bye, darling," Tabitha said, kissing Sharon on the lips and giving her nipple one exciting tweak. "A word of warning. Some parts of the dungeon are so exciting, you might never want to leave. That's how we get our girl-toys."

Consumed with excitement, Sharon trembled suddenly. She already knew she was game for anything, and now her desire could trap her as a victim forever.

"See you on the other side!" Tabitha smiled as Kelly led her victim back into the darkness of the corridors.

6

"Is little Woody ticklish?" Susan cooed.

"Ha-ha-ha-no! Hee-hee-hee-please!" He choked and twisted as four sets of girlish fingers tormented his helpless nude body. No sooner had he begun squirming under Susan's teasing fingers than the other girls joined in—teasing Tiffany and the two new cheerleaders. His cock was still rockhard, saluting its captors, but his mind was overloaded with the powerful tickling. He hated being tickled and he was very ticklish; this was true torture for him.

He howled and pleaded and guffawed and laughed uncontrollably; he jerked at the inflexible mechanical cuffs that held him to the leather exercise bench. Susan and Tiffany were still seated on either side of him, working on his sides and neck and underarms and nipples. One of the new girls, short with light brown, sandy hair and brown eyes, worked on his stomach and inner thighs, while the other new girl, another cruel looking brunette, tall and classy, had pulled a stool up to the foot of the bench and attacked the soles of his feet. It was a tickle orgy with himself at the center, and he wasn't enjoying the attention one bit.

"Please…ha-ha-ha-ha…I can't—ha-ha—take anymore!" he begged. Tears of agonized laughter ran down his cheeks. His arm muscles hurt where he had jerked them, trying desperately to get free.

The girls weren't in any hurry to show mercy; they were clearly enjoying themselves, delighting in his agony and competing to see who could draw the most helpless laughter from his body. He continued to beg and plead for mercy. Wrong move. That only inflamed them more. These girls had a helpless male at their mercy, and they planned to take full advantage. And there wasn't a single thing Bobby could do except go nuts.

"Nooooo! Please!" he cried, continuing his struggle against the merciless cuffs. Their wriggling fingers tickled his underarms, his stomach, his nipples. He writhed in helpless, uncontrollable laughter, squirming desperately to escape the tormenting sensations. "Ha-ha-ahaha-ha! Oh-ha-ha-ha-stop, please ha-ha-stop, no, no-haaha-ha!" It was hard to breathe; he felt himself gasping for lack of oxygen. They didn't even notice; they were wrapped up in the torture.

His brain was completely short-circuited. Seconds passed by like hours in the agony of being a truly helpless tickle-victim. He had never imagined that; Sharon tickled him from time to time, but he could always get away. By now, he was completely hysterical, but his cock stayed hard as an iron bar.

The four cheerleaders continued to play Bobby's helplessly strapped body like a piano. They tickled him all over—underarms, nipples, the inside of his thighs, his kneecaps, everywhere. The more he begged, the more they laughed with fiendish glee and redoubled their efforts.

The cheerleader who scratched his soles with her fingernails made him screech and scream with tormented agony. Susan drew designs in his armpits and made slow, tormenting circles around his rockhard nipples. Every touch, every stroke turned a new area of his body into a ticklish zone until there wasn't a square inch of nonticklish flesh on his body. Tiffany alternated between gentle tickle and rough tickle, digging her fingers into his sensitive sides, making Bobby howl with laughter as she slid her devilish digits up and down his shackled body.

"Oh, ha-ha, I ca-can't stand-ha-ha any more!" Bobby howled. Meanwhile, the sandy-haired girl at his middle traced the contours of his legs and inner thighs, stopping for an agonizing eternity in the hollow of his knees. Bobby never imagined that such sensations could be drawn out of that part of his body. Slowly and tormentingly, she moved her tickling fingers higher up his thighs, tantalizingly, avoiding his rigid, straining cock, then back down his inner thighs and calves, then up again. Throughout this, his cock was standing straight up, pulsing hotly, leaking drops of clear pre-come.

He was desperate for relief from the terrible tickling and his incredible frustration. Twisting and turning, he struggled to get free, but the shackles were relentless. He was just about to pass out when the four grinning sadists finally decided they'd had enough.

The girls were panting with their exertion; driving him insane with tickling torture took energy. "Let's stop before he has a heart attack on us," Susan chuckled.

Even then, as he started to calm down, panting as if he'd just finished running a marathon, one of the girls would give him another tweak or tickle, sending him back into paroxysms.

Naked and helpless, Bobby's heart pounded as he awaited their next move.

"We just came by to tell you to have him ready for the party tonight," the sandy-haired girl said. "Looks like he may not survive, though." She tweaked his side, making him jerk in helpless reflex.

Susan laughed. "If he has trouble with this part, he really will have trouble later. This is just a little warm-up." She planted a kiss on his lips; her teasing eyes focused on his. "Just a little warm-up."

He gulped; he could believe anything now.

The brunette at his feet came up. Her luscious body showed to great advantage in the scanty Valentine cheerleading outfit. She smiled. "Your girlfriend's having a good time. Her initiation is beginning right now. You know she gave you to us as a toy, don't you?"

Susan smiled. "I think he was beginning to figure that out, but we haven't made it official yet. That's right, Woody. You're really going to be our mascot. Sharon's initiation required that she give us a boy-toy. She volunteered you. That's OK with you, isn't it? Tell us you like being our boy-toy."

Bobby blushed yet again, revealing the truth even before he spoke. "Oh, God, yes...just don't tickle me anymore."

"We'll do anything we want, and you'll like it," Susan said, giving his right nipple a hard pinch. "Besides, I bet I can make you beg for us to tickle you again."

"Oh, no...no..." he pleaded.

Susan grabbed his throbbing erection and began pumping it, slipping one finger over the leaking head to rub the seminal fluid over the entire shaft. She stimulated him quickly toward an orgasm, then slowed down. "Would you like to come right now?" she asked.

Deliriously aroused, he looked into her teasing eyes, "Yes...yes...please..." He knew this was some sort of new tease, but he couldn't help it. He needed to come so badly.

"Just beg for us to tickle you again, twice as long and twice as hard, and I'll make you come. OK?"

He was silent. Nothing was worth being tickled... except the way her hand continued stroking him, teasing him up to the edge, then backing off, up to the edge and backing off again....

"Yes! Yes! Tickle me twice as long and twice as hard! Just make me come! Please!"

She released him. "See? There are worse things than being tickled. And this is one."

He moaned again with frustration.

The brunette asked Tiffany, "Got any pot?"

Tiffany smiled. "Of course I do. Have you ever known me not to?"

The girls giggled as Tiffany produced another joint from an endless secret stash in her skirt waistband; obviously, there was a hidden pocket.

The brunette moved her stool up next to the other girls. The name on her cheerleading outfit read "Marcia." She had an intimidating quality to her sexuality. Her perfume was sensual and powerful. Julie, the sandy-haired cheerleader, straddled his hips and kneeled over him. His cock was under her skirt, brushing against her panties.

The joint traveled around the circle of girls.

"Yeahhhh..." Marcia murmured. "That hits the spot."

Julie smiled in agreement. "How about you, Bobby?" Julie said, "Want a hit?" He nodded. He was so crazy that even more marijuana could hardly do more damage.

Instead of placing the joint in his mouth, Julie took a hit herself, leaned over, and pressed her lips against his, forcing his mouth open and breathing the thick smoke into his lungs in a reverse mouth-to-mouth resuscitation. He felt the effects of both pot and kiss, and her large breasts pressing against his naked chest. His cock throbbed and twitched as it rubbed against her panties.

"Oooh, Bobby," she giggled, feeling it twitch, then reaching down and giving it a playful squeeze. "Did that get you all turned on?"

He could only blush. Julie said, "Marcia, why don't you give him a toke?"

"Sure, I'd love to." She took a hit, then kissed him deeply, breathing the smoke deep into his lungs.

"Oh, God! This pot has got me so horny I could burst!" Julie moaned. "I really need to get off...*now*." She sat up and rubbed her hands up over her round breasts, cupping them in her hands, rubbing her nipples until they stood up through the thin sweater. She squeezed her thighs together rhythmically around his torso as she ground against his cock with her silk-covered pussy.

Julie pulled her thin sweater up over her head, revealing large, shapely breasts. She unfastened the clasp on her skirt, unzipped it and slipped it off without ever leaving the table. The other girls looked on with amusement. Bobby was utterly entranced. Naked except for panties and socks, Julie ground her nether regions against him. She was so wet that the moisture was visible between her legs.

"You need some attention for that cock?" she drawled softly. His moans and thrusting hips answered her. "Well, if you take care of us, we'll take care of you. Be a good boy, and maybe we won't have to tickle you anymore." She goosed him just for emphasis.

Julie looked at the other girls. "I sure hope this boy knows how to lick pussy."

"He does," said Tiffany. "His girlfriend was pretty happy."

"He'd better," Susan said firmly, "or he knows what will happen to him."

He gulped, but he didn't have much time to think about consequences, because Julie moved up to straddle his face, sliding her panties down, then rubbing her hand over her pussymound and between her legs. "God, I'm so wet," she giggled. "I want you to lick me and make me come. Then maybe…just maybe…you'll get yours."

Opening her slippery soft netherlips with her fingers, she slowly lowered her open, wet pussy to meet his lips. As Bobby's tongue licked up her wet slit, she moaned with pleasure. "Aaah…that's right…do it good. Yes. Yes. Yes!" He drew her netherlips into his mouth and licked the full length, up and down her pussy. His blood was boiling as he kissed and sucked at her. She tilted her head back with a smile of undisguised pleasure as his tongue probed her sensual depths. She reached her hands up to begin tweaking her own pulsing nipples, slowly grinding her hips in delight.

She moaned, urging her shackled victim to greater efforts. He moaned, too, thrusting his cock up into the empty air. Marcia began to tease it; and then, to his delight, she began to suck it. Wetly, hotly, she engulfed his desperately throbbing cock in her hot mouth as he groaned with rapture. That completely made up for the tickling.

Julie's pussy grew wetter and wetter as she neared her own climax. Her sensual moaning became more insistent. "Aaah. Oooh. Yes. Yes. Oh. Oh! *Oh! Yes! Yes!*

That's it! Yes! Ooooh!" Her orgasm shook her young body as she ground her hips against his face. Viscous fluid bathed Bobby's cheeks and lips as he furiously licked and sucked her through the convulsions of orgasm. Marcia's cocksucking drew him closer and closer to his own long-denied orgasm; but when Julie finished coming, she stopped.

With a final shudder, the tension left Julie's body and she collapsed over him. His heart pounded and his hips bucked slowly with the frustration and sensuality of the moment; she lay calmly against him, recovering from her orgasm.

"Move over, girl, it's my turn!" Marcia ordered. Julie looked up as if to argue, then moved aside. With one hand she reached between Bobby's thighs to softly feather his agonizingly sensitive cock. He moaned. "Please, I'm so close!"

Julie laughed. "Poor baby. Not until Marcia's had her turn."

Then Marcia stripped for him, making it a little show, grinding her hips and staring hotly into Bobby's inflamed eyes as she wriggled out of her tight cheerleader costume.

Then her dark pubic hair and rich, full pussylips were above him, and with deep pleasure he began licking and sucking. He loved sucking pussy; it was almost enough to make up for all the teasing he had been subjected to. Julie's tantalizing fingers teased his enraged cock as he lost himself in the pleasures of Marcia's pussy. He sucked her clit gently into his mouth, then slid his tongue deep within her inner lips. He opened his eyes and watched her playing with her own nipples, her head thrown back, eyes closed, the tip of her tongue penetrating between her lips. The incredibly sexy sight was nearly enough to send Bobby's cock spurting in waves of come, but Julie's careful teasing kept him from the brink. Then—"Ooh! Ah! Ah! Ah!" And Marcia was in the midst of orgasm.

There were more moans, and he looked over to see Tiffany with her skirt up over her waist, her hand deep inside her panties, petting herself to her own simultaneous orgasm. Susan watched the group lust with amused pleasure until finally all the girlish moans subsided, leaving only Bobby to suffer from his denied orgasm.

He writhed helplessly, every centimeter of his body alive with erotic need. "Please…please…" he moaned.

"I don't know, girls," Julie said. "He licks pussy well. Should we be nice to him?"

"Well," Marcia drawled slowly, "I think he probably deserves something. Tiffany?"

The masturbating brunette was still rubbing herself after her orgasm. "Let him wait for a while longer."

"Susan?"

"I haven't gotten off yet. Certainly not until I finish."

"Two to two. That's a tie," Julie observed. "Unfortunately, Woody, ties go to the teaser. You lose. Maybe later. Listen, we really just came by to give you the message about timing, so we should get going. Thanks a lot for lending him to us for a little while. I'm really nice and relaxed now." She stretched languorously, showing off her body and smiling wickedly when she caught Bobby's needy stare.

"You're cute, you know," she smiled, pursing her lips and blowing him a kiss. "I really liked tickling you. Maybe we can have some fun later."

"I almost forgot," Marcia said. "I brought a harness set for you." She pulled out a gym bag. "We'd better help you get him all rigged out."

Tiffany stood up, pulled up her panties, and smoothed down her skirt. She rubbed her wet finger over his lips and pushed it into his mouth; he eagerly sucked her pussyjuices. "Mmm," she said. "That just warmed me up. You have to take care of Susan when she's ready. Then I'll need some extra attention." She pushed the button to release the fasteners on the exercise bench. His arms were trembling and weak; Susan and Tiffany had to help him stand.

Tiffany produced still another joint, and Bobby eagerly joined the girls. Being stoned took away some of the embarrassment, making his sex-slavery easier to take. There he was, a college senior, fairly good-looking, naked and helpless as four tantalizing teases, all fully dressed, took advantage of him. He blushed as the humiliating situation became apparent to him.

"Oooh, look!" Julie saw it immediately. "Our little sex toy is blushing. How cute!" The giggling reaction of the other girls only inflamed his face more. This was like the naked nightmare, only worse—it was real. His cock stayed like iron, pursuing its own agenda.

Susan, pressing her petite body up against him kittenishly, her hips brushing lightly against his straining naked cock, whispered, "Put your hands over your head."

Marcia produced a strange contraption from the gym bag. First came a leather harness that fit around his waist and shoulders, meeting in a large metal O-ring in the middle of his chest. It included a leather belt with metal rings hanging from it. Then she produced leather ankle and wrist cuffs, each with a ring, and a leather collar, also ringed. A leather strip came down his back, parted his buttocks, with a circular ring around his anus, allowing access there. Then it split into a studded leather circle that went around his cock and balls. There were snaps on the leather circle that allowed them to fasten a leather cup—making this a male chastity belt. The cup was small; they experimented, but could not get his full erection inside.

"It's OK; we don't want to put it on right now anyway. When we use it, we'll put it on you when you're soft. Then wait until you get a hard-on," Susan giggled. He winced at the thought. It would hurt.

They fastened a metal clasp to the rings on his waistband, locking his hands behind his back. He realized that the rings and clasps would allow the girls to put him in virtually any sort of bondage they could think of, all in seconds. He was fast losing any hope of freedom.

"We also brought a blindfold, a leash, and this." She produced a silver cock ring.

"Oh, yes," Susan said. "Perfect." She knelt in front of him and to his delight took his rigid straining organ into her mouth, sucking it warmly and wetly. He could feel the surging orgasm building. She pulled her mouth away and slid the ring down to the base of his cock.

TABITHA'S TICKLE

"Let's see if it works." She smiled up at him knowingly. She returned to sucking. Tiffany stood behind him, reached around, and began playing with his nipples. It felt so good. He closed his eyes and leaned back. The two other cheerleaders watched. His hips moved under her oral attentions. There was something serious in her cocksucking that allowed him to believe this time she meant for him to come.

It didn't take long. He realized with great delight that she had taken it finally past the point of no return. "Yes...yes..." he moaned. "Now! Aaah!"

His long-delayed orgasm hit in a wave of convulsive surging pleasure. "Unnhh!" he grunted, thrusting his hips as he went over the edge. "Aaah!"

The first pulse of his orgasm hit; it was delicious. But something strange was happening—there was no sperm, no jet of milky viscous come. Just the quivering delight of "Oooh!" and "Arrhh!" and "Ungh!" as each convulsion hit. There was orgasm—but, to his horror, no release! He quivered through a long orgasm, the best cocksucking of his life—but he was just as aroused, just as tormented as before.

"God...God...God...please...help!" he pleaded with his blonde tormentress. He was quivering with unfulfilled need when she released his cock, leaned back, wiped her lips with the back of her hand, and smiled.

"Like it?" she laughed. "Is that what poor horny Woody needed?"

"No...please...I didn't really come..."

"Of course you didn't come," Susan chided him.

"Why would I want to make you come? I told you you weren't going to come, didn't I? I just wanted to make sure the silver cockring did its purpose. It did. As long as it's on, you can have all the orgasms I decide you deserve, but you'll stay ready for everything else I have in mind. Understand?"

She had a devilish grin that enslaved his very soul. He had fallen victim to a strange secret sorority of teasing cheerleaders who were subjecting him to torments undreamed of…and in his secret heart, he loved it.

"Now," Susan said, standing, teasing his helpless nipples while smiling a withering smile of total control, "it's time to introduce you to the real initiation. All this has just been a little warm-up. Think you can take it?"

"No, Mistress Susan," he sighed. "But I will."

"What a good boy you are," she said, taking his cock in her hands and squeezing it. "Feels nice, doesn't it?" He moaned. "It's nicer when you really need it, isn't it?" she giggled. "Remember, we're just getting started!"

Taking him by the leash, she led her victim into the hall. Julie and Marcia turned left; Tiffany and Susan led Bobby to the right.

7

"I have a few minutes to spare." Tabitha smiled as she looked down on her helpless, spread-eagled fiancé. "I think I want something only you can provide." The look on her face was slightly vampiric.

Utterly under the spell of the dominating vixen, Count Felipe de la Roche gulped, dry-mouthed with desire. Zoe and Mandy released his oozing cock, thick with viscous fluid from innumerable teasings. They got off the bed, leaving the Count to Tabitha.

The beautiful witch began to unlace the bodice of her leather dress, licking her lips with anticipation. Her slow undressing added to the flame of his desire. A wanton expression on her face made his cock lurch with sudden need. She revealed perfect bare breasts, firm nipples crinkling with passion, an exquisitely tiny waist; then, as she slid off the leather skirt, long sensual legs in black silk stockings and red garter belt over red bikini panties.

She pirouetted for her bound lover, showing off her body with pride. "Do you love me?" she giggled.

"I do," the Count sighed.

"Do you remember having me stretched out and shackled in your secret chamber?" she cooed sexily. "I remember how hot I was, how wet your teasing had made me. I remember you going through your manuals, figuring out new delights and trying each one out on me. You were really cruel, you know, but I loved it. Now, of course, the tables are turned. Do you regret it?"

"No, I don't."

"That's good. That's so good." She stretched out on the bed beside him, her face next to his, the heat of her body inflaming his senses, the smell of her rich scent filling his nostrils. She kissed him softly while using her hand to tease his nipples and slip farther down to his cock. Then she began sucking on his nipples while playing with his engorged tool. He moaned with ecstasy.

"It's time to turn silver into gold," she whispered, looking teasingly into his eyes. He trembled with anticipation and fear; he knew what that meant.

Tabitha slid open the bedside table drawer and produced a golden ring. She slipped the silver ring of orgasmic denial from his cock and slid the golden ring on in its place. He arched his hips with the sudden sensation as the golden ring began its own magic.

"I want to drink your come," she said wickedly, and in that moment she did look like a vampire, the sexiest vampire in all history.

The juice of his frustration was the source of her witch powers. Fully teased and denied, it formed a storehouse of magickal energy. She licked her lips in anticipation and slid down between his legs. Zoe and Mandy, turned on from their tease, had slipped away to make love. He arched his hips with a low guttural moan as her hungry mouth began to suck his life juices from him. He was being devoured, consumed, as all his energy and focus centered on his imprisoned cock.

The geyser of hot come began to rumble and build in his groin. He was so close. She sucked hard and deep, pulling his soul out through his penis. *"Aaah!"* His moan of passionate release echoed in the bedroom as the first explosion of rich, thick come spurted into Tabitha's hungry, devouring mouth, and then the second and then the third. His orgasm hit him with volcanic force; she swallowed deeply and repeatedly. His head was so sensitive that he began to cry out in sensual agony; her tongue was affecting him like a cat's tongue, rough and sandpapery on his tender purple cockhead.

His energy was drained; he lay weak, like a kitten. His bonds were no longer necessary; he could barely move. Tabitha sat up and licked her lips catlike, catching stray bits of sticky manjuice. She looked down at his wet, dripping cock, still hard. "Again?" She smiled, knowing that the golden ring would pull load after load of come from him until he was truly drained. He looked up at her weakly, desperately. She glowed, radiated with new energy, the magic of his frustrated seed.

She slid off her panties, straddled him, took his still-rigid cock in her hand and sat down on him, devouring his penis in her second mouth. She rode him slowly, deliberately, squeezing her inner muscles to force his second load. She pinched the nipples on his chest as she increased her speed, fucking him harder and harder until: "Unnhh!" his second load jetted into her nether depths, sucking into her female sexual center.

Still, she kept riding, now grinding her clit against the wiry hair around his penis, stimulating herself to her own orgasm. She cried out with her release, simultaneously drawing out a third spurt from her victim.

The magical ring made each come full and rich and thick. He had spurted nearly half a cup in his three orgasms. Tabitha sucked him to a fourth and a fifth before even magick failed. He seemed weaker, older, a shadow of himself, nearly blacking out under the strain. She smiled and patted his head, then slipped off the gold ring and returned the silver ring to its normal place.

Tabitha felt the incredible energy of well-being, of power surging in her system. She had a special enchantment to prepare for the party. Felipe's contribution was the most important part; maybe she'd have to drain another slave or two to get the rest of the energy to put her over the top. Poor Robin had been teased for a long time, she mused. And she had never, ever made him come. Maybe this was his day—or maybe she'd choose someone else just to continue Robin's torment. She'd have to decide later.

She untied her helpless lover and pulled the sheet up over his naked form. She'd send someone up later to bring him something nutritious; he'd need to get his strength back up.

"This is the secret door to the dungeons," Kelly announced, pulling a lever in the library that made a section of the bookcases swivel out. A sudden draft of cold air made the naked Sharon shiver. She could hear moans and even screams from the darkness below—or was it her imagination? She was still in the grips of the aphrodisiac.

"Go ahead!" Kelly commanded. Tentatively, since her hands were still fastened behind her, Sharon stepped into the gloom. The stone steps led down into darkness. On the second step down, suddenly the stairs collapsed under her and she was sliding down a ramp. She shrieked with shock and fear, and slid helplessly into darkness.

Tumbling, disoriented, Sharon was breathless when she landed with a thud. The light was dim. Her heart pounded loudly. She shrieked with terror when hands grabbed her, pulled her naked form to her knees. Then there were more hands, feeling her up, caressing her. Her eyes began to adjust—she was surrounded by boys, horny boys who had a naked girl at their disposal. Hands groped her breasts, followed by mouths suckling her nipples, other hands probed between her thighs, spreading her legs. She was drowning in a sea of hands and tongues, of frustrated lust. The waves of arousal triggered her own; she reached out, wanting a cock in her hands, in her pussy, in her ass, in her mouth—and she heard the answering male grunts of pleasure as she began to masturbate two at once. Then a cock penetrated between her legs. Other hands cradled her head and she could turn side to side to suck two rigid cocks, back and forth. She could feel her own orgasm building; the boys, of course, wore the silver cockrings. The first waves of a long multiple orgasm swept over her; she moaned her ecstasy through a mouthful of hard, dripping cock as endless contractions of orgasm swept over her. The groping, devouring attack went on; the lust-engorged cocks continued their relentless pursuit of release.

Then the lights came on, suddenly, blindingly. Gasping from the delightful spasms of her long orgasm, Sharon was writhing under the continuing erotic assault, but suddenly it stopped. The boys were frozen in their position, turned into human statues. She was trapped with hands and mouths and cocks frozen around her in a grotesque erotic tableau.

The door opened. There was Kelly, accompanied by another girl; this one a green-eyed redhead wearing a micro-length red leather miniskirt and matching red fishnet hose under knee-high red leather stiletto-heeled boots. Around her neck she wore a studded leather collar. Her tight yellow tank top was cut low, revealing the swell of her breasts and hard, jutting nipples. She held a wand in her hand.

"Welcome to the dungeons!" Kelly laughed.

Sharon wriggled and squirmed, managing finally to free herself from the cage formed by the paralyzed hands and arms of the slaveboys. She brushed her tousled, tangled hair with her fingers and looked around with confusion.

"What was that?"

The redhead replied, "Magick, of course. I'm Mistress Amber; the dungeons are my domain."

"Wow," Sharon whistled as she looked at the mass of helpless boy-flesh. With her missing from the center it looked odd—the erect males straining for something not even there. "You can really do that?"

"And more," Amber replied. "This is the center for the male energy we trap, so all of us witches are more powerful here."

Sharon looked at the frozen tableau. "Are they hurt?"

"Oh, no, just frozen until I release them. They can still feel; they just can't move. Take a look."

Sharon explored the nearest human statue, contorted in the same position he used to ravish her. His was one of the cocks she had been sucking. He had dark brown hair and a slim body; the hair on his chest went in a straight line to his straining cock. She touched his cock; it was soft and warm. She looked into his eyes. Could she see longing and awareness? She wasn't sure. Suddenly everything was too strange for her.

"This is only a small part of what we have in store,"

Amber said. "Come, I'll show you around." Kelly unhooked Sharon's wrist cuffs and took her hand. They left the enchanted boys frozen in their awkward positions.

The tiny cell led to a long hallway. Most of the cells had large glass windows that revealed what was going on inside. "One-way mirrors," said Amber. "You never know when you're being watched here. Plus there are video cameras and other ways, not so obvious, for me to keep an eye on events."

Sharon looked curiously through the nearest window. A boy was shackled to what looked like a high-tech exercise machine, a leather-covered mechanical X. His head was strapped into a strange helmet; nipple clamps trailed electric wires; another wire led from silver ring to silver anal vibrator. His body was quivering.

"The rack can be moved into any position," Amber commented. "Very convenient. The rest of the equipment is our new, improved Tease-o-Matic. The helmet is a virtual reality device that transmits 3-D erotic video and audio, the nipple, cock and ass devices give off constant stimulation. The silver cockring keeps the victim from coming; the vibrator also gives off electric shocks as punishment."

"I know." Sharon winced from her memories. "Is that punishment?"

"No, just training. If we left someone hooked up long enough, they'd probably go insane, though."

"I was wondering where you get all these cute boys. Are they all contributed by pledges like me?"

Amber replied, "Some are, but you'd be surprised

how many boys volunteer to be slaves once they hear about us. Some are true submissives; some think the sex part is going to be more to their liking. They learn better, of course. Some, like Robin, whom you met earlier, are captured. One problem we don't have is getting enough boys down here."

"God, they're cute!" Sharon said. "You do a good job picking them."

"They aren't all cute. That's another benefit of the sex magick we're developing. Have you noticed we're all drop-dead gorgeous down here?" Kelly and Amber both laughed, but Amber wasn't kidding.

"Well, yes," Sharon said. "I feel a little bit like the Ugly Duckling around you. I know I've got a good body and all, but nothing like you two."

"You will. That's part of the magick. As you become part of our society, you'll find that your sexiness and physical appeal grow dramatically. Yours and your boyfriend's. You'll end up drop-dead gorgeous, just like us." She gave Sharon an appraising once-over. "You don't have too far to go."

"Wow!" Sharon said. "What a fringe benefit!"

"Yes," added Kelly, "and all the sex you could hope for. What could be better?"

Sharon could see the boy's cock strain nearly to the bursting point, the head swelling purple and angry, then his entire body convulsed in electric shock. His erection lost part of its stiffness; but as he relaxed, the stimulation continued and he began the tortuous writhing that would lead him inexorably to his next electroshock.

The next window revealed another boy on a similar rack, but without the Tease-o-Matic harness. As the three girls watched, another door opened and a cute brown-haired coed came in, dressed in a parody of a nurse's uniform: starched white cap, ultrashort white dress with white stockings, so short the stocking tops showed, white heels. She posed sexily, bending over as she pretended to putter about his cell.

"That's Abbi," Amber pointed out. "She usually likes to masturbate about this time."

Abbi pulled up a leather chair and sat back, spreading her thighs wide, making her tight dress ride up virtually to her hips. She stuck out her long, sexy leg and used her toes to tease the inside of her victim's thighs. She smiled at his look of desperate need as she unzipped the top of her bodice and slipped her hand in to toy with her large nipples. She squeezed her breasts gently, sexily, getting herself warmed up. Finally, she slid off her panties, spread her legs wide again, and began masturbating wetly and openly, never taking her eyes off her victim, who was suffering greatly as she pleasured herself. Soon she came, passionately, but she continued rubbing herself faster and faster until she came again. Breathless, she sat for a while, recovering, then put on her clothes and left, never deigning to touch the now-dribbling cock she had teased so effectively.

"Hot stuff," Amber said. "The boys dread being Abbi's audience. She never touches a single one of them; having them watch her is all she needs to get off."

TABITHA'S TICKLE

They continued down the hall. "This is our exercise room," Amber announced. "We have to keep our slaves toned up. Why don't we go inside and check it out for ourselves."

Petite raven-haired twins dressed in tight tank tops and short-shorts carrying whistles around their necks were putting a slaveboy through an exercise regimen. He was working on various weight machines as they teased him mercilessly. Sharon, whose libido had fully recovered from her time with the paralyzed boys, found herself wanting to participate.

"Don't let us stop you, Denise and Amy," Amber said.

The twins looked up. "Don't worry," they laughed and returned to their victim. Sharon noticed they were armed with ice cubes.

He was trying to do a leg workout with a machine that forced him to spread his legs then squeeze them together while lifting weights. The weight stack was set at a hundred pounds. Whenever he spread his legs, one of the twins pressed an ice cube on the sensitive ridge between penis and anus. He would clench, hard, but the heavy weights kept him from protecting the area quickly. As his legs came together, the twin took away the ice cube, then the other would touch one of his nipples with her cube until he spread his legs again. He was sweating, tired, nearly exhausted, but the motivation of the ice forced him past his limits. Finally, he couldn't force his legs together with the weights, even when both cock and nipples were chilled together. "There!" one of the twins said. "Now for chin-ups!"

One twin stood in front of him. The other grabbed a wooden paddle and stood behind him. "Come on, baby, chin up for us," the first called out. He strained upward. As his chin came over the bar, the twin in front began to suck his cock while the other counted to five. Then the first twin released his cock and he lowered himself, only to be greeted with a firm *whack!* from the paddle until he began to lift himself up. Again and again, the combination of pain and pleasure continued until his muscles were so exhausted that neither the promise of oral sex nor the threat of the paddle could make him do another.

"They say that for exercise to be effective, muscle groups have to be totally exhausted," Amber observed dryly.

There was one more one-way mirror room before the corridor branched left and right. The boy victim here was standing, his arms stretched to the ceiling; his legs in a spreader bar forced apart and chained to the floor, his feet nearly on tiptoe. Two girls, dressed identically in black shiny leotard tops, velvet hot pants, and laced calf-high leather high-heeled boots, were engaged in tickling him to death. His body contorted and his mouth was open; the soundproof room muffled the screams of laughter and pleading Sharon could easily imagine. There was something odd...

"Wait a minute," Sharon said. "I know him!"

"Really?" asked Kelly.

"Sure! That's Tom Joyce. I went to school with him. He was this big poet-intellectual, and he was just too good to hang out with dumb cheerleaders like me. I had

TABITHA'S TICKLE

a big crush on him. Wow! I can't believe he's one of your sex slaves."

"Want some revenge?" Kelly suggested.

Sharon turned to her with bright eyes. "Could I? That would be fantastic. I've always wanted to show that bastard what he missed out on."

Amber laughed. "Let's go inside."

Tom was so distracted by his excruciating tickle torture that he wouldn't have recognized anybody, much less a girl from his past. Sharon immediately dug her fingers into his sides, attacking him vehemently. The two ticklers said, "There's plenty of ticklish flesh for everybody. Join in!"

Kelly and Amber joined the party, too. Each of the ticklers had her own style: Sharon's aggressive attack on his exposed flanks was combined with Kelly's wicked and subtle approach of getting down on her knees so she could work on the back of his knees and inner thighs, points of particular and excruciating ticklishness. The two booted temptresses switched to quill feathers, one around his belly and hips, the other moving from neck to underarms. He shrieked and babbled and pleaded for mercy, which was, of course, not forthcoming.

Amber looked on with amusement as Tom was overwhelmed by the attack of four beautiful ticklers, screaming and writhing in sensual agony. She pulled a thin dildo made from a clear red transparent material from a pouch on her wide leather belt. She touched it lightly with her wand; it began to quiver as if alive. It began to sprout nubs all over its length. Quickly, before the nubs could grow too large, she thrust it into his anal passage. Suddenly he let out a shriek of tickled agony far more tortured than any previously—the device was a real French tickler; it tickled. He jerked and writhed so hard that if the bonds had not been metal, he would have broken free; if mere human strength had been enough, he would have been able to relieve the tickling, but as it was, he could only scream in hysterical laughter as his senses completely overloaded.

He hadn't been slated for this level of torment today, Amber mused, but that didn't matter when he was serving as such a good toy for Sharon's initiation. She let the tickling go on for a long, long time, much longer than he could truly bear. Tears were running down his cheeks; he was in agony. Sharon seemed tireless in her aggressive attack; the other girls enjoyed watching her and gave her the leadership role as they tickled their helpless male victim past the point of no return.

Finally, she rested, panting, and Amber stopped the French tickler. "Good job," Amber said, patting Sharon's arm.

"I'm not finished with him yet," she said defiantly, standing in front of the limply hanging boy. "Tom, I'll bet you don't even remember who I am." But the look on his face told a different story.

"Sharon—I—" he stammered.

"Oh, you do remember me. You didn't seem to know who I was back in school."

Amber interrupted. "I think you might be surprised. Here, take my wand and touch it to his face."

Sharon did, and suddenly she felt herself linked into his mind. He did know who she was. In fact, he had fantasized about her for years. Images of her in her cheerleading outfit, images of her naked in his arms, images of him fucking her filled her mind, and she realized she had tapped into a well of his deepest fantasies.

"Why didn't you ever ask me out?" she said in wonderment. The answer flooded into her mind: images of being rejected, images of being condemned by his friends for dating a cheerleader—and then, to her surprise, images of her dominating him sexually.

"Oh," she said. "I understand. You didn't think I'd be willing to do this sort of thing to you. Well, as you can see, you're wrong. Very wrong. I'll prove it to you."

She looked at her companions. Amber and Kelly were both smiling at her. "Of course you can borrow him," Amber said. "That's what slaves are for."

Kelly whispered in her ear.

"What a great idea," Sharon laughed. "Of course, Tom won't like it very much, but that makes it perfect."

Amber gestured to the two ticklers. "Let's leave these three alone, shall we? Kelly, I'll send your cousin down shortly."

"OK," Kelly said. "Well, Tom, looks like you're in for the treat of your life, whether you like it or not."

8

Like most people, Bobby had experienced naked-in-school nightmares before, but the stark reality was really too much to bear. He balked when his captors reached the door to the gym, but a sharp tug on his leash and a spank on his rear made him cooperate. He had no choice. Out into the afternoon sun in the middle of a girls' school, naked, erect, cuffed and collared, led like a prize animal by two gorgeous cheerleaders, their cute rears wiggling in their scanty skirts as they walked ahead of him.

The coeds were still lounging on the quad in their brief summer outfits, sunbathing, studying, relaxing in the lovely weather. As he passed, they noticed, sitting up and pointing, laughing, giggling at his obvious need and helplessness. It was an exquisite symphony of humiliation; the blush traveled down his body but his cock tingled. He was getting used to being embarrassed, exposed, teased. In one hidden part of his mind, he liked it.

In the rest of his mind the painful embarrassment was still real, however. When the catcalling began he felt like he was shrinking.

"Hey, cutie, did you forget your clothes?"

"Susan, leave something for the rest of us!"

"Come over here and we'll help you with that hard problem of yours."

Wolf whistles echoed in the quad. His face burned; his cock twitched. It seemed to take forever before he was safely back in the dorm.

Unfortunately, the dorm, like all the others, was female, and now he was being led through a narrow hallway. Doors opened and girls came out.

"Ooh, cute! Can we borrow him for a while?"

"Nice ass."

"Good cock, too." Susan and Tiffany let the dorm residents borrow their victim; the press of young girls forced Bobby up against the wall as hands explored his chest and groin. His own hands clenched and unclenched behind his back as he closed his eyes under the onslaught.

The girls caressed and grabbed at him, groping his flesh, squeezing and twisting his cock, sucking his nipples, running their fingers along his lips and forcing them into his mouth. Susan and Tiffany looked on with amusement. Bobby slumped against the wall, surrendering to the hands and mouths of the hungry coeds. His cock, roughly handled and squeezed, progressed quickly to the edge of orgasm. He could feel the pressure building, then the attack of convulsions his strangled orgasm hit, sending his body through waves of ecstatic pleasure without the release of jetting hot sperm. He trembled and shivered as his body clenched; he fucked his hips against the teasing pressure of girlish hands; he moaned and gasped but gained no final relief.

After the clenches and pulses of his orgasm, he needed a brief respite, but the girls continued their ravenous attack on his naked, shackled body. Now their hands began to tickle, and when they discovered his ticklishness, he screamed and shrieked and wriggled as hands and fingers competed to drive him crazy. He was seized with an overpowering need to piss and was terrified that the tickling would make him wet himself—that would be the ultimate unbearable public humiliation, and one he could not stand nor find sexy.

"Help! Ha-ha-ha-ha! I have to go! *Ha-ha-ha*," he called out in between gasps of helpless laughter.

Finally, Susan made the girls stop. "Careful, or he'll start to pee all over you," she said.

"Euu," one of the girls said, backing away in disgust. "Gross!"

Bobby blushed again as Susan led him into the group bathroom, followed by several of the dorm residents. There were no stalls or urinals. "He tried to wax his woody last time we left him alone," Susan said to the group, to jeers and catcalls. "Now we have to help him go."

She grabbed his cock and pointed it toward the toilet. It was erect, and he couldn't piss easily. "Come on!" she ordered bossily. "You told us you have to go. So go."

"I-I can't—not with everybody watching—and it's hard…" he stammered.

"You'd better, or I'll turn you back over with instructions to really tickle you this time," Susan said.

The threat made him quiver, but his hard-on would not diminish.

Tiffany chimed in. "I've got an idea. I'll be right back."

His cock continued to throb in Susan's tiny hand; the girls watched eagerly at his continuing humiliation until Tiffany came back armed with a wooden paddle. *Thwack!* The first blow landed hard and stinging on his bare ass. *Thwack! Thwack!* She spanked fast and ruthlessly, quickly bringing tears to his eyes. Under the paddling, his erection began to go limp. When he was soft, she stopped. "Now, pee," she ordered. He could. Susan shook it off, then dabbed away the remaining droplets with a square of toilet tissue. The girls applauded.

"Is that everything?" Susan asked.

"Y-yes," he replied shakily. She kept hold of his limp cock, which quickly started swelling until his erection was nice and firm again.

"There we go. Now, say thank you to all the girls who helped, and we'll go on."

"Thank you," he said meekly, his eyes downcast, his cock throbbing.

The girls giggled and laughed at his humiliation. One flushed the toilet, and they all left the bathroom.

"Bring him back soon," called one girl, a cute brunette with a crooked, sexy smile.

He thought he was safe when they were back in the original dorm room he ostensibly shared with Sharon—at least, there were no other girls around. The calculating, controlling smiles on the faces of his delicious coed captors was enough to disabuse him of that notion. His stomach had that lurching sensation, like going over the top on a roller coaster. Like it or not, he was on board for the entire ride.

Tiffany had made him drink a strange-tasting potion. Combined with the effects of all the marijuana, he could tell that there were even more psychedelics in his system, but he was so completely overloaded by all the dominating sexuality that it hardly made a difference.

Their cruel, hungry smiles made him realize again the depths of his own helplessness and he shivered with fear and anticipation. He didn't have long to wait. Tiffany slid a chair over and stood on it, removing a hanging flower basket from a ceiling hook while Susan unclasped the metal lock that held his wrists together. "Hands up!" Susan ordered. Taking another clasp, they fastened his wrists to the hook above, stretching him out. Fastening a short length of chain to the rings on his ankle bands, they stretched his legs to the corners of the bed. He was dangling dangerously; the strain on his arms and legs was on the edge of painful.

Susan stood in front of him, smiling up into his face

with wicked controlling delight. Her eyes sparkled and flashed as she regarded her helpless prisoner. She liked being in control. She moved forward, step by step, hips swinging, lips smiling, aware of the devastating tease in her approach. He felt even more exposed and vulnerable, if that were possible.

Her sharp fingernails slid up his chest to his nipples, affecting him like an electric current, making his cock jump and brush against her skirt. Her body was inches from his.

"Do you want me?" she purred.

"Oh, God, yes!" he moaned. As her fingernails stroked and teased, he found it difficult to talk.

"How much?"

"Completely…absolutely…more than anything…please…" He was babbling, trying to obey. Her voice seemed detached from her, registering in the wrong parts of his brain. He was on fire. The drugs in the potion were more powerful than he first thought. He didn't believe there was any higher level of arousal to which he could climb; he was wrong. Now he wondered whether there was a peak to his sensations.

Hanging from the ropes, he twitched and moaned as her fingers scratched at his white-hard nipples.

"Tell me what you'd do for an orgasm," she teased.

"Anything…be your slave…do whatever you want…"

"But you'd do that right now for me, wouldn't you?"

"Yes…yes…"

"You'd do that even without an orgasm, just for me teasing you."

TABITHA'S TICKLE

"Yes…yes…"

"So, why should I give you an orgasm?"

"Please…I need it…I'll do anything…"

"We already went through that. I know you need it. But what will you do for me?"

"Anything…name it…I don't know…"

Cut loose by his passion and the strange drug, the anchors of his mind let bits of feeling and memory drift out and then vanish with each electric flick of her fingernails against his nipples. The feeling was maddening and wonderful.

"Well, we'll just keep teasing you until we think of something, then," Susan laughed throatily.

Meanwhile, Tiffany stroked and tickled his rear, making him squirm forward, trying to brush his straining erection against Susan's skirt. Susan looked down and slapped his cock stingingly. "I see some precome leaking. If you get even a drop of it on my skirt, you'll regret it big time."

But he couldn't help squirming. Susan continued to torment his nipples, Tiffany stroking his rear. When Tiffany let her fingers trail up over his hip and onto the ridge above, he gasped with the ticklish sensation. Tiffany pressed her entire body up against his back, making him shiver with the delicious sensations. Her hot breath teased the nape of his neck. Her hair tickled. She made him squirm under the tickling fingers along the ridge of his hip.

His cock was lurching wildly, swinging up and down, jerked and pulled as if it were connected to puppet strings. He had come before with less stimulation; he was ready to scream for release.

"I think it's tickle time again," Tiffany whispered. Susan's eyes twinkled with evil delight as she looked at her victim, who recoiled in horror.

The muscles in Bobby's arms, legs, and asshole tightened. He tried to pull his arms down to his sides and strained to free himself from the ceiling hook that held him firmly. He could feel soft, trailing fingers moving up his sides, approaching his rib cage, raising gooseflesh over his stretched and helpless body, and then…

He shrieked with laughter as the wiggling fingers began their relentless attack, forcing endless guffaws. Each tickle session was more devastating than the one before; he felt as if his heart would explode. "No…stop, please…ha-ha-ha!"

"You said 'anything,'" Susan pouted as she kept tickling. "This is part of anything. Remember, you asked to be tickled twice as long and twice as hard for an orgasm—and you've had two!"

"No! No! I didn't really have—ha-ha-ha-ha—an orgasm!"

"Oh, yes you did. For lying, we'll tickle you extra!"

"Oh, God oh, God hahaha *nooo!*" He babbled and laughed with growing hysteria as the relentless tickling continued.

Finally, they stopped, and he sagged against the shackles, shoulders straining under the weight of his body, most of his conscious mind and sanity swept away.

Tabitha's Tickle

The girls had stopped and simply looked amused. A lock of blonde hair had fallen on Susan's forehead. Her smile had vanished and her breathing was a little irregular. Her mouth was slightly open, her full red lips in a sensual pout.

"God, this boy-toy stuff has got me so hot, I haven't gotten off yet." she said.

Tiffany came over, embraced her, and began kissing her neck hungrily and caressing her stomach. Their mouths came together in a hard, passionate kiss. Bobby strained toward them, his cock drawn toward the sexy coeds.

Tiffany slid down the zipper of Susan's short cheerleader skirt; it poodled to the ground. She slid off her midriff top, revealing Susan's pert, bare breasts, then took off her own clothes while keeping her lips locked to Susan's. They groped and petted each other; then Tiffany slid down Susan's panties. They fell on the bed together. Tiffany slid down Susan's naked torso as Susan stretched her arms over her head languorously and slowly. Susan arched her body as Tiffany's mouth worshiped lower and lower.

Bobby strained forward and tugged helplessly; his prick reached out to the two women as his wrists twisted in vain.

Susan glanced at him sideways, eyes bright, and gave him a little, teasing smile, as if to say she understood his desperate plight.

Tiffany was in no hurry as she attended to Susan. She took infinite time stroking and pleasing her. As she kissed Susan's mound, covered with soft blonde fur, her hands and fingers rubbed and stroked from the calves up to the backs of her thighs. Susan's legs were spread wide; they climbed up over Tiffany's shoulders and Tiffany caressed her plump, rounded bottom. Her mouth hardly seemed to move, but Bobby could see Susan's eyes clenching shut, focusing on the pleasure she received.

The pleasure built in Bobby, too. Unattended, bound and left hanging, he felt a part of the sensation in a strange way, as if he were connected telepathically to the lovers. Susan began to moan as Tiffany's tongue had a devastating effect. With some surprise, Bobby realized he was moaning, too, in rhythm with Susan. "God... God...God...yes...*yes!*" Susan moaned as she arched in orgasmic release.

Tiffany licked Susan through another orgasm, then slid up beside her to fasten her wet mouth on her lover. Susan's hand slid up to cup Tiffany's large breasts; she squeezed and petted, then rolled her partner over slowly. She slid down, kissing breasts, stomach, belly, until she was between Tiffany's legs, returning the favor of oral delights.

Bobby's cruelly teased cock throbbed and leaked from the visual stimulation. His hips bucked back and forth of their own accord, fucking an invisible lover; his hands clenched and twisted in the bonds that stretched him wide.

Finally, Susan looked up at him. "Enjoy the show?" she said in a voice without a trace of viciousness or teasing.

Bobby nodded.

"Poor baby, I bet you'd really like some attention right now. You look like you're really turned on." She slid out of bed, magnificently nude, and walked to him slowly. She placed her hands on his shoulders and snuggled up to him, her face uptilted. She kissed him gently on the lips but drew back when his hungry mouth tried for more. Her soft breast inflamed the sensitive skin of his chest; the prickling of her damp pubic hair against his erection maddened him. Watching the girls make love was incredibly arousing; Susan's body pressed against his drove him to utter madness.

She toyed teasingly with the nape of his neck and his sensitive ears. "Tell me," she cooed, "now that we're both relaxed and in such a good mood, is there anything you'd like us to do for you?"

He was gasping; he tried to speak normally and not be tongue-tied with his passion.

"Yes...yes...please..."

"Tell me what it is."

"Please...make me come for real...I can't take any more of this."

"But we can't do that, you know. That's Sharon's job. We can do anything else, but you won't come until Sharon decides to make you come. What else would you like?" Her hips began a slow, grinding movement against his groin.

"Please...I beg you...you're driving me half-crazy..."

She pouted and stepped back. "Only half-crazy? I'm offended."

"No…no…completely crazy…totally insane…I'm burning up!"

"That's better," she smiled, and returned to her previous stance, rubbing her naked form against his. "We were going to find out what you wanted us to do next—except make you come. Tell us."

"Oh, God," he moaned, his emotions bursting like a dam. "Do anything you like—just keep rubbing my cock!"

His painful sincerity made the girls laugh.

"Wait a minute," Tiffany said, scrambling out of bed and padding naked across the carpeted floor. "I've got an idea!" She whispered in Susan's ear. Susan laughed delightedly.

"Great!" she said. Bobby looked on with trepidation. "Oh, don't worry, Woody. You'll probably enjoy this almost as much as we will. We've got an hour or two to kill before we get ready for the party tonight, so we want to make the most of it."

Susan began necking with him, naked body against naked body, rubbing herself against him catlike, tongue-kissing him deeply and passionately. His cock slid between her legs and began rubbing along the wet opening of her netherlips.

He didn't see, or care, where Tiffany had gone, until he suddenly felt her presence at his back. There was a cold, tingling contact as the metal head of a vibrator touched the top of his back. It began to hum. The vibrating sensations sent a new thrill of pleasure coursing through his body as Tiffany slid it down, down, and into the valley between the cheeks of his exposed rear.

It slid along the strap that parted his buttocks, then touched the hole in the leather and slid inside. The buzzing made his anus clench and his body strained to escape, pressing farther into Susan's arms.

The pressure on his anus increased; he felt the narrow passage force open in spite of his resistance. He moaned and struggled; he dreaded a repeat of the tickling device they had used previously. The vibrator was large and long; he felt stuffed and stretched as if it protruded a foot into him. The vibrating sensations against his prostate drove him wild; Susan continued to kiss and caress him. His cock slid back and forth in her wet crevice; he could not quite maneuver himself to slip all the way inside, but the sensation was still delightful.

He quickly began to approach another of his limited orgasms; to his everlasting delight, he felt Susan's passion growing, too, measured by the increasing passion of her hips grinding against his, by her hand slipping down to grab him just *so*, stimulating her clit, and they exploded together—Susan's writhing a real, satisfying orgasm, his a series of passionate clenches and wriggles as the top of his mind exploded, but his body remained filled with sexual energy.

As Susan slipped satisfied from his arms, Tiffany began her attack, first with tickling fingers that completely destroyed him, making him scream with laughter all the while his helpless cock fucked the empty air, looking fruitlessly for warm, wet solace. Tiffany was the crueler of the two in physical terms; Susan in psychological terms. She compounded the cruelty by hand-fucking his cock roughly while continuing her relentless tickling campaign—searching for new areas to attack on his totally exposed body. "I know—how about...underarms?" She suited actions to words.

When tickling bored her, she got out her sorority paddle and began spanking him, masturbating him, and allowing the vibrator to continue its devastating work. He was crying with frustration, pain, lust. Susan sprawled on the bed and looked on with amusement at his suffering.

Bobby had reached a point in his arousal that took him beyond sex and beyond reality; part of his mind had ceased to function: he was an animal, a creature of pure lust. The vibrator had raped the vestiges of his self-control and even his ego. His legs, strained and tired, became rubbery and weak; the strain on his arms increased but he could not continue to stand. The hellish vibrator continued to wring sanity from him. His cock was impossibly big, impossibly hard, swollen, tender, ready for an explosion that would finally tear him apart. The world was shifting to red and in his tormented eyes his mistresses were changing, metamorphosing into strange, demonic creatures—succubi—still impossibly lovely, more wicked and crueler than mere reality could accommodate. The last shreds of his ego disappeared as he fell into unconsciousness.

9

"Your cousin?" Sharon asked curiously as she and Kelly stepped into the anteroom of the dungeon cell to make wicked plans.

Kelly laughed. "Do you really want to get revenge on that boy?"

"Do I!" Sharon answered with a combination of anger and delightful anticipation. "Do you know how many nights I couldn't get to sleep from dreaming about that boy? How many times I fingered myself off over him? I never had any trouble getting any other boy to ask me out. In fact, I usually had too many. That's part of why I was such a pricktease. If someone pestered me enough, was hot enough for me, I'd show them what it meant to be hot. But Tom wouldn't give me the time of day. He'd hang out with his intellectual friends—most of them were nerds, but Tom was real dramatic, always in black, that sort of thing—and if I tried to talk to them he'd treat me like I had an IQ of eighty. I was so pissed!"

"And you didn't know he was into being dominated?"

"How could I? I didn't know about domination or bondage or any of this stuff. Petting, masturbating, maybe oral sex—that I knew about. Pretty naïve, huh?"

"Well, they don't really teach that stuff in school."

"They do here!" They both laughed. "I'm getting a graduate education in kinky sex!"

"You want kinky?" Kelly asked seriously. "You haven't seen kinky yet."

"Really?" Sharon said with eager curiosity. "Right now, I'm game for anything."

Kelly put her hands on Sharon's nude shoulders. "You know I want to make love with you," she said, looking straight into Sharon's eyes.

"Yes," Sharon said. "I want it, too. It's weird; I never wanted a woman that way...I knew about it, of course, but now I want it."

"But that's not your main fantasy."

"Well, no, but it turns me on. You turn me on."

Kelly smiled. "Thanks. You turn me on, too. The difference is, that's my main fantasy."

"Are you a lesbian?" Sharon said. "I mean, it's OK and everything. I just didn't know."

"Basically I am," Kelly replied. "I think males have

their uses, but for me the uses are primarily for teasing. I prefer girls for actual sex. Of course, I like submissive girls the same way I like submissive boys. I'm definitely dominant."

"Well, it's cool with me. I don't know that I'm going to be the same way, but..." Sharon stepped forward to give Kelly a kiss; the tall blonde responded with deep passion. "Ooh! Do you want to make love and make him watch? That would be hot."

Kelly grinned, "Yes, I would, but that's not all I had in mind. Remember, I have a cousin."

"Yeah. What's that about? Is he a slave?"

"Yes and no. You know that our pledges are supposed to bring us a male victim as part of their own initiation. I gave them my cousin."

"Whoa, that is kinky," Sharon said. "Like, do you two have sex?"

"Yes and no. See, he's gay, too."

"Wait a minute. You're into girls, I understand, and you like to tease boys, and that makes sense; but if your cousin is gay, what about being around all these girls?"

"Once you're teased enough, it doesn't really matter who's there to get you off," Kelly laughed. "But the most important thing is, my cousin is a transvestite, too, and thinking about becoming a transsexual."

"Wow!" Sharon was stunned. This was really outside her experience. She turned it around in her mind. She wasn't shocked; she was well past that. She was discovering how kinky she was, and that didn't leave room for a lot of judgment about other people.

"Coming here has been perfect for him. You see, the sex magick is letting him have the best of both worlds—he's turning into something of both genders. Plus, he's the nastiest little tease in the place, and he really gets off getting some absolutely straight boy all gender confused."

Sharon turned that around in her mind for a moment until suddenly she exclaimed, "Oh, my God! I get it! You're going to turn him loose on Tom while we watch! Oh, my God! Kelly, that's the dirtiest trick I've ever heard in my life! It's way too cruel! I love it!" She danced around the room gleefully. "Oh, my God!" she said over and over again. "When do we start?"

"Any minute now," Kelly said. She was laughing at Sharon's excitement, secretly pleased. This would be fun—except for Tom, and even he would enjoy it whether he wanted to or not.

Back in the dungeon cell, Tom was now shackled to the wall by means of the rings on the leather harness set he wore. The room contained various tools for whatever games the girls had in mind. The walls had hooks at various strategic locations, including the ones that imprisoned Tom. There was a hook-and-pulley combination overhead that when combined with the two rings protruding from the floor allowed freestanding bondage, as when they tickled him. A mechanical X-shaped rack was rigged to be moved into a wide variety of positions that would put any desired body part wherever wanted. There was a brass bed with handcuffs conveniently prepared. A spanking bench complete with a medieval neck and arm restraint, a closet filled with a range of sex devices, whips, and extra restraints, and the large, full mirror that Sharon and Kelly knew was one-way glass completed the room.

Tom glanced in the mirror when they reentered the room, then glanced away. The sight of himself in naked, erect bondage with his new tormentors was too much for him. Tom wore such a vulnerable expression, one of fear and longing, that if Sharon didn't already know about his tastes, she would be moved to pity. Instead, she wore a wicked expression, teasing eyes and pouting lips which she licked ostentatiously as she regarded her captive prey.

She pulled a chair between his legs and sat down. Kelly reclined on the brass bed to watch. Sharon raised one gloriously nude leg carelessly and ran her toes along the sensitive inside of Tom's leg, sending a shiver through him.

"Well, Tom, long time no see," she said. "What have you been up to lately?" At the word "up" she flicked his cock with her toes, watching it bob helplessly.

Tom was virtually speechless with shock, fear, humiliation, and arousal. "Sharon...please...I can't take it..." he moaned.

"Can't take what? I haven't even done anything yet. I'm just visiting, catching up on old times." She continued sliding her toes up and down his legs, occasionally sliding up over his hips. Her pussylips were clearly visible. She felt like such an outrageous show-off. She liked the feeling.

"So, Tom," she commanded, "tell me all about it. Tell me about your fantasies and how they brought you here. I want to know the truth. Tell me the truth and we can have some fun together. If you lie, you'll be in deeper trouble than you can imagine, and I'll bet you've got a great imagination, don't you?"

He gulped. How had the cute cheerleader he used to know turned into such an accomplished, wicked, dominating tease? The smile on her face was utterly serious.

"I've always had these fantasies," he said, speaking in slow and distracted tones as she kept up the foot teasing. "I never dreamed about seducing and screwing girls; I wanted them to seduce me, then tie me up, tease me, not let me come, use me, make me beg, humiliate me..."

"Really," said Sharon. "What kind of girls?"

"Cheerleaders. Majorettes. Girls in uniforms, costumes. Classy, pretty, in control. Like you."

"Like me?" Sharon said. He nodded, shamefaced. "That's nice. Then, why didn't you ask me out?"

"I was afraid it would turn out that you weren't like my fantasy at all. Even if we had sex, it wouldn't be the way I wanted. So I didn't ask."

"What did you do for sex, then?" Sharon asked. She was curious. The poor guy. Of course, he would have been right. She might have fucked him, or she might have teased him; but she never would have thought about tying him up, not in those days.

"I masturbated, bought pornography, daydreamed a lot. I daydreamed about you, doing...this. There were girls in my group, some nice. I had regular sex. It was

OK. It was better than OK. But it wasn't my fantasy. I asked a couple of girls to tie me up. Some were too upset to do anything kinky like that; some were willing, but they just didn't understand what was going on. It wasn't the same. Once I went to a prostitute, but it wasn't like my fantasy."

"Wow!" Sharon said sympathetically. "You did have it tough. So, how did you get here?"

"There were rumors, mostly guy jokes, you know, about this wild fuck-palace, but the rumors about teasing and female dominants were the part I heard most clearly. I was studying this sort of thing, and I started to read about some of the sex magick and how it depended on male frustration. I did some of it…to myself, you know, and then I got an affinity. A spirit, something that let me know. I was drawn to Valentine College. I listened to the gossip, and about boys being part of the initiation. So I worked at meeting a girl, dated her, had sex, just to get her to give me to the sorority. She nearly didn't, you know…she felt guilty setting me up, I guess…so I deliberately cheated on her and let her find out. She got so angry with me, my fate was sealed." He was silent for a while, his mind obviously on his initiation.

"I let her lead me on, set me up. My heart was pounding. I was so scared, I nearly ran away from it even though I wanted it so much. I almost couldn't go through with it, but I did. Barely. She got me to take my clothes off. We were in the dark, she teased me into playing tag, and then…"

Sharon watched his cock. It had gotten so purple the head looked as if it were going to burst. Droplets of precome were drizzling from the head, all from the power of his fantasies.

"I was in the dark, naked, and then a part of the floor dropped out from under me. I slid and slid, and then I was attacked by a group of girls waiting for me. I started shrieking with fear as they tickled me. At that moment, I would have given anything to get away—"

"And now?" Sharon prompted, nudging his cock with her foot.

"Oh god, I hate to say this, but I'm still so scared, so overloaded, that if I got a chance I'd be out of here like a shot, but at the same time it's all of my fantasies come to life. I can't believe how aroused I've gotten."

Kelly spoke up from the brass bed. "You know, that happens frequently. Most of our initiates, male and female, aren't really that much into bondage or fantasies before they get here. It's hot, it's frustrating, sometimes it's a little overwhelming. But it's OK. When somebody like Tom, who's into the fantasy scene in a deep way, suddenly finds his fantasies coming out of his id into the real world, it's much more disturbing. Raw sexual fantasy is dangerous. It's probably worse now that you're here, since he knows you."

Tom nodded. "Yes, that's right. My wet dreams have come true, and it's scary. And you..." He was speechless. He couldn't put into words the complicated feelings that having her in the room created.

Sharon thought about that for a minute. "Poor baby.

Part of me is tempted to have pity on you, but I think in my heart that wouldn't be the right thing to do. Do you?"

His blush was all the confirmation she needed.

"I didn't think so. In fact, what you want is for me to make it worse for you. Lots worse."

He shook his head, eyes wide. "I don't know if I can take it."

"I don't know either," said Sharon, flashing her teasing eyes at him, seized by wickedness she had never previously imagined. "But let's find out, shall we?"

Kelly, on the bed, laughed. "Sharon, you're coming along faster than expected. If you want to blow Tom's mind, I'm all for it."

"I'm going to blow a lot more than your mind before I'm finished with you," Sharon said in her sexiest voice. She stood up, pushed the chair back, then pressed her naked body against his, squirming against him in a devastating tease. She looked up into his eyes, capturing him in her wicked gaze. "You know you have to be punished for not telling me all your secrets back in school. Who knows? You might have awakened it all in me and started living your fantasies that much earlier. But I'm here now, I'm in your fantasy, and I promise I'll make you suffer more than you could ever imagine."

She trailed a hand down his hard, muscular chest, teasing his nipples, which seemed as sensitive as poor Bobby's. With a start, she remembered she hadn't even thought about Bobby for hours and hours. Obsessed with her old flame, she felt momentarily guilty. She wondered what was happening with him. He was probably suffering as much as Tom. The thought pleased her. *I'm really getting kinky in a hurry*, she realized. *I like it*. She wondered whether she would ever get together with Bobby as they used to. Probably not, she thought. She pushed relationship thoughts out of her mind and returned to the current situation.

"Mmm"—she continued to caress him—"your body is nicer than I remember. You used to be too skinny."

"Magick. It does a body good." Kelly called out. Sharon laughed; the ripple of her body against Tom's made him moan with agonized pleasure. She bit one of his nipples, hard, then sucked it and flicked her tongue over it. His cock pressed up against her belly; it radiated heat and pulsed with his twitching arousal.

Teasing Tom sent new rushes of arousal through her body. "Maybe I should fasten you down on the rack so I can fuck your cock," she murmured, continuing her assault on his helpless nipple. "Ride it until I burst and know you can't come."

Tom's eyes were screwed shut. His head was thrown back, and every muscle in his body was taut with passion. He was barely able to keep control, to avoid being washed completely away in the sea of his lust. Sharon was overloading his senses.

Finally Sharon stopped and moved away. She looked at her victim with smug satisfaction. Her tease was obviously effective. She might be new at this, but she wasn't going to be an amateur for long. She looked over at Kelly, lounging on the bed. "I'm ready," she murmured, and walked toward her sorority mentor, hips swaying, strutting for the pleasure of two people she had turned on. She crawled up on the bed on all fours, looking like a sleek jungle cat, to kiss Kelly hungrily. Kelly responded, slipped up her hand to caress Sharon's breast, purred in welcome to her pledge's attentions. Sharon slid down and Kelly rolled over; they were side by side. "Let me help you out of that," Sharon said as she began unzipping Kelly's skirt, pulling the cropped sweater over her head, stripping her.

They were naked, necking on the bed. Sharon could feel Tom's eyes devouring her, feel the passion of his cock as if by remote control, but right now Kelly was the center of her attention. The girl-girl petting progressed slowly, wetly, at its own pace.

There was a knock. Kelly said, "It's Serena." She put a finger on Sharon's lips to caution her.

Serena was one of the hottest young girls Sharon had ever seen. A petite bundle of supercharged energy, Serena had waves of blonde hair over a heart-shaped face, wicked flashing eyes, and ruby-red lips. She wore a scandalously short black leather miniskirt over a lacy red bodice; her breasts were at least C-cups, and the nipples showed clearly through the thin lace. Her legs were luscious in wildly patterned red stockings, thigh-highs, the tops clearly revealing another two inches of skin before the skirt began, over red ankle boots with laces. She was ultrafeminine and incredibly sexy. Sharon was confused. There was simply no way that this could be a boy.

Serena's voice was a rich contralto, very feminine with a sultry bedroom quality. "Hi, cousin," she said, kissing Kelly in a very uncousinly manner.

Kelly introduced her to Sharon, still reclining on the bed; Serena gave her an equally warm, wet, and sexy kiss. "Cute," she said, giving Sharon an appraising once-over, for "she" seemed to be the appropriate word. "Kelly, you always knew how to pick them. Oh, and this must be Tom," she added brightly, focusing her laserlike grin on the shackled pleasure victim. "Well, aren't you something!" She giggled knowingly as she examined her new toy.

Tom's cock twitched under Serena's sexy attention. He was ready to be ravished. The petite sexpot sashayed over to her victim and ran her hands over his torso, hefted his erection in her petite hand. "Nice," she said. "I'm going to enjoy this."

Sharon's attention was riveted on the situation. It was unbelievably hot. Her crush on Tom had been quite an obsession for her; now that she knew about his fixations, she found herself with confused, swirling emotions to possess him and to torture him. The two directions blurred together. She squeezed her legs together in her growing passion. Kelly, kneeling on the bed behind her, slid her arms around the young girl to caress her full breasts. Sharon moaned and leaned back into the caress.

Serena unfastened her victim from his shackles, deliberately pressing her body against his, teasing him. "On your knees, like a good slaveboy," she ordered once he was free. "Would you like me to punish you?" she asked.

"Yes...please," he said in a tiny voice, the combination of humiliation and arousal choking him. He was red-faced; Sharon's presence had taken his torment to absolutely unbearable levels. He wanted to break and run, but he was too weak to move.

"Please what?" Serena asked imperiously, nudging the toe of her boot under his downcast face.

"Please, Mistress Serena, punish me," he said.

"I can't hear you."

He repeated it, louder, then louder still until she was satisfied. Sharon couldn't help bursting into giggles, which only made the situation worse for Tom.

"Kiss my boot, then," she ordered. He complied, kissing the red leather boot over and over. "Follow me," she commanded. "Stay on your knees." She led him over to the rack. "Now, climb aboard and stretch your arms and legs out. You know what to do."

He scrambled to obey. It was difficult for him to stretch out; his muscles didn't want to obey. He was tense, red, scared. Serena clipped the chains on the mechanical frame to the rings on his ankles, wrists, neck, waist, shackling him down. She fastened more restraints on him than needed, just to increase his sensation of total helplessness. She moved slowly, deliberately, enjoying the work of bondage, building suspense.

Once Tom was completely shackled, she touched the controls. First, she lowered the rack until he was completely horizontal, then turned him upside down. The motorized rack spun him in a circle, like a human windmill, slowly disorienting him. Then she laid him on his back, fully horizontal, and made the branches of the X stretch apart, pulling him painfully in all directions until the tension was scary, before releasing the pressure. She walked between his outstretched legs to insert a silver shocking vibrator, then put painful alligator clips on his nipples, wires dangling from them. She put another clip on the sensitive flesh under his cockhead.

He moaned and squirmed as she built up the sensation carefully. She stroked his forehead, now beading with sweat. "There, there," she cooed. "We've nearly finished the preliminaries. Soon we'll be ready to put on a show for your old girlfriend. We want to entertain her very well. You'll be a good boy, won't you?"

He was still tongue-tied, not only because of the overwhelming arousal of emotion, but also for fear of humiliating himself further in Sharon's presence. He barely muffled a shriek of pain and surprise when Serena pushed the control button that sent a random pattern of shocks and vibration through the clips and dildo. He thrashed helplessly in his shackles, grunting when each shock took him by surprise.

Sharon's emotions became more complex by the second. Part of her wanted to rush over, free him, make love to his body and kiss all the pain, suck all the pent-up passion from his overteased cock. Part of her wanted to take over the punishment from Serena, be the cruelest bitch-goddess he had ever imagined. Part of

TABITHA'S TICKLE

her wanted to watch, totally obsessed with his torment.

Part of her wanted to make out passionately with Kelly, both from her own desire and from the additional desire to make Tom watch and suffer. Kelly's hands continued to caress her breasts; Sharon leaned her head back into her arms to accept her deep kiss. Kelly's hand slipped down between Sharon's leg to finger her wet pussy, stroking in slow, sensual circles.

Serena tilted the rack so Tom could see the two girls making love on the brass bed. At first, Kelly was the initiator, suckling Sharon's pear-shaped breasts, sliding down to lick at her wet center; then Sharon, giving herself over completely to the sensations, rolled her lover over to begin giving sexual attention where it was needed. Kelly moaned and arched as Sharon's hot mouth fastened on her stiff nipples. Both as receiver and initiator, Sharon was constantly aware of her audience. She let her passion express itself in her voice and body. "Yes. Yes. Do it. Oh, God! It feels so good! Oh, yes. Do that some more." The girls were sharing equally, grinding and rubbing against each other, petting and stroking and fingering every inch of exposed flesh.

Tom's agony of desire and fear increased as he saw how truly passionate Sharon was, how much she was getting into her relationship with Kelly, how aggressively she sucked and licked her partner. His real attention, though, was consumed by the temptress Serena.

"Comfy now?" Serena purred, bending over her victim

to stroke his forehead. She gave him a sweet, sensual kiss and a lovely, warm smile. For a minute, relief swept over him. This wasn't going to be too bad after all. But then the wicked smile returned to her face. "Don't get too comfy. Serena has big plans for that big cock of yours." His stomach lurched. He went over the top of the roller coaster yet again.

Her first weapon of choice was a wooden ruler. She slapped it into her palm, hard, as she looked into his transfixed eyes. "Time for your sex-education lesson," she laughed cruelly. "First lesson: You don't have permission for that hard-on. Lose it. Now."

Of course, he could do no such thing. "Six strokes penalty!" Serena held his penis lightly in position, then spanked it with the ruler. It stung; he gasped. She aimed the second blow right after the first. The pain was real, but it inflamed his erection rather than softened it. He suffered through the six strokes, gasping with each one.

"Bad boy," Serena said. "You didn't go soft. Penalty number two." She pressed the electroshock button on the control panel; jolts shot through his cock, nipples, and anus. His eyes opened wide; he hissed with pain and barely contained a shriek. Serena smiled again. It was a cruel smile.

The shock did soften him for a moment. "Now keep it that way for sixty seconds," she ordered. She removed an alligator clip from one nipple and began to suck the sore, tender flesh. He moaned under the erotic stimulation and tried to concentrate on something else—anything else. He felt himself swelling uncontrollably.

"Uh-oh," Serena said. "That's failure number two. Ten stroke penalty, and you'd better be soft at the end."

Smack! Smack! The penis punishment stung worse than before; she was spanking harder. He squinched his eyes so hard tears came out; he managed to lose at least part of his erection.

She smiled. "Very good. Keep it soft for sixty seconds." This time she swept her hair back over her shoulder and bent down to take his limp cock in her hot, hungry mouth. Her tongue swirled. She sucked with passion. He was stiffening in seconds. She kept sucking until he was nearing the culminating edge, then with a wet *plop!* let it drop from her mouth.

"You obviously have a self-control problem," she said. The penalty was twelve more strokes. His penis was red from the punishment, but so charged up that the pain wasn't enough to make him limp. Two shocks did the trick.

Then she sucked him again, and he was rampant again. "You aren't doing very well," she grinned. The sentence was another twelve strokes. They stung even more, but his erection wouldn't diminish.

When Serena let his cock go, it throbbed and pulsed. She stroked her finger down it; it jerked up to meet her hand. "Good," she said. "Can you hold it up in the air for me? Hold it just like that." She tickled the shaft with her fingers, then trailed her long, silky hair over it. She teased it carefully and thoroughly. At first it was no problem holding his cock in the air because he was so aroused. Soon those muscles began to tire. His cock dropped to his belly for just a second.

"Ah, ah, ah!" Serena chided. "Serena said, 'Hold it up.'" Three spanks with the ruler. His cock elevated again. She kept up the teasing until he dropped back to his belly. Soon his cock was painfully on fire from its punishment, repeated spanks each time he let himself relax. Serena was thoroughly in control, taking infinite delight in her calculated sadism.

"Now for the third game." She smiled and licked her lips. "Don't let yourself come, whatever I do." She began sucking his cock deliciously while at the same time her hands played up and down his naked sides, tweaking his nipples. He moaned with pleasure, and quickly found himself with mounting passion. He knew the silver cockring would defeat his ejaculation, so he relaxed and enjoyed it. Serena was a marvelous cocksucker, inventive, almost telepathic in the way she knew how to drive him crazy. He knew his comeless orgasms only added to his frustration, but they were all he could have. The first wave hit. *Bzzzz!* The electroshock modules all went off. This time a shriek was torn out of his throat.

Serena looked up. "I told you. Don't let yourself come again. It's set for higher shocks each time."

"Oh, God!" he moaned, tugging at his restraints. "I can't take that...please!" Serena returned to her pleasant task of forcing her victim to an unwilling second orgasm.

He tried to concentrate on anything but sex, controlling his impending explosion by force of will. It was at that point that Sharon began to come, loudly and passionately, from Kelly's cunnilingual expertise. "Oh!

Oh! *Oh! Yes!*" she cried, and that sent him back over the top. *Bzzzz!*

He moaned, a terrible cry of pain. "Please...no more...oh, God, I can't take it...please...I beg you..."

His begging went for naught. Sharon came again, stimulated by his cries of pain and her occasional glances at his torment. Her newfound sadism raged in her blood. She began kissing Kelly roughly, assuming a dominant role. Kelly allowed herself to be swept away as Sharon began suckling at her body, driving the tall cheerleader to another exquisite orgasm.

The passionate moans and orgasmic cries of the the lesbian lovers sent Tom over the top for the third time in spite of all his attempts at control. His entire body jerked and twitched as jolts of electricity coursed through him. His cock softened.

Serena relented at last. "That was a fun game," she laughed. "But I saved the best for last. Before I tell you what it is, let's get you hard again." She removed the electrodes and then gave him a delicious new round of oral sex, sucking his cock, playing with his nipples. Instead of triggering new convulsions, this time she contented herself with teasing: up to the edge and back away, up to the edge and back away, until that, too, became torture. "Please...please...please..." He could only moan repeatedly, begging helplessly.

"Girls, I think you might want to watch this," Serena giggled. Sharon and Kelly, now in a languorous postorgasmic glow, rose from the bed, both gloriously nude, to watch Serena's performance.

Serena stroked Tom's nipples. "Would you like to really come, little boy?" she asked.

"Yes...yes," he moaned.

"Would you do anything I asked?" she smiled, keeping up the nipple torment.

"Yes...anything..."

"Anything? I've got a pretty kinky imagination, you know." She pouted prettily at him.

His eyes went even wider. "Yes...please...you know I will."

"What a good boy you are," she said. "I'm very horny, and I want you to get me off. When you do, I'll let you come. I'll even let Sharon do the honors. Is that all right with you, Sharon?"

"You bet!" giggled the young coed. This was prick-teasing far beyond anything she had conceived. She had an idea of what to expect, and the thought of Tom's ultimate humiliation made her quiver with renewed lust.

Tom blushed at the sight of Sharon, but his arousal knew no limits. "Please," he moaned. "Let me get you off. You're so beautiful. I want to please you. Let me."

"OK," Serena laughed. She unzipped the leather skirt slowly and let it drop to the floor. She wore the red bodice, her thigh-high stockings, boots, and red panties. She pulled down the panties, and her hard, jutting cock sprang out. It was long and thick. "Ready to get me off?" she laughed.

"No...oh, God!" Tom recoiled in horror as the three vixens burst out in uncontrollable gales of laughter.

Serena made the rack tilt so his head was lower than his feet, just in the right position to take her cock in his mouth. He struggled against his bonds in shock and fear.

"I just love to see little straight boys when they are confronted with a hard cock," Serena said. "I'll let you suck my cock, Tom, but only if you beg for it."

Tom was still consumed with shock and horror, but his cock stayed distressingly hard, and got harder when Serena began sucking it again, playing with his nipples, inflaming him. He was so sexy that Tom couldn't think straight. But he couldn't…he just couldn't.

He looked to Sharon for help and mercy, but she was excited by his impending fate. "Go ahead," she teased. "Suck Serena's cock. I want to watch."

"Oh, God…oh, God…" he cried out as his furious lust took possession of his senses. "OK…please… Serena, let me suck your cock. Please, I beg you. Let me suck your cock."

"Ooh," the little blonde tease said. "That's the kind of dirty talk I like to hear. OK, but only because you beg. By the way, tell me to unload all my come in your mouth."

Tom could barely choke out the words, but he knew he was doomed. "Please…unload all your come in my mouth."

Kelly removed his silver cockring. "Sharon, make sure you don't let him come until he's swallowed all of Serena's. He's very hair-trigger by now."

Sharon giggled. "Don't worry. In fact, I don't know if I'll make him come even then."

Serena stood with her cock near Tom's face. He opened his mouth to take her and began sucking. Sharon hand-fucked his cock with slow, teasing deliberation. Serena played with his nipples with one hand and teased her own fat nipples with her other. "Mmm, nothing I like better than straight-boy blowjobs," she laughed. Her cock fucked his mouth slowly.

Tom could feel her cock swell, her hips push more insistently. Suddenly the cock was pushing back in his mouth, threatening to trigger his gag reflex. She was close, close. Sharon's careful stroking goaded his cock; sucking Serena's cock was humiliating and exciting simultaneously. Then Serena moaned and jets of come spurted into his mouth; he swallowed deeply as her cock pushed hard against the back of his throat. Sharon kept teasing him until the last jolts of Serena's orgasm leaked away.

"There, there," Serena smiled, kissing his lips and licking away stray drops of sperm. "That wasn't so bad, was it? In fact, you liked it, didn't you."

He couldn't lie. "Yes…yes, I did."

"Good. Now Sharon will finish you off."

Sharon was so inflamed by the sexy vision that she began sucking Tom's cock. Kelly and Serena each took one of his nipples. The three girls attacked their victim with vampirish delight, devouring him, taking him until with *"Oh God!"* a deep and terrible moan as he exploded into Sharon's hungry mouth. Sharon had sucked boys' cocks, but never swallowed; this time she drank down the thick spurts of come with passion nearly equal to her own orgasm.

TABITHA'S TICKLE

Tom was drained, weak, helpless when the girls unfastened him and placed him on the brass bed. His cock was still erect. Sharon needed more. "Put your hands over your head; grab the bars and hold them until I say to let go," she ordered. He looked so vulnerable as she straddled him and sat down on his hard cock. She fucked him in deep strokes, finally falling on him, her hair spilling over his face, tonguing him deeply as she rode faster and faster until *"Oh! Oh!"* her orgasm hit and he spurted again. She smiled down at him. "That's all for now," she said. "But I'll be back."

Tom trembled unresistingly as Serena and Kelly hooked his wrist and ankle cuffs to the bars on the brass bed. The three temptresses left their limp victim naked and drained and closed the cell door behind them.

10

Tabitha prowled the corridors of the dungeon, deciding on her next victims. Tonight's party was the culmination of her study of witchcraft; the sexual energy being harvested in the dungeon would be put to good use—to create the hottest, wildest, strangest, most erotically charged party in history. She smiled at the thought. Her own erotic charge was building; she had absorbed the pent-up come from her lover Felipe and kept her own orgasm in check. She felt the magickal power surging within her. Inside the walls of the dungeon there was far more power, the waves of frustrated delight and erotic agony charged her even more. Suddenly there was a tremble...an orgasm. Her witchy senses reached out; it was Sharon and Tom. Good, she thought. Those two needed to meet. Sharon's life would certainly become more complicated, and that fit Tabitha's plan perfectly.

Rather than put back on her red leather party dress, she had slipped on the dungeon uniform of shiny black leotard top, velvet hot pants, and laced calf-high leather high-heeled boots. Her thick waves of golden-red hair spilled over her shoulders; her luscious body strained against the tight fabric; her long, booted legs were a fetishist's dream. She looked wicked, hot, and dangerous.

She checked out the one-way mirrors. There was a boy strapped to the Tease-o-Matic. Here was a girl, undergoing her own initiation as a tease-toy, being caressed with fur gloves while a vibrator worked on her sensitive parts. Two dungeon mistresses, garbed as she was, worked over a crawling boy on his hands and knees. Next, a couple—a girl who chickened out and tried to free her boyfriend. They were being teased together and soon the girl would have to decide which one got release. Tabitha was fairly sure what her choice would be. In another room, the boys who had been paralyzed by Amber's magic found the spell wearing off; their hard cocks throbbed from having a cute naked girl at their mercy, then having her taken away. *Six boys*, Tabitha thought. *That's a good start.*

She would have Robin brought in, too. She felt a certain fondness for the boy; he was so easy to tease, so responsive to her wickedness. Felipe was her bondage lover, Robin her toy, but she cared in her own way for them both. Robin had never even seen her naked. He was in for a treat. And if six boys weren't enough…well, perhaps Robin would really get lucky.

She gave the orders to Amber. In the meantime, she drank a potion of her own, one to stimulate her own erotic sensitivities and get her ready. She settled into a meditative trance to harness her Tantric energies.

Soon the word came. She went to a special chamber, a large dungeon room with a padded floor. The six boys were dressed in their leather harnesses, their cocks fully teased into readiness. They were kneeling, hands cuffed to their collar rings. Robin was shackled to the wall; he had also been teased hard. He was leaking. Tabitha felt a wildness, a hunger. This would be fun.

She strode into the room like a stripper in control. She caught a glimpse of herself in the mirror; she knew several of the dungeon staff had gathered to watch. *Good*, she thought. *The more the merrier.* She strutted for the pleasure of all her watchers. The lovestruck expression on Robin's face was particularly priceless.

She felt wonderfully slutty. "Come on boys, boys, boys," she taunted. "Wanna fuck? Wanna fuck me? Fuck me hard, fuck my pussy, fuck my ass?" Their saluting cocks gave the answer. She ran her hands over her body, preening in the mirror. She was hot, gorgeous, a wet dream with a knowing smile.

She gestured hypnotically and spoke a single word of power, freeing the hands of the six boys. "Come and get me," she said in her best Lauren Bacall voice. They were up on their feet, surrounding her eagerly, ready to devour her just the way she wanted. She played with them like a matador, teasing one and then another, grabbing a cock in each hand and pumping wildly, taking one for a tongue-kiss and rubbing her ass against the cock of another. Their hands began to caress her, squeeze her, maul her. "Yeah, that's the way. Do it. Do it to me," she urged hotly. Hands were pulling at her leotard top. "Tear it off!" she ordered, and hands were pulling, tearing until her large breasts fell free.

She leaned back into the sea of hands as they tore at her hot pants, leaving her naked except for boots, each hand filled with a cock. Cocks were at her face to the right and to the left; she sucked on one and then another. The hands spread her legs wide and then a mouth fastened itself to her pussy and began devouring her. Other mouths fastened on each breast. Cocks, hands, mouths were all that existed. "Yeah, do it. Lick my pussy. Give me your cocks. Give me all your come." The boys had each been equipped with golden cock-rings that stimulated the production of seminal fluid; their orgasms were guaranteed to be huge and they would not stop until every drop of comejuice had squirted out for Tabitha's pleasure and Tabitha's power. She was playing with fire, but it was her magickal fire.

She felt the first surges of her own first orgasm and let it sweep over her; her power surged with it. She got on her hands and knees, feeling particularly dirty and hot, spread her legs, and one of the boys shoved his cock in her doggy-style as she leaned over to suck off a spread-legged boy sitting in front of her. The other boys continued to feel her up, grab her, use her body. The

Tabitha's Tickle

cock in her pussy began to spurt; then she had a mouthful of hot, creamy come to swallow. The power was building. She let the boys lift her up; there was a new cock in her pussy and now another cock was pushing against the tight ring of her asshole. The double penetration triggered her again; she found herself in a state of continuous orgasm, pulse after pulse, quiver after quiver. Back and forth they rocked, making a sandwich out of her, until both her pussy and ass each took a load of come. She was hand-fucking two of the boys and one of them shot off; she licked the come off her hand.

Tabitha had never felt so outrageous, so hot. She wanted more, much more.

She was on her knees sucking two cocks together, forcing them both into her mouth while hand-fucking a third; her pussy had swallowed up another cock beneath her and she rode it until all four cocks shot off. Her mouth was running over with come, and it was beginning to leak from her pussy. She was getting sticky with male seed. It was glorious!

Tabitha hefted the fat balls beneath one of the cocks. There was still more come to draw out. She had never felt so much power, and still she wanted more. She *needed* more. Her mouth fastened on that cock, determined to drain it dry; it shot under her determined sucking and she kept on, pulling more out of it. She could hear the whimpering of the cock's owner, but she didn't care. There was more for her. And here it came. She could see his quivering legs; he was almost done for. One more should do it. She kept on sucking.

Another boy entered her ass again, filling her up and fucking her hard. The cock in her mouth spurted its weak last; the boy sagged; she let it go. There was another cock waggling at her, and she began sucking it eagerly. When the cock in her ass shot again, she grabbed another boy, pulled him on top of her and spread her legs wide to take his pumping cock as he fucked her, used her pussy as a vessel for his pent-up sperm, spat his load into her. She hand-fucked two more boys and got two more handfuls of sticky sperm.

Her power raged hot and wild within her. Her boy-toys continued their ravenous attack, no matter how much they came they needed more. They couldn't get enough of her. She couldn't get enough of them. Their energy spurted out in waves of cream.

One by one, the boys were drained dry; they dropped out until finally she was fucking one victim for the fifth time; his weak spurts were the end. She was trembling slightly when she stood up, but inside her was a surge of magickal power like nothing she had ever felt. She was a living flame, a cosmic power. She glowed with unbelievable sexuality.

Her senses widened. Through the one-way glass, she could sense the stimulation of her dungeon staff. Some were playing with themselves, some necking and petting, some merely transfixed with lust. She turned to face her final victim.

Shackled to the wall, Robin was utterly transported. Already mesmerized by his tormentress, he was blissed out completely by the wild orgy he had witnessed. His cock was straining and forming drops of pearly liquid. His hips quivered; his body trembled uncontrollably. Tabitha could feel the pain in his swollen cock, could sense the come churning in his balls. She licked her lips at the thought of it.

Robin knew he was in the presence of a goddess. In the months of his imprisonment, he had never seen Tabitha naked. She planned it that way. She had blindfolded him while she made love in the same room, undressed just out of range, teasing him relentlessly with what he couldn't have. Her naked body was fully as gorgeous as he had imagined—more so. His body quivered and went rigid in the grip of a restrained orgasm that would not quit. Fireworks exploded in his skull. His body convulsed as she walked toward him. What would she do now? He could barely hope.

Tabitha licked her lips at the thought of drawing out weeks of frustrated come. Robin would be good for a gallon, at least. She looked at him thoughtfully, then came to a decision.

"No, Robin, not yet." The stricken look of pain on his face made her laugh. "I'll make you a promise, though. At the party, I'll find the most humiliating, sexy, embarrassing, nasty, frustrating, and teasing way to make you come. You'll come tonight, at the stroke of midnight. Something to look forward to." She gave him a wicked grin. "I'm glad you watched. I've never felt so nasty or so hot. I thought about your cock, and I really wanted it inside me. But, you know, you're just too much fun to tease."

One of the other dungeon girls brought Tabitha a

towel; she wiped herself off. Other girls carried out the limp boys, useless for hours to come. Two girls took Robin away; they had eager looks. Tabitha knew they would play more games with her toy, torture him even further before tonight. She expected to keep her promise about his coming at the party, especially the humiliation part. She already had some ideas.

It was dusk; time for magick to begin. Time for the transformation. Time for the Goddess to rule again.

A pentagram was already inscribed on the floor in the secret chamber set aside for spell casting. Felipe, her coach and mentor in the ways of magick as well as her slave and lover, held open an ancient tome. Tabitha was naked, as befits a witch. So were the two others who formed a triangle inside the pentagram: Amber and Veronica. Veronica was a dark-haired senior who had been a sorority member for several years.

Tabitha joined them and the three began to chant through the long spell. Incense wafted through the chamber. They could see the beginnings of the power forming in the pentacle's center; Tabitha fed it more and more of her power. Having absorbed so much power, she was the main engine of the magic. Amber and Veronica, who frequented the dungeons, tended also to have good reserves. The power was a glowing orb; it grew brighter, brighter. The presence of the magick was sexy, since it was, after all, erotic magic. It built and built as the chant continued.

Then a silent explosion and a bright flash of light! The transformation began.

Tabitha's Tickle

Tabitha's spell had opened the gateway to the sex dimension—only a small way, not enough to merge the realms, but enough. For the rest of the night the impossible would be real, the fantastic immediate, the erotic manifest.

Book 2
The Party

1

Queen of her domain in red leather, her red-gold hair forming a halo around her tanned features, her body radiating sexuality from every pore, Tabitha led her two leashed slaves like dogs kneeling beside her: Felipe on the left, Robin on the right, both with swollen cocks laced into painfully tight leather tubes, both naked except for their humiliating leather slave harnesses, this time in red to match her outfit.

Amber wore her own open harness, revealing pussy and breasts, but tough and dominant in style. She carried a whip and strutted with sexy self-confidence. Veronica was a sleek black cat in her formfitting jumpsuit, a large silver zipper from high collar to crotch.

The long paneled corridor was lined with alternating

slaves, male and female, the males teased erect and the females spread and open. An eerie red glow filled the room. The magick had begun.

Tabitha smiled down at her lover. "Tonight should increase our power remarkably," she said quietly.

Felipe nodded. It was Tabitha's power, not his, but he gloried in his mistress's witchy achievements. His cock had revived from his earlier draining; the leather bonds were tightening around him. Robin, whose balls hung full and aching, felt the tight lacing cut cruelly into his swollen shaft.

With a tug on her leash, Tabitha began the procession. As Robin crawled along meekly at her side, he was just at the height of the cocks and pussies of the bound slaves. He could get a glimpse of faces drawn tight with lust. Tabitha's glowing magick made each cock twitch with need, each pussy drip with excitement. He could feel them looking at him: the humiliation of being a slave in front of slaves, a toy in front of toys. Their presence added to his torment; his to theirs.

Ornately carved heavy wooden double doors led into the main chamber. Two dungeon mistresses, garbed in leather hot pants and metallic silver tops, opened the doors.

Dante and Hieronymus Bosch might have envisioned the scene, but few others could. Pulsing light and loud music, the first waves of intricately costumed boys and girls, each trying to top each other with outrageous sexual display, strange erotic devices undergoing imaginative uses. The first couplings began as night fell.

Robin's hips twitched uncontrollably in time to the music; he longed to be part of the massive orgy. He followed Tabitha to an elevated dais: her throne. The Witch-Queen was here to inspire her subjects. Sex-magick was alive. The Goddess was afoot.

David's costume embarrassed him. It was his stepsister's idea: an old-fashioned schoolboy outfit right out of a Red Skelton sketch, complete with ribboned boater and dorky Bermuda shorts—they didn't let him wear underwear, and the shorts were so tight that the outline of his cock showed clearly. He was tall, thin, attractive. His girlfriend Brandi, a freshman, wore a fetish version of a Catholic schoolgirl outfit with a short plaid skirt, blue button-down blouse and knee-high socks. Brandi looked around with eager nervousness. She was cute, small breasts and pert bottom, petite, with great legs.

His stepsister was the schoolteacher: hair in a tight bun, long, straight skirt slit all the way up, granny glasses, and a ruler to discipline unruly students. They fit right in as they entered the party, joining miniskirted nurses, jackbooted girl cops with nightsticks, a genie in diaphanous harem pants that were totally transparent.

David looked hesitantly at his girlfriend. This wasn't the evening he had planned. This was their night: their planned first time making love. Until his stepsister showed up. Now he was afraid that his secret would be revealed, and he didn't know how Brandi would react. His cock ached.

David's secret was that he had been under the spell of his gorgeous stepsister for years. Monica was three years his senior, with dark red hair. She was tall, with a cruel mouth, a terrible tease. He couldn't keep his eyes off her from the time his father remarried and she moved in. She caught him staring and smiled back boldly. She wore sexy clothing: skintight shorts and tight tops, miniskirts with a sheer blouse with one too many buttons unbuttoned. Around the house she was a torment in her short nightie and even just a towel from the shower, giving him a quick peek and a thrill. A teenage wet dream with knowing eyes that caught him every time he stared lustfully at her. He masturbated two or three times a day, but it wasn't enough.

Then one day he sneaked into her bedroom and went into her hamper, fished out satin panties to wrap around his cock. He rubbed the wool of her cheerleading sweater as he masturbated. She was supposed to be safely out of the house, but she wasn't, and he was caught. His punishment was a bare-ass spanking and then he came while bent over her lap. They were both surprised, but she decided that this was an experience worth repeating.

During a long, erotic summer, she turned him into her slave, making him run errands, serve her, wait on her hand and foot. One day her girlfriends visited. She made him kneel on the floor at her feet, patting his head like a dog. His face was a permanent red. She made him fetch drinks, patting his ass, ordering him around as the girls giggled. Then they began to boss him around, teasing him until his cock swelled, making them giggle some more. There was no real sex, just lots of giggling at his hard-on showing through his summer shorts.

In private, though, Monica would explore her dominance by having him pull down his pants, fondling his cock, playing with it, having him lick her to repeated orgasms, but she never fucked him. She loved to see his cock spurt. She made him masturbate for her often. Sometimes she made him stand naked before her, hands clasped behind his back and legs spread as she played with his cock for hours until his legs trembled and he begged for mercy, finally making him shoot for her.

Monica was accepted at Valentine. When it came time for her initiation, she had to give them a boy-toy, so David served his time in the dungeons. Unlike girls who used the dungeons to train their boyfriends, David was not Monica's boyfriend, merely a toy. She went wild with sexual opportunities; he suffered the delights and agonies that Tau Zeta Rho specialized in. He couldn't think of his time in the dungeons without an instant erection. He never spoke of it. The dungeons hadn't turned him into a submissive fetishist, but they had awoken desires in him he didn't know he had. That's why he was so afraid of Brandi's knowing.

David now attended Tech, the nearby college. He was surprisingly successful with the coeds—possibly because his training under Monica and Tau Zeta had made him a very capable and considerate lover. He was certainly a world-class cunnilinguist.

Brandi was the first girl he was completely serious about; he was in love. That night they had been petting for a while on a blanket near the lake. He was ready; so was she. But when they returned to his dorm room for the culmination, there were Monica and two of her Valentine friends lounging on his bed.

"It's party time, darling," Monica smiled cruelly, coming over to give him a hug. The two watching girls smiled as David's cock stiffened. He knew them; they had enjoyed him in the dungeon. He blushed a painful red.

Brandi looked quizzical, but he was too overwhelmed to speak. "I'm his stepsister," Monica said. "We're all off to Valentine College for a party. Ready to party? You do want to come, don't you?" The emphasis on "come" was her deliberate way of sending him a message. He was trapped.

Brandi looked at David. Then she looked at the three girls in the room. There was something going on, and she took David's arm. "Come on, David. You don't have to go if you don't want to. We can go to my room," she said sympathetically.

"How sweet," Monica drawled as her two companions giggled. "But you know you both want to come, don't you? It's a Tau Zeta Rho party, and it's going to be the hottest party of the year."

Brandi was tempted. She always heard about Tau Zeta's parties. There was a really sexy secret she hadn't quite figured out. "If you want to, I'm game," she said, smiling prettily at her blushing boyfriend. "But if you want to go somewhere else, that's OK. I just want to do what you want."

David looked at her with gratitude, but also with fear. How would she react if she knew about his relationship with Monica, or his dungeon experiences.

"Listen, loverboy," Monica said sternly. "You know you want to come. Get with the program! Or do we have to have a long personal chat with your little girlfriend?"

She was capable of anything, David thought, with a combination of fear and a wave of overpowering lust. He looked at Brandi. She was excited about the party.

"I promise…later…" Brandi whispered, her voice trailing off, leaning up to kiss his cheek.

David knew full well what the likely result of that promise would be, but he also knew that Monica wouldn't hesitate to embarrass him if he failed to cooperate. One way or another, he was positive that the evening would end with Brandi's learning his secret. How she would react was anybody's guess, but his fate was cast. "Sure," he said stoically. "Let's party."

Anthony was a stranger to Valentine, and so was his girlfriend Stephanie. Stephanie hoped to transfer in her junior year and was particularly pleased to get this invitation. Anthony had heard rumors about wild orgies and easy women, and really looked forward to the evening. He was another Tech student, and so was she. He fancied himself quite a cocksman. He liked Stephanie a lot and thought she was a good fuck. Stephanie thought he could be something more for her, but spent much of her time annoyed at him.

Anthony's cock jutted out in his lace-front leotard

pants; he had shifted it carefully to make the bulge as obvious as possible. He wore a white pirate shirt with puffy sleeves, the lace open to show his hairy chest. Black boots, a wide black belt, and a matching eye patch made him feel piratical and aggressive. Stephanie, rich blonde hair spilling over bare shoulders, wore a low-cut period gown—the noblewoman captured by her pirate lover. He could see down to her nipples. He knew she wore no underwear. He wanted to fuck her in her costume, but she kept saying, "Later...later." He looked around the antechamber of the party. Every gorgeous woman in the state was there: cheerleaders, vampires, nurses, science fiction aliens, secret agents, cops...a fantasia of fetishes.

"Don't wear your eyes out," Stephanie said with annoyance. "I've got to powder my nose," she said. "Don't get into any trouble."

Anthony *wanted* to get into trouble, to get into the panties of virtually every woman he saw around him. This was every boy's fantasy. After all, men were polygamous, and this was Pussy Central.

Then his eyes were drawn to the cage.

It was a wooden cage about the size of a phone booth with iron bars forming the front. In it was a girl, a prisoner in black leather. Wide black collar with an imprisoning ring, a leather laced-up corset revealing naked breasts and pussy, long raven hair and ruby-red lips. With a shock, he noticed that she was masturbating! Her eyes closed, lips parted with just the tip of a pink tongue protruding, one hand pinching her nipple, hard, two fingers of her other hand sliding roughly back and forth in her wet pussy. He was drawn to her. She opened her eyes, heavy with lust. "Give me your... cock," she breathed, sliding down in her cage. "Give me your cock...fuck my mouth with it...please...I need it so much...fuck my mouth with your cock...I can see it in your pants...pull it out...fuck my mouth...please..." She was gasping with passion.

Without even thinking, Anthony moved up to the cage and unlaced his pants, fumbling inside to pull out his cock, now purple and engorged. Her mouth opened, widely, wetly. As he moved his hips forward, his cock slid inside. Her mouth was hot—so hot and wet that the sensation nearly triggered an instant orgasm. He reached up to grab the bars for stability, standing closer and closer. She was really hungry for cock, sucking him passionately. He closed his eyes; his head spun with passion. His orgasm approached quickly. "Yes...yes... suck my cock..." he moaned.

Suddenly he felt his entire body twist, his cock released to throb wetly and helplessly in the cold air. He was standing on a trapdoor! He slid down a metal slide, clutched in the darkness by waiting hands. Disoriented, stunned at the nearness of his orgasm, he could not resist as knowing female hands stripped him naked, tweaking his nipples and stroking his cock, tickling his sides with light squirming pleasure—he surrendered to it. Then the shackles fastened around his wrists, and he found himself spread-eagled against a wooden wall, ankles pulled apart and imprisoned as well. One last squeeze of his cock and he was being lifted on a platform and then... "Oh, my God!" he gasped as he realized he was back in the party, naked and fastened to a board, his cock bobbing as waves of girlish laughter drew a blush of humiliation from him.

With a flourish, a girl dressed as a circus ringmaster—fishnet stockings and black pumps, black leotard, with a tuxedo shirtfront, a jacket with clawhammer tails and a top hat—announced, "Ladies, our first victim! Here he is, unable to resist an opportunity to get his ashes hauled, a typical out-of-control sex maniac, Anthony!" Applause, whistles, and catcalls drove him crazy with the desire to escape; he struggled against his heavy iron shackles to no avail. As his head whipped back and forth, he stopped suddenly—Stephanie! Her expression was angry.

"Less than five minutes, and look what you're into," she said.

The ringmistress put her arm around the young blonde. "His fate is now in our hands. He must pay a forfeit to be released—he has to be jerked off in front of everybody. When he spurts, he's free." With a wicked glance at Anthony, she whispered quickly in Stephanie's ear. The young blonde's expression changed at once.

With a smile, she walked toward her helpless lover and kissed him. The rustle of stiff satin against his nude form drove him crazy. Their kiss was long. Stephanie slowly reached her hand down and captured his long erection. "I have to jerk you off," she whispered. "Jerk you off in front of everybody, or they won't let you go."

Her eyes were bright, her smile teasing. His cock was throbbing.

"OK," he whispered back. "I'm sorry."

"I know," she smiled. "You just couldn't help yourself, right?"

"That's right," he nodded eagerly as her hand began its slow, sensual work. "Baby, that's nice. So nice. You're the best."

"I'm glad you realize it," Stephanie smiled. "You really owe me one, you know."

"Yes...yes...I owe you one. I'll lick you really nice, fuck you, anything...please...yes..." He was beginning to moan with pleasure. He imagined all the girls watching his cock, getting hot, wanting him. Stephanie studied his face carefully. The girls were whistling and catcalling as she masturbated him. She was angry and humiliated at his unfaithfulness.

"Don't let him spurt all over that nice dress!" one called.

Stephanie looked over her shoulder. "Don't worry." She turned back to Anthony. "I didn't think about that. You'll get that come all over me."

Lost in a growing fog of sensuality, he could barely hear her. "Mmm...yes...OK..." he moaned, his hips fucking her hand as the slow masturbation continued.

He was close. He moved his hips faster, spurring her on. From humiliation to arousal, he was at the point that spurting an orgasm in front of a crowd of girls seemed very sexy, very masculine. He imagined them all envying him, wanting his cock.

"You aren't listening to a word I say," Stephanie teased, her other hand toying with his right nipple. "Tell me what I just said."

He racked his brain. "Don't get come...on your dress..." he gasped.

"That's right," Stephanie smiled. "Are you close?"

"Yes..."

"Very close?"

"Yes...yes..."

"Just about ready to come? Let me know just exactly when, OK?"

"Yes...yes...just a little more...almost...faster... faster...faster...yes! *Yes! Now!*"

Stephanie let go of his cock as if it were a hot iron. Anthony's eyes flew open.

"April fool, lover," she laughed. "I told you I didn't want to get your dirty come all over my dress. I'm going to leave you here just like this as a lesson. Maybe you'll learn to behave."

He tore at his shackles. "Damn it! Stephanie! You can't...you just can't."

"Oh, yes I can," Stephanie giggled. "Tough luck, baby. Maybe one of the other girls will have pity on you. I'm going to go party. 'Bye!"

"Wait! Stephanie...come back here! Right now! Damn it, you can't leave me like this! I'm sorry! Really! I'll make it up to you! Come back!"

The ringmistress gestured at the crowd of girls. "He's unredeemed, available for your pleasure! Keep him hard and tied, or make him come and own him for the rest of the evening!" The girls clustered around, teasing and tickling. "Hard and tied!" one girl cried out, and the rest chanted along. "Hard and tied! Hard and tied!" He screamed as the first tickling fingers attacked.

Stephanie gave a quick glance back as his tickled laughter shrieked in the crowded room. She liked the idea of his torment. The girls would tickle him senseless, then tease him until he couldn't see straight, and nobody, but nobody—would let him come. She planned to return, all right, but he'd be surprised at his little pussycat's claws. She smiled at what she had planned for him. She'd never been this way—dominant, teasing, cruel. Even a few hours ago, she would have pleased him, just to be nice. *There must be something in the air*, she thought, as she went into the main party room, prowling for her own pleasures.

2

Trapped naked in the back of the van between two outrageously costumed coeds, Bobby was continuing his descent into erotic madness. By now, the repeated teases, humiliations, and tickling sessions had short-circuited his brain completely. To his surprise, however, he was still able to feel keen moments of embarrassment.

Once he had recovered from his fainting spell, Susan and Tiffany shifted gears, getting the threesome ready for the party. The girls dressed up as Satanic imps. Both girls somehow made their skin glow an erotic and slightly evil shade of red. Tiffany wore a black ciré spandex costume that consisted of a low-cut V-shaped bottom with high-cut legs, dipping far below her navel in front to rest at the leading edge of her pubic mound. Her midriff was bare; thin bands of cloth hugged her skin like wide suspenders, covering the outer edge of her breasts, dipping in to barely cover the nipples, leaving the deep cleavage gloriously nude. From the upper part of her pert rounded ass protruded a devil's tail with forked end. It seemed alive, not at all fake, and matched her skin perfectly. It twitched. Susan wore the same basic costume in gold, to match her hair.

"We're succubi," Susan said breathily, squirming her lithe body against him. "We visit young boys in their sleep and give them wet dreams. Then we lick up all the come. We're come-vampires."

"I-I've got plenty for you," replied Bobby, trembling with overpowering lust. "You can have it all."

Susan chortled. "Ooh, I'll bet. Let me weigh your balls. Mmm, so heavy. Full of come, rich and thick. Tiffany, feel."

Tiffany's hand joined Susan's. "Mmm. Maybe I'll take a taste," she said, sliding down on her knees to suck his straining shaft deeply into her mouth, sucking hard, until he quivered with desperate need—then she quit. His hips continued to fuck the empty air like a phantom lover. Both girls laughed.

"Ready to party?" Susan teased.

"Where's my costume?" Bobby asked innocently.

"Why, Woody!" Susan said with mock shock. "You're already in costume!"

He looked down at the leather harness, his bobbing cock protruding. "I-I can't go out like this!" he protested.

Tiffany chimed in. "You're right, lover. Of course you can't. We haven't finished the costume yet." She opened the drawer of the study desk and pulled out two sheets. They were decals—temporary tattoos. Soon, he wore an inscription on his chest—SLAVE—and another on his back—PROPERTY OF VALENTINE CHEERLEADING SQUAD. The blush on his face nearly matched the red skin of the costumed imps.

Susan looked him up and down. "Cute," she laughed, giving his cock a sexy squeeze. Then she said more seriously, "Woody, here are tonight's rules. You're not part of the party, you're part of the entertainment. We're going to keep the silver cockring on until midnight. Then we'll bring Sharon in. She gets to decide whether or not to make you come; if you come, she'll do it. Now, you're getting a little overwhelmed; you haven't been here that long, so you're not used to this yet. That actually makes you a lot more amusing. But we're going to help you out. Tiffany..."

Tiffany produced another joint, a huge one, and a strange-smelling concoction. "This is our special slave-boy aphrodisiac," she laughed. "It makes you willing, eager, and able. You'll like it. It's got LSD, THC, Ecstasy, and even real magick." He gulped. "Drink it down. It'll make the evening much easier for you. Then smoke up."

He complied.

The van was filled with coeds, all in costume. There were two girls dressed as rock video vixens, skintight leather and trashy lingerie. An Indian princess in war paint and buckskin leather that barely covered bikini areas. A buxom construction worker in hard hat, an unbuttoned flannel shirt tied off at the midriff, and frayed jeans shorts cut so short that they left nothing to the imagination. Susan and Tiffany were in the seat in front of him; he was between the video vixens.

Leather and lace rubbed up against him. His hands were once again shackled, this time to the rings at his waist. As the van left the dorm, he felt the hands of his seatmates begin a wicked attack, sliding up his legs, stroking him. His erection, never completely soft, raged once again. One hand began pumping him in a regular, evenly paced masturbation, an excruciatingly slow jerk-off. The other hand of the same girl toyed with his right nipple. The girl on his left played with his left nipple and used her tongue to stimulate the nape of his neck and his ears, blowing gently, nipping at his earlobe, stimulating the tiny hairs on the back of his neck. It was delicious; he opened his legs and leaned back to enjoy the sensation.

Tiffany had been right about the pot; it made his sexy torment much easier to bear. The potion had scared him, and now with the tracings coming on, the first signs of a psychedelic episode, he discovered that the aphrodisiac really worked. Right now, in his heart, he was a slave, a toy, a victim—and it gave him surprising pleasure. He couldn't think about anything else; this was normal.

His hips squirmed under the attack of the rock vixens; they took turns kissing him and began trading off his cock. One ran long-nailed fingers over the swollen head, taking the precome drippings and smearing them all around. Despite the array of sexy, scandalous costumes, Bobby's fetish was still operative: he imagined them all in cheerleading outfits. He moaned with delight, leaning back to enjoy the attention. Had it not been for the silver cockring, he would never have held out under the slow masturbation. But he had no choice. He had to suffer excruciating pleasure at the girls' teasing hands. This kind of suffering he liked.

The van jerked to a stop and the side door slid open. Light flooded the interior of the van. "Enjoy the ride?" Susan teased, leaning over the seat to look at her boy-toy being fondled so brazenly by the young rock vixens. His mouth was open and slack, his legs were spread wide and his cock jutted wetly upward in the sensual grip of his costumed playmates. Susan laughed. "I guess you did. Girls, it's party time."

They looked up at Susan. One of them said, "He's so cute. Can't we keep him for a while?"

Susan smiled. "He'd like it too much. But maybe later. He'll be available for general use."

The vixens laughed knowingly. "Ooh, that'll be fun," said the second vixen, tweaking Bobby's nipple sexily. "We'll come get you when you're all tied up and humiliated. Maybe we'll jerk you off in front of an audience. Would you like that?"

The combination of blush and twitching erection spoke volumes. He moaned in sensual desperation, thrusting his cock in hopes of finding a willing hand, mouth, or pussy.

"See you later, baby," the other vixen said, giving him a last wet kiss and quick pump of his cock. The girls slid out of the van, leaving Bobby once again in the hands of his captors.

Bobby was shaking as he climbed out of the van. With his arms shackled, it took the support of Tiffany and Susan to help him out. His aching cock, head glistening with precome ooze, bobbed in the chilly night air. He developed goose bumps all over; his balls tightened.

The van had parked in the driveway of an imposing mansion, far larger than he imagined the Tau Zeta sorority house to be. The formal driveway circled past the front entrance of the mansion; a fountain spouted in the center of the circle. The sculpture was of Prometheus bound on his rock, blindfolded and stretched wide. The fountain spurted from his cock. Instead of eagles tearing at his liver, this Prometheus's torture was a never-ending orgasm. A lovely Grecian goddess gripped his cock as it arched out its passion.

The moon was full and ripe; its yellow light illuminated the courtyard. Cars, vans, and limousines pulled up; exotically costumed guests climbed from them to proceed up the wide steps to the columned entrance. He noticed a Hindu goddess with multiple arms waving, a sultana with a male harem in golden chains, a circus ringmaster in fishnets and top hat, her companion a naked man with a lion's head.

Several of the arrivals noticed Bobby; one girl dressed as a miniskirted nurse snickered as she read the

TABITHA'S TICKLE

PROPERTY OF VALENTINE CHEERLEADING SQUAD tattoo. He blushed.

"Come on," Susan said bossily. "We haven't got all night." Bobby started toward the mansion until he got a sharp pull on his lease. "No, silly. The front entrance is for guests. Servants, slaves, and toys use the rear entrance. Follow us."

As the two succubi led their hard-cocked sex toy around the side, Bobby's torment grew. Both girls were so lovely, so sexy—he wanted to fuck either of them or both of them over and over again. By now the aphrodisiac concoction had hit him fully. The night was filled with tracings and hallucinations; his body trembled with the intense passion and desire brought on by the powerful drugs. His feet stumbled with uncertain balance on the cold stone walkway. In the bushes, on the expanse of formal lawn, in bowers behind hedges, numerous costumed couples were playing erotic games. One girl dressed in a Roman toga led two male satyrs on a merry chase: they darted from the bushes, ran across the stone path, then back into the bushes. A sexy female pirate had her male companion, dressed now only in the remnants of a ruffled shirt and tight pants, tied as she worked him over with a cat-o'-nine-tails.

Behind the house was a large swimming pool; skinny-dippers and bikini-clad coeds frolicked in the water. Couples spread on blankets necked, petted, and even made love.

In addition to the main pool, a series of grottoes lined the path. As the trio crossed a short wooden bridge,

Bobby looked down into a bubbling Jacuzzi containing two naked girls—twins—who looked up at him. "Wanna play?" they giggled, splashing him with warm water. "Come join us," they teased. Bobby stopped, wanting more than anything to slide into the hot bubbling water with the two lovely water nymphs, but a quick tug on the leash made him follow once again.

Susan laughed cruelly. "Poor Woody. I bet you'd really like to be in their hands for a few hours. But we have much more interesting things planned for you."

At the servants' entrance there were a number of costumed waitresses, dressed as French maids, in fishnet stockings and flouncy skirts, stiletto-heeled fuck-me pumps, and tuxedo jackets over tight, low-cut cleavage. The male waiters wore tuxedo slacks, bow ties, but no shirts. One waitress came over to the trio as they approached.

"Here's a toy for the entertainment booths," Susan laughed wickedly, handing Bobby's leash over to the raven-haired waitress, who looked him over with a calculating smile.

"So you're a toy." The waitress giggled knowingly, sliding her hand over his chest in a casual ownership way. "Don't worry," she said to Susan. "I'll get him where he belongs."

Susan took Bobby's face in her hand. Her blue eyes twinkled with amusement. "You're entertainment, but we're guests. It's party time. Be a good boy, do what everybody tells you, and we'll be back for you at the stroke of midnight."

TABITHA'S TICKLE

"Please!" Bobby moaned. "Please, don't leave me like this! I'm going completely crazy!"

"Oh, poor baby," Tiffany said, pouting with mock sympathy. "Has to be teased and hand-fucked and tickled by all the cute coeds. Well, that's the way it goes." She reached over to muss his blonde hair.

Bobby devoured her with his eyes. Her costume had become the single sexiest sight he'd seen in his life; he needed her more than he could imagine. But she just laughed at his helpless lust. Susan and Tiffany left, arms linked, to join the party. Bobby remained behind in the custody of the raven-haired waitress.

"Come on, slaveboy," she ordered. "Time to go to work." She led him in through the kitchen, filled with the clatter of pots and pans, waiters and waitresses trooping in and out. She pulled him into a pantry. "Here's your first assignment," she said, jumping up on an empty table. She spread her legs: she wore fishnet stockings fastened to a black garter belt, but no panties. Bobby knew what to do. He knelt in the tight quarters and leaned forward. His arms were still fastened to his sides, but his tongue was free. He licked up the length of her slit slowly; she shivered. "Mmm," she whispered breathily, "do it good!"

Betty loved getting head; he began kissing and nibbling the delicate folds of her labia. She was already aroused; her lips began to pout open under his slow, sensual attention. Soon her wet core was open and glistening; his tongue probed her center over and over, sliding up the ridge just under her clit, then backing off to tease just at the tip of her pleasure center. He glanced up: she had slid down her top and was playing with her nipples, tweaking them with thumb and forefinger, then cupping her entire breasts and squeezing gently. Her eyes were closed. He continued to lick and nibble. As her arousal grew, he flicked his tongue fast over her clit, then backed off to sensual strokes up and down the full length of her, over and over again. Her passion built; so did his.

She panted, faster and faster. He could tell she was getting close...close...he backed off to tease her, then close again, then back and again, the cycle between near-orgasm and backing off getting shorter and shorter until... "Nnnhhh!" she moaned and twisted as her orgasm began. He dove in, licking and stroking with his tongue faster and faster, sucking in the entirety of her outer lips until—finally—the waves subsided.

His heart pounded as he waited; mouth holding her erotic center. Finally she reached down to rub his tousled hair. "Good boy," she said sensually, stretching her gorgeous body. She slid down off the table to face him.

He got the first full look at her body. Her large, full breasts had plump nipples, slightly bruised from her own pinching. Her legs were long and lovely, still netted in the sexy black stockings, set off by the tall heels. Her eyes were dark and piercing, her lips red and full. Her hair was in slight disarray from her passion. She smiled at him, licking her red lips. "I shouldn't do this, but I feel like it. Spread your legs, lean against the wall, and smile."

Tabitha's Tickle

She stroked and teased his torso first, discovering how sensitive his nipples were and then tormenting them until he quivered all over. With excruciating slowness she slid her red-nailed hands down to tickle through the wiry hair surrounding his protruding erection, finally toying with his balls. She wrapped her other hand around his erection and began to stroke it, pressing her body close to his, rubbing her bare breasts against him. She kissed his bare shoulder and sucked on the nape of his neck. Kissing slowly, she went up his neck to his earlobe, sucking it, then teasing and blowing into his ear, driving him insane with delight.

"Too bad about your cockring," she whispered in his ear as she stroked him faster and faster. "I'd make you come; I really would. Does it feel good?"

"Yes...yes..." he moaned. "Oh, God, does it feel good. Please...I'm so close!" Bobby was in an agony of delight and passion. The waitress began to slither down his body, kissing all the way, suckling his nipple, then his bare belly, then reaching his shaft, kissing and licking its length, getting it wet, then enveloping it with her hot mouth. He fucked her mouth with his rocking hips; it was heavenly. But he couldn't come, couldn't reach the moment of climax, couldn't explode his pent-up passion. She let him go, his glistening erection throbbing.

She smiled. "I would have made you come, but I also like teasing. Did that make you crazy?"

"Yes," he moaned, then looked down at the beautiful girl crouched between his spread legs. "But I loved it."

She laughed, then gave him a deep tongue-kiss. "I'd better put you to work. If you get loose, come find me. I'll trade you a lick for a suck."

He laughed. It was the first time in this long day he'd felt any equality with a woman. "You got it."

He followed her to his fate.

3

"Like the costume?" Kelly asked, twirling for her audience. Sharon whistled. It was completely outrageous.

Kelly was dressed as a cop—a sex fantasy in blue. She wore a stiff-billed police officer's hat with silver insignia, tipped at a jaunty angle. Her long blonde hair was drawn into a severe bun. Mirror shades gave her a stern, dominant look. Her starched blue uniform shirt stretched tight over her ample chest; the last four buttons were unbuttoned so that the ends could be tied off, exposing her midriff. She wore a Sam Browne belt with a leather holster, a billy club, and handcuffs hanging from it. A high-cut leotard bottom, also in blue, exposed her legs as far as they would go. Her legs were covered in opaque striped hose, blue and white. High-heeled leather boots hugged her calves to just below her knees.

The girls had left the dungeons and were in an upstairs dressing room in the sorority house. More evidence of the wealth of Tau Zeta was everywhere—beautiful curtains, antique wardrobes, classical art on the walls. They were there to get ready for the party, but Sharon was in a playful mood.

"Arrest me now, Officer!" Sharon giggled, putting her hands behind her back and making her firm breasts jut out sexily.

"OK, you asked for it. Up against the wall and spread 'em," Kelly growled in return.

Sharon obeyed quickly, leaning against the wall and spreading her legs wide. She was still naked. "Frisk me, Officer," she said in a little-girl voice. "Oooh," she moaned as Kelly began her work. "Check all my hiding places. Yes. That's right."

Kelly laughed. "Maybe I'll give you a taste of my billy club." She brandished it as Sharon peeked behind her. The billy club was a huge black dildo, extremely realistic in design.

"Mmm," said Sharon, licking her lips. "Now, *that's* what I call a billy club!"

"You haven't seen the best part yet," said Kelly. She slid the club between Sharon's spread legs. It was part of Tau Zeta's magic; Sharon's pussy clenched immediately in paroxysms of near-orgasmic transport.

"Oh, my God!" she panted. "Oh! Oh! *Oh!*"

Kelly withdrew the club before Sharon's orgasm was

TABITHA'S TICKLE

fully triggered. She whimpered as it was withdrawn. "Do that some more," she pouted.

"You'd better save it for the party. You'll have a lot better opportunities than this. You don't want to wear yourself out with the appetizers before you get the main dish. Come and give me a nice kiss. Then we'll see about your costume."

Sharon slid into her pledgemistress's arms. The feel of the police uniform against her nakedness aroused her. She leaned into a deep kiss.

"You're going to think I'm so bad," Sharon breathed through her kisses, "but I'm burning up. Please…spank me. I'd really like it if you spanked me."

"You are a bad girl," Kelly whispered. "So very bad. Tau Zeta is really bringing it out in you. Yes, I'll spank you, but you'll have to lick me. On your knees!"

Sharon obeyed, leaning down to kiss Kelly's leather boots, working her way slowly up the slick nylon hose, finally nuzzling between Kelly's thighs. She popped open the crotch snaps, rubbing through the pantyhose at the growing wetness. She pulled down the hose eagerly and began to lick and suck the wet pussy before her. She was consumed by lust; feelings had awakened in her that she didn't know she had. She was rewarded quickly by Kelly's orgasm.

"Now me," she breathed. Kelly sat up and pulled Sharon roughly over her lap, then began to spank her. She spanked hard; Sharon squirmed in sudden pain, and then again as the pain merged with arousal. The spanking drove her crazy, nearly enough to prompt an orgasm by itself. Finally Kelly slipped the billy club dildo between Sharon's legs to rub her clit while continuing to spank her. Sharon moaned and cried out loudly, wriggling her hips as she came strongly.

There was a discreet throat-clearing noise, and Sharon turned to see Serena, costumed as Marilyn Monroe in her famous white dress. "Did I interrupt something naughty?" he/she asked.

Sharon was sweaty. She looked up at the hermaphrodite tease and smiled weakly. "Very naughty. I think I've turned into a complete slut."

"And you make a very cute slut," Serena said, smiling. "Don't worry. Around here, we learn to give in to our passions. It's only the slaves who have to wait."

"God, I know. I couldn't stand it. But it's fun making them stand it. By the way, you look really hot," Sharon observed. "That costume really works on you."

Serena smiled. "Thanks. How about you? Or are you just going naked because anything else is just gilding the lily?"

Sharon laughed. "I think Kelly is about to show me some outfits."

"And, by the way, thanks for letting me mess around with Tom," Serena said. "He's a good-looking boy."

"Mmm, yes," Sharon replied. "I think I'm not nearly finished with him."

"I could tell," Serena said. "If you need more help, I'm your man. Or woman. Just pass the word."

"I've got a few ideas about your costume," Kelly interjected. "Want to see?"

"Oh, yes," said Sharon. Serena was interested, too.

"As a new sister, you've learned that Tau Zeta is about sexual witchcraft. Let's make you a witch." Sharon nodded eagerly.

Kelly and Serena both helped costume her. Soon Sharon was dressed, in a manner of speaking. She wore a low-cut black minidress with a pointed handkerchief hem over black fishnets and black high-heeled granny boots. A pointed hat and a magic wand completed the outfit.

"The wand is real magick," Kelly said. "Use it carefully."

"What does it do?" Sharon asked, looking at the foot-long ebony rod.

"It's packed with a sexual charge," Kelly replied. "When you use it, every sexual nerve in your victim's body fires at the same time. They may have an orgasm, or they may not, but they won't forget it. They won't be able to move or do anything but twitch for a few minutes."

"Cute," smiled Sharon. "How does it work?"

"Just point and fire," Kelly said.

Sharon immediately pointed at Serena's crotch and squeezed the rod end gently. "Zap! You're it!" she laughed.

The effect was amazing. Serena's body suddenly went into a seizure. Every muscle stiffened; her eyes closed; her body began to twitch spastically. Her Marilyn skirt flew up; Sharon saw the outline of her bulging cock in her tight white panties. It began to spurt, staining the white cotton fabric. Sharon rushed to grab Serena before she fell.

It took a few minutes for her to recover. Sharon held her carefully. "I'm sorry," she said, "I didn't realize…"

"Oh, darling," Serena smiled weakly. "Don't apologize. It was an amazing moment. I'll have to have you do that again. Don't worry about the panties—I knew I'd need extras; and later in the party, I don't plan to wear any at all."

"You know, you're going to end up as one of the most sadistic girls in the sorority," Kelly observed wryly.

Sharon looked up, momentarily serious. "I don't know what's coming over me," she said.

"Oh, don't worry. I meant it as a compliment."

"No, really," Sharon said. "I'm serious. You know, this is the sexiest thing that ever happened to me, and I'm loving every minute of it. But I'm really getting caught up in this. Take Tom, for example."

"Mmm, yes," Serena teased. "I'll take him any time and any way."

"He's so sexy, and I really have had a crush on him for years. But the way I treated him! And then there's Bobby. I gave him to you to play with, and I really don't even know what you've done with him. And the truth is, I don't care. I mean, I do care, but only that I wish I could see what you're putting him through. And now, I don't know whether I want Bobby back, or whether it's going to be Tom. Kelly, I loved what we did and I want more. I knew I had a little bit of curiosity about girls that way, but not this much. And...while you were spanking me, I imagined taking a girl who didn't want to have sex with me and forcing her. I'm turning into a lesbian rapist and a dominatrix—and I've been here only a few hours!"

Kelly put her hand on Sharon's shoulder. "I understand, truly. You're the sort of girl we want in Tau Zeta. I know about the confusion you're going through, but you're not really a sadist. What we do isn't really sadism. It's the world's sexiest practical joke. You're a tease and a game player. That's different."

"Yeah? But isn't game playing bad?"

"Depends on who's playing and what they're playing for. You tortured Tom with pleasure, not pain. You messed with his mind and his cock. And I didn't hear Tom protest—at least not seriously. A few 'No! No!' cries add a little spice to it all. Tau Zeta's mission isn't to dominate the world, just add a little wicked fun to the mix. We turn people upside down and inside out. We play with pussies and pricks, but basically we play with minds. You understand mind games. You know how to mind-fuck. Sure, it's confusing right now, but you're not making anybody do anything that in their heart of hearts they don't like. We don't take victims who don't enjoy what we do. We take victims who like being taken, who want to be surprised. They have a submissive streak that welcomes what we do. Enjoy yourself. Let yourself go. Drive some helpless boy out of his mind with lust, and watch him crawl to kiss your feet in gratitude."

Sharon looked at her pledgemistress. "I can't help it. What a sexy image! I want some boy crawling at my feet. Maybe a girl, too. Maybe several all at once. I want them begging for it. Oh, God...what a sick girl I've become—but I still like it!"

"That's the spirit!" Kelly laughed. "As far as Bobby versus Tom, don't worry about it right now. Bobby's going crazy right now, but he is having fun. You'll see. And Tom...well, you know this is what Tom wants, even though it scares him in much the same way it scares you."

Serena spoke up. "Kelly's right. I had to go through all kinds of hell to find my sexual identity. I'm a magickal transsexual cockteaser. Innocent young boys are my specialty, and I haven't found one yet who ended up regretting my attentions. I blow their minds...among other things, of course."

Sharon looked from one to the other, then took a deep breath. "You're right. Robin was having fun, and so was Tom. And so am I. I like being in control, but I liked being spanked and played with, too. If I like it, so must they."

"There you go!" Kelly smiled. "This party will be just the thing for you. Try out various recreations. Let your witchy self rule for tonight. Find Tom, then find Bobby when midnight comes. I think it'll all work out."

"OK," Sharon said. Her face brightened in a wicked grin. "Let's go tease some cocks!"

"Go, Teasers!" the other two chanted.

The party was heating up. The huge ballroom was

filled with exotic and expensive Halloween decorations, all with erotic and witchy motifs. Tabitha, in her tight red leather, sat on her throne looking with amusement as the party turned into an exotic orgy of dominance and submission. Lashed to pillars on either side of her were her two personal slaves—Felipe on the left, Robin on the right—the cocks still painfully laced into their constricting leather tubes. Robin's hips writhed helplessly with his overwhelming passion; Felipe, better trained and more recently relieved, suffered in silent dignity. From time to time, Tabitha trailed the end of a braided whip down one of their backs, causing a shiver of erotic delight to ripple through their helpless bodies.

Games of every persuasion filled the room. One group of girls spun a large wheel of fortune to which were shackled four male slaves. Around and around it went; bets were placed. When it stopped, one male was removed and turned over to a group of gleeful giggling girls. They pulled him over to a felt-covered pool table and fastened him down with his hands pulled over his head and legs pulled apart at the foot of the bed, securing him with cold metal cuffs.

Each of the girls in turn perched on the bed beside the naked young prisoner. They kissed his mouth and nipples, stroked his cock, caressed his chest, nibbled his neck and ears, each inflaming him to renewed jutting passion, giggling and taunting him in his desperate need. It was going to be a long night.

Another group—this one of both boys and girls—were playing a simple board game. Each point won caused the other player to lose an article of clothing. Each trip to a "Lose a Point" space gave the other player three minutes to do or have done anything they pleased. When one player lost all his or her clothes, the other player also got three minutes per point. The first to score twelve points was the master or mistress. One of the boys, already naked, lost a point as Tabitha watched. His female counterpart, who still had on bra, panties, stockings, and garter belt, was in a fiendish mood, practicing nipple torture on her companion. She made him put his hands behind his back as she tweaked and rubbed them. He writhed in sensual agony. His cock was hard and leaking.

When he returned to the game, he was shaking. He couldn't concentrate. On the next roll of the dice, he lost completely. His companion smiled and licked her lips. He was really in for it.

Not all the activity was female dominant. Tabitha noticed a particularly cute young thing dressed as a seventeenth-century lady. She wore a hoopskirt and petticoats, with a low-cut bodice that revealed deep cleavage, a powdered wig, and lots of costume jewelry. She looked like a rich, pampered lady, arrogant and spoiled. Her male companion, dressed as a cruel pirate, handkerchief tied around his head, an eye patch, wore a white pirate's shirt with puffy sleeves, a tricorne hat, tight breeches, and tall boots, with a wide leather belt holding a sword. They were in an exhibitionist mood, and a small crowd had gathered to watch her public ravishment.

Her hands were tied in front of her. The pirate

pulled her roughly onto a small stage. There were several scattered throughout the ballroom for just such situations. "Ohhhh!" she moaned loudly, playing to the audience. "You brute! I demand that you free me at once! At once, do you hear?"

The pirate merely smiled. "Ah, my haughty beauty, be careful. You're at the mercy of Captain Blood and must watch your step."

She tossed her head disdainfully. "I am not afraid of the likes of you. My father's fleet will hunt you down like the dog you are, and soon enough you'll be clasped in chains, on your way to the gallows."

He laughed. "Perhaps. But not soon enough to spare you from the fate you so richly deserve." He looked her over slowly, calculatingly. "Such elegant clothes covering such a fine body. I wonder what you'd look like without them."

She put a shocked look on her face. "You wouldn't *dare!* You inhuman beast!"

"I've dared much worse, milady, and what sort of beast I am you'll soon see." With that he pulled her toward him. She struggled wildly to escape, but he was far too strong for her. He grasped her firmly and kissed her. At first she resisted and pulled away, but soon she found herself kissing back. "You see?" he said. "Soon you'll be my own little wench."

"Never!" she said. "Never!"

To the applause and encouragement of the audience, the pirate passed the rope that bound her hands over a bar that arched over the stage. He slowly contemplated the beauty that was now his for the ravishing. Slowly, he unfastened the stays of her dress and removed it, leaving her only in petticoats. She moaned and screamed and demanded her freedom. The crowd watched raptly and silently as the petticoats went next, and then she was revealed in her tight corset alone. He displayed her for the audience, circling her slowly, kissing the nape of her neck, stroking her taut, restrained body. She closed her eyes and her demands became muted as the pirate continued his sensual assault. Her weight shifted from foot to foot as his fingers tickled her pleasure centers—her neck, her earlobe, her lips, her arms, and down her sides, and eventually to the swell of her taut young breasts that were now aching for a pirate's touch. He recited the dirty, wicked things he planned to do to her helpless body. By the time he finally touched her nipples, she moaned with pleasure. Her protests continued, but they grew weaker and weaker. He slipped a hand down to check below and felt her wetness. She was ready.

He removed her corset, revealing her nude form for the crowd's delectation. Then he stripped off his outfit to reveal his rigid cock, straining from its long imprisonment. His victim's eyes fastened on it through lowered lashes, revealing her innocent embarrassment. Clasping her bound form in his manly arms, she moaned once again as their mouths locked. He stroked the wet center of her pleasure and moved down to suckle her nipples into stiffness. Soon she was gasping for pleasure, nearing the moment of climax.

"No...you mustn't enter me...no...don't...please..." She begged for mercy, but her passion betrayed her. She writhed under the gentle manipulation of his fingers and tongue. One finger entered her, and she gasped.

"You have no choice," the pirate muttered firmly, sliding between her legs. She tried to wriggle free, but her tight bonds only allowed her to squirm in delicious helplessness. "There's nothing you can do but submit," he said cruelly, and then pushed his intruding organ through her maidenhead.

"Ooohh," she wailed with a mixture of pleasure and pain. He fucked her with slow, deep strokes as the audience watched, rapt with sensual delight.

"How is the viceroy's daughter now?" he demanded. "The precious young virgin? All your wealth and power counts for nothing now. Now you're just a bed wench, here as a vessel for my lusts."

She was writhing, no longer fighting to get free, but to push herself upward to meet his hard thrusts. "Yes," she moaned. "Yesss...I'm just your bed wench. Make love to me. Aaah. Oh...oh...oh...*Oh! Oohh!*" She shrieked as her passion overtook her. As her writhing subsided, he pulled his wet cock from her. Looking at the audience, he grabbed his shaft and began pumping it.

"Feel the hot passion of my love on your sated body," he moaned as he jerked himself to orgasm and spurted his viscous seed over her helpless form.

There was general applause. The pirate bowed; the shackled heiress could only nod. Several audience members climbed onto the stage; two males and one female began caressing the bound girl. Another female knelt to suck the still-hard cock of the pirate.

David and Brandi, still dressed as schoolboy and schoolgirl, were among the watchers. Brandi grabbed his arm. "Oh my God! That was so incredibly hot," she moaned. "I'm really turned on. Is there somewhere private we can go? I know I said we'd wait until after the party, but I'm ready. I wish you could treat me just like the pirate girl."

David looked down at his girlfriend with surprised pleasure. "I'd love to, my proud beauty," he said, twirling an imaginary mustache. "I'm sure the way this place is set up there must be lots of private rooms. We have to be careful, though. Some things are set up as practical jokes. We don't want to become part of the entertainment, do we?"

Brandi was silent. *What an interesting idea*, she thought, but she said nothing. She just looked at David and smiled. He was hiding something; she knew it. But that was for later. Right now, they had to get away. She was burning up inside. Perhaps there was something in the punch....

As the couple moved away, arm in arm, Monica, standing nearby, smiled evilly. Little stepbrother was going to have an evening he'd never forget. And so would his little cupcake. She whispered to her female companion, who laughed.

4

Bobby followed the cute waitress into the ballroom. His hands were once again shackled to the leather harness, his ankles were hobbled, and a humiliating leash tugged at his leather collar. His cock throbbed as his eyes devoured her sexy legs in their fishnets, following the line of her curvy legs up under her stiff skirt, imagining the wet pussy he'd so enjoyed licking. He wanted her badly; it made it worse that she was willing if only he were free.

The noise and light hit him strongly as he entered the main party area. Throbbing dance music and sweeping strobes filled the room, setting off the psychedelics coursing through his system. His nakedness and bondage seemed to fit right in with the mass of erotic costuming on both males and females, but the knowledge he was part of the entertainment kept his sense of humiliation high. He looked around avidly as he followed his delicious escort.

"Are you a mouse?" purred a sexy cat-woman—feline ears and whiskers over a tight leotard; a tail protruding behind.

"I-I—" he stuttered, not sure if she meant him.

"Are you a mouse?" she repeated, stroking her hand sensually over his chest, "I play with mice and eat them."

He was entranced. His cock strained toward her. "You can eat me," he sighed with passion as her clawed gloves found his sensitive nipple.

The cat-girl laughed. "I'll bet."

"Sorry," the waitress chimed in. "He's going to serve in one of the pleasure booths. You can visit him there."

"Maybe I'll come eat you later, little mouse." She smiled and left.

Entranced, he followed her with his eyes until a stinging slap on his rear brought his attention back to the cute waitress. She looked at him with amused sternness. "Be good, or I'll have to punish you." At the lurch of his cock, she laughed and amended her words. "Be good, or I *won't* punish you." She looked him up and down. "You are a cutie pie, you know." She wrapped her long fingers around his cock and squeezed. He went weak in the knees. "I like the way you react. You know, they have big plans for you."

He gulped with fear and delight. "They can do anything...if they just take off that damned cockring!"

She laughed and released him. "Sorry, baby. No chance of that, at least for a while. Tell the truth. It's fun being so desperate, isn't it."

He sighed and trembled. "Yes, but I like to come, too!"

She laughed. "Don't worry. That will happen in the long run. I'm finishing up my time as a Tau Zeta slave, myself. You know they capture girls, too."

"No, I didn't," he said, instantly imagining the cute waitress as a sex slave, stretched out in bondage, writhing in desperate need of an orgasm. His cock twitched.

She laughed. "I can see you like that idea. Oh, yes. Actually, I did it for a scholarship. Tau Zeta got me for a semester. The first couple of weeks was the tease-and-torment route—what you're going through. Then I joined the dungeon staff. There are full-time sorority officers, regular members, who finish their initiations and get to enjoy the slaves whenever they like, and staff. We work regular shifts, take care of routine training, and help out at special events, like this. Of course, we get access to the toys, too." She grinned wickedly. "Like you. I've developed a taste for girls, too." Images filled Bobby's mind—dungeons filled with sex toys, his waitress teased to insanity, his waitress playing with girls and boys together.

"If you're part of the staff, I'll be your slave whenever you like," he said.

"Oh, yes, you will," she smirked. "I'm glad you want to, but you'd have to do it anyway."

"What's that?" Bobby suddenly asked, observing a bank of strange machines. At first glance they looked like Victorian-era pinball machines—golden cases in elaborate curves, flashing lights and colors.

"Oh, those? That's part of the game room. You've been very good. Would you like to check them out?"

He nodded, fascinated. They *were* pinball machines! The golden shapes were familiar—they were shaped like men and women! The female machines had spread legs; their torsos were the playing surfaces. The male machines had a jutting metal cockseat. One girl was playing a male machine. Her skirt was puddled around her ass, her legs straddled the seat, taking the metal cock up inside her. She played the flipper buttons on either side. The writhing of her hips as she played implied that the cock was moving or vibrating in her. Suddenly lights flashed and bells rang; the player threw back her head and arched her back as she went into a convulsive orgasm, then slumped over the machine.

"May I play one?" he pleaded.

"Just one," the waitress said. "Then you go to work."

The machines were named: "Vampire Lady," "Bondage Fantasy," "Kiss and Tell," and "Cheerleaders." He chose the Cheerleaders machine. The waitress unhooked his wrist cuffs. Between the outstretched golden legs was a center hole—a mechanical cunt. He slid his cock inside, and instantly the legs closed around him. The machine gave a sexy female moan as his cock penetrated it. It felt warm, wet, almost human. He looked over the playing field. It was decorated with colorful art of playful, sexy, miniskirted cheerleaders, cheering, dancing, doing pyramid stunts. There was a side bonus chute labeled LOCKER

ROOM. A nest of thumper bumpers at the top led to the main field after a bank of rollovers containing the letters C-H-E-E-R. Below, three targets on each side contained the letters L-E-A and D-E-R. The completed CHEERLEADER obviously activated some kind of bonus play. On the back glass was an erect cock and the words "Special When Lit," which clearly meant orgasm. There was an area labeled "Penalty Box." He wanted to stay out of that. He felt he understood the rules well enough; he was ready. He pulled back the plunger for the first ball.

The metal ball shot out of the chute and hit the upper playfield, rolling over to light the R in CHEER before falling into the nest of thumper bumpers. Bobby gasped as the mechanical cunt began to stimulate him, fucking in and out while gentle vibration drove him crazy. One of the challenges of the machine was continuing to play in spite of the distraction, because the ball shot straight down from the thumper bumper, hit the kicker barrier near the flippers and middle exit chute, ricocheted back and forth, and nearly slipped out. A quick double-flipper hit shot it back up, but it was close. The ball hit a side target, lighting D. A sexy voice cheered, "Hit 'em again, hit 'em again, harder, harder." The cock stimulation increased slightly.

The ball shot down again; he caught it on the left flipper, aimed and shot it up toward an upper flipper on the asymmetrical playing field, and slammed the ball right into LOCKER ROOM. The ball rested in a hole as the back glass turned into a hologram—it was a cheerleader dressing room with lovely half-clad nymphs getting in and out of their outfits. One of them appeared to notice him and walked boldly toward the camera. She was topless, with a pleated cheerleading skirt below. The cheerleaders chanted, "Do it to it! Do it to it!" As she approached, smiling, the display stopped. The ball shot out into the nest of thumper bumpers. He tried to catch it as it flew toward the left outlane, but the stimulation was too distracting. The ball slipped out. The stimulation stopped.

His first ball bonus was 7,000 points. This earned him thirty-five seconds of a cheerleader striptease hologram—but she didn't even get her top off.

The second ball was a dud; it ran over the R once again, fell into the thumper-bumper nest and shot in a terrible straight line right between the flippers and out. The 3,000-point bonus earned him a fifteen-second striptease.

Artful pinball English kept the third ball in the upper playfield to roll over the C, H, and one E while gaining major thumper-bumper action—his cock felt it, too—and finally a carom shot off the upper flipper finished the final E. He had lit C-H-E-E-R, and suddenly the back glass turned into a hot dance number with a squad of wriggling cheerleaders. Unfortunately, the ball continued in play; the distraction was too much, and he lost the ball on the edge of one of the flippers. The dance stopped, replaced by a cheerleader who laughed mockingly at him. He enjoyed a 10,000-point-bonus show, nearly a minute long.

Fourth ball. The play went well, gaining a few thousand

points of bonus, and all but two of the letters in LEADER. A carom off the top flipper nearly sent him into the Locker Room again, but he miscalculated and the ball flew into the Penalty Box. Ominous music began to play. A cheerleader appeared on the back glass, shaking her head sternly. She was joined by others who laughed mockingly as his cock underwent its punishment.

Suddenly the warm, wet mechanical cunt produced hard bristles. Panicked, Bobby tried to pull out, but the legs held him fast. The bristles rotated around his cock in two directions, like an Indian burn—he twisted and pulled but could only endure. The Penalty Box area had three ball catchers. The bristle treatment lasted for about fifteen seconds, then the ball shot from the first into the second penalty area. An electric shock made him scream. He was scared; he couldn't get free; his cock was trapped inside the machine. Then the third penalty area: bristles and shocks together until finally the ball shot free. The penalty had been so disturbing that he lost all concentration, and the ball shot out the right lane.

The fifth and final ball sat in the plunger well for a minute while he composed himself. Finally he launched it. The fifth ball lit the 2X bonus light at the bottom of the playfield. CHEER was waiting to be lit again; only the L and second E in LEADER needed to be hit. He played cautiously this time, less concerned with super points than with avoiding the Penalty Box. He managed to earn 15,000 points, then lost the ball in a Three-Bonus-Advance lane. With the 2X, that amounted to a 36,000-point bonus, which was a complete striptease scene. It was the prettiest cheerleader, and her strip dance was athletically sexy. The machine stimulation grew. The final pouting pose would have triggered a massive orgasm if he only had the ability.

GAME OVER. The back glass match didn't click; the machine's legs parted; he was free. Trembling, he stood still as the waitress refastened him. She toyed with his cock for an excruciating moment. "Did you like it?" she teased.

"Oh, God, that was so hot—except for the Penalty Box!" he gasped. "I didn't know what it was going to do to me!"

She laughed. "Well, you're all heated up. It's time to go into your own penalty box."

The casino action was hot and loud as the partygoers played for sexual stakes. Some played against each other; boys and girls turned into slaves of their partners. Some bet their bodies to win slaves of their own for the evening; the losers joined the victims.

The Pleasure Booths were below the floor level; stairs led down to each cell. The waitress fastened Bobby to a rack in the center of a curtained room. "Ready to be the entertainment?" she teased, sucking him to near explosion.

"Please…oh, God…I can't take any more," he moaned as he twisted in helpless lust.

"Oh, you can." The waitress laughed. "I did. Now you get some public humiliation before you get to serve. Bye-bye, baby. See you on the other side!"

She pressed a button beside the door. To his shock, Bobby felt himself being pulled up. The entire rack assembly rose toward the ceiling, which opened. To his utter horror, he was naked, spread, vulnerable, exposed to the entire gaming crowd. There were several other naked, spread victims, male and female. A male won a big jackpot; lights flashed. He stood up eagerly, looked at the line of sex toys, choosing an innocent-looking redhead with skin so white that her nipples and netherlips were light pink, her pubic hair red-blonde. The mistress of ceremonies touched a button and her rack sank down into her Pleasure Booth. The man went down the steps eagerly to enjoy his prize.

Bobby's public exposure was painfully humiliating to him; it was almost a relief when he looked down to see that he had been chosen by a 1960s–era go-go dancer—Mary Quant mini, white "These Boots Are Made for Walking" vinyl boots with tassels. He felt himself sink back into his booth.

His new tormentress entered the chamber. At a push of a button, his shackles dropped off. "On the bed," she ordered. "Hands above your head, eyes closed, and smile."

He heard the click of handcuffs and opened his eyes to find the go-go dancer straddling his chest. Her skirt had ridden up almost to her ass and her muscular legs imprisoned his thighs. He could see the outline of her panties underneath. She started stroking Bobby's too-sensitive nipples, a hot line to his twitching cock, making him crazy.

"Well, baby, looks like you're really in a fix now. What do you suppose we ought to do about it?" she cooed sexily. He fought against the mercilessly firm handcuffs, dry-mouthed, scared.

"Let's see," she giggled. "How about this?" She slid down between his legs to grab his straining organ. Slowly, deliciously, she licked it, first like a lollipop until every square inch was wet with saliva and precome, then took it in her mouth and swirled her tongue around until Bobby was gasping with pleasure. He was nearly ready for another of his near-explosions—at this level of frustration, even the convulsions of a strangled orgasm were better than nothing. But she wouldn't allow it. "Cool down," she ordered as he began to pulse. "Don't you dare come until I say so."

She got him close and then backed away, again and again until he was swimming in a sea of desperation. "Oh, God, please make me come!" he begged.

Driving him crazy was, it seemed, all she had in mind. She slipped one hand between her legs and played with herself while sucking him; when she came, she stopped, got up and walked out of the room, closing the door behind her.

"Wait..." he moaned. He expected to be hoisted back to public view, but there had been a sequence of winners.

The door opened again, and the girl who stood in the door had jet-black hair, a black vinyl snap-crotch corset and long, evil-looking leather boots with pointed toes and narrow heels that rose to midcalf. Fishnet stockings completed the bizarre outfit. "I'm Cassandra," she announced. She strode firmly to the bed where Bobby lay chained. She carried a black leather riding crop and smacked it into her palm. "Turn over!" she ordered. He obeyed quickly, twisting his hands together in the cuffs. She forced him to kneel, his ass sticking up in the air, and then began to whip him with the riding crop.

Whack! "Owwww!" *Whack!* "Ahhhhh!" *Whack!* With her other hand, she reached between his legs and began milking his hard-on, combining pleasure and pain until he thought he'd go crazy. The hot drops of precome flowed from his shaft; his ass was striped with red where the crop had struck.

Whipping him turned her on; finally she had enough and pushed him roughly down on the bed. She unsnapped the bottom of her corset and straddled his face, leaning forward so that she could play with the rest of his body at whim. Lightly, then harder, she whipped his cock from side to side with her riding crop as Bobby's straining tongue probed her nether depths. "Ahhh, that's right, do it. Lick me. Yesss." She rode his tongue to a deep orgasm, while continuing to whip his cock and his thighs. He was a mass of blazing striped pain when she finished.

This time she fastened him back to the rack and for five minutes slashed his body until he was striped red all over. Then she elevated him back above the crowd. His humiliation was renewed by the crowd's catcalls and cheers.

His mind was threatening to leave its moorings completely. He just couldn't stand it anymore. He hung above the crowd for a while; his cock throbbed and leaked impotently. Finally, after an eternity of waiting, he was chosen again and the rack sank back into the room.

The new coed teaser was dressed as a schoolmistress. She had her hair tied up in a bun; she wore glasses and had on a very conservative blouse and plaid skirt. She stripped silently, undoing her hair and shaking it loose, taking off her glasses to reveal sensuous eyes, and removing her outer garments to reveal scandalously sexy lingerie underneath. She circled the rack, inspecting him like a side of beef, then finally unfastened him. "Kneel!" she ordered. He obeyed. She sat on the edge of the bed and spread her legs wide. She wanted his mouth on her pussy, his cuffed hands playing with her breasts. Her thighs imprisoned his head as she gasped her way to a powerful orgasm.

After a brief elevation, he was forced to serve again, this time a punk rocker in ripped fishnets and black lacy bra as outerwear who toyed with him roughly, grabbing his cock and twisting it, kneeling above his prone body and rubbing the head of his cock against her clit for stimulation until she came. She rode him to another orgasm while pinching his nipples and chest, hard and painfully, then left.

Two girls entered the pleasure chamber together. They were both cat-girls—one was the girl he'd met earlier. "Hi, baby," she said. "Ready to be eaten?" He moaned in delight, but they were in a mood for sensual tease. They mocked his desperate condition. "Tell us how much you want it," one laughed.

Tabitha's Tickle

He moaned and pleaded, begged with all his might. They only laughed and giggled. The first cat-girl teased him, batting innocent eyes at him. "How terrible! Are you asking me to play with your cock? Maybe suck it or fuck it? Is that a nice thing to ask a pussycat to do? I don't think so. We're not nasty cats. Do you think we're nasty pussies?" She wriggled sexily and pressed her body against his, the rough fabric of her skirt stimulating his cock beyond all endurance.

He could only beg in the face of their merciless teasing. "OK," the second girl said. "We'll take pity on you." Their giggling belied their words. They had him lie down between them, the heat of their bodies inflaming him beyond all need. They toyed with his rockhard nipples, making him hold onto the brass bed rails. "If you let go, we'll stop," one giggled.

This was a cruel tease—for once, he would have welcomed the bondage. The nipple torment turned into tickling. He squirmed helplessly, finally releasing the bars to resist the tormenting fingers.

"Bad boy!" one girl laughed. "We were going to be so nice to you. But now you have to be punished, don't you?"

Even without the aid of bondage, he was no match for the two girls. Soon one sat on his hands and the other his legs, imprisoning him as their hands went to work.

At first their fingers dug into his sides, tickling hard, making him shriek hysterically. They were everywhere at once: ribs, underarms, belly, thighs, feet. The young sadists played spider's-legs over his helpless body, convulsing him with helpless, humiliating laughter. He begged desperately, but his pleas were choked off by bursts of helpless laughter. "No—ha-ha—please—nooo!—ha-ha-hah!" he cried.

The young cat-girls laughed with delight at his suffering plight, utterly in control and obviously enjoying themselves in his eternal agony. Merciless fingers continued to tickle his underarms, his stomach, and nipples. He writhed in helpless, uncontrollable laughter, squirming futilely to escape. He begged helplessly, but the torturing tickling continued.

He giggled and sputtered and pleaded with them to stop wiggling their fingers in his armpits, tracing cat claws up and down his arms and chest, and making slow, tormenting circles around his rockhard nipples. They tickled his ribs and tormented the agonizingly sensitive ridge of his hip with sharp fingernails.

They were in no hurry to quit. His salvation came only when the door opened. "Time's up," the assistant announced. "Save some for the rest of the girls."

The devilish cat-girls finally released him, refastening him to the rack with teasing and tickling. The public humiliation was nearly a relief; it took him some time to get his sanity back together.

He saw his next mistress before the rack returned to the room. His heart pounded loudly in his chest. It was a vampire. She looked hungrily at him.

She entered the room silently and looked at him for a long moment. He could feel the fear and lust building in him. "I am a true vampire. When I first drink of your blood, you shall be under my spell; when I drink of it three times, you also become a vampire." He stood frozen on the rack as her soft, small hands stroked his flesh. Her mouth trailed down his bare chest, nipping and biting, leaving a wet trail of pleasurable pain. She took his cock in her long red fingernails, digging them in until he moaned.

Her gaze traveled down his helpless body and she ran one sharp fingernail from his neck down to the inside of his thigh, including the length of his straining cock. Then she took his cock in her hand and gave it a few slow, tantalizing strokes until the first bead of precome oozed from the tip. She dipped her finger in it and touched it to her tongue. "Tastes good," she smiled, "but that's not what vampires want."

She toyed with his body, teasing it with long, rubbing strokes, driving him mad with desire. He started to plead for her to touch his cock, but she silenced him with a finger on his lips. "Be patient, my victim," she cooed. "I haven't taken my pleasures yet."

There was nothing he could do. He dropped his head back and surrendered to whatever games she wanted to play. She was determined to play out her vampire fantasy exactly the way she wanted.

"You must be prepared for your initiation." She smiled. Her eyes were bright, and he could see her nipples were stiff under the black satin bodysuit. Clearly she was getting her own powerful stimulation from the fantasy she'd created. She lit a candle and turned off the room lights, then tipped the burning candle. A drop of hot wax fell against Bobby's bare chest. He moaned with pain, but it wasn't very much—just a flash of heat and an odd feeling as the wax congealed. She moved the dripping candle down his body slowly, the droplets of hot wax forming a red line from just between his nipples down to his rigid, tormented cock. And then down his cock, the molten wax stimulating him in a combination of pleasure and pain until he was writhing in sensory overload. Her eyes were intent on him; she was devouring the pleasurable agony she was causing.

Finally she put the candle aside and stood up. Her eyes were bright. She grabbed his cock tightly; it was wet and glistening with ropy strands of his male fluid. Her hot tongue licked it off. He moaned. "Y-yes. I need it."

"So do I," she said. "But not this." She touched the leaking come once again. Then she looked up and smiled. Her fangs were real. "I need blood."

His eyes bugged out and he started thrashing in his bonds. "No!" he yelled. "Help!" His heart pounded in terror. She took the length of his cock deep into her mouth and he felt her teeth bite down, puncturing his shaft. Her carnivorous mouth sucked his blood. The blood flowing out felt like the long-delayed orgasm—it was painful but also impossibly erotic. "God...God...God..." he moaned as he thrashed in his bonds, his body convulsing with passion.

Her own orgasm hit as she sucked; they came together, vampire and victim; she released him only after her own convulsions stopped. He looked down fearfully, but his cock was still there. Two small puncture wounds adorned the shaft.

Gasping, weak, drained, his body could hardly move as the inexorable rack hoisted him back into public view.

5

"This looks like a good spot!" Brandi giggled, grabbing David's arm and pulling him through a heavy black velvet curtain into a quiet alcove. The party arena, flashing lights, loud music, and constant crowd noise, was suddenly cut off. They were alone.

Brandi kissed him, hard and passionately, pressing her lithe body tightly against him. She was so excited that she couldn't think straight anymore. Ever since she watched the pirate rape his captive maiden, all she could think about was having David do the same thing to her. That she was also under the influence of the strange-tasting drink given her by Monica, David's stepsister, didn't occur to her at all.

David was similarly swept up in passion, but tinged

with nervousness. He knew, unlike Brandi, what might befall them in the strange, dark corners of the Tau Zeta Rho house. But his cock had been hard all day, from their prolonged petting session on the blanket to the jolt of erotic fear produced by Monica's untimely appearance. Whatever his stepsister had planned for him was going to happen no matter what, and David resolved that at least he'd take his pleasure where he could.

"I want you so badly," he murmured between passionate kisses. "I love you."

Brandi looked at him, her eyes bright. She smiled. "I love you, too. I want you inside me, taking me. Look—there's a couch. Looks comfortable, too." She slipped out of his embrace. "Sit down and watch," she whispered.

She reached up and pulled the scrunchie off her ponytail and shook her dark blonde hair so it spilled across her face. Fastening her eyes on his and smiling sexily, she began to unbutton her white blouse, revealing a lacy bra underneath. She pulled the blouse from her skirt and slipped it off. She pulled down the zipper of her pleated skirt slowly, the rasping metal sound sending a quiver through David's cock. When she unfastened the single button, the skirt dropped to the floor. She wore only white cotton panties, knee-high socks, and black patent-leather shoes.

David couldn't take his eyes off her. Such innocent sexuality drove him mad with desire. He wanted to take her right then, push her to the floor and force his cock deep into her tight pussy. He controlled himself with difficulty, waiting for her next move.

Brandi felt wickedly slutty, like a striptease artist. As a young girl, she had fantasized about being Natalie Wood in *Gypsy*; now she was. Her eyes focused on the growing bulge in David's shorts. Her body was turning him on. She reached up to open the front clasp of her bra and teased him by holding her hands over her breasts as she shook the bra loose. She smiled, turned away from him, looking back over her shoulder as she slipped her fingers into the waistband of her cotton panties and worked them over her pert ass and down her silky legs inch by inch, finally pushing them off over her socks and shoes. Then she turned back, still playing the stripteaser, covering her breasts with one arm and cupping a hand over her nether regions. "Like what you she?" she teased.

"Yes," he breathed. "Yes. Come here."

"Not yet," Brandi laughed tauntingly. "Now you."

David was slightly unsteady on his feet, the effects of prolonged arousal. He threw away his ribboned boater and began unbuttoning his shirt.

"Slower," Brandi ordered. "I like it."

He complied, button by button, slipping the shirt off his masculine chest.

"Mmm," Brandi observed. "You work out, don't you?"

David nodded. His chest was good, and so were his legs. He took off his shoes and socks, then stood tall, unbuttoning the top button of his Bermuda shorts and pulling down the zipper. The shorts dropped to the floor. His white briefs bulged under the pressure of his erection. He decided to tease her in return, and began to rub his hand over his cock, squeezing it, sliding the shaft upward so the red tip began to peek out of the top of the elastic band. He slid the briefs slowly down the length of his cock, finally imprisoning the elastic band underneath his balls. He smiled at her. "You do the rest," he ordered.

In an erotic trance, Brandi moved toward her soon-to-be lover, her hands falling away to reveal her naked form. She pressed her body against his, the fullness of her breasts rubbing against the prickly hairs of his chest. She took his cock in both hands, one wrapped around the length of his shaft, the other cupping his balls. She masturbated his length gently as she leaned into a deep kiss. His hands slid down over her ass as the couple slid slowly onto the luxurious couch.

"Well, what have we here?" Monica's loud voice shattered the atmosphere of the quiet room as the black velvet drape was pulled back. "Naked schoolboys and schoolgirls—tsk, tsk."

The sudden noise and shaft of light shocked the two lovers; they sprang apart. Both clutched their modesty. Monica, tall and gorgeous in her stern schoolmistress garb was accompanied by her two friends, Jill, a sultry auburn-haired wench with pouty lips, and Lori, raven tresses and a ripe figure. Jill was dressed as a 1960s go-go dancer in fringed miniskirt and white boots; Lori was a high-stepping chorus girl.

Next to them was Kelly, wearing her police garb: starched blue uniform shirt tied off at the midriff, hot pants with blue and white striped hose, and high-heeled leather boots; and Sharon, still in her witchy mini with black fishnet stockings, pointed hat, and magic wand.

David and Brandi felt completely overwhelmed and helpless at the invasion. Outnumbered better than two to one, not to count the various costumed partygoers who peeked in to watch the show, the would-be lovers were helpless.

Looking sternly at the naked couple, Kelly announced, "You're under arrest for violation of Rule Sixty-nine—being caught naked. Of course, it's not the naked part that's the crime, it's the being caught part. On your feet; put your hands behind your back."

Humiliated and scared, David felt his first impulse to resist flow out of his body. He knew what was likely to happen to them both. Brandi looked over at him. She wished she could let him know that his concern wasn't really necessary—secretly, she hoped something like this would happen. She scrambled to her feet and put her hands behind her back, making her chest thrust forward. "I surrender, Officer," she said.

The naked lovers were handcuffed quickly and marched back onto the party floor, to the accompaniment of catcalls and caresses from passersby. David's rigid cock, still cupped by the elastic of the white briefs below his testicles, was the subject of several squeezes. Brandi, wearing only white knee socks and black patent-leather shoes, the picture of young innocence, felt hands crawling over her naked flesh. It was ticklish, delightful, sinful, erotic. She loved it!

Tabitha's throne was on the dais in the center of the room. Brandi was amazed at the sight of the gorgeous coed in her exotic red leather harness looking so utterly dominant and in control. Brandi's fantasies had included being dominated by a beautiful woman; Tabitha inflamed her. The two shackled male slaves lashed to the pillars on either side amazed her—the dignified older man and the young man, about her own age, both with painfully rigid erections restrained in their constricting leather tubes. As the couple was forced to kneel, Brandi found herself next to the young student, his cock at the level of her face. She couldn't keep her eyes off it, or off David's cock. Her pussy was wet and open; she had never been so aroused.

Tabitha smiled at her latest victims. Kelly told the story of their capture; Tabitha laughed. "Poor babies. David, I would have thought you knew better."

Brandi looked at her companion with surprise. Did David know this beautiful creature? A pang of jealousy swept through her. The quizzical look on her face prompted Tabitha to ask, "Didn't you know that David had been one of our toys for a while?"

"Toys?" Brandi asked, blushing deeply as she realized how eager she sounded.

"Toys. Like poor Robin here." Tabitha reached out to squeeze the leather-clad penis. Robin moaned desperately; the sight of a young girl falling into Tabitha's torments was always particularly arousing for him. "We keep toys—boy-toys—for our pleasure, you know. David had been Monica's toy, and she loaned him to us during her initiation."

Brandi looked over her shoulder at Monica, who smirked knowingly. "That's right, sweetie," she drawled. "David's a boy-toy pretending to be a lover. He really just wants to be teased and tormented—don't you, David?" Monica nudged the tip of David's cock with the pointed toe of her black pump.

David's face was stricken with utter humiliation and embarrassment. He could barely look at Brandi. He could feel her contempt for him growing as he slipped back under the spell of the girls of Valentine. His traitor cock remained hard.

Tabitha looked down with amused pity. "For the crime of private nakedness, I sentence you each to thirty minutes of torture. Take them away!"

Kelly pulled the two victims to their feet and marched them off to their fate.

Sharon felt the dynamics of the situation between David, Brandi, and Monica. Kelly had whispered a few of the details in her ear as she marched her prisoners to Tabitha. Although the situation was different, she was reminded of her confusion about Tom and Bobby. She wanted to be a creature of pure sex, but emotions and relationships kept creeping into it. She felt sorry for David, but not for Brandi. In a way, Brandi seemed eager, much like Sharon herself. A new wave of erotic cruelty swept over Sharon. She wanted to be one of Brandi's tormentors.

The torture chamber was a glass booth in one corner of the party; it contained two metal frames for victims and a cabinet filled with toys of punishment and pleasure. While Kelly, assisted by Monica and Lori, shackled David to his frame, Sharon, along with Jill, took care of Brandi.

Brandi's libido was afire. Every molecule of her body tingled in erotic fever as the hands of the young witchy blonde fastened her wrists and ankles into the cold metal cuffs. This was too sexy. David's muscular form spread-eagled on the other frame excited her as well; the hangdog expression on his face filled her with a mix of empathy and desire. His cock, purple and thrusting, jutted in her direction; she wanted it. Maybe that would be her punishment—to feel that cock inside her.

But no. Kelly produced two cat-o'-nine-tail whips, long leather straps tied to a handle. Sharon took one and stood behind Brandi; Kelly took the other over to David. *Thwack! Thwack!* Brandi screamed, more in shock than pain—it stung, but no more than that. David screamed, "No! Don't!" and tore at his shackles, trying to get free to save his girlfriend, but to no avail. Then his own blows began to land, forcing a gasp and then a cry from him.

An audience gathered around the glass torture chamber to watch the humiliating torture of the two young lovers. They laughed and chanted the count of each blow.

Both their asses were red and striped when the whipping finished. The crowd shouted suggestions for the next round of torment. "Tickle-time! Tickle-time!"

TABITHA'S TICKLE

Brandi's eyes widened and she screamed again, "Please don't tickle me*eee!*" Then her body suddenly convulsed with shock as the first attack of tickling fingers grabbed her rib cage. "Oh, God, oh, God, *Ha-ah-ha!*" she screamed as fear and laughter took control of her body. She thrashed helplessly in her bonds.

Sharon found herself overcome once again with sadistic delight. She dove into the helpless exposed sides of her innocent girl victim with a sense of evil delight. Each scream and wiggle she produced—and she produced many—had its counterpart in the tingling of her cunt. More restrained in her approach, Jill began toying with Brandi's exposed nipples, combining the terrible tickling with a charge of erotic pleasure. Brandi wriggled and squirmed to escape the overpowering stimulation.

Meanwhile, Monica, Kelly, and Lori were torturing David the same way—a three-way tickle orgy with an erect male victim at the center. He screamed and writhed, gasping and choking with laughter; his cock remained rigid throughout.

The crowd continued to hoot and call out new torment ideas. Lost in gales of laughter and the overwhelming and mind-blowing sensations of the long tickle-torture, David and Brandi were oblivious to the suggestions.

Sharon felt herself once again confused about her role. On the one hand, being the evil torturess was wildly exciting; on the other, she could identify strongly with Brandi and imagined herself, naked, helpless, spread-eagled, tickled for the amusement of an audience. She looked at Jill, still carefully teasing Brandi's nipples. Arousal took over from the desire to torture, and Sharon began to kiss Brandi's exposed neck, slipping her hands to toy between her legs. Brandi was wet, open; her eyes closed, her head dropped back; she moaned with pleasure.

Monica was thoroughly enjoying tormenting her stepbrother in front of his new girlfriend. *Let's make sure we know who's boss*, she thought. David's stiffie made an amusing playtoy, and his body squirmed so well. She grabbed it, letting her fingernails sink into the reddened shaft. "Want to stick it into something nice and wet? Like your little girlfriend? Enjoy watching her get it at the same time you do? Ooh, look. She's getting played with very nicely. Girl-girl sex seems to turn her on, doesn't it. And here you are, all swollen with nowhere to go." She laughed.

As Monica teased, Kelly and Lori continued to tickle. Ass, inner thighs, underarms, ribs, neck—nothing escaped their calculating torment. David had screamed with hysterical laughter so long he was getting hoarse. Finally, Kelly and Lori switched to teasing, Lori stroking his shaft in a cruelly slow and sensual masturbation while Kelly played with his nipples, hard and white as stones.

Monica went over to Brandi, squirming with delight as Sharon and Jill continued to arouse her young, innocent body. Monica stroked Brandi's cheek softly. "Look at your boyfriend, all helpless. He likes what the girls are doing to him, doesn't he."

Brandi could only look, transfixed with jealousy and

lust as she watched David's cock toyed with by the two coed vixens who dominated him so completely. "Boys are like that, you know," Monica observed, stroking one of Brandi's nipples casually. "All they want is someone to play with their cocks. That's how I got David in the first place—I caught him jerking off into my panties; can you believe it? What a dirty boy. So I punished him, and you know, he liked it. He liked it so much he became my little sex-pet. I played with his cock all the time, and he couldn't get enough. So finally I had to give him to the girls of Tau Zeta sorority. They keep male sex toys."

Brandi's mind kept flashing on images of David in various bondage positions, teased, tortured, whipped, spanked. She saw the come forced from him in one position after another, long, ropy streams of white spurting come. Her tongue dipped out over her cute pouting lips. "Y-yes, I see..." she gasped, the pleasure about to completely unhinge her mind.

"You can have him; I'm through with him. But you need to know about the special care he needs. He needs to be used, just like this. Make sure not to let him come more often than once a month; it just spoils a man, you know."

David squirmed in sexual agony as the two teases who worked him over brought him close to the edge of orgasm, only to keep him there in continued straining desperation. He saw Monica talking to Brandi and imagined the conversation. He thought of Brandi as his newest tormentress; the girl he'd fallen in love with becoming just another cruel tease. It was sexy, deliciously sexy, but disappointing at the same time. He flashed back on the pirate and his captive princess. He imagined himself in that role. His cock pulsed with renewed need.

Gasping with desire, the two lovers got a brief minute to recover. Then Kelly decided to let the crowd in. "OK! Everybody who wants to can have a minute with the prisoners. Get in line, either for the boy or the girl. Take any item from the rack and enjoy yourself!"

Most of the men and several of the women lined up for Brandi; most of the women and a few men lined up for David.

Brandi looked at the line of people ready to abuse her. The combination of tease and desire was too much. "Oh! Oh! *Ooooh! Oh, God!*" Without direct stimulation, she began to convulse in the throes of orgasm. "Hot stuff," Kelly observed. Then the torment began anew. The first in line, a girl, chose a sorority paddle. *Whack! Whack!* came the blows on Brandi's already-reddened ass. Then a couple, boy and girl, decided to repeat the tickle-torment. A cruel blonde in a miniskirted nurse's uniform, starched white cap, and white shoes, took an ice cube. "No!" screamed Brandi, her eyes wide, as the cold ice pressed against her neck, traveling slowly down her body, drawing screams of shivery agony all the way down her sides. It was even worse than the tickling.

David's tormentors followed their own pattern. A girl dressed all in leather took a penis whip to his erection, slashing down hard enough to leave stripes. Then there was a man dressed in a leather harness, his own cock hard, who looked at him with dominant delight, running his hand over David's nipple and grabbing his cock. David blushed beet-red in utter humiliation; he wanted desperately to control his arousal, but couldn't. Brandi, noticing David being dominated by a man, found the sight of the two cocks together enough to drive her to the edge of another spontaneous orgasm. After the man, two girls team-tickled him again, then a paddle session, then another tickle.

The two victims were sagging in their bonds, blown away by the constant torment, when finally their thirty minutes of slavery ended. Kelly unfastened them from their shackles; they needed assistance to sit down. Monica and her cronies laughed and laughed with delight at the sight of their shattered victims. "See you later, cutie," she said sarcastically, patting David's cheek. They left.

Once seated, Sharon brought them each a drink; they were laced again with the aphrodisiac—based on one last suggestion from Monica.

"Your time is up, but be careful that you don't get caught again. Next time, we'll really put you through the wringer," Kelly counseled.

"C-can we have our clothes back?" David asked.

"Nope. Naked for the rest of the evening, that's the rest of your punishment. Remember, we can arrest you for being naked." Kelly laughed.

"What should we do?" Brandi asked.

Kelly looked at David. "The dungeons are empty tonight. That's about the only safe place to stay out of sight."

The dungeons? The thought caused Brandi to tingle with arousal yet again. "Yes, David. Let's go to the dungeons."

"You don't know what they are," David said. "I'm not so sure I want to go there."

Kelly smiled. "Tonight you get a free pass. Promise. Of course, if you're caught there after dawn, it's a different story. Besides, I think Brandi ought to see them, don't you?"

David looked at his girlfriend and sighed. "Yes, I suppose so. It wouldn't be fair for her not to know the whole story." He squared his shoulders. "Come with me."

Brandi stopped him and took his face in her hands. "David, I know you have some big dark secret, and I think I know what it is. Don't worry. I love you, and I have a few secrets to share with you, too. OK?" She gazed into his eyes and tried to transmit sincerity with them.

David looked back into her eyes. "OK. I love you, too." He took her hand.

Kelly said, "Let me lead you down there. Sharon, I'll see you later. Maybe you should try to find Tom."

"Mmm, sounds like a good idea," Sharon said, smiling.

Kelly led her charges through a set of wooden double doors into a darkened chamber. "Bye-bye!" she said, pulling a lever that caused the floor to fall away. Brandi screamed as the naked lovers slid into the darkness below.

6

Sharon wandered into the formal gardens that surrounded the Tau Zeta mansion, relieved to get a few minutes of privacy to think about the strange experiences of the day. Right now, she didn't quite feel like herself. Who was she? Dominant vixen or innocent cheerleader? Fucker or fuckee? All she was certain of was that she would never be the same person again. Tau Zeta, in a few brief hours, had changed her forever.

She followed a stone pathway at random, which led her around a carved hedge to a wooden bridge arching over an artificial pond. Lights under the water created an eerie fantasy world, occupied by satyrs and nymphs partaking of exotic delights. Two naked coeds made love to a young man who was lost in transports of delight; they kissed and suckled his nude body and played slowly with his towering shaft. Beside the pool, another girl was riding her lover, taking his cock deep inside while sitting upright on his body. His hands reached up to caress her breasts. As she noticed Sharon's gaze, the girl blew her a kiss.

Across the bridge, the pathway led to a small gazebo. Hanging from a hook in the ceiling was a naked boy being attended to by two sexy girls wearing togas made from bedsheets. One girl was armed with a whip and lashed her helpless captive while the other knelt in front of him, sucking his cock with delicious passion. He moaned and twisted under the stimulation. After a while, the girls switched places as Sharon continued to watch. The whipping and sucking went on for a long time. Finally, they released their prisoner and forced him on his knees. One girl wriggled her toga up over her hips and the boy began to worship at her sex as the other picked up the whip again.

In an overload of desire, Sharon found each vision a new stimulation, but somehow all the strange sexuality seemed normal to her. She walked on. The path led into a copse of trees. The remaining sounds of the party, which had formed a backdrop to her wandering, were completely screened out, replaced by the sounds of nature: crickets, birds, a gust of wind. Most of the grounds were lit with elegantly placed artificial light; here she experienced natural darkness, the swollen white light of the full moon casting a gentle glow over the surroundings.

Tabitha's Tickle

Then she heard the beat of a tom-tom and saw a flickering glow of firelight ahead through the trees. She approached quietly. The pathway ended suddenly in a wall of trees. Carefully, she pulled several branches aside.

At the center of the copse was a fairy circle—a clear expanse of green marked with a circle of stones. In the center was a bonfire, around which were wild women from some exotic primitive fantasy, shredded clothes and streaks of tribal war paint, looking like jungle cats in the flickering firelight. There was a tall wooden pole next to the bonfire, and to the pole was lashed a handsome, well-muscled man. His hands were tied above his head and long cords wrapped around his body, holding it tight. He was naked. His cock was swollen and red. It was Tom.

The wild women had evidently been abusing Tom for a long time. His body was covered from chest to shin in red stripes and welts from the long whips each of the wild women carried. They were dancing in wild Dionysian abandon around the campfire, lashing their male victim in rhythm to the primitive beat. One wild woman, hair forming a golden frizzy halo, raked his chest with her long fingernails, drawing welts of blood all the way down his torso to the base of his cock.

Tom struggled and twisted in the tight bonds; not so much to escape them, but to let his own sensations sweep over him. His eyes were glazed; his mouth gaped open. The woman who had clawed his chest took her whip and lashed his chest. He moaned deeply, consumed by the sensation. The wild women continued their demonic dance of delight.

Sharon's first impulse was to save Tom from this awful torture, but her second impulse was another rush of evil erotic sensation. She wanted to watch the abuse and then to join in, to whip and defile him, to draw screams of subjection from his naked body, to feel his sexual agony and make it her own. One hand slid up to caress her right nipple; the other slid between her legs and into her panties to rub her wet clit. She was once again at the edge of orgasm.

The beat of the tom-tom grew faster and faster and louder and louder, and the dance of the wild women turned into a whirl of light and movement and sound and the bonfire raged and the crack of the whips and torment grew and grew and—

Suddenly the tom-tom stopped. The wild women flung themselves panting and gasping onto the greensward. The dance had ended, at least for now.

The wild women passed around a wineskin, shooting long streams of golden liquid into each others' mouths, some falling onto their skin. One stood up to pour liquid into Tom's mouth, then squirted more into the welts that covered his body; he tensed in the burning agony of sensation. The Tau Zeta aphrodisiac or something similar made the touch of liquid against skin also a carrier of the erotic sensation, for soon the panting and gasping of exhaustion turned into the moans and gasps of pleasure as the wild women stripped off their few remaining clothes to slither slowly into a huge orgy.

One wild woman poured liquid from the wineskin onto the growing writhing mass. Mouths and cunts and breasts and wet naked skin flowed together in a sight of unbelievable erotic power, the lights and shadows of the bonfire and its crackling sound mixing in with moans of pleasure and delight and the noises of the night. Above the orgy, lashed and engorged, Tom entered a new phase of erotic agony as his cock strained for pleasure denied.

Sharon couldn't resist. She stripped off her witch's costume and walked boldly naked into the circle. She picked up the wineskin where the wild women had dropped it and poured a generous stream into her own mouth. It tasted like liquid fire. She squirted some over her chest and rubbed it in. Each nerve tingled with special pleasure and deep erotic charge. She walked over to Tom, whose eyes were unfocused in his trance of delightful agony, and slapped him. His eyes widened and then focused on her. "Sharon!" he gasped. "Oh, my God!" With satisfaction, she noticed his cock lurch with pleasure.

She smiled. Staring boldly and wickedly into his eyes, she picked up a thin strip of torn cloth and tied it around the shaft of his cock. She tugged at it experimentally, making his foreskin slip up over his cockhead, then back again when she released it. He groaned at the teasingly slow masturbatory sensation. She pulled the cloth a few more times, grinning at the effect she was having. Then she tied her end of the cloth around her wrist and slid down into the writhing mass of wild women.

Sharon was buried in a mass of sensation as the naked wild women caressed and licked her from head to toe. She was part of the orgy. A naked breast shoved itself into her mouth; her hands and fingers found nipples and clitorises and acres of sensual skin. As the hand with the cloth strip tied to it moved, she glanced up; she was teasing Tom with cruelly slow masturbation with each movement. The occasional fast jerks of her hand caused him pleasurable pain.

A tongue busied itself between her legs; her breasts were suckled and her skin caressed and kissed—she floated in a warm, wet sea of women. Her body clenched and convulsed in sudden delight, but unlike normal orgasm didn't stop. It was an ocean of orgasmic nonstop delight for her.

Suddenly she felt warm drops from above and looked up—she had masturbated Tom to an orgasm. She opened her eyes just in time to see the warm drops of drizzling precome turn into the first jet of thick, ropy come, then another and another. A guttural groan tore from Tom's throat as he came in the throes of primal passion.

The band of cloth continued to pull; Tom continued to shoot his pent-up seed spraying over the naked wild women, who writhed even more passionately under the spell of his orgasm.

The orgy subsided after an endless period of sensual delight, the women sprawled on the grass, falling into blissful sleep. Sharon stood on shaky legs in front of Tom. She untied the cloth strip from his penis and fondled the shaft. Tom gasped with pleasure as it quickly firmed to hardness once again.

"I would have thought you'd had enough," said Sharon, gloriously naked, her skin glistening in the firelight.

Tom shook his head. "Never. Not here. They make me wait so long until all I can do is dream about it, then when I do come it's not enough to make up for all the teasing. Besides, when your fantasies come true, you can't get enough."

"I guess that's true." Sharon continued to fondle his erection as they talked. "I've lost track of how many times I've come today, and each one is as powerful as the first. But I thought it was different for boys. You run out of juice."

Tom smiled ruefully. "That's magic for you," he said. "You saw them whip me. Now look."

Indeed, the whip marks were already fading from his body, the bloody welts turning into thin red lines and then fading completely.

"Wow!" Sharon exclaimed. "So no matter what I do, you're still ready for more."

Tom nodded. "Oh, yes. Just speed up your hand a little bit, and you'll see."

She giggled and released him, producing another moan. "Oh, no you don't. Not now, anyway. Maybe later." She could see his hips pull against the tight bonds. She loved the feeling of arousing him when there was nothing he could do about it.

"Tom, you've been here longer than me.... How long have you been here?"

"Nearly a month, I guess. It's hard to keep track of time. It seems like forever."

"Wow. And it's all been like this?"

"No. At first it was just tease and tickle, plus some mind games. Each time I got used to it, they would escalate. That, plus the lack of orgasms, keeps it all hot. Tonight, well, this is the first time I've experienced anything like this. The maenads, you know."

Sharon didn't know about the wild women of Dionysus, but didn't want to be distracted with a mythology lesson. "Are you still scared?"

"All the time," Tom replied. "I've had these fantasies for so long, and the reality is sometimes just too much to bear. Besides, I feel funny giving myself up like this. The Tau Zeta sisters have put me through things I never imagined before. Some of it's quite disturbing."

Sharon nodded. "I wanted to hear you say that, because I'm feeling the same way. I kind of knew that something was going to happen in the way of an initiation when I came to Valentine, especially when they asked me to lend them my boyfriend."

"Your boyfriend?" Tom asked with anxious interest.

Sharon nodded. "Bobby. They've got him now, and I guess they're working him over, but he's not like you—I mean, I don't think he's into the same things. But you know, what's bothering me is my feelings. I mean, I really like this—I mean, I *really* like this, you know? I'm having fantasies and feelings I never knew I had, and I'm doing things I would never have thought of. I'm turning into a sick little puppy, you know?"

Tabitha's Tickle

"Don't think like that," Tom said. "I mean, I understand how you can, because sometimes I think that about myself—but I've always been a sick little puppy that way. But Valentine is a really sexy place, and it's natural to be turned on, and it's natural to have feelings that you might not have otherwise. I mean, you and your boyfriend can enjoy this and then go back to your regular lives afterward."

"But I don't *want* to go back to my regular life," Sharon complained. "And I don't want to go back to Bobby, either."

Tom brightened with hope. "Why not?" he asked.

"Well, Bobby's cute and sexy and all, but I've changed since I've been here and I think it's a real change. I want this lifestyle. I want to be a prickteaser and a dominatrix, and sometimes I want to get spanked and played with; but mostly I want to be one of the sisters and have my own personal slave and use him any way I like whenever I like." She ran her fingers down Tom's muscular chest and looked into his eyes. "Any way I like and whenever I like."

His cock pulsed. "What about Bobby?" He didn't want to ask. He didn't want the answer he feared, but he had to get it out of the way.

"It's not about Bobby. Bobby's just got a cheerleader hard-on. It's about you, OK?"

"Thank God!" Tom breathed. "Because I need you desperately."

Sharon looked at him, eyes bright. "Really?"

"Really. Even though other girls have done things to

me, the most incredible moments I've had have been today. Here. Now. With you."

"Oh, God!" Sharon cried. "I think I love you."

"I love you, too," Tom replied.

"But I want to do awful things to your body."

"I *want* you to do awful things to my body," he replied.

"Really?"

"Really. I want to be your slave."

Sharon paused. "My slave?" she asked.

Suddenly Tom was afraid he'd gone too far, but there was no stopping now. "Yes. Your slave. Mistress Sharon, may I be your slave? To serve you and give you pleasure, and be used by you in whatever way you desire?"

Sharon looked at him. "Do you really mean it? You see how mean and nasty and evil I've become in just one day. And I know I haven't finished changing yet. You may really be getting yourself into deep trouble."

"I hope so," Tom replied. "In fact, if you don't get mean and nasty and evil enough, I'll help you."

She laughed. It was a good feeling. "All right, Tom. You can be my slave. But you'd better know I'm serious."

"I certainly hope so," he said. "There is a catch, though."

"What's that?"

"I'm already a slave. A slave of Tau Zeta Rho. You're just a pledge, not even a full sorority sister. I want to be your slave, completely and absolutely, but remember—they own me right now."

Tabitha's Tickle

Sharon paused. "I didn't think of that. But it's OK. I'll talk to Tabitha. I'm sure I can convince her. Or maybe I can buy you."

"Buy me?"

"Yeah. Give them my nubile young body for a week or two. They'd probably go for that."

He looked at her glorious naked form. "*I* sure would."

She giggled and simpered. "Thanks. Or, I could give them Bobby permanently. Oh, God—I'm so wicked! I can't believe I said that!" She laughed. "But I *am* that wicked. I really would give them Bobby. Poor baby. I'll bet he's had his mind totally blown. I hope he's enjoying it."

"I'm sure he is," Tom said. "They know how to make sure of it. Not all the slaves are basically submissive, like me."

"Well," Sharon said resolutely, "the first thing we have to do is talk to Tabitha. Here, let me untie you. We'd better be quiet, in case the wild women wake up."

"I think they're out for a long time, but you're right."

As Sharon worked at the knots, her naked form brushed up against Tom. The press of flesh against flesh inflamed both their young bodies. As soon as he was partly untied, Tom bent his face toward hers and kissed her. Their tongues swirled together; his cock slithered wetly against her belly, lubricated by his drizzling fluid. She slid her hands up to toy deliciously with his nipples. "Oh, God!" he moaned into her mouth.

She broke the kiss. "Later. Besides, I call the shots, remember?" She squeezed his erection, then led him away, ropes trailing from his body. Once in the bushes, she laced his hands together in front of him, leaving a leash. She draped the leash over a bush and retrieved her clothes, dressing in front of him.

"You make a sexy witch," he observed. "You certainly cast a spell on me."

Sharon laughed as she finished dressing, and picked up her ebony wand. "Cast a spell? Like this?" With an expression of innocent teasing, she touched him with the tip of her wand. Tom instantly convulsed with pleasure, falling backward onto the ground. His cock leaked pure, clear fluid.

"Zotz! You're it!" she laughed. He twitched like the victim of a huge electric shock, recovering slowly.

"Oh, God!" he whispered. "That was incredible."

"That's just a warm-up. I plan to torture you, tease you, whip you, tickle you, and rub ice cubes all over your naked body until you scream. Then I'll let several guys and girls fuck me at the same time and make you watch. And that's just the beginning. Still want to be my slave?"

"More than ever," Tom said.

"Then follow me!" she commanded.

The gazebo at the edge of the copse was empty, but the shackles that had imprisoned the boy still hung from the hook in the ceiling. Sharon led Tom into the gazebo. There was a large mat on the ground; she could smell the sex on it. "Lie down," she ordered. "Hands above your head and close your eyes. I just had a fantasy I want to tell you about."

She knelt beside his prone body and began stroking his nipples. "I want you to imagine that we're back in school together. I'm still a cheerleader, and you're now my slave. It's the last period of the school day. That's when the cheerleading squad has its practice. You're stark naked, hands tied. I'm wearing a red miniskirt and a tight white sleeveless cashmere sweater; my legs are bare. I'm pulling you into the girls' locker room. You're deeply humiliated, especially when all the girls cluster around you. They're laughing at you. I make you confess that you like being teased and tied up. They think that's hysterically funny. You're blushing so much you can barely stand up."

Tom moaned and twisted. Throbbing and in agony, his cock pulsed impotently, needing her touch. She looked at his desperate, aching cock with sadistic pleasure. "I know you want me to hand-fuck you, but this is nipple-tease time. If you keep your cock perfectly still, I might do something for it later. If it keeps twitching like that, I'll have to punish you. Understand?"

He nodded and furrowed his brow in concentration, trying to hold his cock still.

"I back you up against the wall of gym baskets and cuff you to them. The metal is cold against your back. I spread your legs apart and cuff each ankle. You're in an upside-down 'Y' position. I tell you to behave yourself. All the cheerleaders start changing clothes. I strip down to my panties; I don't have on a bra. Then I put on my shortest, cutest cheerleading outfit. The other girls are stripping, too. Gina—you remember Gina—comes over to you. She is wearing a bra; with those breasts, she needs one. She takes off her bra and trails it over your front. Oops! Your cock twitched. Bad boy. No cockplay for you. The other girls enjoy watching you being teased. Finally, all the girls are in their cheerleading outfits, and your cock hasn't been touched at all. Tammi picks up her pom-poms and shakes them in your face. Oops! There goes your cock again. Tsk. No self-control. Your cock is leaking." She continued her cruel nipple torment.

"It's time for cheerleader practice, so we all go out on the field. You're going to be the measure of how sexy we are. I wrap a cuff around your cock to let us know how swollen you get. Then we dance and do our routines, watching the meter to make sure we're as hot as possible. Other students come by to watch. Several of the cheerleaders' boyfriends are watching. I think they envy you.

"Finally, practice is over and we go back into the locker room. Kara and Tammi ask for permission to play with you for a while. I grant it. They play with your nipples, just like I am right now. Then they want to tickle you. Oops! There you go again. You like the idea of being tickled by Kara and Tammi, don't you? They're great ticklers. You know, they once tickled Wayne, the football player, until he nearly wet himself. Oops! You're getting worse, not better. Now, they're tickling you. The other girls see you laughing and

Tabitha's Tickle

decide to join in. Now you're being tickled by the entire cheerleading squad. I'm watching, enjoying your humiliation."

Sharon reached down to grab Tom's twitching cock. It was hot, swollen, and near to exploding even though she hadn't touched it. She was ready for his cock; she wanted it inside her. "I'm going to fuck you now," she said breathily. "I'm going to fuck you slowly, and if you come before I do, I'll spank you. If you hold out, I'll spank you and tickle you both."

"Y-yes, Mistress," he whispered.

With excruciating slowness, she took his hardness into her tight pussy, inch by inch. It filled and stretched her going in. She felt her own orgasm close. Finally she took the entire length of his cock inside her. Her clitoris pressed against his wiry pubic hair. Slowly she lifted herself up, slowly she sat back down on him, riding him for her pleasure. She rode his rigid erection again and again.

"You're being tickled all over by the cheerleading squad. In the middle of your tickle session, I come over. I take your cock in my hand and begin masturbating you. I lean down and fasten my mouth around one of your nipples and play with the other one with my free hand. You're squirming and screaming and begging, and it really turns me on. Getting close?"

"Yes…yes…careful…"

"Don't come yet. It won't be long now." She sped up. She felt her own orgasm nearly upon her. She felt his cock pulsing inside her; his orgasm was near, too.

"Just another minute," she said. "Now I'm straddling you just like this, and all the girls are clustered around, petting you and tickling you and using you and it's so humiliating and here I...*Oh, God, oh yes! Ooh!*" She exploded on his cock, writhing and twisting, pinching his nipples hard. "Come for me now!" she ordered, and he did, arching his back and shooting his pulsing orgasm deep inside her.

Finally the two lovers fell back, hearts pounding.

"You know," Tom said dreamily, "I've had more orgasms today than in all the time I've been a slave. You're my kind of mistress."

Sharon giggled. The rippling effect could be felt in both cock and pussy. "That's just for today. After today, I think it will be at least three weeks before you come again. Maybe longer, especially if you're really suffering."

"That's when Tabitha gives me to you," he observed.

"I'll get you, no matter what it takes. You're my slave now, even if I have to buy you," Sharon promised.

"That's wonderful," Tom said. "I love you."

"I love you, too...my little sex toy."

7

With a breathless thump, David and Brandi landed in one of the dungeon cells deep beneath the Tau Zeta mansion. Brandi clung to him with fear and shock. "W-what happened?" she gasped.

"We're in the dungeons," David said. "God knows if we'll ever get out." He stood and stumbled around the tiny room until he found a light switch. It was a small padded cell; a metal chute behind a spring-loaded door was their entrance; a locked and barred door the only possible exit. The room contained two racks, elaborately mechanical devices that could display and twist their prisoners into any position, a padded spanking stool, and an assortment of pleasure and torment devices hanging from a wall-mounted rack.

"Look at the bright side," said Brandi. "At least we have some privacy. She patted her hair into shape while standing in front of the large wall mirror.

David shook his head. "Not necessarily. That mirror is one-way glass."

Brandi giggled and primped, turning her body sexily. "That's OK. I'm getting used to having an audience." She turned to her lover. His face was drawn and haggard. "What's the matter, darling? Everything's OK, really. I think this whole thing is fun."

David looked at her. "Fun. Well, some of it is fun. Some of it is unbelievably sexy. But you don't understand. They keep prisoners here...slaves."

Suddenly Brandi felt a wave of pity for David. He felt responsible for her situation and deeply humiliated at his own, all at the same time. She went over and placed her hands on his shoulders and smiled sweetly. When a thin grimace answered her smile, she hugged him. With delight, she felt the swelling of his erection once again.

"So, you were a prisoner here. A slave. Is that right?"

"Yes," he said solemnly. "Monica used me as her initiation ticket to join the Tau Zetas."

"But you were already her slave. That's what she said, anyway."

"True again. I guess I'd better tell you the whole story. You have a right to know. Monica always walked around half-dressed, and I was young. I couldn't help myself...I watched her. One day, after she'd come out of the shower wrapped only in a towel, she flashed me.

I...well, I stole a pair of her panties and her cheerleading sweater and jerked off. She caught me. As punishment, she spanked me. But that wasn't enough. She wanted a sex toy of her own. I licked her and she played with my cock, embarrassed me in front of her girlfriends, drove me crazy. I didn't date much in those days, and when I did, she teased me with threats to tell the girl about what we did."

"Did you like it?"

David paused before answering. "Yes. It was incredibly sexy. She only had to blackmail me a little bit at first. Afterward, I'd do anything, as long as she played with my cock."

"It's hard right now," Brandi said. She clasped it in her small hand.

David continued. "Then she was accepted at Valentine, and the rules for initiation into Tau Zeta include giving them a boy-toy. She had me drive over from Tech during a week break. At a party, the girls fed me their special drink—it's an aphrodisiac, you know."

"Oh," Brandi said. "That explains a few things. Keep going."

David's voice took on a faraway quality; he still had trouble focusing on his time in the dungeon. "After teasing me for a while, they made me take off my clothes. I thought it was just another one of Monica's games. Then I was in the dark, blindfolded, and then I was in a room just like this, fastened to the rack. Monica came by to let me know that I'd be a pet for the next week, then went away. Then the games started."

"What kind of games?"

"Tickling, spanking…a really nasty game with ice cubes…I gave a lot of head, which was the best part—making the girls come, you know. I like that a lot. They have a machine they call the Tease-o-Matic. Basically, their rule is that their toys don't get an orgasm for the first week. It seemed to take forever. I was completely insane." His cock pulsed hot and red in Brandi's hand; the first drops of precome glistened on her fingers.

"And then?"

"The end of the week, they had a show. I was the star—or the animal act, I guess. They made me show how well trained I was. Then, finally, right at the stroke of midnight, they made me come. And come. They kept stroking me and sucking me until I was completely drained. Then they set me free. I could come back if I liked, but I didn't. And Monica, I thought, had finally found her own niche and didn't need me anymore. I don't know what tonight was all about."

"Maybe she's jealous. Maybe she still wants you for herself."

"I guess," David replied. "She's beautiful and sexy and my stepsister, and we'll always have some sort of relationship, but she's older than I am and has her own interests. I don't know why she'd still want me."

"Maybe it's just that she doesn't want anyone else to have you."

"Or maybe she just likes the idea of letting you in on our secret."

"You mean, so I would do this?" With a teasing

smile, still gripping his cock, Brandi pushed David back against the rack. She stretched his hands into the waiting cuffs, then did the same with his ankles. "You look very sexy that way, you know." She stroked his cock gently. "I can imagine you all tied up and horny. I would have enjoyed fucking you that way. But I'd gladly fuck you any way. You know I've wanted you all night. Tell me the truth about something, will you?"

"Anything," David sighed. "Anything at all."

"Would you like me to dominate you like the girls of Tau Zeta?"

"Whatever pleases you."

"No, that's not the answer I wanted. What pleases *you?*"

"The truth? The truth is that I never had fantasies about being dominated until it happened to me. It's sexy, it's hot. I can't deny it. And I guess I found out that I might enjoy it occasionally. But the truth is, I always fantasized about it the other way. *Me* doing the dominating."

Brandi smiled a secret smile. She slid his wrists and ankles out of the loosely constricting shackles. She backed over to her own rack and slid her hands and ankles into the restraints. "That's what I hoped you'd say, because that's what I want. Yes, it would be fun to occasionally use your body. But what I really want is for you to use mine. I had already guessed your secret and it doesn't bother me. I don't want to be your next mistress; I want to be your conquest. I want to be like the princess and the pirate we saw outside. I want the fantasy of Tau Zeta, but I want to be its object. Do you understand?"

"You want me to dominate you, just like Tau Zeta but in reverse?"

"That's right."

"Wow. You know I've got a lot of pent-up energy and I've had a lot of inspiration."

"Exactly what I hoped for."

"I might turn out to be really cruel."

"Ooh, please do!"

"I might spank you."

"Mmm."

"Rape you."

"Ooh!"

"Strip you naked in public, throw you to the floor and fuck your brains out with a crowd standing around, then threaten to share you with the crowd, and whip you without mercy if you dared to protest."

"Now you're talking," Brandi laughed. They both laughed. It was intensely liberating after the long evening of torment and frustration. When they finally calmed down, Brandi looked at him with innocent eyes. "Now that you're naked in a dungeon with a beautiful woman who wants to be dominated, what are you going to do about it?"

Her innocent expression inflamed him. David placed his hands on her naked shoulders. Firmly, irresistibly, he pulled her forward into his embrace, forcing his lips against hers in a burning kiss. She put her hands on his chest and tried to struggle out of his arms. "No! Stop it, please! What do you think you're doing?" Brandi's acting drove him even crazier.

"God, I want you," he said.

She pushed away again. "If you don't stop *right now*, I'll scream!"

He merely smiled. "Go right ahead. There's no one around. You're helpless. The door is locked. Will you submit voluntarily, or do I have to rape you?"

She continued to protest. "You'll go to jail!"

"Not until I've fully enjoyed your body," he said. "I've wanted you for a long time, and you can't do anything about it. No one is here. No one can hear you. No one can rescue you. You're mine. I want you. I need you. And I'm going to have you."

Brandi felt his erection pressing against her and a wave of erotic helplessness overcame her. She really couldn't stop him if she wanted to. The thought excited her. "Please, don't..." she moaned, rubbing her body against him in a way that belied her words.

Nothing was going to stop him. With one strong hand, he bent her head back to kiss her. She wriggled in his arms in a combination struggle and play. This was her fantasy come true.

David picked her up in his strong, muscular arms, her naked form pressed against his chest. With a touch of a button, the rack folded down into a horizontal surface—a bed with shackles. Her heart pounded loudly. Her nipples stiffened; her pussy tingled. She felt so helpless. So sexy.

Once she was on the bed, David straddled her,

grabbed her hair with one hand, and pulled her against him for a hard, ruthless kiss. His lips fastened against hers, his tongue probed her mouth. His erection pressed insistently at her belly, rubbing against the soft fur of her mount of Venus, ready to invade her.

She felt herself responding to his kiss, her pussy quickly moistening. His grip became less rough, and he stroked one hand gently down her back, then reached down to cup her asscheeks with both hands, pushing her lower body against his cock. She moaned. He smiled wickedly. She was at his mercy and would be his erotic toy.

With one knee he forced her legs apart, laying on top of her with the tip of his cock pressing insistently against her pulsing clitoris. He kissed her sensually and deeply, stroking his hands over her gently rounded breasts, then leaning down to kiss her right nipple and suck it into his hot mouth.

"Ooh!" she moaned. A wave of pleasure coursed through her young, desperately aroused body. She reveled in her helplessness, giving herself up to the fierce joy of being dominated.

His other hand slipped between her legs, stroking the length of her wet slit, already tantalized by his cock's nearness. Insistently, his finger rubbed gently over her clit, then took it between two fingers and massaged the little node of pleasure. That drew another deep moan from her. His cock rubbed between her legs, sliding the length of her wet slit. Then he reached his arm underneath her and kissed her left breast, suckling her nipple, while one hand played with her right nipple and the other hand slid down her belly, between her open thighs, to gently stroke the center of her sex. Her pussy was wet and throbbing with desire. She moaned, closed her eyes, and gave herself up to the pleasure of being masturbated by his expert hand. He rubbed her pussylips, then stroked wetly and gently over her clitoris. She could feel his erection pressing against her thigh. The whole experience was so sexy that she couldn't believe it. Within minutes, she felt her orgasm building. "Oh...oh...oh...*oh...oh!*" she moaned. But just as she got close, he stopped.

She moaned with disappointment and frustration, but then he started again. It took only a minute or two to get her close. Then he stopped again. He was teasing her, toying mercilessly with her passion and need. The sensation drove her crazy. "Please, oh, please, don't stop... ooh...*oh!*" she cried as he tormented her once again.

Finally, he stopped completely. She looked at him passionately, wordlessly, wishing he would stroke her to orgasm. But David had something else in mind. "I want you to suck my cock," he said.

Brandi scrambled shakily onto her knees as David reclined on the rack, his cock pulsing in the air. She could see pearly beads of come glistening from the head. His cock was purple and rigid, twitching like a live thing, burning to her touch. She reached out to stroke it. The skin was soft, and underneath the strong muscle, and pulsing blood made it hard. He grabbed her head, and slowly forced it down on his cock.

She took his cock in both hands, stroking it softly. It

was very large. She leaned over and kissed it on the angry red head, tasting a little bit of the glistening precome against her lips. She looked up. He closed his eyes and leaned back, ready for her to pleasure him. The thought excited her. Again, she kissed it, this time licking around the head. He moaned. Emboldened by his response, she licked his cock up and down, getting it wet, while playing with it with her hands. She stroked his hairy balls, then opened her mouth wide to take it in. "Yes...yes!" he moaned. "Suck my cock, Brandi," he murmured. He began playing with his own nipples.

His arousal awakened a response in her. Wet and throbbing from his teasing fingers, she was deeply turned on, and the pleasure she was giving his cock turned her on even more. She began sucking and licking deeply, letting his cock fuck her mouth. It was delicious.

His moaning grew louder as his orgasm approached. She could feel the beginnings of his pleasure ooze from the sensitive head of his cock. Brandi had never let a boy come in her mouth; for the first time, the idea turned her on. She felt his cock ravaging her mouth, taking his pleasure. His hips began to buck underneath her. She could feel him getting closer...closer...

"Unnhh!" he moaned gutturally as the first hot spurts of his passion filled her mouth. She gulped his orgasm, feeling his cock pulse and shoot its seed. Her own passion mounted as she rode out his climax, his cock pulsing, his hands busy on his nipples, his hips rocking and bucking.

Finally, he stopped pulsing, and she released his softening cock gently from between her lips. Her heart pounded as she looked up into his face, contorted with pleasure, eyes closed. She felt on fire with passion, desperately wanting his cock deep inside her. Was it all over so soon?

Panting, he said, "Brandi, you are a great little cocksucker. I like that in a slavegirl."

Brandi blushed. "That's the first time I've ever… swallowed." It embarrassed her to admit her innocence.

He was surprised. "Really? That was unbelievable. Now it's your turn."

Startled, she looked up at him. She had thought it was all over after he had come in her mouth. But it wasn't. Now David knelt before her, spreading her legs, lowering his face to her wet and throbbing pussy. When his fiery tongue began to lick and suck at her innermost recesses, she nearly went out of her mind with pleasure. It was ten times sexier than his earlier toying with her. She cried aloud at the sensations that racked her young body. He reached his hands up around her hips to cup and stroke her breasts, kneading them gently, then stroking her nipples in a circular rhythm. She looked down at his hard, muscular body. She could see his cock stiffen again as he licked her, and she knew her passion turned him on. The thought excited her. Again, he brought her to the edge, and again he denied her, driving the young beauty crazy with desire and need. "Please…please…please…pleasepleaseplease!" Her moans turned into begging as his cunnilingual feast continued.

Time and time again, his hot, flicking tongue drove Brandi insane with pleasure. He took one hand from her breasts and slid it between her legs, slipping it inside her pussy, fucking her depths with his finger, making her long for his cock. When was he going to fuck her? When was he going to stick his cock inside her?

At last he was ready. He sat up, wiped his mouth, and looked into her eyes. "I'm going to fuck you now." She looked down at his cock, as hard as before. She needed it inside her.

"Ask for it!" he demanded. "Beg me to fuck you."

"F-fuck me," she said in response. "P-please, fuck me." The words were deeply arousing and fueled her submissive fantasies. "Please fuck me. I want you to fuck me. Fuck me now."

He sat up between her legs, and slowly rubbed the head of his hard cock against her lips. "I'm going to fuck you," he said. "I've been wanting to fuck you for a long time."

She looked up into his eyes. "Yes, I want you to fuck me. Fuck me hard. I need you to fuck me."

He slid his hard, aching penis between her pouting wet pussylips. Her pussy was tight, and he pressed hard to enter her. "Mmmh," she moaned, with a combination of pleasure and pain as he forced his way into her wet center. *"Ooh!"* she cried.

He was in her. The entire length of his hard cock was deep within her. He drew his cock out slowly, then entered her depths again. Again he withdrew, then

Tabitha's Tickle

plunged inside, a little faster. "My little Brandi, you've got my cock inside your tight pussy. I'm fucking your pussy just like I fucked your mouth earlier. Do you like being fucked by my cock?"

She looked up into his gray eyes. "Yes, I like being fucked by your hard cock. Fuck me, David, please fuck me. Fuck me, fuck me, fuck me," she murmured.

He continued to fuck her, building in speed, each thrust penetrating to her core. He stroked her wet clit with one hand, and played with his own nipples with the other. "Play with your nipples!" he commanded. She obeyed.

Her passion built. She could feel his own orgasm approaching, and she imagined his hot come inside her pussy as it had filled her mouth. His experienced hand on her clit drove her wild, along with the sensation of his cock fucking her pussy. She felt her orgasm close once again.

"Oh, fuck me!" Brandi cried, twisting her hips underneath him. His own passion stimulated by the sight of the beautiful coed, his cock so hard it would burst, he began to fuck her faster and faster, playing with his nipples, with her clit, building both their orgasms to the peak....

"I'm fucking you; I'm going to come in your pussy; oh, God!" he moaned as he thrust inside her faster and faster.

"Oh, fuck me, fuck meeee, fuck meeeeee!" Brandi moaned wildly. Both their orgasms were near.

And then the climax. "Oh...*oh*...*oh!*" she cried wildly

as the first pulses of her long-denied climax exploded in waves deep inside her body, radiating from her clit.

"*Aaah!*" David cried, as pulsing waves of orgasm spurted from his cock. "I love you!" he cried out in the midst of his passion.

"I love you, too," she moaned.

Their simultaneous orgasm filled the air with cries and moans of pleasure, until the two lovers finally collapsed, sweating, on the rack. Panting, trying to catch their breath, they kissed and held each other, his still-hard cock buried deep within her pussy, grinding against her in a motion that could never stop.

Finally, they relaxed. "Is that what you wanted?" David asked.

Brandi smiled. "You know it is. There's only one thing more…"

"What's that?"

"Do it again!"

The lovers laughed.

And soon they did, heedless of the possibility of watching eyes behind the glass of the one-way mirror.

8

By now, Bobby thought his night of erotic torment would never end. His mind was shattered; his cock ached with a world-class case of blue balls. The silver cockring had kept him from innumerable orgasms—he could hardly imagine what it would feel like to get sexual relief. Whenever he thought he was getting used to being a sexual prisoner and toy, the sadistic vixens of Tau Zeta Rho would escalate to a new and unexpected level. Exposed above the laughing crowd, a toy to be won and used, Bobby experienced the stark humiliation of being merely a sex object. When the mechanical whirring sound signaled that he was being lowered once again into the sex chamber below, he trembled with fear and anticipation. His nipples tingled; his still-rigid erection throbbed. After the vampire, the cat-women, and the endless parade in, what new and exotic pleasures could they have for him?

To his shock, it was his original captors: Susan and Tiffany, still dressed as succubi. "Welcome back, darling," Susan laughed mockingly. "Miss us?"

Desperate with need, he could only beg, even though he knew it would probably only inflame her sadistic nature. "Please...please...I can't take any more. You've got to help me!"

Susan strutted over to the helpless, shackled boy-toy and cupped his balls gently, weighing them. "Ooh, you're really full of come right now. I'll bet you feel really backed up." She giggled at the thought. "But don't worry about not being able to take any more. I'm sure you can, especially with help. Right, Tiff?"

"That's right!" Tiffany chimed in cheerfully. "We'll help you out." She undulated across the room, her pointed tail twitching as her ass wiggled with each high-heeled step. Bobby couldn't keep his eyes off her. She was a fetishist's dream, as was Susan—two beautiful, scantily clad costumed succubi, with the deep cleavage between their pert breasts peeking from the thin bands of ciré spandex that formed the brief costumes. The two girls pressed against Bobby, one on either side. Tiffany encircled his swollen organ with one tiny hand as Susan continued to fondle his aching balls. "Let's help the boy out," she breathed, winking at Susan.

With that, the two demonic succubi began to devour

TABITHA'S TICKLE

Bobby's helpless body once again. One set of succulent lips fastened on each of his ultrasensitive nipples. Tiffany's hand began to slowly, slowly pump his aching cock. Susan continued to fondle his balls but slipped a finger down to massage his perineal ridge. Bobby arched his back and let out a deep moan of pleasure that reached near-orgasmic heights. While frustrating, it was also delicious. "Please...please...more...just like that...oh, God...please!" he babbled in his desperate need to climax.

Of course, it was another tease, though a delightful one. With skill and sensitivity, the two tormenting temptresses worked their helpless victim along the crumbling edge of passion, licking and sucking and stroking and fondling and rubbing until passion yielded to agony. Bright bursts of color seemed to explode before Bobby's tormented eyes as he was swept away in a psychedelic tide of pleasure.

"You know you can't come until Sharon gets here, no matter how much we want to make you come," Susan taunted. "We do want to make you come, don't we, Tiff?"

"That's right, Woody. We want your come. We want to make you squirt all your come all over the place. Wouldn't you like that? Wouldn't you like to come for us? Maybe I could suck you off, make you explode in my mouth. You'd like that. I'm a hot cocksucker, you know."

"Or you could fuck my pussy and come in my pussy," Susan teased. "I'll bet your cock would feel so good in my pussy, all swollen and big. You'd really fill me up, wouldn't you?"

"Yes...yes...yes..." Bobby moaned. "Please...I'll do anything you want!"

"I know, Woody," Susan said. "I know you would. Even if I offered to trade one orgasm right now for an entire week of frustration, you'd take it, wouldn't you?"

Bobby gulped, then agreed.

"You'd let us tickle you nonstop as long as we felt like it for just one little orgasm, wouldn't you?"

"Oh...no...no...*Yes! Yes!*" Bobby cried, as Susan stimulated him carefully to the edge of explosion.

She studied his face and laughed. "Poor Woody. You don't have any willpower left at all, do you?"

"No...no..." Only the simplest responses remained for him.

"Then it's a good thing Sharon's here," Tiffany giggled.

"Sharon?" Bobby lifted his head weakly in shock, disbelief, arousal, and fear. What would she think? What would she do when she found him like this? Was he really going to get an orgasm at long last?

As Sharon opened the door, her mind was filled with confusion as well. After she and Tom had finished making love in the gazebo, she had led him back to the party to talk to Tabitha. As they entered the main party area, she saw a line of restraints along the wall. Several males were chained up; party girls amused themselves toying with victims at random. "You'd better wait here," she told Tom. "I'll lock you up and take the key, and I'll be back soon…I hope." His cock swelled as she fastened his hands into cuffs above his head and locked his legs into a spreader bar. She squeezed his cock tightly, making it rage to full erection. "If you still have this hard-on when I get back, I'll punish you for it," she said loudly, knowing full well that the teasing costumed party girls would make sure that his erection was still strong for her.

Tom's stricken expression of lust, love, and fear sent a surge of pleasure through her. "Yes, Mistress," he sighed, lost in the delights of submissive slavery.

Tabitha's majestic presence in red leather filled Sharon with awe, but she approached her anyway. "I know this is a big favor for a new pledge to ask," she began, "but I've fallen in love and want one of your slaves."

Tabitha smiled wickedly. "Come, dear, sit beside me and tell me all about it." Haltingly, Sharon blurted out the whole story. "How delightfully romantic and sexy!" Tabitha laughed. "I wouldn't want to stand in the way of young love, but maybe you need to prove yourself. I've got a little game for you to play, and if you win, Tom is yours. If not, you both can be mine for a week. Are you willing to gamble your body for Tom's?" Tabitha reached over to fondle Sharon's breast. Her touch, augmented by her witchcraft, was amazingly erotic.

Sharon gasped, nearly orgasmic. "Oh, God!" she gasped. "Yes! Yes!"

Tabitha gave a low, sexy laugh. "If you lose, you and

Tom are both mine for a week. A very *long* week. If you win, you and Tom are mine for a night. A very *long* night. That's the price. Do you agree?"

"Yes," Sharon said, recovering. "I'll enjoy it."

"We both will, darling. There is another problem, though. Your boyfriend, Woody."

Woody. Sharon shook her head. "I just don't know what to do. I got him into this, but I don't know how to get him out."

Tabitha smiled. "I've got an idea, darling. What if…" She whispered softly to Sharon, who brightened instantly.

"That's wonderful!" Sharon laughed. "Cruel, but wonderful. Think he'll go for it?"

"If my instincts are right, and they always are, I think he'll love it," Tabitha replied. "And you may enjoy it, too."

"Thank you," Sharon said.

"You're welcome. I look forward to the night—or the week—we're going to be together."

"So do I," Sharon said. She leaned into Tabitha for a deep, deep kiss. As she rose, she noticed the two bound men on either side of Tabitha's throne: Count Felipe and Robin. She looked at Tabitha, who nodded.

First, Sharon went over to Count Felipe. She took his large cock in her hands, then dropped to her knees to suckle it. She looked up at him; he moaned deeply. "That's to make up for the last time," she said around her mouthful, then swirled her tongue and moved her head back and forth, drawing him inexorably to the edge and then beyond. Only the power of the silver cockring kept the Count's come from exploding into Sharon's waiting mouth.

Then she approached Robin. The cruelly teased slaveboy had only been a watcher in the evening's festivities. He instantly recognized the new sorority initiate who had prick-teased him so well in the mansion earlier. His cock hadn't been sucked at all that day, and he looked forward to getting what Count Felipe had gotten—even a strangled orgasm was better than none. But Sharon had grown in cruelty and sophistication: she merely teased his nipples, standing so close that the heat of her body served to inflame him. She smiled at him. "I'm still a prickteaser, you know. If I become a sorority sister, I promise to spend a day with you. I'll make you suffer like nobody else has."

Robin's cock lurched with the threat; his body shook with pleasure. Carefully, wickedly, Sharon touched him with her magic wand. It was like an electric shock—his body convulsed, twisted and shook with indescribable ecstasy.

Then, filled with lust, cruelty, power, and hope, the beautiful blonde coed went to find her old boyfriend.

"Hi, Bobby." Sharon smiled. "Miss me today?"

"Sharon!" he cried. "Thank God you're here! I'm going crazy! Help me! What have you gotten us into?"

The two coeds looked at each other. How much had changed in less than a day! Bobby saw his innocent cheerleader girlfriend turned into an exquisitely sexy witch, her black mini revealing every curve of her body, a cruel and knowing smile turning her into a vixen every bit as wicked as the girls who had been torturing him for this endless day.

Sharon had last seen her boyfriend naked on the dorm bed, his cock swollen. Not much had changed. Bobby was naked, except for his bizarre leather harness, the same kind Tom wore. His cock was, if anything, even more swollen, imprisoned in the silver cockring that denied his explosion. Red stripes and marks all over his body revealed the evidence of whippings. The look of desperate sexual agony wasn't new, either, but now it had the appearance of near-insanity.

Susan and Tiffany in their succubi costumes were different, too. Sharon experienced a moment of jealousy seeing her old boyfriend so obviously turned on by the two beautiful coeds. Then she strutted over to him. "Well, Bobby baby, looks like you're really in a fix."

He struggled. "Sharon, you've got to help me! You don't know what they've done to me today. I'm going crazy...please...they told me I couldn't come until you got here and you made me come. Please...I'm going crazy."

"Oh?" Sharon asked innocently. "You want me to make you come?"

Bobby paused. His eyes widened in horror. "Oh, God—you aren't going to make me come! You're one of them! Sharon—you can't... No! No!" He thrashed in his bonds.

"Shush," Sharon smiled. "It's OK. You're going to get what you need—soon. First, tell me about your day. Tell me all about it."

Tabitha's Tickle

Bobby quieted down. He was filled with a combination of fear and desperate need. He wasn't sure he believed Sharon's reassurances, but she was his only hope. With the three girls clustered around him, he began to talk. Sharon reached out to stroke his chest and play with his nipples. Tiffany continued to masturbate his cock. The story of his endless teasing and torment came out in halts and stutters—it was a source of incredible embarrassment, not only to tell his girlfriend, but to tell the story in front of the two who had orchestrated so much of it. Whenever he stuttered and stopped, the girls stopped playing with him, urging him to continue. Whenever he omitted parts of the story, Susan and Tiffany added the missing details.

Sharon found the entire situation too funny; she couldn't help laughing at several points. "So, Bobby baby, here you are. You really need something for that swollen stiffie, don't you?"

"Yes...yes...please...I'm going insane!"

"I'll bet. Unfortunately, I've got some bad news for you."

His eyes widened in horror yet again. "No! Please, don't! I can't take any more."

"Shush. Calm down. It's OK. I've got some good news, too."

He quieted down, though his heart was pounding.

"Bobby, I'm afraid that I have to break up with you."

"What!? Sharon, you can't—especially not now!"

"I have to. I've met someone else."

"Who?"

"His name is Tom. He's a slave here, like you. But I knew him before."

"Damn it, Sharon—this isn't fair!"

"I know, Bobby. It isn't fair. But it happened anyway. When I decided to let Tau Zeta have you for my initiation, I didn't know how far things were going to go. I also figured that you'd enjoy being played with by a bunch of cheerleaders. Things have gotten out of hand, but I want to try to make it up to you."

"Make it up to me? You come in here and tell me we're breaking up after putting me through all of this? How can you make it up?"

"Be quiet for a minute and I'll tell you. I talked to Tabitha. It seems that the Valentine Cheerleading Squad needs a manager."

"A manager?"

"Someone to take care of logistics, fetch and carry, run errands. It needs someone organized, hardworking, someone who loves being around cheerleaders."

Bobby blushed.

"That's why I thought of you. Tabitha told me that they initiate their managers, and after the initiation, they play with them, use them, and abuse them. You'll have to go into the locker room to help the cheerleaders with every game. You'll travel on long bus rides; you'll stay in hotels with them. You'll even have to room in the cheerleaders' dormitory on campus here. Want the job?"

His face was so red it looked as if it would explode. "Oh, God! You're kidding, right?"

"Nope. Susan, Tiffany, tell him."

"That's right, Woody," Susan said, smiling inches from his face. "You can 'manage' us, and we'll play games like this all the time. You know, we sometimes get sore after putting on an exhibition, and the manager gets to massage us. Naked. If one of us gets horny and there's nobody else around, you'll have to get us off. Of course, you'll have to go for long periods without orgasm and keep us amused any way we want." The images of steamy locker rooms and cheerleaders, combined with Tiffany's devilish hand, defeated him utterly.

"Oh, God! Yes—I'll be your manager."

"Great!" Susan said. "Go, Teasers!"

"Now, about your orgasm," Sharon added.

Bobby stopped dead. "What about it?" he demanded.

"I planned to fuck you all tied down, and I have to admit, the thought of it is still sexy. But I have another boyfriend now."

"Wait a minute!" he cried. "You can leave me if you like, but you have to do something for me at least one more time—you owe me that much!"

"You wouldn't want me to be unfaithful, would you?" Sharon teased.

"Yes…please…do anything you want, but do something!"

"Well…"

"Pleaaase!" he begged.

She giggled as he humiliated himself; Susan and Tiffany joined in. "Well, OK. But I won't fuck you."

"That's all right. Please. Anything you like. I need it so badly."

"OK. Girls, come here." Sharon, Susan, and Tiffany huddled as Bobby watched in desperate need and anxiety. He no longer trusted any promise or any person. Finally, the three girls broke their huddle and grinned wickedly at him. "We'll be right back," Tiffany giggled. "Don't go anywhere!"

"Wait!" Bobby cried out, but it was too late. The girls were heading for the door. Susan gave him a farewell wink and turned out the lights. He was left alone in the darkness with his throbbing cock.

Endless minutes ticked by; then the door opened again. There were the three girls—they had changed into their cheerleading costumes just for him. Susan and Tiffany wore their Valentine cheerleading outfits—hot scarlet with white trim, flouncy pleated miniskirts and cropped sweaters just a size too tight. Sharon was wearing her Kittens costume—short purple and white pleated skirt and matching high-necked sleeveless sweater. For an exotic touch, the girls all wore high-heeled fuck-me pumps, the Valentines' in scarlet and Sharon's in purple. Bobby's cock lurched dangerously. "Oh, God!" he cried out. "You're beautiful!"

The girls giggled. "Cheerleader fetish," Sharon observed. "Just like I told you."

"Don't worry, Woody," Susan said. "We like that in a boy. Now lie back and smile. We cheerleaders will make you feel all better."

They unfastened him from the rack and tied him to

the rails of the large brass bed. Then all three perched around him: Susan on his right, Sharon on his left, and Tiffany crouched between his spread legs.

Then the torment began. Before the girls would let him spurt, all three were determined to drive him to new heights of madness.

Sharon and Susan began to tease his ultrasensitive nipples, sending delicious waves of pleasure through his needy body. At the same time, Tiffany slowly captured his leaking purple shaft in her tiny hand. Veins stood out in sharp relief. She smiled wickedly as she lowered her head to lick his cock in a ritual of slow moistening, combining her tongue's moisture with his precome ooze to make his shaft glisten with desire. He was gasping and in preorgasmic territory in seconds. "OhGodohGod!" he murmured as his eyes and voice glazed over with passion. Once his cock was thoroughly wet, Tiffany slid the restricting silver cockring off his straining shaft. He moaned again.

Meanwhile, Sharon and Susan teased his nipples. Each leaned down in turn to tongue-kiss him. They smiled at his helpless form. His entire body was tensing in precome territory, but Tiffany's slow, slow cocksucking kept him below the climactic edge.

"Please...please...make me come," he whined.

"Shush. You know you want us to make it last. After all, this is the last orgasm I'll give you—and probably the last you'll get for a while if you're going to be the new cheerleader manager."

Bobby wriggled and squirmed under the relentless

teasing. His lust-dazed mind could think of nothing but spurting, spurting endlessly.

"No...no...please keep going. I'll behave."

Tiffany continued to torture his cock with the slowest cocksucking he'd ever experienced. She smiled. "Let's play a little game," she laughed.

Bobby didn't want to play any games, but he had no choice.

"What did you have in mind?" Sharon asked.

"Let's see if our new manager has any self-control. He's pretty close right now, but let's see if he can hold out for one little minute." She sped up her mouth action, and his hips lifted from the bed.

"No, no, Woody. I want you to control yourself. Here's the rest of the game. If you wait one minute, Susan and I will take turns fucking you until you come. If you *can't* wait one minute, all three of us will tickle you senseless. Got it?"

He gulped with horror. "No! No!"

"Control yourself. Just think about getting thoroughly fucked by us."

Unfortunately, that was exactly the wrong image. Combined with everything else the stimulation sent him thoroughly and completely over the edge. His hips rose uncontrollably from the bed as he bucked them for the final stimulation he needed to trigger uncontrollable spurting.

He was in heaven, his body one large sex organ, every nerve filled with indescribable pleasure. And then it was here—the final tidal wave.... "*Aaaaahhhh!*" he screamed as the first jet of spurting come arched a foot into the air. *"Aaaarrgh!"* he yelled as the second jet shot as high as the first—then a third and a fourth; the pressure subsiding slowly as the ache of hours of desperate teasing was finally released. He was spattered in come all over his chest; strands of come were in Susan's hair and on Sharon's uniform. His chest heaved and his heart pounded as the waves of convulsive orgasm subsided, and then...

"Ha-ha-ha-hee-hee-*hee-hee!*" Bobby convulsed again as three sets of tickling fingers attacked his come-soaked, exhausted body. "Nooo!" he yelled. He twisted and squirmed to escape the maddening fingers of his tormentors.

"We warned you," Tiffany said. "Now you have to pay the consequences."

In the middle of the terrible tickling, he looked up into Sharon's eyes. His now-ex-girlfriend was clearly enjoying tormenting him. His cock swelled again. With a look of amused pity and simultaneous sadism, Sharon began masturbating him in the middle of the tickle-party. His cock grew and grew and grew. Sharon produced a thin ebony shaft. She gave him one last cruel smile and jabbed him in the side with it. *"Oh, God!"* he screamed as another wave of orgasm hit—every bit as strong as the first wave, jets of come spurting high in the air as his body convulsed under the stimulation of the magic wand.

"Oooh, messy!" Susan said, pulling a string of come out of her blonde hair. The other girls laughed.

Bobby blushed once again.

9

"Attention, boys and girls," came the announcement. "It's time for the Grand Masturbation Contest!" Eagerly, the costumed partygoers clustered about the central stage to watch as the victims and their masturbatrices were lined up for display.

Each masturbation stand was a metal bar anchored to the floor. Near the base of the pole, a crosspiece had two metal cuffs for ankles—they would be elevated off the floor when they were fastened. At the top of the pole was a strange seat consisting of a dildo that would fit into the ass of the victim and a frame to hold his body straight and balls forward. The crowd cheered as a line of shackled men was led out by women wearing circus ringleader costumes: tux and tails over leotard, fishnet stockings, and heels. The line included Tom and Bobby and Anthony and David, all naked, hard, collared and chained, arms cruelly pulled together by long single gloves laced up behind their backs.

The men were forced to climb steps to straddle their dildo seats. They rocked awkwardly and unsteadily as the dildos slid into their tight assholes. Their legs were spread and fastened into the ankle cuffs. Leather straps came out from below the seat and fastened over their thighs. They were unsteady, but completely helpless. Cocks jutted out rigidly. Then came the masturbatrices who would participate in the contest. Sharon for Tom, Susan and Tiffany both for Bobby, Stephanie for Anthony, and Brandi for David. The girls lined up beside their males.

Tabitha smiled wickedly as she walked down the line. "The rules are simple. When I say 'go,' masturbate your boy-toy. The first boy to come will be a slave for a month. The second boy to come will be a slave for a week. The girl who makes her boy come last will be the slave of that boy for a week. Other prizes will be awarded at my whim. Got it?"

The girls nodded.

This was a particularly wicked contest, and Tabitha was proud of herself for thinking it up. Each couple had something to win or lose.

Sharon's heart pounded. She had to win—first or second place, at least—or she wouldn't get Tom as her personal slave. The four orgasms Tom had gotten today would surely serve as a handicap. "If you come for me quickly, I promise you that I'll think up the most humiliating and outrageous tortures you've ever experienced," she whispered in his ear.

Susan and Tiffany just planned to enjoy themselves. Just to tease their victim, Susan whispered in Bobby's ear, "If you can hold out, we'll have to be your slaves. I'd like to be your fuck-toy for a week. If you want me, just resist whatever Tiffany and I do. OK?" Bobby gulped. He'd sure like to win, but the thought of winning was so arousing it served as a handicap to him. Besides, he saw Sharon with Tom, her new boyfriend. She looked so sexy in her cheerleading costume.

Anthony had spent the entire party shackled and teased. Stephanie was mad at him. He didn't want to end up a slave—he couldn't take any more—but he was so incredibly horny after everything that he didn't know how he could hold out.

David and Brandi had made love in the dungeon cell several times before the door flew open and they were taken prisoner again. Once again, Monica was the ringleader. "Poor babies!" she mocked. "David, you know you want to spend a month as a slave. Brandi, you can watch, and if you're very good, we may let you join us." But Brandi had a simple plan. She would just go slow in masturbating David. She would lose, and she'd be the slave and he the master, just as she wanted. She smiled a secret smile.

"Hold on!" Tabitha announced. "There's been a last-minute change in the lineup. Instead of Brandi, for David we now have…Monica!" There was a loud cheer, and with a sense of horror, Brandi and David turned around. Monica strode sexily on stage and rubbed her body against David's. "Good luck holding out, baby stepbrother," she laughed cruelly. "I know all your weak spots!" Nearly in tears, Brandi was forced to leave the stage. In the audience, she could only watch with hope.

Tabitha laughed. "One more little catch!" She gestured magically, and suddenly all the erect male penises went limp. "That should make things more challenging. OK—ready, set, go!" Tabitha announced, and the masturbation contest began. Female hands, slick with baby oil, grasped the rigid members and began to work them as the audience applauded, cheered, and whistled.

Sharon rubbed her baby-oiled hand over Tom's limp cock and was pleased to feel it begin to stir, even after four orgasms. She whispered, "You're naked and exposed in front of a huge audience, being masturbated so you'll shoot a huge load of sperm in front of everybody. They know you'll be a slave. They're laughing at you. Just imagine that it's the Kittens cheerleading squad. There's Gina and there's Tammi. Ooh, yeah. Swell up. Humiliate yourself in front of everyone. That's the ticket!" As he stiffened, she began to masturbate him in long, liquid strokes. She reached her free hand around to toy with his nipples.

Bobby squirmed as his two mistresses began their erotic attack. "Don't come for us," Susan giggled. "No matter how much we tease your poor cock, no matter how good it feels when we pump it for you, don't come. Hold it back. Watch all the other boys come. Watch

Sharon with her new boyfriend. That's right. Imagine that's you. You'd be a slave for sure. Instead, you're going to hold out, and then we'll have to be *your* slaves. We'll have to suck you off on command. Won't that be sexy?" His cock was rampant instantly. He knew their hands could defeat him easily; he could only hope they would misjudge or that the other boys would be even more hair trigger. He tried to concentrate on something—anything—but the teasing hands of his two masturbatrices.

"Baby, I'm sorry," Anthony begged. "You've got your revenge. Don't do this to me."

Stephanie smiled as her oiled hand began to stroke him. "You don't like the way this feels?"

"Yeah, baby, yeah, so good.... Just be careful. I want to get out of this, and then we can go somewhere so you can finish it."

"Go somewhere so I can jerk you off?" Stephanie said innocently. "Is that what you want?"

"Or suck me off, whichever you like," Anthony replied.

"Oh, how generous. Suck or masturbate. My choice, huh?"

"Yeah, baby, yeah." He felt his cock swelling uncontrollably at the touch of her teasing hand. "Whichever you like."

Wickedly, she increased the speed of her hand. "What if I like the idea of making you a slave?"

"Baby, no! Damn it, be careful. Haven't you done enough already?"

Stephanie laughed. "You started it, baby. Now I'm going to finish it." She flogged his penis faster and faster.

David gritted his teeth as Monica's talented fingers took possession of his cock. "Just like old times, darling," Monica chuckled. "I've got your cock and I can make it spurt whenever I want. Baby, you're mine, and don't you ever forget it."

"Please, Monica," he pleaded. "Let go. You're beautiful and you're sexy, but it's over. I'm not a submissive. Besides, I love Brandi."

"I know you do, Davy-boy," Monica laughed. "Don't worry. I have plans for her, too. A nice little submissive girl to go with my sex toy of a stepbrother. I've got lots of ideas. Fight me if you like, but you know I've got you. See? Your cock is already hard. What's this? A drop of precome. Baby, you've already lost. Surrender now."

David caught sight of Brandi, still gloriously nude and beautiful, standing in the front of the crowd. She looked at him with an expression of total confidence and gave him a thumbs-up sign. "You can hold on, David! Do it for us!" she called to him.

Tom felt the overwhelming sensations of Sharon's masturbating hand mixed with the glorious humiliation of being exposed and abused in public. He would normally be right at the edge of orgasm just at her touch, but he felt emptied by his four previous orgasms. For a moment he worried—he needed to lose this contest for his sake and Sharon's. What if he couldn't come again? The thought concerned him enough to take the edge off his orgasm—he was stuck in a downward spiral. "Sharon—help me," he begged. "I-I'm losing it!" Even under her best manipulation, he began to wilt.

Susan and Tiffany left Bobby's cock right at the edge of orgasm to tease his nipples. His aching cock bobbed impotently in the empty air. The twisting of his hips agitated the dildo that stretched his asshole; he got closer and closer to his orgasm even without being touched. Susan giggled. "We're trying to help you out. We want to be your sex slaves and let you fuck us any time and any way you want. But you bad boy—you just can't control yourself, can you? You must really want to be a slave and tease-toy yourself." Bobby moaned, "No...no...careful...don't...oh, God..." and bit his lip to keep from coming.

"Please, Stephanie! Please! I'll do anything you like. I'm sorry! I'll lick you to a hundred orgasms—just stop doing this to me! Let me go! Oh, God! *Oh, God! Oh, God!*" Anthony felt the inexorable build of pressure in his balls. His orgasm was inevitable now.

Stephanie masturbated him so quickly that her hand was a blur. "I've been talking with the Valentine girls, Anthony. We've got a whole plan mapped out for you for your month of slavery. You'll come right now, and then you won't come again until the month is up. Like the thought? I'll make sure you spend each day with a hard-on and you'll never...never...never get off." With each "never" she jerked his cock by the roots hard enough to hurt.

Through focus and concentration, David slowly

mastered the overwhelming sensations of Monica's hand. She was a particularly talented masturbatrix who had earned a reputation in the dungeons for her talent in drawing a man to the edge and beyond. She worked the entire shaft, finally sliding her oily fingers in a ring just under the ultrasensitive head of his cock, a maneuver well known to bring any man to his knees. David moaned, but resisted.

"Baby brother, you might as well give up now. I've got an insurance policy," Monica laughed haughtily. She reached down to touch a secret button below the dildo that penetrated her stepbrother. It began to vibrate and slide in and out, fucking his ass and rubbing over his prostate. His eyes widened. It was too much! He felt his orgasm breaking through his control...he was just about to—

Suddenly Sharon had an inspiration. She pulled the magic wand from the waistband of her cheerleading costume and touched it directly to the shaft of Tom's cock. *"Oh, God, yes!"* he screamed. His eyes widened. His body convulsed. His throbbing cock shot a huge jet of come out into the audience.

Waves of applause greeted the first victim to explode. "To the dungeons! To the dungeons!" the crowd chanted. To their mutual surprise, the platform segment on which they were standing began to descend. Sharon had the presence of mind to raise her hands in a boxer's victory gesture. She had won. She had her slave.

"You're in for it now, lover," she whispered as the couple sank into the depths.

"I know. Thank you," he replied.

The pressure in Anthony's balls grew and grew as his masturbatrix triggered his inevitable climax. "No! Baby! Please! Please! Don't! Oh! Oh! *Oh! Aaah!*" The long-delayed orgasm from his cruelly teased cock jetted into the crowd. At the first pulse of orgasm, Stephanie released his cock. "No! Touch it! Please!" he begged, but it was too late. His orgasm was left incomplete and hanging as he continued to shoot. He moaned in frustration and blue-ball agony. Why had he ever cheated on Stephanie in the first place? More cheers and raucous laughter greeted the second slave and his new mistress as they descended for a week in the dungeons.

"Enjoy the ride, darling," Stephanie laughed gaily. "I sure will."

Two victims were left: David, who was on the verge of orgasm at Monica's hands and Bobby, still being played with by Susan and Tiffany. Susan and Tiffany looked at each other with surprised horror. Perhaps they had delayed too long. "Oh, my God!" Tiffany cried, starting to stroke him faster and faster.

"Come for us! Come for us!" Susan urged, playing with his nipples, driving him toward the edge. At last, victory was in sight for Bobby. He imagined what he would do with his two slavegirls. It was a great feeling.

Monica was annoyed that she had failed to get David as a slave, but at least she could escape becoming his. The vibrator in his ass and her calculating hands had defeated him. His orgasm was upon him. She could feel his cock stiffen and pulse in the moment before his final explosion. Then—suddenly—he slid back. His entire trip to the edge reversed. She pumped his cock wildly.

Bobby's eyes grew wider and wider. "Oh, God! Oh, God! *Aaah!*" His orgasm hit and his come began to spurt and spurt. Susan and Tiffany laughed as he sagged in his cruel bondage.

"Guess you won't get two slavegirls for a week after all," Susan mocked. "But don't worry. You're still our manager, and we'll do lots of things to keep you entertained."

Monica's hand slid up and down David's shaft, but suddenly nothing she could do—not the vibrator, not all her skill—would get him closer to orgasm. Wild-eyed, she suddenly saw Brandi climb up on the platform. "What did you do?" she asked, suddenly suspicious.

Brandi smiled knowingly. "Valentine doesn't have a monopoly on witchcraft, you know. Every woman is a witch—especially when she needs to be."

"That's unfair!" Monica protested.

"As opposed to the vibrator dildo in David's ass?" Tabitha asked, joining the trio on the platform. "All's fair in love and perverse sexuality. Congratulations, Monica. You just earned a week in the dungeon." Tabitha gestured hypnotically. Monica suddenly found herself naked and impaled on the platform; David stood next to her.

Brandi hugged David's arm and smiled sweetly. "I'm David's slave and always will be, but I think I'll enjoy being a mistress for a week where you're concerned."

Tabitha's Tickle

Monica's heart sank along with the platform.

Tabitha laughed sexily. Things had worked out exactly as she planned. There was only one more thing to do to complete the evening.

10

The swollen moon cast its golden light over the grounds of the Tau Zeta Rho sorority house. The party had ended, the guests were gone, and the new slaves were undergoing their first initiations in the dungeons. An eerie quiet had settled over the surroundings. The fantasy areas had returned to normal, but the echoes of passionate moans and cracking whips could be heard faintly in the recesses of the gardens.

Only Robin was left, shackled to his post on what had been the dais holding Tabitha's throne in what had been the main party ballroom, now returned to normal size in the elegant sorority. He had been ignored through most of the evening, except for random humiliation and teasing. Sharon's magic wand had been the highlight of the evening's stimulation for him.

Robin had had a long journey from captured boy-victim to complete and utter sex slave. From the moment of his arrival at Valentine, Robin had fallen under the spell of the gorgeous, sexy coeds who populated the campus. He had been caught masturbating, was punished in a most humiliating fashion, and stripped naked and left in a public place to find his way back home. But he had become distracted by peeping through a window at another show and had been captured again. Since then, his life had been one excruciating tease after another. He escaped once, but fell into the clutches of the cheerleaders of a rival school. He was abused there as well, before finding his way back to Valentine.

Tabitha had punished him for the crime of his escape. During the long, tantalizing torment, he found in himself a deep submissive nature. His one vice was the pleasure he found watching a girl being dominated by other girls; his attempt to pleasure one such girl was responsible for his current situation. Normally, he came every week or so, at Tabitha's whim, but now he was on punishment. He spent most of his days tied up near wherever Tabitha was, teased when she was in the mood. She loaned him out regularly to one or more girls needing a tickle victim or party servant. He had been the prize in several competitions, devoting himself to the service of one pretty girl or another. It was a delicious slavery.

Tied to his post, his cock permanently hard (some of Tabitha's magic, he felt sure), he rubbed his ass against the pole. Any stimulation was better than none. He didn't need an orgasm right now as much as he just needed to be played with. Tabitha had promised him an orgasm tonight. "I'll find the most humiliating, sexy, embarrassing, nasty, frustrating, and teasing way to make you come. You'll come tonight, at the stroke of midnight. Something to look forward to." He could hear her ghost voice in his head. It was after midnight. Perhaps this was another tease. It wouldn't surprise him, but then nothing much would any more. Sometimes Tabitha delighted in making promises, then simply changing her mind about them. She was entitled to. She was in charge.

He resigned himself to another night of endless frustration. He was a slave.

Just then a single spotlight came on. He blinked, blinded by the sudden light. Then he saw her. As always, she was a walking wet dream, an impossible beauty. Her royal blue eyes twinkled with amusement. She was wearing her Valentine College cheerleading costume. Her amazing figure threatened to burst the tight and revealing confines of the cute costume. His cock jolted at the sight.

"You thought I forgot you, didn't you." It was simply a statement. "But how could I forget an opportunity to torture my very favorite sex-pet?"

Behind him he saw the rest of the full Tau Zeta sorority members filing into the room. All were wearing their cheerleading costumes. They formed a wide circle around him. He counted. There were exactly thirteen, counting Tabitha.

The girls joined hands. Tabitha entered the ring right in front of him. The circle closed about him. "Now the coven is complete. Sisters," Tabitha announced, "it is time for the Great Sacrifice."

Robin's heart pounded. Whatever Tabitha had planned for him, it was sure to be humiliating, degrading...and painfully sexy.

"Sisters, the traditions of magick and witchcraft have revolved around sacrifice. Sacrifices of blood, sacrifices of animals—and, above all, the sacrifice of virgins. Tonight, we have a rare animal for our sacrifice: an authentic male virgin." She smiled at Robin and licked her lips.

He blushed a painful shade of red. It was true. He was a virgin, in spite of everything that had happened. He had been a virgin when he arrived at Valentine, and with everything they had done to him, they had never, not once, allowed him to ejaculate inside a pussy. He was still a virgin.

"We are on the verge of the ultimate female power—the power to instantly arouse and tease, to utterly dominate through our sexuality alone. We need a final spell to complete the pattern. Tonight's event created a web of passion that surrounds the mansion. With the appropriate sacrifice, all the power will be ours. Here is our sacrifice—a carefully prepared male virgin, full of semen. Let us use our sacrifice to open the gateway fully."

She gestured magically. Robin found himself free of the pole at last. Naked, except for his leather slave harness, he found his hands imprisoned by his side. He

TABITHA'S TICKLE

floated up into the air. Underneath him there appeared a draped altar. Tabitha levitated him over the altar and lowered him upon it. Two of the cheerleader witches took his hands and shackled them in cold iron above his head; they did the same with his feet. He was pulled from both ends.

Another cheerleader brought in a large silver chalice filled with liquid—another magical concoction. She passed it around the circle. Robin could feel the growing sensuality. They brought another chalice, this one filled with thick purple liquid. This one they gave to Tabitha, who proceeded to pour it over Robin's body. It was cold and slimy. He nearly cried out at the shock; only his slave training kept him quiet.

The liquid warmed and caressed his body, flowing like something alive, inflaming every nerve of his body. This time he cried out in lust that was almost painful.

Tabitha smiled down at him. "Robin, darling, we need all your virgin sperm for our magic spell. Do you understand?"

"Yes, yes," he breathed. "It's all yours."

She laughed. "I know it's all mine. But I need it all, every last drop. It's like a bottle of soda pop. If you shake it and shake it, finally everything gushes out at once." She abused his penis gently with her soft hand; he gave himself up to the sensation. She slipped the silver cockring off his slithery cock, slimed with the strange liquid. Now he could explode for real—when she decided to let him. But she would certainly put him through his paces first.

His body taut and stretched, Robin looked up at the gorgeous cheerleaders whose complete slave he was. His heart pounded in his chest. The cold iron bands at wrists and ankles made him acutely aware of his servitude.

"Are you ready to be our virgin sacrifice?" Tabitha asked gently.

"Yes," he replied. "Yes. Yes."

"That's so nice." She smiled. "You really are a good slaveboy. That's why I torture you so much."

The cheerleaders of the Tau Zeta coven surrounded the altar, clustering on all sides of the helpless Robin, their scantily clad bodies radiating heat that stimulated his skin. Their sweet perfume tickled his nostrils.

"Now it begins," Tabitha breathed. Slow, sensual music began to play, and Tabitha performed a breathtakingly erotic dance to inflame the virgin slaveboy even more. She arched her body sensually, stroking her hands over her breasts, twisting to display herself in every position. She teased him by bringing her body close to his, moving so that her body was within inches, then writhing without making the final contact. She slowly peeled off her cheerleading outfit with the élan of a true striptease artist, exposing each inch of flesh with as much drama and power as possible.

The other cheerleaders were aroused by the performance. Under the spell of the ritual, the remaining twelve paired up, taking off each other's clothes slowly, petting each other. Tabitha finally began to touch Robin, rubbing his nipples in soft circles, slapping his cock back and forth playfully.

When all the cheerleaders were nude and aroused, the next phase of the ritual began. From a vase holding ostrich feathers, each cheerleader took a single long plume. Head to toe, no inch of Robin's flesh was free of a stroking, teasing, tickling ostrich plume. At first the tickling was a gentle titillation; then it escalated. He squirmed and wriggled, and then the first helpless giggles escaped him. It was maddening. He moaned helplessly under the onslaught of the thirteen tickling cheerleaders. His hips twitched involuntarily, his cock fucking the empty air. He leaked slowly, constantly, the pent-up seminal fluid oozing from the tip of his rigid, straining purple cock.

Tabitha's sparkling blue eyes regarded him with amusement. She played with him as if he were a pet. His eyes devoured her as she displayed her body; her amusement at his plight and his total lack of control made him even more aroused.

The feathers gave way to fingers. The cheerleaders pinched his nipples, slapped his cock from side to side, slid their fingers around in the viscous fluid that covered his body and drew patterns in the purple liquid, tickling the ridge of his hips to make him squirm helplessly, tickling the soles of his feet, licking his ear, driving him insane.

"Lick me!" Tabitha ordered. He had never before touched her sexually, though she had freely explored his body many times. She was breathtaking. She straddled his prone body, knees on either side of his chest, and cupped her breasts. Dry-mouthed, helpless, he watched as she slid her panties down, revealing close-cropped blonde pubic hair and pale pink lips, red and pouting, with a few drops of moisture glistening in the dim red light.

Robin stared hungrily at her. She weighed very little as she sat on his chest. She opened her slippery, soft netherlips with her fingers. She was wet. She lowered her pussy to his lips. He opened his mouth to take in her sensitive flesh. This was the torment he liked best. He was determined to give her pleasure, kissing her softly and deeply, licking his tongue up and down her wet slit, gently sucking the ridge that hid her clitoris, feeling it swell. The fingers and feathers that played with the rest of his body were only part of the background as he lavished oral adoration on his mistress.

Tabitha moaned with pleasure. Robin was a talented cunnilinguist; she'd heard that from the other girls, but she had to wait until this night to draw out the come she needed. At the edge of her orgasm, she pulled away; she couldn't come yet.

His heart pounded loudly in his chest. He looked up at Tabitha with awe and delight. She gestured to another cheerleader. This one produced an egret feather, hard and stiff.

To his horror, they planned one of the worst torments in his experience: the feather was for his balls.

He clenched and screamed at the first touch of the maddening sensation; it was the worst possible kind of tickling for him. In vain he writhed and twisted to escape the relentless tormenting feather. He gasped for breath. The cruel cheerleader drew the feather back and forth slowly across his balls. She stroked the sensitive flesh between his balls and his anus, wriggling the feather in the narrow passage, then touching the tip of the feather to his clenching asshole. His screams echoed in the darkened chamber. His tormentress continued the feathery attack, locating the exact spots that caused him the most agony.

Finally she relented, only to stroke the feather up and down his swollen organ. Up and down she stroked, around the underside of the head of his cock, back down the shaft. A pearly drop of precome oozed from the head of his cock. His hips wriggled helplessly.

As his orgasm approached, she returned to his balls and anus. The agony was worse the second time. Then to his cock. It took less time than before to draw him to the crumbling edge of release.

He was trembling with agony and desire when the long torment ended. And there was Tabitha, looking down at him. "Now it's time for the virgin sacrifice. We're going to sacrifice your virginity. Will you sacrifice your virginity to me?"

He took a moment to puzzle out what she meant. Then he answered, "With all my heart and soul."

Tabitha smiled. "Then don't come until I say so."

She reached down to grab Robin's twitching and swollen cock. He bit his lip at the overwhelming sensation. With excruciating slowness, she took his hardness into her tight pussy, inch by inch. Each inch was heaven to the much-teased slaveboy. This was what he imagined fucking would be like—but it was even better.

The cheerleaders began to chant. "Nevaeh ni tra ohw rehtaf ruo/Eman yht eb dewollah..." Robin didn't recognize the Lord's Prayer backwards. He was too busy finally losing his virginity.

When Tabitha finally took the entire length of his cock inside her, she began a slow, rhythmic fuck in time to the solemn chant. "Goddess," she prayed, "by offering the sacrifice of the virginity of this young man, we ask for the gifts You have promised us."

Afterward, Robin never knew how he managed to refrain from spontaneous orgasm. It was certainly the peak erotic experience in an environment filled with peak erotic experiences. He held out because Tabitha wanted him to. Again and again she rode him, taking him deep inside her with each stroke.

Tabitha felt her orgasm nearly upon her. His orgasm was there for the taking. She had to time this perfectly, else all would be for naught. She looked down at her erotically suffering victim. He was so close; a touch of his nipples would trigger him. Her passion built, built... She started rubbing his sensitive nipples. "Now," she smiled. "Give me your virginity."

Robin's eyes widened and his hips rose off the altar. At the moment Tabitha's orgasm began, so did his. The pent-up flow of come filled her so much she came again; the come leaked out, staining the altar. At the same time, a radiant glow made the fucking couple illuminate the room, then the glow spread to the other cheerleaders in the coven, then swept through the sorority house.

Tabitha's Tickle

"We did it!" Tabitha cried, leaning down and kissing Robin spontaneously. The cheerleaders kissed and hugged each other.

"W-what did we do?" Robin asked, weak and drained.

"We have liberated the power of the Goddess, silly," Tabitha said. "The things you've experienced—now we can bring them into the world. Thanks, baby. Because of you, more men can be slaves. Like the idea?"

"As long as I can stay *your* slave," Robin sighed.

"Of course you can, baby," Tabitha promised. "Forever."

You've heard of the writers
but didn't know where to find them

Samuel R. Delany • Pat Califia • Carol Queen • Lars Eighner • Felice Picano • Lucy Taylor • Aaron Travis • Michael Lassell • Red Jordan Arobateau • Michael Bronski • Tom Roche • Maxim Jakubowski • Michael Perkins • Camille Paglia • John Preston • Laura Antoniou • Alice Joanou • Cecilia Tan • Michael Perkins • Tuppy Owens • Trish Thomas • Lily Burana • Alison Tyler • Marco Vassi • Susie Bright • Randy Turoff • Allen Ellenzweig • Shar Rednour

You've seen the sexy images
but didn't know where to find them

Robert Chouraqui • Charles Gatewood • Richard Kern • Eric Kroll • Vivienne Maricevic • Housk Randall • Barbara Nitke • Trevor Watson • Mark Avers • Laura Graff • Michele Serchuk • Laurie Leber • John Willie • Sylvia Plachy • Romain Slocombe • Robert Mapplethorpe • Doris Kloster

You can find them all in
Masquerade

a publication designed expressly for the connoisseur of the erotic arts.

ORDER TODAY
SAVE 50%
1 year (6 issues) for $15; 2 years (12 issues) for only $25!

Essential. —*Skin Two*

The best newsletter I have ever seen! —*Secret International*

Very informative and enticing. —*Redemption*

A professional, insider's look at the world of erotica. —*Screw*

I recommend a subscription to **MASQUERADE**... It's good stuff. —*Black Sheets*

MASQUERADE presents some of the best articles on erotica, fetishes, sex clubs, the politics of porn and every conceivable issue of sex and sexuality. —*Factsheet Five*

Fabulous. —*Tuppy Owens*

MASQUERADE is absolutely lovely ... marvelous images. —*Le Boudoir Noir*

Highly recommended. —*Eidos*

MASQUERADE DIRECT

Masquerade/Direct • DEPT BMMQC6 • 801 Second Avenue • New York, NY 10017 • FAX: 212.986.7355
MC/VISA orders can be placed by calling our toll-free number: 800.375.2356

☐ PLEASE SEND ME A 1 YEAR SUBSCRIPTION FOR $30 *NOW* $15!
☐ PLEASE SEND ME A 2 YEAR SUBSCRIPTION FOR $60 *NOW* $25!

NAME _____
ADDRESS _____
CITY _____ STATE _____ ZIP _____
TEL (___) _____
PAYMENT: ☐ CHECK ☐ MONEY ORDER ☐ VISA ☐ MC
CARD # _____ EXP. DATE _____

No C.O.D. orders. Please make all checks payable to Masquerade/Direct. Payable in U.S. currency only.

MASQUERADE BOOKS

MASQUERADE

ATAULLAH MARDAAN
KAMA HOURI/DEVA DASI
$7.95/512-3
Two legendary tales of the East in one spectacular volume. *Kama Houri* details the life of a sheltered Western woman who finds herself living within the confines of a harem—where she discovers herself thrilled with the extent of her servitude. *Deva Dasi* is a tale dedicated to the cult of the Dasis—the sacred women of India who devoted their lives to the fulfillment of the senses—while revealing the sexual rites of Shiva.

"...memorable for the author's ability to evoke India present and past.... Mardaan excels in crowding her pages with the sights and smells of India, and her erotic descriptions are convincingly realistic."
—Michael Perkins,
The Secret Record: Modern Erotic Literature

J. P. KANSAS
ANDREA AT THE CENTER
$6.50/498-4
Kidnapped! Lithe and lovely young Andrea is whisked away to a distant retreat. Gradually, she is introduced to the ways of the Center, and soon becomes quite friendly with its other inhabitants—all of whom are learning to abandon restraint in their pursuit of the deepest sexual satisfaction. This tale of the ultimate sexual training facility is a nationally bestselling title and a classic of modern erotica.

VISCOUNT LADYWOOD
GYNECOCRACY
$9.95/511-5
An infamous story of female domination returns to print. Julian, whose parents feel he shows just a bit too much spunk, is sent to a very special private school, in hopes that he will learn to discipline his wayward soul. Once there, Julian discovers that his program of study has been devised by the deliciously stern Mademoiselle de Chambonnard. In no time, Julian is learning the many ways of pleasure—under the firm hand of this demanding headmistress.

CHARLOTTE ROSE, EDITOR
THE 50 BEST PLAYGIRL FANTASIES
$6.50/460-7
A steamy selection of women's fantasies straight from the pages of *Playgirl*—the leading magazine of sexy entertainment for women. These tales of seduction—specially selected by no less an authority than Charlotte Rose, author of such bestselling women's erotica as *Women at Work* and *The Doctor is In*—are sure to set your pulse racing. From the innocent to the insatiable, these women let no fantasy go unexplored.

N. T. MORLEY
THE PARLOR
$6.50/496-8
Lovely Kathryn gives in to the ultimate temptation. The mysterious John and Sarah ask her to be their slave—an idea that turns Kathryn on so much that she can't refuse! But who are these two mysterious strangers? Little by little, Kathryn not only learns to serve, but comes to know the inner secrets of her stunning keepers.

J. A. GUERRA, EDITOR
**COME QUICKLY:
FOR COUPLES ON THE GO**
$6.50/461-5
The increasing pace of daily life is no reason to forgo a little carnal pleasure whenever the mood strikes. Here are over sixty of the hottest fantasies around—all designed to get you going in less time than it takes to dial 976. A super-hot volume especially for couples on a modern schedule.

ERICA BRONTE
LUST, INC.
$6.50/467-4
Lust, Inc. explores the extremes of passion that lurk beneath even the coldest, most business-like exteriors. Join in the sexy escapades of a group of high-powered professionals whose idea of office decorum is like nothing you've ever encountered! Business attire not required....

VANESSA DURIES
THE TIES THAT BIND
$6.50/510-7
The incredible confessions of a thrillingly unconventional woman. From the first page, this chronicle of dominance and submission will keep you gasping with its vivid depictions of sensual abandon. At the hand of Masters Georges, Patrick, Pierre and others, this submissive seductress experiences pleasures she never knew existed....

M. S. VALENTINE
THE CAPTIVITY OF CELIA
$6.50/453-4
Colin is mistakenly considered the prime suspect in a murder, forcing him to seek refuge with his cousin, Sir Jason Hardwicke. In exchange for Colin's safety, Jason demands Celia's unquestioning submission—knowing she will do anything to protect her lover. Sexual extortion!

AMANDA WARE
BOUND TO THE PAST
$6.50/452-6
Anne accepts a research assignment in a Tudor mansion. Upon arriving, she finds herself aroused by James, a descendant of the mansion's owners. Together they uncover the perverse desires of the mansion's long-dead master—desires that bind Anne inexorably to the past—not to mention the bedpost!

BUY ANY 4 BOOKS & CHOOSE 1 ADDITIONAL BOOK, OF EQUAL OR LESSER VALUE, AS YOUR FREE GIFT

MASQUERADE BOOKS

SACHI MIZUNO
SHINJUKU NIGHTS
$6.50/493-3
Another tour through the lives and libidos of the seductive East, from the author of Passion in Tokyo. No one is better than Sachi Mizuno at weaving an intricate web of sensual desire, wherein many characters are ensnared and enraptured by the demands of their long-denied carnal natures. One by one, each surrenders social convention for the unashamed pleasures of the flesh.

PASSION IN TOKYO
$6.50/454-2
Tokyo—one of Asia's most historic and seductive cities. Come behind the closed doors of its citizens, and witness the many pleasures that await. Lusty men and women from every stratum of Japanese society free themselves of all inhibitions....

MARTINE GLOWINSKI
POINT OF VIEW
$6.50/433-X
With the assistance of her new, unexpectedly kinky lover, she discovers and explores her exhibitionist tendencies—until there is virtually nothing she won't do before the horny audiences her man arranges! Unabashed acting out for the sophisticated voyeur.

RICHARD McGOWAN
A HARLOT OF VENUS
$6.50/425-9
A highly fanciful, epic tale of lust on Mars! Cavortia—the most famous and sought-after courtesan in the cosmopolitan city of Venus—finds love and much more during her adventures with some of the most remarkable characters in recent erotic fiction.

M. ORLANDO
THE ARCHITECTURE OF DESIRE
Introduction by Richard Manton.
$6.50/490-9
Two novels in one special volume! In The Hotel Justine, an elite clientele is afforded the opportunity to have any and all desires satisfied. The Villa Sin is inherited by a beautiful woman who soon realizes that the legacy of the ancestral estate includes bizarre erotic ceremonies. Two pieces of prime real estate.

CHET ROTHWELL
KISS ME, KATHERINE
$5.95/410-0
Beautiful Katherine can hardly believe her luck. Not only is she married to the charming and oh-so-agreeable Nelson, she's free to live out all her erotic fantasies with other men. Katherine has discovered Nelson to be far more devoted than the average spouse—and the duo soon begin exploring a relationship more demanding than marriage! Soon, Katherine's desires become more than any one man can handle.

MARCO VASSI
THE STONED APOCALYPSE
$5.95/401-1/mass market
"Marco Vassi is our champion sexual energist."—VLS
During his lifetime, Marco Vassi praised by writers as diverse as Gore Vidal and Norman Mailer, and his reputation was worldwide. The Stoned Apocalypse is Vassi's autobiography; chronicling a cross-country trip on America's erotic byways, it offers a rare glimpse of a generation's sexual imagination.

ROBIN WILDE
TABITHA'S TICKLE
$6.50/468-2
Tabitha's back! The story of this vicious vixen—and her torturously tantalizing cohorts—didn't end with Tabitha's Tease. Once again, men fall under the spell of scrumptious co-eds and find themselves enslaved to demands and desires they never dreamed existed. Think it's a man's world? Guess again. With Tabitha around, no man gets what he wants until she's completely satisfied—and, maybe, not even then....

TABITHA'S TEASE
$5.95/387-2
When poor Robin arrives at The Valentine Academy, he finds himself subject to the torturous teasing of Tabitha—the Academy's most notoriously domineering co-ed. But Tabitha is pledge-mistress of a secret sorority dedicated to enslaving young men. Robin finds himself the utterly helpless (and wildly excited) captive of Tabitha & Company's weird desires! A marathon of ticklish torture!

ERICA BRONTE
PIRATE'S SLAVE
$5.95/376-7
Lovely young Erica is stranded in a country where lust knows no bounds. Desperate to escape, she finds herself trading her firm, luscious body to any and all men willing and able to help her. Her adventure has its ups and downs, ins and outs—all to the undeniable pleasure of lusty Erica!

CHARLES G. WOOD
HELLFIRE
$5.95/358-9
A vicious murderer is running amok in New York's sexual underground—and Nick O'Shay, a virile detective with the NYPD, plunges deep into the case. He soon becomes embroiled in an elusive world of fleshly extremes, hunting a madman seeking to purge America with fire and blood sacrifices. Set in New York's infamous sexual underground.

CLAIRE BAEDER, EDITOR
LA DOMME: A DOMINATRIX ANTHOLOGY
$5.95/366-X
A steamy smorgasbord of female domination! Erotic literature has long been filled with heartstopping portraits of domineering women, and now the most memorable have been brought together in one beautifully brutal volume. A must for all fans of true Woman Power.

MASQUERADE BOOKS

CHARISSE VAN DER LYN
SEX ON THE NET
$5.95/399-6
Electrifying erotica from one of the Internet's hottest and most widely read authors. Encounters of all kinds—straight, lesbian, dominant/submissive and all sorts of extreme passions—are explored in thrilling detail.

STANLEY CARTEN
NAUGHTY MESSAGE
$5.95/333-3
Wesley Arthur discovers a lascivious message on his answering machine. Aroused beyond his wildest dreams by the acts described, Wesley becomes obsessed with tracking down the woman behind the seductive voice. His search takes him through strip clubs, sex parlors and no-tell motels—and finally to his randy reward....

AKBAR DEL PIOMBO
DUKE COSIMO
$4.95/3052-0
A kinky romp played out against the boudoirs, bathrooms and ballrooms of the European nobility, who seem to do nothing all day except each other. The lifestyles of the rich and licentious are revealed in all their glory.

A CRUMBLING FAÇADE
$4.95/3043-1
The return of that incorrigible rogue, Henry Pike, who continues his pursuit of sex, fair or otherwise, in the most elegant homes of the most debauched aristocrats.

CAROLE REMY
FANTASY IMPROMPTU
$6.50/513-1
A mystical, musical journey into the deepest recesses of a woman's soul. Kidnapped and held in a remote island retreat, Chantal—a renowned erotic wirter—finds herself catering to every sexual whim of the mysterious and arousing Bran. Bran is determined to bring Chantal to a full embracing of her sensual nature, even while revealing himself to be something far more than human....

BEAUTY OF THE BEAST
$5.95/332-5
A shocking tell-all, written from the point-of-view of a prize-winning reporter. And what reporting she does! All the secrets of an uninhibited life are revealed, and each lusty tableau is painted in glowing colors.

DAVID AARON CLARK
THE MARQUIS DE SADE'S JULIETTE
$4.95/240-X
The Marquis de Sade's infamous Juliette returns—and emerges as the most perverse and destructive nightstalker modern New York will ever know. One by one, the innocent are drawn in by Juliette's empty promise of immortality, only to fall prey to her strange and deadly lusts.

ANONYMOUS
NADIA
$5.95/267-1
Follow the delicious but neglected Nadia as she works to wring every drop of pleasure out of life—despite an unhappy marriage. A classic title providing a peek into the secret sexual lives of another time and place.

NIGEL McPARR
THE STORY OF A VICTORIAN MAID
$5.95/241-8
What were the Victorians really like? Chances are, no one believes they were as stuffy as their Queen, but who would have imagined such unbridled libertines!

TITIAN BERESFORD
CINDERELLA
$6.50/500-X
Beresford triumphs again with this intoxicating tale, filled with castle dungeons and tightly corseted ladies-in-waiting, naughty viscounts and impossibly cruel masturbatrixes—nearly every conceivable method of erotic torture is explored and described in lush, vivid detail.

JUDITH BOSTON
$6.50/525-5
Young Edward would have been lucky to get the stodgy old companion he thought his parents had hired for him. Instead, an exquisite woman arrives at his door, and Edward finds his lewd behavior never goes unpunished by the unflinchingly severe Judith Boston! Together they take the downward path to perversion!

NINA FOXTON
$5.95/443-7
An aristocrat finds herself bored by run-of-the-mill amusements for "ladies of good breeding." Instead of taking tea with proper gentlemen, naughty Nina "milks" them of their most private essences. No man ever says "No" to Nina!

P. N. DEDEAUX
THE NOTHING THINGS
$5.95/404-6
Beta Beta Rho—highly exclusive and widely honored—has taken on a new group of pledges. The five women will be put through the most grueling of ordeals, and punished severely for any shortcomings—much to everyone's delight!

LYN DAVENPORT
THE GUARDIAN II
$6.50/505-0
The tale of Felicia Brookes—the lovely young woman held in submission by the demanding Sir Rodney Wentworth—continues in this volume of sensual surprises. No sooner has Felicia come to love Rodney than she discovers that she must now accustom herself to the guardianship of the debauched Duke of Smithton. How long will this last? Surely Rodney will rescue her from the domination of this stranger. Won't he?

BUY ANY 4 BOOKS & CHOOSE 1 ADDITIONAL BOOK, OF EQUAL OR LESSER VALUE, AS YOUR FREE GIFT

MASQUERADE BOOKS

DOVER ISLAND
$5.95/384-8
Dr. David Kelly has planted the seeds of his dream—a Corporal Punishment Resort. Soon, many people from varied walks of life descend upon this isolated retreat, intent on fulfilling their every desire. Including Marcy Harris, the perfect partner for the lustful Doctor....

THE GUARDIAN
$5.95/371-6
Felicia grew up under the tutelage of the lash—and she learned her lessons well. Sir Rodney Wentworth has long searched for a woman capable of fulfilling his cruel desires, and after learning of Felicia's talents, sends for her. Felicia discovers that the "position" offered her is delightfully different than anything she could have expected!

LIZBETH DUSSEAU

THE APPLICANT
$6.50/501-8
"Adventuresome young women who enjoys being submissive sought by married couple in early forties. Expect no limits." Hilary answers an ad, hoping to find someone who can meet her special needs. The beautiful Liza turns out to be a flawless mistress, and together with her husband, Oliver, she trains Hilary to be the perfect servant. Scandalous sexual servitude.

ANTHONY BOBARZYNSKI

STASI SLUT
$4.95/3050-4
Adina lives in East Germany, where she can only dream about the freedoms of the West. But then she meets a group of ruthless and corrupt STASI agents. They use her body for their own perverse gratification, while she opts to use her talents and attractions in a final bid for total freedom!

JOCELYN JOYCE

PRIVATE LIVES
$4.95/309-0
The lecherous habits of the illustrious make for a sizzling tale of French erotic life. A widow has a craving for a young busboy; he's sleeping with a rich businessman's wife; her husband is minding his sex business elsewhere! Scandalous sexual entanglements run through this tale of upper crust lust!

SARAH JACKSON

SANCTUARY
$5.95/318-X
Sanctuary explores both the unspeakable debauchery of court life and the unimaginable privations of monastic solitude, leading the voracious and the virtuous on a collision course that brings history to throbbing life.

THE WILD HEART
$4.95/3007-5
A luxury hotel is the setting for this artful web of sex, desire, and love. A newlywed sees sex as a duty, while her hungry husband tries to awaken her to its tender joys. A Parisian entertains wealthy guests for the love of money. Each episode provides a new variation in this lusty Grand Hotel!

LOUISE BELHAVEL

FRAGRANT ABUSES
$4.95/88-2
The saga of Clara and Iris continues as the now-experienced girls enjoy themselves with a new circle of worldly friends whose imaginations match their own. Perversity follows the lusty ladies around the globe!

SARA H. FRENCH

MASTER OF TIMBERLAND
$5.95/327-9
A tale of sexual slavery at the ultimate paradise resort. One of our bestselling titles, this trek to Timberland has ignited passions the world over—and stands poised to become one of modern erotica's legendary tales.

MARY LOVE

MASTERING MARY SUE
$5.95/351-1
Mary Sue is a rich nymphomaniac whose husband is determined to declare her mentally incompetent and gain control of her fortune. He brings her to a castle where, to Mary Sue's delight, she is unleashed for a veritable sex-fest!

THE BEST OF MARY LOVE
$4.95/3099-7
Mary Love leaves no coupling untried and no extreme unexplored in these scandalous selections from *Mastering Mary Sue*, *Ecstasy on Fire*, *Vice Park Place*, *Wanda*, and *Naughtier at Night*.

AMARANTHA KNIGHT

THE DARKER PASSIONS: THE PICTURE OF DORIAN GRAY
$6.50/342-2
Amarantha Knight takes on Oscar Wilde, resulting in a fabulously decadent tale of highly personal changes. One young man finds his most secret desires laid bare by a portrait far more revealing than he could have imagined....

THE DARKER PASSIONS READER
$6.50/432-1
The best moments from Knight's phenomenally popular Darker Passions series. Here are the most eerily erotic passages from her acclaimed sexual reworkings of *Dracula*, *Frankenstein*, *Dr. Jekyll & Mr. Hyde* and *The Fall of the House of Usher*.

THE DARKER PASSIONS: THE FALL OF THE HOUSE OF USHER
$6.50/528-X
The Master and Mistress of the house of Usher indulge in every form of decadence, and initiate their guests into the many pleasures to be found in utter submission.

THE DARKER PASSIONS: DR. JEKYLL AND MR. HYDE
$4.95/227-2
It is a story of incredible transformations achieved through mysterious experiments. Explore the steamy possibilities of a tale where no one is quite who—or what—they seem. Victorian bedrooms explode with hidden demons!

MASQUERADE BOOKS

THE DARKER PASSIONS: FRANKENSTEIN
$5.95/248-5
What if you could create a living human? What shocking acts could it be taught to perform, to desire? Find out what pleasures await those who play God....

THE DARKER PASSIONS: DRACULA
$5.95/326-0
The infamous erotic retelling of the Vampire legend. "Well-written and imaginative, Amarantha Knight gives fresh impetus to this myth, taking us through the sexual and sadistic scenes with details that keep us reading.... A classic in itself has been added to the shelves." —Divinity

PAUL LITTLE

THE BEST OF PAUL LITTLE
$6.50/469-0
One of Masquerade's all-time best-selling authors. Known throughout the world for his fantastic portrayals of punishment and pleasure, Little never fails to push readers over the edge of sensual excitement.

ALL THE WAY
$6.95/509-3
Two excruciating novels from Paul Little in one hot volume! *Going All the Way* features an unhappy man who tries to purge himself of the memory of his lover with a series of quirky and uninhibited lovers. *Pushover* tells the story of a serial spanker and his celebrated exploits.

THE DISCIPLINE OF ODETTE
$5.95/334-1
Odette's was sure marriage would rescue her from her family's "corrections." To her horror, she discovers that her beloved has also been raised on discipline. A shocking erotic coupling!

THE PRISONER
$5.95/330-9
Judge Black has built a secret room below a penitentiary, where he sentences the prisoners to hours of exhibition and torment while his friends watch. Judge Black's House of Corrections is equipped with one purpose in mind: to administer his own brand of rough justice.

TEARS OF THE INQUISITION
$4.95/146-2
The incomparable Paul Little delivers a staggering account of pleasure and punishment. "There was a tickling inside her as her nervous system reminded her she was ready for sex. But before her was...the Inquisitor!" One of history's most infamous periods comes to throbbing life via the perverse imagination of Paul Little.

DOUBLE NOVEL
$4.95/86-6
The Metamorphosis of Lisette Joyaux tells the story of a young woman initiated into a new and incredible world world of lesbian lusts. *The Story of Monique* reveals the twisted sexual rituals that beckon the ripe and willing Monique.

CHINESE JUSTICE AND OTHER STORIES
$4.95/153-5
The story of the excruciating pleasures and delicious punishments inflicted on foreigners under the leaders of the Boxer Rebellion. Each foreign woman is brought before the authorities and grilled, much to the delight of their perverse captors. Scandalous deeds and shocking exploitation!

CAPTIVE MAIDENS
$5.95/440-2
Three beautiful young women find themselves powerless against the debauched landowners of 1824 England. They are banished to a sexual slave colony, and corrupted by every imaginable perversion. Soon, they come to crave the treatment of their unrelenting captors.

SLAVE ISLAND
$5.95/441-0
A leisure cruise is waylaid by Lord Henry Philbrock, a sadistic genius. The ship's passengers are kidnapped and spirited to his island prison, where the women are trained to accommodate the most bizarre sexual cravings of the rich, the famous, the pampered and the perverted.

ALIZARIN LAKE

SEX ON DOCTOR'S ORDERS
$5.95/402-X
Beth, a nubile young nurse, uses her considerable skills to further medical science by offering incomparable and insatiable assistance in the gathering of important specimens. Soon, an assortment of randy characters is lending a hand in this highly erotic work. No man leaves naughty Nurse Beth's station without surrendering what she needs!

THE EROTIC ADVENTURES OF HARRY TEMPLE
$4.95/127-6
Harry Temple's memoirs chronicle his amorous adventures from his initiation at the hands of insatiable sirens, through his stay at a house of hot repute, to his encounters with a chastity-belted nympho!

JOHN NORMAN

TARNSMAN OF GOR
$6.95/486-0
This controversial series returns! *Tarnsman* finds Tarl Cabot transported to Counter-Earth, better known as Gor. He must quickly accustom himself to the ways of this world, including the caste system which exalts some as Priest-Kings or Warriors, and debases others as slaves. A spectacular world unfolds in this first volume of John Norman's Gorean series.

OUTLAW OF GOR
$6.95/487-9
In this second volume, Tarl Cabot returns to Gor, where he might reclaim both his woman and his role of Warrior. But upon arriving, he discovers that his name, his city and the names of those he loves have become unspeakable. Cabot has become an outlaw, and must discover his new purpose on this strange planet, where danger stalks the outcast, and even simple answers have their price....

BUY ANY 4 BOOKS & CHOOSE 1 ADDITIONAL BOOK, OF EQUAL OR LESSER VALUE, AS YOUR FREE GIFT

MASQUERADE BOOKS

PRIEST-KINGS OF GOR
$6.95/488-7
The third volume of John Norman's million-selling Gor series. Tarl Cabot searches for the truth about his lovely wife Talena. Does she live, or was she destroyed by the mysterious, all-powerful Priest-Kings? Cabot is determined to find out—even while knowing that no one who has approached the mountain stronghold of the Priest-Kings has ever returned alive....

NOMADS OF GOR
$6.95/527-1
Another provocative trip to the barbaric and mysterious world of Gor. Norman's heroic Tarnsman finds his way across this Counter-Earth, pledged to serve the Priest-Kings in their quest for survival. Unfortunately for Cabot, his mission leads him to the savage Wagon People—nomads who may very well kill before surrendering any secrets....

RACHEL PEREZ

AFFINITIES
$4.95/113-6
"Kelsy had a liking for cool upper-class blondes, the long-legged girls from Lake Forest and Winnetka who came into the city to cruise the lesbian bars on Halsted, looking for breathless ecstasies...." A scorching tale of lesbian libidos unleashed, from a writer more than capable of exploring every nuance of female passion in vivid detail.

SYDNEY ST. JAMES

RIVE GAUCHE
$5.95/317-1
The Latin Quarter, Paris, circa 1920. Expatriate bohemians couple with abandon—before eventually abandoning their ambitions amidst the intoxicating temptations waiting to be indulged in every bedroom.

GARDEN OF DELIGHT
$4.95/3058-X
A vivid account of sexual awakening that follows an innocent but insatiably curious young woman's journey from the furtive, forbidden joys of dormitory life to the unabashed carnality of the wild world.

DON WINSLOW

PRIVATE PLEASURES
$6.50/504-2
An assortment of sensual encounters designed to appeal to the most discerning reader. Frantic voyeurs, licentious exhibitionists, and everyday lovers are here displayed in all their wanton glory—proving again that fleshly pleasures have no more apt chronicler than Don Winslow.

THE INSATIABLE MISTRESS OF ROSEDALE
$6.50/494-1
The story of the perfect couple: Edward and Lady Penelope, who reside in beautiful and mysterious Rosedale manor. While Edward is a true connoisseur of sexual perversion, it is Lady Penelope whose mastery of complete sensual pleasure makes their home infamous. Indulging one another's bizarre whims is a way of life for this wicked couple, and none who encounter the extravagances of Rosedale will forget what they've learned....

SECRETS OF CHEATEM MANOR
$6.50/434-5
Edward returns to his late father's estate, to find it being run by the majestic Lady Amanda. Edward can hardly believe his luck—Lady Amanda is assisted by her two beautiful, lonely daughters, Catherine and Prudence. What the randy young man soon comes to realize is the love of discipline that all three beauties share.

KATERINA IN CHARGE
$5.95/409-7
When invited to a country retreat by a mysterious couple, two randy young ladies can hardly resist! But do they have any idea what they're in for? Whatever the case, the imperious Katerina will make her desires known very soon—and demand that they be fulfilled... Sexual innocence subjugated and defiled.

THE MANY PLEASURES OF IRONWOOD
$5.95/310-4
Seven lovely young women are employed by The Ironwood Sportsmen's Club, where their natural talents are put to creative use. A small and exclusive club with seven carefully selected sexual connoisseurs, Ironwood is dedicated to the relentless pursuit of sensual pleasure.

CLAIRE'S GIRLS
$5.95/442-8
You knew when she walked by that she was something special. She was one of Claire's girls, a woman carefully dressed and groomed to fill a role, to capture a look, to fit an image crafted by the sophisticated proprietress of an exclusive escort agency. High-class whores blow the roof off in this blow-by-blow account of life behind the closed doors of a sophisticated brothel.

N. WHALLEN

TAU'TEVU
$6.50/426-7
In a mysterious land, the statuesque and beautiful Vivian learns to subject herself to the hand of a mysterious man. He systematically helps her prove her own strength, and brings to life in her an unimagined sensual fire. But who is this man, who goes only by the name of Orpheo?

COMPLIANCE
$5.95/356-2
Fourteen stories exploring the pleasures of ultimate release. Characters from all walks of life learn to trust in the skills of others, hoping to experience the thrilling liberation of sexual submission. Here are the many joys to be found in some of the most forbidden sexual practices around....

THE CLASSIC COLLECTION

PROTESTS, PLEASURES, RAPTURES
$5.95/400-3
Invited for an allegedly quiet weekend at a country vicarage, a young woman is stunned to find herself surrounded by shocking acts of sexual sadism. Soon, her curiosity is piqued, and she begins to explore her own capacities for cruelty. The ultimate tale of an extraordinary woman's erotic awakening.

MASQUERADE BOOKS

THE YELLOW ROOM
$5.95/378-3
The "yellow room" holds the secrets of lust, lechery, and the lash. There, bare-bottomed, spread-eagled, and open to the world, demure Alice Darvell soon learns to love her lickings. In the second tale, hot heiress Rosa Coote and her lusty servants whip up numerous adventures in punishment and pleasure.

SCHOOL DAYS IN PARIS
$5.95/325-2
The rapturous chronicles of a well-spent youth! Few Universities provide the profound and pleasurable lessons one learns in after-hours study—particularly if one is young and available, and lucky enough to have Paris as a playground. A stimulating look at the pursuits of young adulthood, set in a glittering city notorious for its amorous excesses.

MAN WITH A MAID
$4.95/307-2
The adventures of Jack and Alice have delighted readers for eight decades! A classic of its genre, Man with a Maid tells an outrageous tale of desire, revenge, and submission. This tale qualifies as one of the world's most popular adult novels—with over 200,000 copies in print!

CONFESSIONS OF A CONCUBINE III: PLEASURE'S PRISONER
$5.95/357-0
Filled with pulse-pounding excitement—including a daring escape from the harem and an encounter with an unspeakable sadist—*Pleasure's Prisoner* adds an unforgettable chapter to this thrilling confessional.

CLASSIC EROTIC BIOGRAPHIES

JENNIFER
$4.95/107-1
The return of one of the Sexual Revolution's most notorious heroines. From the bedroom of a notoriously insatiable dancer to an uninhibited ashram, *Jennifer* traces the exploits of one thoroughly modern woman as she lustfully explores the limits of her own sexuality.

JENNIFER III
$5.95/292-2
The further adventures of erotica's most daring heroine. Jennifer, the quintessential beautiful blonde, has a photographer's eye for details—particularly of the masculine variety! One by one, her subjects submit to her demands for sensual pleasure, becoming part of her now-infamous gallery of erotic conquests.

RHINOCEROS

KATHLEEN K.

SWEET TALKERS
$6.95/516-6
Kathleen K. ran a phone-sex company in the late 80s, and she opens up her diary for a very thought provoking peek at the life of a phone-sex operator—and reveals a number of secrets and surprises. Transcripts of actual conversations are included.

"If you enjoy eavesdropping on explicit conversations about sex... this book is for you." —Spectator

"Highly recommended." —Shiny International
Trade /$12.95/192-6

THOMAS S. ROCHE

DARK MATTER
$6.95/484-4
"*Dark Matter* is sure to please gender outlaws, body-mod junkies, goth vampires, boys who wish they were dykes, and anybody who's not to sure where the fine line should be drawn between pleasure and pain. It's a handful." —Pat Califia

"Here is the erotica of the cumming millenium: velvet-voiced but razor-tongued, tarted-up, but smart as a whip behind that smudged black eyeliner—encompassing every conceivable gender and several in between. You will be deliciously disturbed, but never disappointed." —Poppy Z. Brite

NOIROTICA: AN ANTHOLOGY OF EROTIC CRIME STORIES
$6.95/390-2
A collection of darkly sexy tales, taking place at the crossroads of the crime and erotic genres. Thomas S. Roche has gathered together some of today's finest writers of sexual fiction, all of whom explore the murky terrain where desire runs irrevocably afoul of the law.

ROMY ROSEN

SPUNK
$6.95/492-5
A tale of unearthly beauty, outrageous decadence, and brutal exploitation. Casey, a lovely model poised upon the verge of super-celebrity, falls for an insatiable young rock singer—not suspecting that his sexual appetite has led him to experiment with a dangerous new aphrodisiac. Casey becomes an addict, and her craving plunges her into a strange underworld, where bizarre sexual compulsions are indulged behind the most exclusive doors and the only chance for redemption lies with a shadowy young man with a secret of his own.

BUY ANY 4 BOOKS & CHOOSE 1 ADDITIONAL BOOK, OF EQUAL OR LESSER VALUE, AS YOUR FREE GIFT

MASQUERADE BOOKS

MOLLY WEATHERFIELD
CARRIE'S STORY
$6.95/485-2
"I had been Jonathan's slave for about a year when he told me he wanted to sell me at an auction. I wasn't in any condition to respond when he told me this..." Desire and depravity run rampant in this story of uncompromising mastery and irrevocable submission. A unique piece of erotica that is both thoughtful and hot!

"I was stunned by how well it was written and how intensely foreign I found its sexual world.... And, since this is a world I don't frequent... I thoroughly enjoyed the National Geo tour." —bOING bOING

"Hilarious and harrowing... just when you think things can't get any wilder, they do." —Black Sheets

CYBERSEX CONSORTIUM
CYBERSEX: THE PERV'S GUIDE TO FINDING SEX ON THE INTERNET
$6.95/471-2
You've heard the objections: cyberspace is soaked with sex. Okay—so where is it!? Tracking down the good stuff—the real good stuff—can waste an awful lot of expensive time, and frequently leave you high and dry. The Cybersex Consortium presents an easy-to-use guide for those intrepid adults who know what they want. No horny hacker can afford to pass up this map to the kinkiest rest stops on the Info Superhighway.

AMELIA G, EDITOR
BACKSTAGE PASSES
$6.95/438-0
Amelia G, editor of the goth-sex journal *Blue Blood*, has brought together some of today's most irreverant writers, each of whom has outdone themselves with an edgy, real tale of modern lust. Punks, metalheads, and grunge-trash roam the pages of *Backstage Passes*, and no one knows their world better...

GERI NETTICK WITH BETH ELLIOT
MIRRORS: PORTRAIT OF A LESBIAN TRANSSEXUAL
$6.95/435-6
The alternately heartbreaking and empowering story of one woman's long road to full selfhood. Born a male, Geri Nettick knew something just didn't fit. And even after coming to terms with her own gender dysphoria—and taking steps to correct it—she still fought to be accepted by the lesbian feminist community to which she felt she belonged. A fascinating, true tale of struggle and discovery.

DAVID MELTZER
UNDER
$6.95/290-6
The story of a 21st century sex professional living at the bottom of the social heap. After surgeries designed to increase his physical allure, corrupt government forces drive the cyber-gigolo underground—where even more bizarre cultures await him.

ORF
$6.95/110-1
He is the ultimate musician-hero—the idol of thousands, the fevered dream of many more. And like many musicians before him, he is misunderstood, misused—and totally out of control. Every last drop of feeling is squeezed from a modern-day troubadour and his lady love.

LAURA ANTONIOU, EDITOR
NO OTHER TRIBUTE
$6.95/294-9
A collection sure to challenge Political Correctness in a way few have before, with tales of women kept in bondage to their lovers by their deepest passions. Love pushes these women beyond acceptable limits, rendering them helpless to deny anything to the men and women they adore. A volume dedicated to all Slaves of Desire.

SOME WOMEN
$6.95/300-7
Over forty essays written by women actively involved in consensual dominance and submission. Professional mistresses, lifestyle leatherdykes, whipmakers, titleholders—women from every conceivable walk of life lay bare their true feelings about explosive issues.

BY HER SUBDUED
$6.95/281-7
These tales all involve women in control—of their lives, their loves, their men. So much in control that they can remorselessly break rules to become powerful goddesses of the men who sacrifice all to worship at their feet.

TRISTAN TAORMINO & DAVID AARON CLARK, EDITORS
RITUAL SEX
$6.95/391-0
While many people believe the body and soul to occupy almost completely independent realms, the many contributors to *Ritual Sex* know—and demonstrate—that the two share more common ground than society feels comfortable acknowledging. From personal memoirs of ecstatic revelation, to fictional quests to reconcile sex and spirit, *Ritual Sex* provides an unprecedented look at private life.

TAMMY JO ECKHART
PUNISHMENT FOR THE CRIME
$6.95/427-5
Peopled by characters of rare depth, these stories explore the true meaning of dominance and submission. From an encounter between two of society's most despised individuals, to the explorations of longtime friends, these tales take you where few others have ever dared....

AMARANTHA KNIGHT, EDITOR
SEDUCTIVE SPECTRES
$6.95/464-X
Breathtaking tours through the erotic supernatural via the macabre imaginations of today's best writers. Never before have ghostly encounters been so alluring, thanks to a cast of otherworldly characters well-acquainted with the pleasures of the flesh.

MASQUERADE BOOKS

SEX MACABRE
$6.95/392-9
Horror tales designed for dark and sexy nights. Amarantha Knight—the woman behind the Darker Passions series—has gathered together erotic stories sure to make your skin crawl, and heart beat faster.

FLESH FANTASTIC
$6.95/352-X
Humans have long toyed with the idea of "playing God": creating life from nothingness, bringing life to the inanimate. Now Amarantha Knight collects stories exploring not only the act of Creation, but the lust that follows....

GARY BOWEN
DIARY OF A VAMPIRE
$6.95/331-7
"Gifted with a darkly sensual vision and a fresh voice, [Bowen] is a writer to watch out for."
—Cecilia Tan
Rafael, a red-blooded male with an insatiable hunger for the same, is the perfect antidote to the effete malcontents haunting bookstores today. The emergence of a bold and brilliant vision, rooted in past and present.

RENÉ MAIZEROY
FLESHLY ATTRACTIONS
$6.95/299-X
Lucien was the son of the wantonly beautiful actress, Marie-Rose Hardanges. When she decides to let a "friend" introduce her son to the pleasures of love, Marie-Rose could not have foretold the excesses that would lead to her own ruin and that of her cherished son.

JEAN STINE
THRILL CITY
$6.95/411-9
Thrill City is the seat of the world's increasing depravity, and this classic novel transports you there with a vivid style you'd be hard pressed to ignore. No writer is better suited to describe the extremes of this modern Babylon.

SEASON OF THE WITCH
$6.95/268-X
"A future in which it is technically possible to transfer the total mind...of a rapist killer into the brain dead but physically living body of his female victim. Remarkable for intense psychological technique. There is eroticism but it is necessary to mark the differences between the sexes and the subtle altering of a man into a woman." —The Science Fiction Critic

GRANT ANTREWS
MY DARLING DOMINATRIX
$6.95/447-X
When a man and a woman fall in love, it's supposed to be simple and uncomplicated—unless that woman happens to be a dominatrix. Curiosity gives way to desire in this story of one man's awakening to the joys of willing slavery.

JOHN WARREN
THE TORQUEMADA KILLER
$6.95/367-8
Detective Eva Hernandez gets her first "big case": a string of vicious murders taking place within New York's SM community. Eva assembles the evidence, revealing a picture of a world misunderstood and under attack—and gradually comes to understand her own place within it.

THE LOVING DOMINANT
$6.95/218-3
Everything you need to know about an infamous sexual variation—and an unspoken type of love. Mentor—a longtime player in scene—guides readers through this world and reveals the too-often hidden basis of the D/S relationship: care, trust and love.

LAURA ANTONIOU WRITING AS "SARA ADAMSON"
THE TRAINER
$6.95/249-3
The Marketplace—the ultimate underground sexual realm includes not only willing slaves, but the exquisite trainers who take submissives firmly in hand. And now these mentors divulge the desires that led them to become the ultimate figures of authority.

THE SLAVE
$6.95/173-X
This second volume in the "Marketplace" trilogy further elaborates the world of slaves and masters. One talented submissive longs to join the ranks of those who have proven themselves worthy of entry into the Marketplace. But the delicious price is staggeringly high....

THE MARKETPLACE
$6.95/3096-2
"Merchandise does not come easily to the Marketplace.... They haunt the clubs and the organizations.... Some are so ripe that they intimidate the poseurs, the weekend sadists and the furtive dilettantes who are so endemic to that world. And they never stop asking where we may be found...."

DAVID AARON CLARK
SISTER RADIANCE
$6.95/215-9
Rife with Clark's trademark vivisections of contemporary desires, sacred and profane. The vicissitudes of lust and romance are examined against a backdrop of urban decay in this testament to the allure of the forbidden.

THE WET FOREVER
$6.95/117-9
The story of Janus and Madchen—a small-time hood and a beautiful sex worker on the run from one of the most dangerous men they have ever known—The Wet Forever examines themes of loyalty, sacrifice, redemption and obsession amidst Manhattan's sex parlors and underground S/M clubs. Its combination of sex and suspense led Terence Sellers to proclaim it "evocative and poetic."

BUY ANY 4 BOOKS & CHOOSE 1 ADDITIONAL BOOK, OF EQUAL OR LESSER VALUE, AS YOUR FREE GIFT

MASQUERADE BOOKS

MICHAEL PERKINS
EVIL COMPANIONS
$6.95/3067-9
Set in New York City during the tumultuous waning years of the Sixties, *Evil Companions* has been hailed as "a frightening classic." A young couple explores the nether reaches of the erotic unconscious in a shocking confrontation with the extremes of passion.

THE SECRET RECORD: MODERN EROTIC LITERATURE
$6.95/3039-0
Michael Perkins surveys the field with authority and unique insight. Updated and revised to include the latest trends, tastes, and developments in this misunderstood and maligned genre.

AN ANTHOLOGY OF CLASSIC ANONYMOUS EROTIC WRITING
$6.95/140-3
Michael Perkins has collected the very best passages from the world's erotic writing. "Anonymous" is one of the most infamous bylines in publishing history—and these steamy excerpts show why! Includes excerpts from some of the most famous titles in the history of erotic literature.

LIESEL KULIG
LOVE IN WARTIME
$6.95/3044-X
Madeleine knew that the handsome SS officer was a dangerous man, but she was just a cabaret singer in Nazi-occupied Paris, trying to survive in a perilous time. When Josef fell in love with her, he discovered that a beautiful woman can sometimes be as dangerous as any warrior.

HELEN HENLEY
ENTER WITH TRUMPETS
$6.95/197-7
Helen Henley was told that women just don't write about sex—much less the taboos she was so interested in exploring. So Henley did it alone, flying in the face of "tradition" by writing this touching tale of arousal and devotion in one couple's kinky relationship.

ALICE JOANOU
BLACK TONGUE
$6.95/258-2
"Joanou has created a series of sumptuous, brooding, dark visions of sexual obsession, and is undoubtedly a name to look out for in the future."
—*Redeemer*
Exploring lust at its most florid and unsparing, *Black Tongue* is a trove of baroque fantasies—each redolent of forbidden passions. Joanou creates some of erotica's most mesmerizing and unforgettable characters.

TOURNIQUET
$6.95/3060-1
A heady collection of stories and effusions from the pen of one our most dazzling young writers. Strange tales abound, from the story of the mysterious and cruel Cybele, to an encounter with the sadistic entertainment of a bizarre after-hours cafe. A complex and riveting series of meditations on desire.

CANNIBAL FLOWER
$4.95/72-8
The provocative debut volume from this acclaimed writer. "She is waiting in her darkened bedroom, as she has waited throughout history, to seduce the men who are foolish enough to be blinded by her irresistible charms.... She is the goddess of sexuality, and *Cannibal Flower* is her haunting siren song."
—Michael Perkins

PHILIP JOSÉ FARMER
A FEAST UNKNOWN
$6.95/276-0
"Sprawling, brawling, shocking, suspenseful, hilarious..."
—Theodore Sturgeon
Farmer's supreme anti-hero returns. "I was conceived and born in 1888." Slowly, Lord Grandrith—armed with the belief that he is the son of Jack the Ripper—tells the story of his remarkable and unbridled life. His story begins with his discovery of the secret of immortality—and progresses to encompass the furthest extremes of human behavior.

THE IMAGE OF THE BEAST
$6.95/166-7
Herald Childe has seen Hell, glimpsed its horror in an act of sexual mutilation. Childe must now find and destroy an inhuman predator through the streets of a polluted and decadent Los Angeles of the future. One clue after another leads Childe to an inescapable realization about the nature of sex and evil....

DANIEL VIAN
ILLUSIONS
$6.95/3074-1
Two tales of danger and desire in Berlin on the eve of WWII. From private homes to lurid cafés, passion is exposed in stark contrast to the brutal violence of the time, as desperate people explore their deepest, darkest sexual desires.

SAMUEL R. DELANY
THE MAD MAN
$8.99/408-9
"Reads like a pornographic reflection of Peter Ackroyd's *Chatterton* or A. S. Byatt's *Possession*.... Delany develops an insightful dichotomy between [his protagonist]'s two worlds: the one of cerebral philosophy and dry academia, the other of heedless, 'impersonal' obsessive sexual extremism. When these worlds finally collide...the novel achieves a surprisingly satisfying resolution...." —*Publishers Weekly*

For his thesis, graduate student John Marr researches the life of Timothy Hasler: a philosopher whose career was cut tragically short over a decade earlier. On another front, Marr finds himself increasingly drawn toward shocking, depraved sexual entanglements with the homeless men of his neighborhood, until it begins to seem that Hasler's death might hold some key to his own life as a gay man in the age of AIDS. Unquestionably one of Delany's most shocking works, *The Mad Man* is one of American erotic literature's most transgressive titles.

MASQUERADE BOOKS

EQUINOX
$6.95/157-8
The Scorpion has sailed the seas in a quest for every possible pleasure. Her crew is a collection of the young, the twisted, the insatiable. A drifter comes into their midst and is taken on a fantastic journey to the darkest, most dangerous sexual extremes—until he is finally a victim to their boundless appetites. An early title that set the way for the author's later explorations of extreme, forbidden sexual behaviors. Long out of print, this disturbing tale is finally available under the author's original title.

ANDREI CODRESCU
THE REPENTANCE OF LORRAINE
$6.95/329-5
"One of our most prodigiously talented and magical writers." —*NYT Book Review*
By the acclaimed author of *The Hole in the Flag* and *The Blood Countess*. An aspiring writer, a professor's wife, a secretary, gold anklets, Maoists, Roman harlots—and more—swirl through this spicy tale of a harried quest for a mythic artifact. Written when the author was a young man, this lusty yarn was inspired by the heady days of the Sixties. Includes a new introduction by the author, detailing the events that inspired *Lorraine*'s creation. A touching, arousing product from a more innocent time.

TUPPY OWENS
SENSATIONS
$6.95/3081-1
Tuppy Owens tells the unexpurgated story of the making of *Sensations*—the first big-budget sex flick. Originally commissioned to appear in book form after the release of the film in 1975, *Sensations* is finally released under Masquerade's stylish Rhino*eros* imprint.

SOPHIE GALLEYMORE BIRD
MANEATER
$6.95/103-9
Through a bizarre act of creation, a man attains the "perfect" lover—by all appearances a beautiful, sensuous woman, but in reality something far darker. Once brought to life she will accept no mate, seeking instead the prey that will sate her hunger for vengeance.

LEOPOLD VON SACHER-MASOCH
VENUS IN FURS
$6.95/3089-X
This classic 19th century novel is the first uncompromising exploration of the dominant/submissive relationship in literature. The alliance of Severin and Wanda epitomizes Sacher-Masoch's dark obsession with a cruel, controlling goddess and the urges that drive the man held in her thrall. This special edition includes the letters exchanged between Sacher-Masoch and Emilie Mataja, an aspiring writer he sought to cast as the avatar of the forbidden desires expressed in his most famous work.

BADBOY

WILLIAM J. MANN, EDITOR
GRAVE PASSIONS
$6.50/405-4
A collection of the most chilling tales of passion currently being penned by today's most provocative gay writers. Unnatural transformations, otherworldly encounters, and deathless desires make for a collection sure to keep readers up late at night—for a variety of reasons!

J. A. GUERRA, EDITOR
COME QUICKLY: FOR BOYS ON THE GO
$6.50/413-5
Here are over sixty of the hottest fantasies around—all designed to get you going in less time than it takes to dial 976. Julian Anthony Guerra, the editor behind the phenomenally popular *Men at Work* and *Badboy Fantasies*, has put together this volume especially for you—a busy man on a modern schedule, who still appreciates a little old-fashioned action.

JOHN PRESTON
HUSTLING: A GENTLEMAN'S GUIDE TO THE FINE ART OF HOMOSEXUAL PROSTITUTION
$6.50/517-4
The very first guide to the gay world's most infamous profession. John Preston solicited the advice and opinions of "working boys" from across the country in his effort to produce the ultimate guide to the hustler's world. *Hustling* covers every practical aspect of the business, from clientele and payment options to "specialties," sidelines and drawbacks. No stone is left unturned—and no wrong turn left unadmonished—in this guidebook to the ins and outs of this much-mythologized trade.

"...Unrivalled. For any man even vaguely contemplating going into business this tome has got to be the first port of call." —*Divinity*

"Fun and highly literary. What more could you expect form such an accomplished activist, author and editor?" —*Drummer*
Trade $12.95/137-3

MR. BENSON
$4.95/3041-5
A classic erotic novel from a time when there was no limit to what a man could dream of doing.... Jamie is an aimless young man lucky enough to encounter Mr. Benson. He is soon led down the path of erotic enlightenment, learning to accept this man as his master. Jamie's incredible adventures never fail to excite—especially when the going gets rough! One of the first runaway bestsellers in gay erotic literature, *Mr. Benson* returns to capture the imagination of a new generation.

BUY ANY 4 BOOKS & CHOOSE 1 ADDITIONAL BOOK, OF EQUAL OR LESSER VALUE, AS YOUR FREE GIFT

MASQUERADE BOOKS

TALES FROM THE DARK LORD
$5.95/323-6
A new collection of twelve stunning works from the man *Lambda Book Report* called "the Dark Lord of gay erotica." The relentless ritual of lust and surrender is explored in all its manifestations in this heart-stopping triumph of authority and vision from the Dark Lord!

TALES FROM THE DARK LORD II
$4.95/176-4
The second volume of John Preston's masterful short stories. Includes an interview with the author, and a sexy screenplay written for pornstar Scott O'Hara.

THE ARENA
$4.95/3083-0
There is a place on the edge of fantasy where every desire is indulged with abandon. Men go there to unleash beasts, to let demons roam free, to abolish all limits. At the center of each tale are the men who serve there, who offer themselves for the consummation of any passion, whose own bottomless urges compel their endless subservience. The thrilling tale of the ultimate erotic club, brought to vivid life by anw of gay erotica's masters.

THE HEIR•THE KING
$4.95/3048-2
The ground-breaking novel *The Heir*, written in the lyric voice of the ancient myths, tells the story of a world where slaves and masters create a new sexual society. This edition also includes a completely original work, *The King*, the story of a soldier who discovers his monarch's most secret desires. A special double volume, available only from Badboy.

....

THE MISSION OF ALEX KANE

SWEET DREAMS
$4.95/3062-8
It's the triumphant return of gay action hero Alex Kane! In *Sweet Dreams*, Alex travels to Boston where he takes on a street gang that stalks gay teenagers. Mighty Alex Kane wreaks a fierce and terrible vengeance on those who prey on gay people everywhere!

GOLDEN YEARS
$4.95/3069-5
When evil threatens the plans of a group of older gay men, Kane's got the muscle to take it head on. Along the way, he wins the support—and very specialized attentions—of a cowboy plucked right out of the Old West. But Kane and the Cowboy have a surprise waiting for them....

DEADLY LIES
$4.95/3076-8
Politics is a dirty business and the dirt becomes deadly when a political smear campaign targets gay men. Who better to clean things up than Alex Kane! Alex comes to protect the dreams, and lives, of gay men imperiled by lies and deceit.

STOLEN MOMENTS
$4.95/3098-9
Houston's evolving gay community is victimized by a malicious newspaper editor who is more than willing to sacrifice gays on the altar of circulation. He never counted on Alex Kane, fearless defender of gay dreams and desires.

SECRET DANGER
$4.95/111-X
Homophobia: a pernicious social ill not confined by America's borders. Alex Kane and the faithful Danny are called to a small European country, where a group of gay tourists is being held hostage by ruthless terrorists. Luckily, the Mission of Alex Kane stands as firm foreign policy.

LETHAL SILENCE
$4.95/125-X
The Mission of Alex Kane thunders to a conclusion. Chicago becomes the scene of the right-wing's most noxious plan—facilitated by unholy political alliances. Alex and Danny head to the Windy City to do battle with the mercenaries who would squash gay men underfoot.

....

MATT TOWNSEND

SOLIDLY BUILT
$6.50/416-X
The tale of the tumultuous relationship between Jeff, a young photographer, and Mark, the butch electrician hired to wire Jeff's new home. For Jeff, it's love at first sight; Mark, however, has more than a few hang-ups. Soon, both are forced to reevaluate their outlooks, and are assisted by a variety of hot men....

....

JAY SHAFFER

SHOOTERS
$5.95/284-1
No mere catalog of random acts, *Shooters* tells the stories of a variety of stunning men and the ways they connect in sexual and non-sexual ways. A virtuoso storyteller, Shaffer always gets his man.

ANIMAL HANDLERS
$4.95/264-7
In Shaffer's world, each and every man finally succumbs to the animal urges deep inside. And if there's any creature that promises a wild time, it's a beast who's been caged for far too long. Shaffer has one of the keenest eyes for the nuances of male passion.

FULL SERVICE
$4.95/150-0
Wild men build up steam until they finally let loose. No-nonsense guys bear down hard on each other as they work their way toward release in this finely detailed assortment of masculine fantasies. One of gay erotica's most insightful chroniclers of male passion.

....

D. V. SADERO

IN THE ALLEY
$4.95/144-6
Hardworking men—from cops to carpenters—bring their own special skills and impressive tools to the most satisfying job of all: capturing and breaking the male sexual beast. Hot, incisive and way over the top, D.V. Sadero's imagination breathes fresh life into some of the genre's most traditional situations. One of the new generation's most exhilarating voices.

MASQUERADE BOOKS

SCOTT O'HARA
DO-IT-YOURSELF PISTON POLISHING
$6.50/489-5
Longtime sex-pro Scott O'Hara draws upon his acute powers of seduction to lure you into a world of hard, horny men long overdue for a tune-up. Pretty soon, you'll pop your own hood for the servicing you know you need....

SUTTER POWELL
EXECUTIVE PRIVILEGES
$6.50/383-X
No matter how serious or sexy a predicament his characters find themselves in, Powell conveys the sheer exuberance of their encounters with a warm humor rarely seen in contemporary gay erotica.

GARY BOWEN
WESTERN TRAILS
$6.50/477-1
A wild roundup of tales devoted to life on the lone prairie. Gary Bowen—a writer well-versed in the Western genre—has collected the very best contemporary cowboy stories. Some of gay literature's brightest stars tell the sexy truth about the many ways a rugged stud found to satisfy himself—and his buddy—in the Very Wild West.

MAN HUNGRY
$5.95/374-0
By the author of *Diary of a Vampire*. A riveting collection of stories from one of gay erotica's new stars. Dipping into a variety of genres, Bowen crafts tales of lust unlike anything being published today.

KYLE STONE
HOT BAUDS 2
$6.50/479-8
Another collection of cyberfantasies—compiled by the inimitable Kyle Stone. After the success of the original *Hot Bauds*, Stone conducted another heated search through the world's randiest bulletin boards, resulting in one of the most scalding follow-ups ever published. Here's all the scandalous stuff you've heard so much about—sexy, shameless, and eminently user-friendly.

FIRE & ICE
$5.95/297-3
A collection of stories from the author of the infamous adventures of PB 500. Randy, powerful, and just plain bad, Stone's characters always promise one thing: enough hot action to burn away your desire for anyone else....

HOT BAUDS
$5.95/285-X
The author of *Fantasy Board* and *The Initiation of PB 500* combed cyberspace for the hottest fantasies of the world's horniest hackers. Stone has assembled the first collection of the raunchy erotica so many gay men cruise the Information Superhighway for.

FANTASY BOARD
$4.95/212-4
The author of the scalding sci-fi adventures of PB 500 explores the more foreseeable future—through the intertwined lives (and private parts) of a collection of randy computer hackers. On the Lambda Gate BBS, every hot and horny male is in search of a little virtual satisfaction—and is certain to find even more than he'd hoped for!

THE CITADEL
$4.95/198-5
The sequel to *The Initiation of PB 500*. Having proven himself worthy of his stunning master, Micah—now known only as '500'—will face new challenges and hardships after his entry into the forbidding Citadel. Only his master knows what awaits—and whether Micah will again distinguish himself as the perfect instrument of pleasure....

THE INITIATION OF PB 500
$4.95/141-1
He is a stranger on their planet, unschooled in their language, and ignorant of their customs. But this man, Micah—now known only by his number—will soon be trained in every last detail of erotic personal service. And, once nurtured and transformed into the perfect physical specimen, he must begin proving himself worthy of the master who has chosen him....

RITUALS
$4.95/168-3
Via a computer bulletin board, a young man finds himself drawn into a series of sexual rites that transform him into the willing slave of a mysterious stranger. Gradually, all vestiges of his former life are thrown off, and he learns to live for his Master's touch....

ROBERT BAHR
SEX SHOW
$4.95/225-6
Luscious dancing boys. Brazen, explicit acts. Unending stimulation. Take a seat, and get very comfortable, because the curtain's going up on a show no discriminating appetite can afford to miss.

JASON FURY
THE ROPE ABOVE, THE BED BELOW
$4.95/269-8
The irresistible Jason Fury returns—this time, telling the tale of a vicious murderer preying upon New York's go-go boy population. No one is who or what they seem, and in order to solve this mystery and save lives, each studly suspect must lay bare his soul—and more!

ERIC'S BODY
$4.95/151-9
Meet Jason Fury—blond, blue-eyed and up for anything. Fury's sexiest tales are collected in book form for the first time. Follow the irresistible Jason through sexual adventures unlike any you have ever read....

BUY ANY 4 BOOKS & CHOOSE 1 ADDITIONAL BOOK, OF EQUAL OR LESSER VALUE, AS YOUR FREE GIFT

MASQUERADE BOOKS

1 800 906-HUNK

THE connection for hot handfuls of eager guys! No credit card needed—so call now for access to the hottest party line available. Spill it all to bad boys from across the country! (Must be over 18.) Pick one up now.... **$3.98 per min.**

LARS EIGHNER

WHISPERED IN THE DARK
$5.95/286-8
A volume demonstrating Eighner's unique combination of strengths: poetic descriptive power, an unfailing ear for dialogue, and a finely tuned feeling for the nuances of male passion.

AMERICAN PRELUDE
$4.95/170-5
Eighner is widely recognized as one of our best, most exciting gay writers. He is also one of gay erotica's true masters—and *American Prelude* shows why. Wonderfully written, blisteringly hot tales of all-American lust.

B.M.O.C.
$4.95/3077-6
In a college town known as "the Athens of the Southwest," studs of every stripe are up all night—studying, naturally. Relive university life the way it was supposed to be, with a cast of handsome honor students majoring in Human Homosexuality.

DAVID LAURENTS, EDITOR

SOUTHERN COMFORT
$6.50/466-6
Editor David Laurents now unleashes a collection of tales focusing on the American South—reflecting not only Southern literary tradition, but the many contributions the region has made to the iconography of the American Male.

WANDERLUST: HOMOEROTIC TALES OF TRAVEL
$5.95/395-3
A volume dedicated to the special pleasures of faraway places. Gay men have always had a special interest in travel—and not only for the scenic vistas. *Wanderlust* celebrates the freedom of the open road, and the allure of men who stray from the beaten path....

THE BADBOY BOOK OF EROTIC POETRY
$5.95/382-1
Over fifty of today's best poets. Erotic poetry has long been the problem child of the literary world—highly creative and provocative, but somehow too frank to be "literature." Both learned and stimulating, *The Badboy Book of Erotic Poetry* restores eros to its rightful place of honor in contemporary gay writing.

AARON TRAVIS

BIG SHOTS
$5.95/448-8
Two fierce tales in one electrifying volume. In *Beirut*, Travis tells the story of ultimate military power and erotic subjugation; *Kip*, Travis' hypersexed and sinister take on film noir, appears in unexpurgated form for the first time.

EXPOSED
$4.95/126-8
A volume of shorter Travis tales, each providing a unique glimpse of the horny gay male in his natural environment! Cops, college jocks, ancient Romans—even Sherlock Holmes and his loyal Watson—cruise these pages, fresh from the throbbing pen of one of our hottest authors.

BEAST OF BURDEN
$4.95/105-5
Five ferocious tales. Innocents surrender to the brutal sexual mastery of their superiors, as taboos are shattered and replaced with the unwritten rules of masculine conquest. Intense, extreme—and totally Travis.

IN THE BLOOD
$5.95/283-3
Written when Travis had just begun to explore the true power of the erotic imagination, these stories laid the groundwork for later masterpieces. Among the many rewarding rarities included in this volume: "In the Blood" —a heart-pounding descent into sexual vampirism, written with the furious erotic power that is Travis' trademark.

THE FLESH FABLES
$4.95/243-4
One of Travis' best collections. *The Flesh Fables* includes "Blue Light," his most famous story, as well as other masterpieces that established him as the erotic writer to watch. And watch carefully, because Travis always buries a surprise somewhere beneath his scorching detail....

SLAVES OF THE EMPIRE
$4.95/3054-7
"A wonderful mythic tale. Set against the backdrop of the exotic and powerful Roman Empire, this wonderfully written novel explores the timeless questions of light and dark in male sexuality. The locale may be the ancient world, but these are the slaves and masters of our time...."
—John Preston

BOB VICKERY

SKIN DEEP
$4.95/265-5
So many varied beauties no one will go away unsatisfied. No tantalizing morsel of manflesh is overlooked—or left unexplored! Beauty may be only skin deep, but a handful of beautiful skin is a tempting proposition.

JR

FRENCH QUARTER NIGHTS
$5.95/337-6
Sensual snapshots of the many places where men get down and dirty—from the steamy French Quarter to the steam room at the old Everard baths. These are nights you'll wish would go on forever....

TOM BACCHUS

RAHM
$5.95/315-5
The imagination of Tom Bacchus brings to life an extraordinary assortment of characters, from the Father of Us All to the cowpoke next door, the early gay literati to rude, queercore mosh rats. No one is better than Bacchus at staking out sexual territory with a swagger and a sly grin.

MASQUERADE BOOKS

BONE
$4.95/177-2
Queer musings from the pen of one of today's hottest young talents. A fresh outlook on fleshly indulgence yields more than a few pleasant surprises. Horny Tom Bacchus maps out the tricking ground of a new generation.

KEY LINCOLN
SUBMISSION HOLDS
$4.95/266-3
A bright young talent unleashes his first collection of gay erotica. From tough to tender, the men between these covers stop at nothing to get what they want. These sweat-soaked tales show just how bad boys can really get.

CALDWELL/EIGHNER
QSFX2
$5.95/278-7
The wickedest, wildest, other-worldliest yarns from two master storytellers—Clay Caldwell and Lars Eighner. Both eroticists take a trip to the furthest reaches of the sexual imagination, sending back ten stories proving that as much as things change, one thing will always remain the same....

CLAY CALDWELL
ASK OL' BUDDY
$5.95/346-5
Set in the underground SM world, Caldwell takes you on a journey of discovery—where men initiate one another into the secrets of the rawest sexual realm of all. And when each stud's initiation is complete, he takes his places among the masters—eager to take part in the training of another hungry soul...

STUD SHORTS
$5.95/320-1
"If anything, Caldwell's charm is more powerful, his nostalgia more poignant, the horniness he captures more sweetly, achingly acute than ever."
—Aaron Travis
A new collection of this legend's latest sex-fiction. With his customary candor, Caldwell tells all about cops, cadets, truckers, farmboys (and many more) in these dirty jewels.

TAILPIPE TRUCKER
$5.95/296-5
Trucker porn! In prose as free and unvarnished as a cross-country highway, Caldwell tells the truth about Trag and Curly—two men hot for the feeling of sweaty manflesh. Together, they pick up—and turn out—a couple of thrill-seeking punks.

SERVICE, STUD
$5.95/336-8
Another look at the gay future. The setting is the Los Angeles of a distant future. Here the all-male populace is divided between the served and the servants—guaranteeing the erotic satisfaction of all involved.

QUEERS LIKE US
$4.95/262-0
"Caldwell at his most charming." —Aaron Travis
For years the name Clay Caldwell has been synonymous with the hottest, most finely crafted gay tales available. *Queers Like Us* is one of his best: the story of a randy mailman's trek through a landscape of willing, available studs.

ALL-STUD
$4.95/104-7
This classic, sex-soaked tale takes place under the watchful eye of Number Ten: an omniscient figure who has decreed unabashed promiscuity as the law of his all-male land. One stud, however, takes it upon himself to challenge the social order, daring to fall in love. Finally, he is forced to fight for not only himself, but the man he loves.

CLAY CALDWELL AND AARON TRAVIS
TAG TEAM STUDS
$6.50/465-8
Thrilling tales from these two legendary eroticists. The wrestling world will never seem the same, once you've made your way through this assortment of sweaty, virile studs. But you'd better be wary—should one catch you off guard, you just might spend the rest of the night pinned to the mat....

LARRY TOWNSEND
LEATHER AD: S
$5.95/407-0
The second half of Townsend's acclaimed tale of lust through the personals—this time told from a Top's perspective. A simple ad generates many responses, and one man finds himself in the enviable position of putting these studly applicants through their paces.....

LEATHER AD: M
$5.95/380-5
The first of this two-part classic. John's curious about what goes on between the leatherclad men he's fantasized about. He takes out a personal ad, and starts a journey of self-discovery that will leave no part of his life unchanged.

1 900 745-HUNG

Hardcore phone action for real men. A scorching assembly of studs is waiting for your call—and eager to give you the headtrip of your life! Totally live, guaranteed one-on-one encounters. (Must be over 18.) No credit card needed. $3.98 per minute.

BEWARE THE GOD WHO SMILES
$5.95/321-X
Two lusty young Americans are transported to ancient Egypt—where they are embroiled in regional warfare and taken as slaves by marauding barbarians. The key to escape from this brutal bondage lies in their own rampant libidos, and urges as old as time itself.

BUY ANY 4 BOOKS & CHOOSE 1 ADDITIONAL BOOK, OF EQUAL OR LESSER VALUE, AS YOUR FREE GIFT

MASQUERADE BOOKS

2069 TRILOGY
(This one-volume collection only $6.95) 244-2
For the first time, Larry Townsend's early science-fiction trilogy appears in one massive volume! Set in a future world, the *2069 Trilogy* includes the tight plotting and shameless male sexual pleasure that established him as one of gay erotica's first masters.

MIND MASTER
$4.95/209-4
Who better to explore the territory of erotic dominance than an author who helped define the genre—and knows that ultimate mastery always transcends the physical. Another unrelenting Townsend tale.

THE LONG LEATHER CORD
$4.95/201-9
Chuck's stepfather never lacks money or clandestine male visitors with whom he enacts intense sexual rituals. As Chuck comes to terms with his own desires, he begins to unravel the mystery behind his stepfather's secret life.

MAN SWORD
$4.95/188-8
The très gai tale of France's King Henri III, who was unimaginably spoiled by his mother—the infamous Catherine de Medici—and groomed from a young age to assume the throne of France. Along the way, he encounters enough sexual schemers and politicos to alter one's picture of history forever!

THE FAUSTUS CONTRACT
$4.95/167-5
Two attractive young men desperately need $1000. Will do anything. Travel OK. Danger OK. Call anytime... Two cocky young hustlers get more than they bargained for in this story of lust and its discontents.

THE GAY ADVENTURES OF CAPTAIN GOOSE
$4.95/169-1
Hot young Jerome Gander is sentenced to serve aboard the *H.M.S. Faerigold*—a ship manned by the most hardened, unrepentant criminals. In no time, Gander becomes well-versed in the ways of horny men at sea, and the *Faerigold* becomes the most notorious vessel to ever set sail.

CHAINS
$4.95/158-6
Picking up street punks has always been risky, but in Larry Townsend's classic *Chains*, it sets off a string of events that must be read to be believed.

KISS OF LEATHER
$4.95/161-6
A look at the acts and attitudes of an earlier generation of gay leathermen, *Kiss of Leather* is full to bursting with the gritty, raw action that has distinguished Townsend's work for years. Sensual pain and pleasure mix in this tightly plotted tale.

RUN, LITTLE LEATHER BOY
$4.95/143-8
One young man's sexual awakening. A chronic underachiever, Wayne seems to be going nowhere fast. He finds himself bored with the everyday—and drawn to the masculine intensity of a dark and mysterious sexual underground, where he soon finds many goals worth pursuing....

RUN NO MORE
$4.95/152-7
The continuation of Larry Townsend's legendary *Run, Little Leather Boy*. This volume follows the further adventures of Townsend's leatherclad narrator as he travels every sexual byway available to the S/M male.

THE SCORPIUS EQUATION
$4.95/119-5
The story of a man caught between the demands of two galactic empires. Our randy hero must match wits—and more—with the incredible forces that rule his world.

THE SEXUAL ADVENTURES OF SHERLOCK HOLMES
$4.95/3097-0
A scandalously sexy take on this legendary sleuth. "A Study in Scarlet" is transformed to expose Mrs. Hudson as a man in drag, the Diogenes Club as an S/M arena, and clues only the redoubtable—and very horny—Sherlock Holmes could piece together. A baffling tale of sex and mystery.

DONALD VINING

CABIN FEVER AND OTHER STORIES
$5.95/338-4
Eighteen blistering stories in celebration of the most intimate of male bonding. Time after time, Donald Vining's men succumb to nature, and reaffirm both love and lust in modern gay life.

"Demonstrates the wisdom experience combined with insight and optimism can create."
—Bay Area Reporter

DEREK ADAMS

PRISONER OF DESIRE
$6.50/439-9
Scalding fiction from one of Badboy's most popular authors. The creator of horny P.I. Miles Diamond returns with this volume bursting with red-blooded, sweat-soaked excursions through the modern gay libido.

THE MARK OF THE WOLF
$5.95/361-9
I turned to look at the man who stared back at me from the mirror. The familiar outlines of my face seemed coarser, more sinister. An animal? The past comes back to haunt one well-off stud, whose unslakeable thirsts lead him into the arms of many men—and the midst of a perilous mystery.

MY DOUBLE LIFE
$5.95/314-7
Every man leads a double life, dividing his hours between the mundanities of the day and the outrageous pursuits of the night. The creator of sexy P.I. Miles Diamond shines a little light on the wicked things men do when no one's looking.

HEAT WAVE
$4.95/159-4
"His body was draped in baggy clothes, but there was hardly any doubt that they covered anything less than perfection.... His slacks were cinched tight around a narrow waist, and the rise of flesh pushing against the thin fabric promised a firm, melon-shaped ass...."

MASQUERADE BOOKS

MILES DIAMOND AND THE DEMON OF DEATH
$4.95/251-5
Derek Adams' gay gumshoe returns for further adventures. Miles always find himself in the stickiest situations—with any stud whose path he crosses! His adventures with "The Demon of Death" promise another carnal carnival.

THE ADVENTURES OF MILES DIAMOND
$4.95/118-7
The debut of Miles Diamond—Derek Adams' take on the classic American archetype of the hardboiled private eye. "The Case of the Missing Twin" promises to be a most rewarding case, packed as it is with randy studs. Miles sets about uncovering all as he tracks down the elusive and delectable Daniel Travis.

KELVIN BELIELE
IF THE SHOE FITS
$4.95/223-X
An essential and winning volume of tales exploring a world where randy boys can't help but do what comes naturally—as often as possible! Sweaty male bodies grapple in pleasure, proving the old adage: if the shoe fits, one might as well slip right in....

JAMES MEDLEY
THE REVOLUTIONARY & OTHER STORIES
$6.50/417-8
Billy, the son of the station chief of the American Embassy in Guatemala, is kidnapped and held for ransom. Frightened at first, Billy gradually develops an unimaginably close relationship with Juan, the revolutionary assigned to guard him.

HUCK AND BILLY
$4.95/245-0
Young love is always the sweetest, always the most sorrowful. Young lust, on the other hand, knows no bounds—as is often the hottest of one's life! Huck and Billy explore the desires that course through their young male bodies, determined to plumb the lusty depths of passion.

FLEDERMAUS
FLEDERFICTION:
STORIES OF MEN AND TORTURE
$5.95/355-4
Fifteen blistering paeans to men and their suffering. Fledermaus unleashes his most thrilling tales of punishment in this special volume designed with Badboy readers in mind.

VICTOR TERRY
MASTERS
$6.50/418-6
A powerhouse volume of boot-wearing, whip-wielding, bone-crunching bruisers who've got what it takes to make a grown man grovel. Between these covers lurk the most demanding of men—the imperious few to whom so many humbly offer themselves....

SM/SD
$6.50/406-2
Set around a South Dakota town called Prairie, these tales offer compelling evidence that the real rough stuff can still be found where men roam free of the restraints of "polite" society—and take what they want despite all rules.

WHiPs
$4.95/254-X
Connoisseurs of gay writing have known Victor Terry's work for some time. Cruising for a hot man? You'd better be, because one way or another, these WHiPs—officers of the Wyoming Highway Patrol—are gonna pull you over for a little impromptu interrogation....

MAX EXANDER
DEEDS OF THE NIGHT:
TALES OF EROS AND PASSION
$5.95/348-1
MAXimum porn! Exander's a writer who's seen it all—and is more than happy to describe every inch of it in pulsating detail. A whirlwind tour of the hypermasculine libido.

LEATHERSEX
$4.95/210-8
Hard-hitting tales from merciless Max Exander. This time he focuses on the leatherclad lust that draws together only the most willing and talented of tops and bottoms—for an all-out orgy of limitless surrender and control....

MANSEX
$4.95/160-8
"Mark was the classic leatherman: a huge, dark stud in chaps, with a big black moustache, hairy chest and enormous muscles. Exactly the kind of men Todd liked—strong, hunky, masculine, ready to take control...."

TOM CAFFREY
TALES FROM THE MEN'S ROOM
$5.95/364-3
From shameless cops on the beat to shy studs on stage, Caffrey explores male lust at its most elemental and arousing. And if there's a lesson to be learned, it's that the Men's Room is less a place than a state of mind—one that every man finds himself in, day after day....

HITTING HOME
$4.95/222-1
Titillating and compelling, the stories in *Hitting Home* make a strong case for there being only one thing on a man's mind.

TORSTEN BARRING
GUY TRAYNOR
$6.50/414-3
Another torturous *tour de force* from Torsten Barring. Some call Guy Traynor a theatrical genius; others say he was a madman. All anyone knows for certain is that his productions were the result of blood, sweat and tears—all extracted from his young, hung actors! Never have artists suffered so much for their craft!

BUY ANY 4 BOOKS & CHOOSE 1 ADDITIONAL BOOK, OF EQUAL OR LESSER VALUE, AS YOUR FREE GIFT

MASQUERADE BOOKS

PRISONERS OF TORQUEMADA
$5.95/252-3
Another volume sure to push you over the edge. How cruel is the "therapy" practiced at Casa Torquemada? Barring is just the writer to evoke such steamy sexual malevolence.

SHADOWMAN
$4.95/178-0
From spoiled Southern aristocrats to randy youths sowing wild oats at the local picture show, Barring's imagination works overtime in these vignettes of homolust—past, present and future.

PETER THORNWELL
$4.95/149-7
Follow the exploits of Peter Thornwell as he goes from misspent youth to scandalous stardom, all thanks to an insatiable libido and love for the lash. Peter and his sex-crazed sidekicks find themselves pursued by merciless men from all walks of life in this torrid take on Horatio Alger.

THE SWITCH
$4.95/3061-X
Sometimes a man needs a good whipping, and *The Switch* certainly makes a case! Packed with hot studs and unrelenting passions.

BERT McKENZIE
FRINGE BENEFITS
$5.95/354-6
From the pen of a widely published short story writer comes a volume of highly immodest tales. Not afraid of getting down and dirty, McKenzie produces some of today's most visceral sextales.

SONNY FORD
REUNION IN FLORENCE
$4.95/3070-9
Captured by Turks, Adrian and Tristan will do anything to save their heads. When Tristan is threatened by a Sultan's jealousy, Adrian begins his quest for the only man alive who can replace Tristan as the object of the Sultan's lust.

ROGER HARMAN
FIRST PERSON
$4.95/179-9
A highly personal collection. Each story takes the form of a confessional—told by men who've got plenty to confess! From the "first time ever" to firsts of different kinds, *First Person* tells truths too hot to be purely fiction.

J. A. GUERRA, ED.
SLOW BURN
$4.95/3042-3
Welcome to the Body Shoppe! Torsos get lean and hard, pecs widen, and stomachs ripple in these sexy stories of the power and perils of physical perfection.

DAVE KINNICK
SORRY I ASKED
$4.95/3090-3
Unexpurgated interviews with gay porn's rank and file. Get personal with the men behind (and under) the "stars," and discover the hot truth about the porn business.

SEAN MARTIN
SCRAPBOOK
$4.95/224-8
Imagine a book filled with only the best, most vivid remembrances...a book brimming with every hot, sexy encounter its pages can hold... Now you need only open up *Scrapbook* to know that such a volume really exists....

CARO SOLES & STAN TAL, EDITORS
BIZARRE DREAMS
$4.95/187-X
An anthology of stirring voices dedicated to exploring the dark side of human fantasy. *Bizarre Dreams* brings together the most talented practitioners of "dark fantasy," the most forbidden sexual realm of all.

CHRISTOPHER MORGAN
STEAM GAUGE
$6.50/473-9
This volume abounds in manly men doing what they do best—to, with, or for any hot stud who crosses their paths. Frequently published to acclaim in the gay press, Christopher Morgan puts a fresh, contemporary spin on the very oldest of urges.

THE SPORTSMEN
$5.95/385-6
A collection of super-hot stories dedicated to that most popular of boys next door—the all-American athlete. Here are enough tales of carnal grand slams, sexy interceptions and highly personal bests to satisfy the hungers of the most ardent sports fan. Editor Christopher Morgan has gathered those writers who know just the type of guys that make up every red-blooded male's starting line-up....

MUSCLE BOUND
$4.95/3028-8
In the New York City bodybuilding scene, country boy Tommy joins forces with sexy Will Rodriguez in a battle of wits and biceps at the hottest gym in town, where the weak are bound and crushed by iron-pumping gods.

MICHAEL LOWENTHAL, ED.
THE BADBOY EROTIC LIBRARY VOLUME I
$4.95/190-X
Excerpts from *A Secret Life*, *Imre*, *Sins of the Cities of the Plain*, *Teleny* and others demonstrate the uncanny gift for portraying sex between men that led to many of these titles being banned upon publication.

THE BADBOY EROTIC LIBRARY VOLUME II
$4.95/211-6
This time, selections are taken from *Mike and Me* and *Muscle Bound*, *Men at Work*, *Badboy Fantasies*, and *Slowburn*.

ERIC BOYD
MIKE AND ME
$5.95/419-4
Mike joined the gym squad to bulk up on muscle. Little did he know he'd be turning on every sexy muscle jock in Minnesota! Hard bodies collide in a series of workouts designed to generate a whole lot more than rips and cuts.

MASQUERADE BOOKS

MIKE AND THE MARINES
$6.50/497-6
Mike takes on America's most elite corps of studs—running into more than a few good men! Join in on the never-ending sexual escapades of this singularly lustful platoon!

ANONYMOUS

A SECRET LIFE
$4.95/3017-2
Meet Master Charles: only eighteen, and quite innocent, until his arrival at the Sir Percival's Royal Academy, where the daily lessons are supplemented with a crash course in pure, sweet sexual heat!

SINS OF THE CITIES OF THE PLAIN
$5.95/322-8
Indulge yourself in the scorching memoirs of young man-about-town Jack Saul. With his shocking dalliances with the lords and "ladies" of British high society, Jack's positively sinful escapades grow wilder with every chapter!

IMRE
$4.95/3019-9
What dark secrets, what fiery passions lay hidden behind strikingly beautiful Lieutenant Imre's emerald eyes? An extraordinary lost classic of fantasy, obsession, gay erotic desire, and romance in a small European town on the eve of WWI.

TELENY
$4.95/3020-2
Often attributed to Oscar Wilde, *Teleny* tells the story of one young man of independent means. He dedicates himself to a succession of forbidden pleasures, but instead finds love and tragedy when he becomes embroiled in a cult devoted to fulfilling only the very darkest of fantasies.

HARD CANDY

KEVIN KILLIAN

ARCTIC SUMMER
$6.95/514-X
Highly acclaimed author Kevin Killian's latest novel examines the many secrets lying beneath the placid exterior of America in the '50s. With the story of Liam Reilly—a young gay man of considerable means and numerous secrets—Killian exposes the contradictions of the American Dream, and the ramifications of the choices one is forced to make when hiding the truth.

STAN LEVENTHAL

BARBIE IN BONDAGE
$6.95/415-1
Widely regarded as one of the most refreshing, clear-eyed interpreters of big city gay male life, Leventhal here provides a series of explorations of love and desire between men. Uncompromising, but gentle and generous, *Barbie in Bondage* is a fitting tribute to the late author's unique talents.

SKYDIVING ON CHRISTOPHER STREET
$6.95/287-6
"Positively addictive." —Dennis Cooper
Aside from a hateful job, a hateful apartment, a hateful world and an increasingly hateful lover, life seems, well, all right for the protagonist of Stan Leventhal's latest novel. Having already lost most of his friends to AIDS, how could things get any worse? But things soon do, and he's forced to endure much more....

PATRICK MOORE

IOWA
$6.95/423-2
"Moore is the Tennessee Williams of the nineties—profound intimacy freed in a compelling narrative."
—Karen Finley
"Fresh and shiny and relevant to our time. *Iowa* is full of terrific characters etched in acid-sharp prose, soaked through with just enough ambivalence to make it thoroughly romantic." —Felice Picano
A stunning novel about one gay man's journey into adulthood, and the roads that bring him home again.

PAUL T. ROGERS

SAUL'S BOOK
$7.95/462-3
Winner of the Editors' Book Award
"Exudes an almost narcotic power.... A masterpiece." —*Village Voice Literary Supplement*
"A first novel of considerable power... Sinbad the Sailor, thanks to the sympathetic imagination of Paul T. Rogers, speaks to us all." —*New York Times Book Review*
The story of a Times Square hustler called Sinbad the Sailor and Saul, a brilliant, self-destructive, alcoholic, thoroughly dominating character who may be the only love Sinbad will ever know.

WALTER R. HOLLAND

THE MARCH
$6.95/429-1
A moving testament to the power of friendship during even the worst of times. Beginning on a hot summer night in 1980, *The March* revolves around a circle of young gay men, and the many others their lives touch. Over time, each character changes in unexpected ways; lives and loves come together and fall apart, as society itself is horribly altered by the onslaught of AIDS.

RED JORDAN AROBATEAU

LUCY AND MICKEY
$6.95/311-2
The story of Mickey—an uncompromising butch—and her long affair with Lucy, the femme she loves. A raw tale of pre-Stonewall lesbian life.
"A necessary reminder to all who blissfully—some may say ignorantly—ride the wave of lesbian chic into the mainstream." —Heather Findlay

BUY ANY 4 BOOKS & CHOOSE 1 ADDITIONAL BOOK, OF EQUAL OR LESSER VALUE, AS YOUR FREE GIFT

MASQUERADE BOOKS

DIRTY PICTURES
$5.95/345-7
"Red Jordan Arobateau is the Thomas Wolfe of lesbian literature... She's a natural—raw talent that is seething, passionate, hard, remarkable."
—Lillian Faderman, editor of *Chloe Plus Olivia*
Dirty Pictures is the story of a lonely butch tending bar—and the femme she finally calls her own.

DONALD VINING
A GAY DIARY
$8.95/451-8
Donald Vining's *Diary* portrays a long-vanished age and the lifestyle of a gay generation all too frequently forgotten. "*A Gay Diary* is, unquestionably, the richest historical document of gay male life in the United States that I have ever encountered.... It illuminates a critical period in gay male American history."
—*Body Politic*

LARS EIGHNER
GAY COSMOS
$6.95/236-1
A title sure to appeal not only to Eighner's gay fans, but the many converts who first encountered his moving nonfiction work. Praised by the press, *Gay Cosmos* is an important contribution to the area of Gay and Lesbian Studies.

FELICE PICANO
THE LURE
$6.95/398-8
"The subject matter, plus the authenticity of Picano's research are, combined, explosive. Felice Picano is one hell of a writer." —Stephen King
After witnessing a brutal murder, Noel is recruited by the police, to assist as a lure for the killer. Undercover, he moves deep into the freneticism of Manhattan's gay highlife—where he gradually becomes aware of the darker forces at work in his life. In addition to the mystery behind his mission, he begins to recognize changes: in his relationships with the men around him, in himself...

AMBIDEXTROUS
$6.95/275-2
"Deftly evokes those placid Eisenhower years of bicycles, boners, and book reports. Makes us remember what it feels like to be a child..."
—*The Advocate*
Picano's first "memoir in the form of a novel" tells all: home life, school face-offs, the ingenuous sophistications of his first sexual steps. In three years' time, he's had his first gay fling—and is on his way to becoming the widely praised writer he is today.

MEN WHO LOVED ME
$6.95/274-4
"Zesty...spiked with adventure and romance...a distinguished and humorous portrait of a vanished age." —*Publishers Weekly*
In 1966, Picano abandoned New York, determined to find true love in Europe. Upon returning, he plunges into the city's thriving gay community of the 1970s.

WILLIAM TALSMAN
THE GAUDY IMAGE
$6.95/263-9
"To read *The Gaudy Image* now...it is to see firsthand the very issues of identity and positionality with which gay men were struggling in the decades before Stonewall. For what Talsman is dealing with...is the very question of how we conceive ourselves gay."
—from the introduction by Michael Bronski

ROSEBUD

THE ROSEBUD READER
$5.95/319-8
Rosebud has contributed greatly to the burgeoning genre of lesbian erotica—to the point that our authors are among the hottest and most closely watched names in lesbian and gay publishing. Here are the finest moments from Rosebud's contemporary classics.

LESLIE CAMERON
WHISPER OF FANS
$6.50/542-5
"Just looking into her eyes, she felt that she knew a lot about this woman. She could see strength, boldness, a fresh sense of aliveness that rocked her to the core. In turn she felt open, revealed under the woman's gaze—all her secrets already told. No need of shame or artifice...." A fresh tale of passion between women, from one of lesbian erotica's up-and-coming authors.

RACHEL PEREZ
ODD WOMEN
$6.50/526-3
These women are sexy, smart, tough—some even say odd. But who cares, when their combined ass-ets are so sweet! An assortment of Sapphic sirens proves once and for all that comely ladies come best in pairs.

RANDY TUROFF
LUST NEVER SLEEPS
$6.50/475-5
A rich volume of highly erotic, powerfully real fiction from the editor of *Lesbian Words*. Randy Turoff depicts a circle of modern women connected through the bonds of love, friendship, ambition, and lust with accuracy and compassion. Moving, tough, yet undeniably true, Turoff's stories create a stirring portrait of contemporary lesbian life and community.

RED JORDAN AROBATEAU
ROUGH TRADE
$6.50/470-4
Famous for her unflinching portrayal of lower-class dyke life and love, Arobateau outdoes herself with these tales of butch/femme affairs and unrelenting passions. Unapologetic and distinctly non-homogenized, *Rough Trade* is a must for all fans of challenging lesbian literature.

MASQUERADE BOOKS

BOYS NIGHT OUT
$6.50/463-1
A *Red*-hot volume of short fiction from this lesbian literary sensation. As always, Arobateau takes a good hard look at the lives of everyday women, noting well the struggles and triumphs each woman experiences.

ALISON TYLER

VENUS ONLINE
$6.50/521-2
What's my idea of paradise? Lovely Alexa spends her days in a boring bank job, not quite living up to her full potential—interested instead on saving her energies for her nocturnal pursuits. At night, Alexa goes online, living out virtual adventures that become more real with each session. Soon Alexa—aka Venus—feels her erotic imagination growing beyond anything she could have imagined.

DARK ROOM: AN ONLINE ADVENTURE
$6.50/455-0
Dani, a successful photographer, can't bring herself to face the death of her lover, Kate. An ambitious journalist, Kate was found mysteriously murdered, leaving her lover with only fond memories of a too-brief relationship. Determined to keep the memory of her lover alive, Dani goes online under Kate's screen alias—and begins to uncover the truth behind the crime that has torn her world apart.

BLUE SKY SIDEWAYS & OTHER STORIES
$6.50/394-5
A variety of women, and their many breathtaking experiences with lovers, friends—and even the occasional sexy stranger. From blossoming young beauties to fearless vixens, Tyler finds the sexy pleasures of everyday life.

DIAL "L" FOR LOVELESS
$5.95/386-4
Meet Katrina Loveless—a private eye talented enough to give Sam Spade a run for his money. In her first case, Katrina investigates a murder implicating a host of society's darlings. Loveless untangles the mess—while working herself into a variety of highly compromising knots with the many lovelies who cross her path!

THE VIRGIN
$5.95/379-1
Veronica answers a personal ad in the "Women Seeking Women" category—and discovers a whole sensual world she never knew existed! And she never dreamed she'd be prized as a virgin all over again, by someone who would deflower her with a passion no man could ever show....

K. T. BUTLER

TOOLS OF THE TRADE
$5.95/420-8
A sparkling mix of lesbian erotica and humor. An encounter with ice cream, cappuccino and chocolate cake; an affair with a complete stranger; a pair of faulty handcuffs; and love on a drafting table. Seventeen tales.

LOVECHILD

GAG
$5.95/369-4
From New York's poetry scene comes this explosive volume of work from one of the bravest, most cutting young writers you'll ever encounter. The poems in *Gag* take on American hypocrisy with uncommon energy, and announce Lovechild as a writer of unforgettable rage.

ELIZABETH OLIVER

PAGAN DREAMS
$5.95/295-7
Cassidy and Samantha plan a vacation at a secluded bed-and-breakfast, hoping for a little personal time alone. Their hostess, however, has different plans. The lovers are plunged into a world of dungeons and pagan rites, as Anastasia steals Samantha for her own.

SUSAN ANDERS

CITY OF WOMEN
$5.95/375-9
Stories dedicated to women and the passions that draw them together. Designed strictly for the sensual pleasure of women, these tales are set to ignite flames of passion from coast to coast.

PINK CHAMPAGNE
$5.95/282-5
Tasty, torrid tales of butch/femme couplings. Tough as nails or soft as silk, these women seek out their antitheses, intent on working out the details of their own personal theory of difference.

ANONYMOUS

LAVENDER ROSE
$4.95/208-6
From the writings of Sappho, Queen of the island Lesbos, to the turn-of-the-century *Black Book of Lesbianism*; from *Tips to Maidens* to *Crimson Hairs*, a recent lesbian saga—here are the great but little-known lesbian writings and revelations. A one volume survey of hot and historic lesbian writing.

LAURA ANTONIOU, EDITOR

LEATHERWOMEN
$4.95/3095-4
These fantasies, from the pens of new or emerging authors, break every rule imposed on women's fantasies. The hottest stories from some of today's newest and most outrageous writers make this an unforgettable exploration of the female libido.

LEATHERWOMEN II
$4.95/229-9
Another groundbreaking volume of writing from women on the edge, sure to ignite libidinal flames in any reader. Leave taboos behind, because these Leatherwomen know no limits....

BUY ANY 4 BOOKS & CHOOSE 1 ADDITIONAL BOOK, OF EQUAL OR LESSER VALUE, AS YOUR FREE GIFT

MASQUERADE BOOKS

AARONA GRIFFIN
PASSAGE AND OTHER STORIES
$4.95/3057-1
An S/M romance. Lovely Nina is frightened by her lesbian passions, until she finds herself infatuated with a woman she spots at a local café. One night Nina follows her, and finds herself enmeshed in an endless maze leading to a world where women test the edges of sexuality and power.

VALENTINA CILESCU
MY LADY'S PLEASURE: MISTRESS WITH A MAID, VOLUME I
$5.95/412-7
Claudia Dungarrow, a lovely, powerful, but mysterious professor, attempts to seduce virginal Elizabeth Stanbridge, setting off a chain of events that eventually ruins her career. Claudia vows revenge—and makes her foes pay deliciously....

DARK VENUS: MISTRESS WITH A MAID, VOLUME 2
$6.50/481-X
This thrilling saga of cruel lust continues! *Mistress with a Maid* breathes new life into the conventions of dominance and submission. What emerges is a picture of unremitting desire—whether it be for supreme erotic power or ultimate sexual surrender.

THE ROSEBUD SUTRA
$4.95/242-6
"Women are hardly ever known in their true light, though they may love others, or become indifferent towards them, may give them delight, or abandon them, or may extract from them all the wealth that they possess." So says *The Rosebud Sutra*—a volume promising women's inner secrets.

MISTRESS MINE
$6.50/502-6
Sophia Cranleigh sits in prison, accused of authoring the "obscene" *Mistress Mine*. What she has done, however, is merely chronicle the events of her life. For Sophia has led no ordinary life, but has slaved and suffered—deliciously—under the hand of the notorious Mistress Malin.

LINDSAY WELSH
SECOND SIGHT
$6.50/507-7
The debut of Dana Steele—lesbian superhero! During an attack by a gang of homophobic youths, Dana is thrown onto subway tracks—touching the deadly third rail. Miraculously, she survives, and finds herself endowed with superhuman powers. Dana decides to devote her powers to the protection of her lesbian sisters, no matter how daunting the danger they face.

NASTY PERSUASIONS
$6.50/436-4
A hot peek into the behind-the-scenes operations of Rough Trade—one of the world's most famous lesbian clubs. Join Slash, Ramone, Cherry and many others as they bring one another to the height of torturous ecstasy—all in the name of keeping Rough Trade the premier name in sexy entertainment for women.

MILITARY SECRETS
$5.95/397-X
Colonel Candice Sproule heads a highly specialized boot camp. Assisted by three dominatrix sergeants, Col. Sproule takes on the talented submissives sent to her by secret military contacts. Then comes Jesse—whose pleasure in being served matches the Colonel's own. This new recruit sets off fireworks in the barracks—and beyond....

ROMANTIC ENCOUNTERS
$5.95/359-7
Beautiful Julie, the most powerful editor of romance novels in the industry, spends her days igniting women's passions through books—and her nights fulfilling those needs with a variety of lovers. Finally, through a sizzling series of coincidences, Julie's two worlds come together explosively!

THE BEST OF LINDSAY WELSH
$5.95/368-6
A collection of this popular writer's best work. This author was one of Rosebud's early bestsellers, and remains highly popular. A sampler set to introduce some of the hottest lesbian erotica to a wider audience.

NECESSARY EVIL
$5.95/277-9
What's a girl to do? When her Mistress proves too systematic, too by-the-book, one lovely submissive takes the ultimate chance—choosing and creating a Mistress who'll fulfill her heart's desire. Little did she know how difficult it would be—and, in the end, rewarding....

A VICTORIAN ROMANCE
$5.95/365-1
Lust-letters from the road. A young Englishwoman realizes her dream—a trip abroad under the guidance of her eccentric maiden aunt. Soon, the young but blossoming Elaine comes to discover her own sexual talents, as a hot-blooded Parisian named Madelaine takes her Sapphic education in hand.

A CIRCLE OF FRIENDS
$4.95/250-7
The story of a remarkable group of women. The women pair off to explore all the possibilities of lesbian passion, until finally it seems that there is nothing—and no one—they have not dabbled in.

BAD HABITS
$5.95/446-1
What does one do with a poorly trained slave? Break her of her bad habits, of course! The story of the ultimate finishing school, *Bad Habits* was an immediate favorite with women nationwide.
"Talk about passing the wet test!... If you like hot, lesbian erotica, run—don't walk—and pick up a copy of *Bad Habits*." —*Lambda Book Repor*

ANNABELLE BARKER
MOROCCO
$6.50/541-7
A luscious young woman stands to inherit a fortune—if she can only withstand the ministrations of her cruel guardian until her twentieth birthday. With two months left, Lila makes a bold bid for freedom, only to find that liberty has its own excruciating and delicious price....

MASQUERADE BOOKS

A.L. REINE
DISTANT LOVE & OTHER STORIES
$4.95/3056-3
In the title story, Leah Michaels and her lover, Ranelle, have had four years of blissful, smoldering passion together. When Ranelle is out of town, Leah records an audio "Valentine:" a cassette filled with erotic reminiscences.

A RICHARD KASAK BOOK

SIMON LEVAY
ALBRICK'S GOLD
$12.95/518-2
From the man behind the controversial "gay brain" studies comes a chilling tale of medical experimentation run amok. Roger Cavendish, a diligent researcher into the mysteries of the human mind, and Guy Albrick, a researcher who claims to know the secret to human sexual orientation, find themselves on opposite sides of the battle over experimental surgery. Has Dr. Albrick already begun to experiment on humans? What are the implications of his receiving support from ultra-conservative forces? Simon Levay fashions a classic medical thriller from today's cutting-edge science.

SHAR REDNOUR, EDITOR
VIRGIN TERRITORY 2
$12.95/506-9
The follow-up volume to the groundbreaking *Virgin Territory*, including the work of many women inspired by the success of *VT*. Focusing on the many "firsts" of a woman's erotic life, *Virgin Territory 2* provides one of the sole outlets for serious discussion of the myriad possibilities available to and chosen by many contemporary lesbians. A necessary addition to the library of any reader interested in the state of contemporary sexuality.
VIRGIN TERRITORY
$12.95/457-7
An anthology of writing by women about their first-time erotic experiences with other women. From the ecstasies of awakening dykes to the sometimes awkward pleasures of sexual experimentation on the edge, each of these true stories reveals a different, radical perspective on one of the most traditional subjects around: virginity.

MICHAEL FORD, EDITOR
ONCE UPON A TIME:
EROTIC FAIRY TALES FOR WOMEN
$12.95/449-6
How relevant to contemporary lesbians are the lessons of these age-old tales? The contributors to *Once Upon a Time*—some of the biggest names in contemporary lesbian literature—retell their favorite fairy tales, adding their own surprising—and sexy—twists. *Once Upon a Time* is sure to be one of contemporary lesbian literature's classic collections.

HAPPILY EVER AFTER:
EROTIC FAIRY TALES FOR MEN
$12.95/450-X
A hefty volume of bedtime stories Mother Goose never thought to write down. Adapting some of childhood's most beloved tales for the adult gay reader, the contributors to *Happily Ever After* dig up the subtext of these hitherto "innocent" diversions—adding some surprises of their own along the way.

MICHAEL BRONSKI, EDITOR
TAKING LIBERTIES: GAY MEN'S ESSAYS
ON POLITICS, CULTURE AND SEX
$12.95/456-9
"Offers undeniable proof of a heady, sophisticated, diverse new culture of gay intellectual debate. I cannot recommend it too highly."—Christopher Bram
A collection of some of the most divergent views on the state of contemporary gay male culture published in recent years. Michael Bronski here presents some of the community's foremost essayists weighing in on such slippery topics as outing, masculine identity, pornography, the pedophile movement, political strategy—and much more.
FLASHPOINT: GAY MALE SEXUAL WRITING
$12.95/424-0
A collection of the most provocative testaments to gay eros. Michael Bronski presents over twenty of the genre's best writers, exploring areas such as Enlightenment, True Life Adventures and more. Sure to be one of the most talked about and influential volumes ever dedicated to the exploration of gay sexuality.

HEATHER FINDLAY, EDITOR
A MOVEMENT OF EROS:
25 YEARS OF LESBIAN EROTICA
$12.95/421-6
—Gertrude Stein
One of the most scintillating overviews of lesbian erotic writing ever published. Heather Findlay has assembled a roster of stellar talents, each represented by their best work. Tracing the course of the genre from its pre-Stonewall roots to its current renaissance, Findlay examines each piece, placing it within the context of lesbian community and politics.

CHARLES HENRI FORD & PARKER TYLER
THE YOUNG AND EVIL
$12.95/431-3
"*The Young and Evil* creates [its] generation as *This Side of Paradise* by Fitzgerald created his generation." —Gertrude Stein
Originally published in 1933, *The Young and Evil* was an immediate sensation due to its unprecedented portrayal of young gay artists living in New York's notorious Greenwich Village. From flamboyant drag balls to squalid bohemian flats, these characters followed love and art wherever it led them—with a frankness that had the novel banned for many years.

BUY ANY 4 BOOKS & CHOOSE 1 ADDITIONAL BOOK,
OF EQUAL OR LESSER VALUE, AS YOUR FREE GIFT

MASQUERADE BOOKS

BARRY HOFFMAN, EDITOR
THE BEST OF GAUNTLET
$12.95/202-7
Gauntlet has, with its semi-annual issues, always publishing the widest possible range of opinions, in the interest of challenging public opinion. The most provocative articles have been gathered by editor-in-chief Barry Hoffman, to make *The Best of Gauntlet* a riveting exploration of American society's limits.

MICHAEL ROWE
WRITING BELOW THE BELT:
CONVERSATIONS WITH EROTIC AUTHORS
$19.95/363-5
"An in-depth and enlightening tour of society's love/hate relationship with sex, morality, and censorship." —*James White Review*
Journalist Michael Rowe interviewed the best erotic writers and presents the collected wisdom in *Writing Below the Belt*. Rowe speaks frankly with cult favorites such as Pat Califia, crossover success stories like John Preston, and up-and-comers Michael Lowenthal and Will Leber. A volume dedicated to chronicling the insights of some of this overlooked genre's most renowned pratitioners.

LARRY TOWNSEND
ASK LARRY
$12.95/289-2
One of the leather community's most respected scribes here presents the best of his advice to leathermen worldwide. Starting just before the onslaught of AIDS, Townsend wrote the "Leather Notebook" column for *Drummer* magazine. Now, readers can avail themselves of Townsend's collected wisdom, as well as the author's contemporary commentary—a careful consideration of the way life has changed in the AIDS era. No man worth his leathers can afford to miss this volume of sage advice and considered opinion.

MICHAEL LASSELL
THE HARD WAY
$12.95/231-0
"Lassell is a master of the necessary word. In an age of tepid and whining verse, his bawdy and bittersweet songs are like a plunge in cold champagne."
—Paul Monette
The first collection of renowned gay writer Michael Lassell's poetry, fiction and essays. As much a chronicle of post-Stonewall gay life as a compendium of a remarkable writer's work.

AMARANTHA KNIGHT, EDITOR
LOVE BITES
$12.95/234-5
A volume of tales dedicated to legend's sexiest demon—the Vampire. Not only the finest collection of erotic horror available—but a virtual who's who of promising new talent. A must-read for fans of both the horror and erotic genres.

RANDY TUROFF, EDITOR
LESBIAN WORDS: STATE OF THE ART
$10.95/340-6
"This is a terrific book that should be on every thinking lesbian's bookshelf." —Nisa Donnelly
One of the widest assortments of lesbian nonfiction writing in one revealing volume. Dorothy Allison, Jewelle Gomez, Judy Grahn, Eileen Myles, Robin Podolsky and many others are represented by some of their best work, looking at not only the current fashionability the media has brought to the lesbian "image," but considerations of the lesbian past via historical inquiry and personal recollections.

ASSOTTO SAINT
SPELLS OF A VOODOO DOLL
$12.95/393-7
"Angelic and brazen."—Jewelle Gomez
A fierce, spellbinding collection of the poetry, lyrics, essays and performance texts of Assotto Saint—one of the most important voices in the renaissance of black gay writing. Saint, aka Yves François Lubin, was the editor of two seminal anthologies: 1991 Lambda Literary Book Award winner, *The Road Before Us: 100 Gay Black Poets* and *Here to Dare: 10 Gay Black Poets*. He was also the author of two books of poetry, *Stations* and *Wishing for Wings*.

WILLIAM CARNEY
THE REAL THING
$10.95/280-9
"Carney gives us a good look at the mores and lifestyle of the first generation of gay leathermen. A chilling mystery/romance novel as well."—Pat Califia
With a new introduction by Michael Bronski. First published in 1968, this uncompromising story of American leathermen received instant acclaim. *The Real Thing* finally returns from exile, ready to thrill a new generation.

EURYDICE
F/32
$10.95/350-3
"It's wonderful to see a woman...celebrating her body and her sexuality by creating a fabulous and funny tale." —Kathy Acker
With the story of Ela, Eurydice won the National Fiction competition sponsored by Fiction Collective Two and Illinois State University. A funny, disturbing quest for unity, *f/32* prompted Frederic Tuten to proclaim "almost any page... redeems us from the anemic writing and banalities we have endured in the past decade..."

CHEA VILLANUEVA
JESSIE'S SONG
$9.95/235-3
"It conjures up the strobe-light confusion and excitement of urban dyke life.... Read about these dykes and you'll love them." —Rebecca Ripley
Based largely upon her own experience, Villanueva's work is remarkable for its frankness, and delightful in its iconoclasm. Unconcerned with political correctness, this writer has helped expand the boundaries of "serious" lesbian writing.

MASQUERADE BOOKS

SAMUEL R. DELANY
THE MOTION OF LIGHT IN WATER
$12.95/133-0

"A very moving, intensely fascinating literary biography from an extraordinary writer....The artist as a young man and a memorable picture of an age."—William Gibson

Award-winning author Samuel R. Delany's autobiography covers the early years of one of science fiction's most important voices. *The Motion of Light in Water* follows Delany from his early marriage to the poet Marilyn Hacker, through the publication of his first, groundbreaking work.

THE MAD MAN
$23.95/193-4/hardcover

Delany's fascinating examination of human desire. For his thesis, graduate student John Marr researches the life and work of the brilliant Timothy Hasler: a philosopher whose career was cut tragically short over a decade earlier. Marr soon begins to believe that Hasler's death might hold some key to his own life as a gay man in the age of AIDS.

"What Delany has done here is take the ideas of the Marquis de Sade one step further, by filtering extreme and obsessive sexual behavior through the sieve of post-modern experience...."
—*Lambda Book Report*

"Delany develops an insightful dichotomy between [his protagonist]'s two worlds: the one of cerebral philosophy and dry academia, the other of heedless, 'impersonal' obsessive sexual extremism. When these worlds finally collide ... the novel achieves a surprisingly satisfying resolution...."
—*Publishers Weekly*

FELICE PICANO
DRYLAND'S END
$12.95/279-5

The science fiction debut of the highly acclaimed author of *Men Who Loved Me* and *Like People in History*. Set five thousand years in the future, *Dryland's End* takes place in a fabulous techno-empire ruled by intelligent, powerful women. While the Matriarchy has ruled for over two thousand years and altered human society, it is now unraveling. Military rivalries, religious fanaticism and economic competition threaten to destroy the mighty empire.

ROBERT PATRICK
TEMPLE SLAVE
$12.95/191-8

"You must read this book." —Quentin Crisp
"This is nothing less than the secret history of the most theatrical of theaters, the most bohemian of Americans and the most knowing of queens.... *Temple Slave* is also one of the best ways to learn what it was like to be fabulous, gay, theatrical and loved in a time at once more and less dangerous to gay life than our own." —*Genre*

GUILLERMO BOSCH
RAIN
$12.95/232-9

"Rain is a trip..." —Timothy Leary
An adult fairy tale, *Rain* takes place in a time when the mysteries of Eros are played out against a background of uncommon deprivation. The tale begins on the 1,537th day of drought—when one man comes to know the true depths of thirst. In a quest to sate his hunger for some knowledge of the wide world, he is taken through a series of extraordinary, unearthly encounters that promise to change not only his life, but the course of civilization around him. A moving fable for our time.

LAURA ANTONIOU, EDITOR
LOOKING FOR MR. PRESTON
$23.95/288-4

Edited by Laura Antoniou, *Looking for Mr. Preston* includes work by Lars Eighner, Pat Califia, Michael Bronski, Joan Nestle, and others who contributed interviews, essays and personal reminiscences of John Preston—a man whose career spanned the industry. Preston was the author of over twenty books, and edited many more. Ten percent of the proceeds from sale of the book will go to the AIDS Project of Southern Maine, for which Preston served as President of the Board.

CECILIA TAN, EDITOR
SM VISIONS: THE BEST OF CIRCLET PRESS
$10.95/339-2

"Fabulous books! There's nothing else like them."
—Susie Bright,
Best American Erotica and Herotica 3

Circlet Press, devoted exclusively to the erotic science fiction and fantasy genre, is now represented by the best of its very best: *SM Visions*—sure to be one of the most thrilling and eye-opening rides through the erotic imagination ever published.

RUSS KICK
OUTPOSTS:
A CATALOG OF RARE AND DISTURBING ALTERNATIVE INFORMATION
$18.95/0202-8

A huge, authoritative guide to some of the most bizarre publications available today! Rather than simply summarize the plethora of opinions crowding the American scene, Kick has tracked down and compiled reviews of work penned by political extremists, conspiracy theorists, hallucinogenic pathfinders, sexual explorers, and others. Each review is followed by ordering information for the many readers sure to want these publications for themselves. An essential reference in this age of rapidly proliferating information systems and increasingly extremes political and cultural perspectives.

BUY ANY 4 BOOKS & CHOOSE 1 ADDITIONAL BOOK, OF EQUAL OR LESSER VALUE, AS YOUR FREE GIFT

MASQUERADE BOOKS

LUCY TAYLOR
UNNATURAL ACTS
$12.95/181-0

"A topnotch collection..." —*Science Fiction Chronicle*
Unnatural Acts plunges deep into the dark side of the psyche and brings to life a disturbing vision of erotic horror. Unrelenting angels and hungry gods play with souls and bodies in Taylor's murky cosmos: where heaven and hell are merely differences of perspective; where redemption and damnation lie behind the same shocking acts.

TIM WOODWARD, EDITOR
THE BEST OF SKIN TWO
$12.95/130-6

A groundbreaking journal from the crossroads of sexuality, fashion, and art, *Skin Two* specializes in provocative essays by the finest writers working in the "radical sex" scene. Collected here are the articles and interviews that established the magazine's reputation. Including interviews with cult figures Tim Burton, Clive Barker and Jean Paul Gaultier.

MICHAEL LOWENTHAL, EDITOR
THE BEST OF THE BADBOYS
$12.95/233-7

The very best of the leading Badboys is collected here, in this testament to the artistry that has catapulted these "outlaw" authors to bestselling status. John Preston, Aaron Travis, Larry Townsend, and others are here represented by their most provocative writing.

PAT CALIFIA
SENSUOUS MAGIC
$12.95/458-5

A new classic, destined to grace the shelves of anyone interested in contemporary sexuality.
"*Sensuous Magic* is clear, succinct and engaging even for the reader for whom S/M isn't the sexual behavior of choice.... When she is writing about the nuances of sex and the technical aspects of it, Califia is the Dr. Ruth of the alternative sexuality set...." —*Lambda Book Report*
"Pat Califia's *Sensuous Magic* is a friendly, non-threatening, helpful guide and resource... She captures the power of what it means to enter forbidden terrain, and to do so safely with someone else, and to explore the healing potential, spiritual aspects and the depth of S/M."
—*Bay Area Reporter*
"Don't take a dangerous trip into the unknown—buy this book and know where you're going!"
—*SKIN TWO*

MICHAEL PERKINS
THE GOOD PARTS: AN UNCENSORED GUIDE TO LITERARY SEXUALITY
$12.95/186-1

Michael Perkins, one of America's only critics to regularly scrutinize sexual literature, presents sex as seen in the pages of over 100 major fiction and nonfiction volumes from the past twenty years.

COMING UP:
THE WORLD'S BEST EROTIC WRITING
$12.95/370-8

Author and critic Michael Perkins has scoured the field of erotic writing to produce this anthology sure to challenge the limits of even the most seasoned reader. Using the same sharp eye and transgressive instinct that have established him as America's leading commentator on sexually explicit fiction, Perkins here presents the cream of the current crop.

DAVID MELTZER
THE AGENCY TRILOGY
$12.95/216-7

"...'The Agency' is clearly Meltzer's paradigm of society; a mindless machine of which we are all 'agents,' including those whom the machine supposedly serves...." —Norman Spinrad

When first published, *The Agency* explored issues of erotic dominance and submission with an immediacy and frankness previously unheard of in American literature, as well as presented a vision of an America consumed and dehumanized by a lust for power.

JOHN PRESTON
MY LIFE AS A PORNOGRAPHER AND OTHER INDECENT ACTS
$12.95/135-7

A collection of renowned author and social critic John Preston's essays, focusing on his work as an erotic writer and proponent of gay rights.
"...essential and enlightening... [*My Life as a Pornographer*] is a bridge from the sexually liberated 1970s to the more cautious 1990s, and Preston has walked much of that way as a standard-bearer to the cause for equal rights...." —*Library Journal*

"*My Life as a Pornographer*...is not pornography, but rather reflections upon the writing and production of it. In a deeply sex-phobic world, Preston has never shied away from a vision of the redemptive potential of the erotic drive. Better than perhaps anyone in our community, Preston knows how physical joy can bridge differences and make us well."
—*Lambda Book Report*

CARO SOLES, EDITOR
MELTDOWN! AN ANTHOLOGY OF EROTIC SCIENCE FICTION AND DARK FANTASY FOR GAY MEN
$12.95/203-5

Editor Caro Soles has put together one of the most explosive collections of gay erotic writing ever published. *Meltdown!* contains the very best examples of the increasingly popular sub-genre of erotic sci-fi/dark fantasy: stories meant to shock and delight, to send a shiver down the spine and start a fire down below.

MASQUERADE BOOKS

LARS EIGHNER
ELEMENTS OF AROUSAL
$12.95/230-2
A guideline for success with one of publishing's best kept secrets: the novice-friendly field of gay erotic writing. Eighner details his craft, providing the reader with sure advice. Because that's what *Elements of Arousal* is all about: the application and honing of the writer's craft, which brought Eighner fame with not only the steamy *Bayou Boy*, but the illuminating *Travels with Lizbeth*.

STAN TAL, EDITOR
BIZARRE SEX
AND OTHER CRIMES OF PASSION
$12.95/213-2
From the pages of *Bizarre Sex*. Over twenty small masterpieces of erotic shock make this one of the year's most unexpectedly alluring anthologies. This incredible volume, edited by Stan Tal, includes such masters of erotic horror and fantasy as Edward Lee, Lucy Taylor and Nancy Kilpatrick.

MARCO VASSI
A DRIVING PASSION
$12.95/134-9
Marco Vassi was famous not only for his groundbreaking writing, but for the many lectures he gave regarding sexuality and the complex erotic philosophy he had spent much of his life working out. *A Driving Passion* collects the wit and insight Vassi brought to these lectures, and distills the philosophy that made him an underground sensation.

"The most striking figure in present-day American erotic literature. Alone among modern erotic writers, Vassi is working out a philosophy of sexuality."
—Michael Perkins, *The Secret Record*

"Vintage Vassi." —*Future Sex*

"An intriguing artifact... His eclectic quest for eroticism is somewhat poignant, and his fervor rarely lapses into silliness." —*Publishers Weekly*

THE EROTIC COMEDIES
$12.95/136-5
Short stories designed to shock and transform attitudes about sex and sexuality, *The Erotic Comedies* is both entertaining and challenging—and garnered Vassi some of the most lavish praise of his career. Also includes his groundbreaking writings on the Erotic Experience, including the concept of Metasex—the premise of which was derived from the author's own unbelievable experiences.

"To describe Vassi's writing as pornography would be to deny his very serious underlying purposes.... The stories are good, the essays original and enlightening, and the language and subject-matter intended to shock the prudish." —*Sunday Times* (UK)

"The comparison to [Henry] Miller is high praise indeed.... But reading Vassi's work, the analogy holds—for he shares with Miller an unabashed joy in sensuality, and a questing after experience that is the root of all great literature, erotic or otherwise.... Vassi was, by all accounts, a fearless explorer, someone who jumped headfirst into the world of sex, and wrote about what he found. And as he himself was known to say on more than one occasion, 'The most erotic organ is the mind.'"
—David L. Ulin, *The Los Angeles Reader*

THE SALINE SOLUTION
$12.95/180-2
"I've always read Marco's work with interest and I have the highest opinion not only of his talent but his intellectual boldness." —Norman Mailer

The story of one couple's spiritual crises during an age of extraordianry freedom. While renowned for his sexual philosophy, Vassi also experienced success in with fiction; *The Saline Solution* was one of the high points of his career, while still addressing the issue of sexuality.

THE STONED APOCALYPSE
$12.95/132-2
"...Marco Vassi is our champion sexual energist."
—*VLS*

During his lifetime, Marco Vassi was hailed as America's premier erotic writer. His reputation was worldwide. *The Stoned Apocalypse* is Vassi's autobiography, financed by his other groundbreaking erotic writing. Chronicling a cross-country roadtrip, *The Stoned Apocalypse* is rife with Vassi's insight into the American character and libido. One of the most vital portraits of "the 60s," this volume is a fitting testament to the writer's talents, and the sexual imagination of his generation.

BUY ANY 4 BOOKS & CHOOSE 1 ADDITIONAL BOOK, OF EQUAL OR LESSER VALUE, AS YOUR FREE GIFT

ORDERING IS EASY

MC/VISA orders can be placed by calling our toll-free number
PHONE 800-375-2356/FAX 212-986-7355/E-MAIL masqbks@aol.com
or mail this coupon to:
MASQUERADE DIRECT
DEPT. BMMQC6 801 2ND AVE., NY, NY 10017

BUY ANY FOUR BOOKS AND CHOOSE ONE ADDITIONAL BOOK, OF EQUAL OR LESSER VALUE, AS YOUR FREE GIFT.

QTY.	TITLE	NO.	PRICE
			FREE
			FREE

We Never Sell, Give or Trade Any Customer's Name.

SUBTOTAL
POSTAGE and HANDLING
TOTAL

In the U.S., please add $1.50 for the first book and 75¢ for each additional book; in Canada, add $2.00 for the first book and $1.25 for each additional book. Foreign countries: add $4.00 for the first book and $2.00 for each additional book. No C.O.D. orders. Please make all checks payable to Masquerade Books. Payable in U.S. currency only. New York state residents add 8.25% sales tax. Please allow 4-6 weeks for delivery.

NAME _____

ADDRESS _____

CITY _____ STATE _____ ZIP _____

TEL( ) _____

E-MAIL _____

PAYMENT: ☐ CHECK   ☐ MONEY ORDER   ☐ VISA   ☐ MC

CARD NO _____ EXP. DATE _____

STUD SHORTS
CLAY CALDWELL

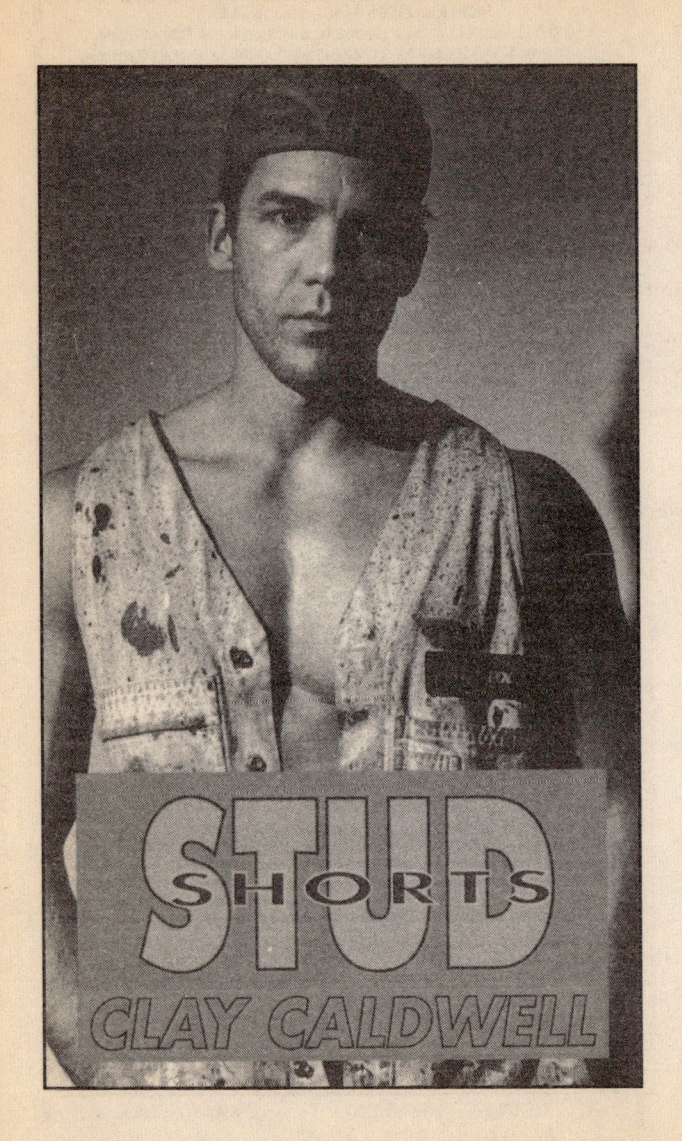

THE STONED APOCALYPSE

MARCO VASSI

"Vassi's the only one of the gang of contemporary erotic writers who should be read."

—NORMAN MAILER

MASQUERADE

MASTERING MARY SUE

MARY LOVE

BOUND TO THE PAST

AMANDA WARE

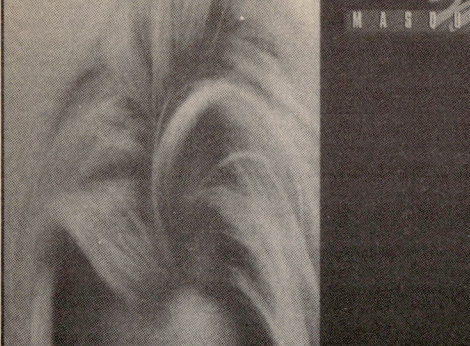

DOVER ISLAND

LYN DAVENPORT

MASQUERADE

TABITHA'S TEASE

ROBIN WILDE

SEASON of the WITCH
JEAN STINE

"A stylistically brilliant psychosexual novel."
—*Isaac Asimov's SF Magazine*

rHINOCERO

ROUGH TRADE

RED JORDAN AROBATEA

MASQUERADE

PROTESTS, PLEASURES, RAPTURES

ANONYMOUS